VENGEANCE

To Eman and Adams.

Enjoy. [signature]

VENGEANCE

A Novel

RONALD A. MOORE

authorHOUSE®

AuthorHouse™ UK
1663 Liberty Drive
Bloomington, IN 47403 USA
www.authorhouse.co.uk
Phone: 0800.197.4150

Published by AuthorHouse 01/02/2015

ISBN: 978-1-5049-3510-4 (sc)
ISBN: 978-1-5049-3509-8 (hc)
ISBN: 978-1-5049-3511-1 (e)

Book Cover Photography, by kind permission of, Photogunphotography (UK) facebook.com/photogunphotography   thesmdavey@gmail.com Fashion Model front cover, Emma Jo Shadbolt. (UK based)

DEDICATION

TO MY BEAUTIFUL EMMA
MY INSPIRATION

A WORD FROM THE AUTHOR

"When the good Lord calls upon your name, he will care not that you won or lost, but how you played the game."

The above words are those of another man's wife, who had the sweetest lips that I ever kissed: my mother.

As the sixth of seven children, I knew from an early age that it would be dog eat dog in our family household. If you wanted anything, you just had to save for it. There was no pocket money or treats; money was too scarce a commodity. We all soon learnt to stand on our own two feet. For me, that meant doing a milk round before school – from six in the morning until eight – and then a paper round when I got home from school. At age 11, I was clocking up a good thirty hours a week. It was a three-mile walk to school, and the same back, so I was walking thirty miles a week, plus twenty for the jobs I did.

We were given jack shit as kids; we were too damn poor. It really was a case of survival of the fittest. Mum kept the family together as best she could. I caught her crying on many occasions, and I often cried too. Our problem was our father. He was an arsehole. He always preferred a drunken night down the pub with his lazy cronies to being a real father to his children. We could never rely on him for anything, and so we never did. We all flew the nest when the opportunity arose.

My slightly older sister, Lynn, was the one I most felt sorry for. She was the only girl, and having six brothers must have made her adolescent years a nightmare, with no private space whatsoever. I felt so sorry for her that I used my first month's wages from my jobs to buy a small shed, which I put up for her down the bottom of the garden. At least that gave her some of her own private space with a lock and key. My mum was so proud of me.

I often dreamt that one day I would have my own big three-storey house, with a bathroom on every floor – all paid for and with no mortgage.

We all turned out to be strong-willed, with even stronger desires to succeed in life. I hated growing up in that domestic nightmare I had been born into. In hindsight, though, it sure did toughen us all up and ready us for our chosen careers. I left home at 18 to play football, and I was also a partner in a garage business. Life was good. My sister had her own fashion boutique before she was 20. I was born with a competitive nature and spirit, and my mother's words instilled in me a philanthropic sense of kindness that I would go on to share with other people as I journeyed through life. My mother's gift of words made each and every morning, every new day dawning, a challenge.

There is no point in waiting for your ship to come in. It never will; you have to swim out and meet it head-on. We make our own destinies, and we shape our own futures. Yes, we make mistakes along the way, but if we learn from them, they served us well. Ultimately, we will be what we want to be, and those with true desire and passion will achieve their ambitions. As we all journey through life, if we can help someone along the way, our living will have not been in vain.

I have brought my life philosophies to this, my first novel. The main character is Steve Hurst. He runs a business called DIRTS, an acronym for Discreet Intelligence Reports and Technical Services. It's a security company that specialises in the horse-racing industry. The company is best described as the unofficial MI5 security arm of the Jockey Club, the governing body for the horse-racing industry in England, Wales, and Scotland.

Let me take you on a white-knuckle roller-coaster ride as the plot thickens from chapter to chapter. Buckle up! If you like fast racehorses, fast cars, sex, drugs, and showjumping – sleepy Sussex, I think not – then I hope you will enjoy my first venture into crime-thriller writing. It has certainly been an adventure for me to put the story together, and I hope you enjoy it.

PROLOGUE

The Jockey Club was fed up to its back teeth with all the adverse publicity it had attracted through its so-called security department; it really was a shambles, constantly ridiculed by the tabloids and the general public on a whole variety of issues. There was even a growing amount of dissension from the club's own stewards. If it wasn't one thing, it was another; enough was enough, and one of the senior stewards, Lord Oakley, needed to take drastic action.

On the last day of the Royal Ascot meeting, a Saturday in June 2000, it was announced at a noon press conference that the security division of the Jockey Club was to be disbanded. After lengthy negotiations with other companies over the previous three months, the Jockey Club members had unanimously agreed to award a four-year contract to Discreet Intelligence Reports and Technical Services (DIRTS), a company that had been working for the club non-contractually since 1996.

DIRTS would operate totally independently from the Jockey Club, and any persons or companies connected to the racing industry could avail themselves of this company's services. Lord Oakley thought that this would protect the integrity of the horse-racing industry; however, the Jockey Club reserved the right to be informed of any breaches of its protocols or rules of racing.

Lord Oakley hoped that the press release would satisfy the press and racing fraternity alike, and also distance the Jockey Club from the adverse publicity it had received over so many years, all through utter incompetence and botched inquiries by its previous inept security division.

Four years later, in June 2004, Lord Oakley was all smiles as he entertained his Jockey Club guests at this prestigious Royal Ascot meeting. He would announce that Discreet Intelligence Reports and Technical

Services had been an amazing success over the past four years. "It is my pleasure to announce a further four-year contract," he said.

Steve Hurst's company, DIRTS, with its dynamic professional approach to a whole host of problems and situations, had indeed been a sensation with the Jockey Club. Steve, along with his fiancée Jane Coe, were official guests at the press conference given by Lord Oakley, and Steve's contract was renewed to June 2008.

Some weeks later, the racing was now at the prestigious Glorious Goodwood, for its five-day festival of summer racing.

Horse racing may well be regarded as the sport of kings; however, it can also provide golden opportunities for some people with a more devious nature. You can get ahead, and you can get even – for some people, though, *vengeance* is all that matters.

CHAPTER 1

Glorious Goodwood. That's what they called it, and on a bright summer's day, with temperatures in the 70s or 80s, they could be right. The weather this Wednesday morning, though, was anything but glorious. It had not stopped drizzling, the rain falling from the early hours. It occurred to me that the meeting today (which was the second day of a five-day meeting) might well be abandoned because of the amount of rain that had already fallen.

As I drove past Arundel Castle, I tuned in to the local radio station, South Coast Radio. It was eleven thirty, and the traffic was surprisingly light. The newsreader on the half hour finished his broadcast with:

> A report is coming in that two people have been found dead in a flat in the Kemptown area of Brighton, the deaths, according to the police spokesman, are thought to be drug related, and there are no suspicious circumstances. And now with the sports news, here is Kelly Simmonds … last night's meeting of Brighton District Council has given the green light for Brighton and Hove Albion to stay at Withdean Stadium indefinitely; today's meeting at Goodwood has at last been given the go-ahead, after a second inspection at 10.30. The going is officially described as heavy.

I tuned back in to Southern Sound and listened to the music.

Jane, my fiancée, had her head buried in the *Horse & Hound* ever since we left home in Sayers Common, now a little village on the old A23, about 9 miles from Brighton.

Jane really enjoyed all the social occasions associated with big race meetings, and I didn't have to ask her twice whether she wanted to attend such events with me. She had been increasingly difficult to get on with in recent months, though. Unbeknown to Jane, I had managed to put behind me the deep hurt I'd suffered through her infidelity in April. I tried really hard to help Jane as much as I could with her showjumping career, all whilst trying to run my own business, Discreet Intelligence Reports and Technical Services (DIRTS). DIRTS had really taken off in recent years as a result of my involvement with the Jockey Club.

As we approached Fontwell, the traffic on the road increased dramatically. I was not unduly worried, though; my guests were not due to arrive until one o'clock, and it was now just before twelve. I had organised a buffet lunch in the Richmond Rooms and expected about 100 to 120 people to attend. Clients both old and new. It was not so much a case of advertising my business; I never advertised. I'd been offered an indecent amount of money, however, for my business at the recent Royal Ascot meeting, as reported later in *The Racing Post* and various financial rags. Although this summer's craze was multimillion-pound buyouts of dot-com and dot-uk businesses, mine was not one of them.

My clients were mainly connected to the horse-racing industry in one form or another: owners, trainers, jockeys, wannabes, and, of course, those Hooray Henry types born with silver spoons in their mouths, the ones who rode in point-to-points for the simple reason that it would look good on their curricula vitae.

To say I loathed these Henrys would be an overstatement, but I certainly did not respect them to any great degree. My belief was that you earned your spurs; you should not just be given them or expect them as a birthright. There were, to my mind, too many people getting a living out of this industry through who they knew and not what they knew – especially this new breed of media hacks on satellite channel racing programmes, who constantly tipped favourites that invariably get beaten day after day.

People like these represented a certain section of my company's clients, and no matter what I thought of them, I had to admit they did pay me really well and quite promptly to sort out their problems when they could not handle them themselves. And believe me, there is not a day that goes by in the racing industry where you will not be shocked or somewhat surprised at the goings-on within the sport itself.

After some forty minutes of bumper-to-bumper queuing, we eventually made it to Goodwood and parked relatively easily. We picked up our badges from the necessary office and made our way to the Richmond Rooms, where I would spend most of the day in conversation and welcoming clients old and new who might be interested in my company's services. Set up some five years earlier, as its full name implied, DIRTS offered discreet intelligence reports and technical services. When there was any dirty washing to be done in the racing industry, invariably, my company would do the laundry, so to speak; collating or collecting evidence, field surveillance, and production of videos to be used in evidence was usually the difference between winning and losing cases. We were the best around. The Jockey Club was by far our biggest account.

It would be equally true to say that for every satisfied client, there was one that would rejoice in dancing upon my grave, and if it were not for some long prison sentences, there would be some who would willingly like to put me there.

My wealthiest client once told me that the establishment – Parliament, the European Union, etc. – were merely pawns with no "real" power. The power to sanction wars or to take out heads of state, the power to move billions of pounds around the world or to enact sanctions, now that was *real* power. However, my wealthiest client did not have such power, nor would he ever, even though his racing interest had so far cost him the best part of £100 million, in the last twenty years or so that he'd been keenly interested in racing and breeding. Robert Argonaut was born wealthy. Before his fortieth birthday, he'd inherited a massive empire of utility companies. His holdings consisted of businesses and properties amassed by his late father who, with various friends, had made fantastic fortunes of unimaginable proportions during their heyday – which included the two world wars, although the exact nature of their business ventures had never been revealed. Robert did tell me one day that the answer to accumulating wealth was supply and demand – if your clients demand it and you can supply it, you will one day own them and all that they have! Robert's father and friends, though, had lived in a nuclear-free world.

Robert Argonaut only had one runner at today's meeting, a stakes race for two-year-old colts with £45,000 in prize money, which meant very little to him. He was more interested in breeding and making sure that the bloodline he'd built over the years, with careful selection of mares and colts, continued in his quest for more classic winners. The blue ribbon of this sport was to win the Derby at Epsom; Robert had told me that a Derby winner could be worth millions every year if his progeny were to be prolific winners as well.

"Supply and demand, my boy", he said now as he pulled me to one side, confiding, "I'm not going to run my horse today. The going is far too soft, and it would not be a nice experience first time out for such a nice horse."

I agreed, nodding intelligently, taking in all that Robert said to me as words of wisdom, golden nuggets of common sense from a man who knew this game inside out, as he always put it.

Robert was drinking champagne; I had my usual cup of tea. I commented on horse number 6, a colt called Hot Tea. The only reason I mentioned the horse was because of the fact that its sire, Northern Lancer, had sired Robert's horse. Robert told me it cost £20,000 to send a broodmare to Northern Lancer, and then your broodmare must have at least been placed in Group Company to entitle you to have your mare covered by such a high-class sire. I asked Robert why Hot Tea had only made £20,000 at the yearling sales the previous year (it said so in the racecard), and Robert said that the horse was a bad walker and looked as though it would need a lot of time before it would come into itself; obviously, the breeders were not too happy with what their broodmare had thrown and were glad just to get their money back at the yearling sales. (I was not entirely convinced Robert had told me the truth; my inner sense told me he was spinning a yarn.)

I'd had some dealings with Hot Tea's trainer in the past; a small-time trainer from just outside Guildford in Surrey. He worked hard for his owners and always turned his horses out well, even if they did not win. Jonathan Ridger liked to have a crack at the big novice chases, at places like Kempton, Sandown, and Ascot, and, invariably, when he had runners, they would get placed at big odds, mainly because the opposition fell by the wayside through being too fearless with their jumping, and also because of overzealous jockeys who seemed to want to win at all costs. Jonathan's jockeys were usually good horsemen; they would take the ride knowing they probably wouldn't win but would get round.

Jonathan schooled all his horses at home, and Rachel and Rebecca, his twin teenage daughters, loved every minute of it. Coming from a showjumping background, their homework on the schooling ground invariably bore fruit when it came to jump racing. Though only 15, both were highly talented horsewomen. Jonathan had told me that both girls wanted to be jockettes in a year's time, when they would be old enough. Jonathan was mainly a National Hunt trainer (jumping). It was seldom he had runners on the flat on turf at grade 1 tracks like Goodwood.

I knew where I would find Jonathan, so I headed for the lads' canteen, after telling Robert I was busting for a pee and had to extricate myself quickly. As usual, there was Jonathan, brown trilby still on his head, (I was sure he slept with it on), white shirt, blue tie, grey suit, brown overcoat, binoculars over his right arm, *The Racing Post* in his overcoat's left pocket.

"Jonathan, can I get you another cup of tea?" I asked.

He replied, "Have you ever known me to refuse?"

He muttered on about the price of pork pies, and since I was after some information, I put Jonathan's freshly brewed cuppa down on the dining table, together with the pork pie and pot of mustard. (The price of that pork pie was one of the best investments I ever made, it later turned out.)

As I sat down, I thought about how much this reminded me of three years ago at Plumpton, when I first met Jonathan and he asked me if I could help him.

One of his horses was bought out of a seller after winning, and to Jonathan's astonishment, made 8,000 guineas. (Horses were always sold in guineas, with a guinea being equal to £1.05.) The buyer, a local jack who owned a café--cum-bar in Brighton, asked Jonathan if he would train the horse for him. Although Jonathan was keen to be without the horse, he didn't mind taking it back with a new owner. A good day's work, it seemed, as he drove back along the A3 in Surrey towards Guildford and home.

As he turned into his drive and up to his yard, there was Stu Ward in his yard looking at the horses. Jonathan got out of the box and enquired as to what he was doing there.

Stu replied, "If you're going to train a horse for my syndicate, I wanted to know exactly where you were situated before the eleven other members come to see the horse on Sunday."

Jonathan was gobsmacked; the thought of twelve people coming to see the horse on Sunday gave him sleepless nights. Sunday came and went: twelve cups of tea, various cakes and biscuits; to Jonathan, a complete waste of two hours, and a parking nightmare. This indeed was the beginning of his worst nightmare.

To be fair, Jonathan did his best with the horse, a six-year-old bay gelding called Trying Times. Since it was bought out of the seller, Jonathan had run the horse twice more and been placed on both occasions in substandard 2-mile handicaps over hurdles. The syndicate had been in operation twelve weeks, and the horse had won them some £850 in place money. However, poor Jonathan had endured twelve weeks of pure hell, with phone calls every day enquiring after the horse's health. Every Sunday, syndicate members and their girlfriends would turn up from Stu's bar, claiming to be part owners. In three months, Jonathan had received no training fees whatsoever from Stu Ward. He was owed somewhere in the region of £2,000.

Jonathan then made me a proposition: if I could get the horse out of the yard, and the £2,000 training fees from Stu Ward, I could have 50 per cent of the fees, and that was a cool £1,000.

It proved quite a simple task. I hired a horsebox for the evening, went to Guildford, loaded him up (Trying Times, that is), and took him to Brighton. I conveniently parked the horsebox outside the Konkordski Bar (as Stu had called his establishment), which was in Marine Parade, 200 yards to the left of the Palace Pier. I put the ramp down, so you could see the horse from the windows of the bar. I then put a banner on the box. It read: "My name is Trying Times. I am a racehorse. My owner won't pay my trainer. Where will I stay tonight?"

Within seconds, Stu was outside, gesticulating. However, it had the desired effect. Trying Times stayed at my stables near Hickstead that night, and Stu got a local trainer, Jamie Bolton, to pick him up the next day, after he had come round to pay me £2,000 for Jonathan, as well as the cost of the horsebox hire, for which I charged him £100. Stu Ward was seething. Jonathan was ecstatic that his problem was no more.

"What you after then?" Jonathan said now as I settled back in my chair.

I replied, "Nothing really."

"You wouldn't buy me a pork pie if you were after 'nothing'. Come on, I know you well enough to know you've got something on your mind, something you want an answer to. And you know I can supply that answer, or you wouldn't be here. Am I right?"

"Yes, Jonathan, you're right," I said with a grin. "You've never been guilty of putting your hand in your pocket when somebody else could pay,

Jonathan, so why did you buy Hot Tea for 20,000 guineas at the yearling sales last year, when the most expensive horse you've ever bought until then was 2,000 guineas?"

"What's it got to do with you?" Jonathan asked. "I suppose you've been talking to that rich money-is-no-object client of yours, Argonaut. Has he put you up to this?"

I told Jonathan the truth, explaining that I had been speaking to Robert Argonaut earlier, and he'd informed me that he was not running his horse in the stakes race. "He's pulling him out because of the ground; he doesn't want to risk the horse first time out," I said.

Jonathan's eyes lit up. "What did you say?"

I repeated what I'd just said, adding that Robert would not be running his horse because the going was far too heavy.

Jonathan grabbed hold of my arm, sending my cup and saucer flying. Luckily, there were only a few people in the canteen, as most of the lads had left to go and see the first race.

"Steve, are you kosher? Are you telling me the truth?"

I said, "Yes, yes. I've no reason to lie to you, Jonathan. I just wanted to know why you suddenly decided to splash out 20,000 guineas on a yearling that's a bad walker, and from what I can gather from professional opinion, needs time to mature. I just couldn't get the horse out of my mind, how you managed to get it to the races today, fit and ready to race."

Jonathan beckoned for me to follow him.

I said, "Where are we going?"

He said, "To the stables to see Hot Tea."

I asked inquisitively, "Why?"

Jonathan said, "I trust you, Steve. If the Jockey Club gave you a security-clearance badge to investigate on its behalf on every racecourse in the country, that's good enough for me. Follow me."

The security guard nodded as he inspected Jonathan's trainer's badge and my security badge issued direct from the Jockey Club.

It had been decided about eighteen months ago that, because the Jockey Club was one of my main clients, full security clearance should be made available to me at all times, to allow any investigation to proceed without hold-up or delay. I did not know what I was about to see or do, but it occurred to me that every job had its perks.

We came up to Hot Tea's box, and Jonathan opened the door. He said to me, "What do you see?"

I said, "A two-year-old colt, probably about 14.2 hands high, with a hard-on." (That was not unusual in midsummer, even though it was still raining, though not as hard as it had been earlier – the rain, that is!) I added, "I am not a horseman. Well, not in your league, anyway, so tell me what made you give £20,000 for this colt?"

He said one word: "Bloodlines."

"Jonathan," I said. "Level with me. Look, I know your horse and Robert's have the same sire, so explain to me why you got excited in the canteen and brought me here to see your little colt."

"Steve," he said. "You just don't see it do you? Metaphorically speaking. Look, get some paper, I'll show you."

After I gave him some paper and a pen, he did show me. He drew a family tree of his two-year-old colt. It showed Hot Tea was sired by Northern Lancer out of Dance for Tea. In layman's terms this simply meant that Hot Tea's father was Northern Lancer and his mother was Dance for Tea.

Jonathan then showed me the family tree for Robert's two-year-old colt, pointing out the similarities: both two-year-olds had the same father (Northern Lancer) but different mothers; Robert's two-year-old, which was called North Star, was by a mare called Northern Lights, which won the Oaks and 1,000 guineas, both Group 1 races at Epsom, and Newmarket some years ago.

I then got the gist of what Jonathan was trying to explain to me. The two-year-olds Hot Tea and North Star were half-brothers: same father, different mothers. Jonathan explained that when Dance for Tea (Hot Tea's mother) was placed in Group Company, it was at Goodwood a few years before, when the going was like today, desperately heavy. He also explained to me that Robert Argonaut had telephoned him (Jonathan) many times, trying to purchase Hot Tea from him. His latest offer had £50,000, just last week.

I asked the obvious question. "Why does Robert want your colt so much, Jonathan?"

Grinning from ear to ear, he replied, "It's simple, Steve. He wants Hot Tea to safeguard his bloodline that he's built up over the years. All Robert's breeding horses are Group 1 winners, both sires and broodmares. All his stock are blue bloods, winners of the Derby, Oaks, etc. – all the English Classics, French Group 1 races, and Irish Group 1 races. He also has Breeders' Cup–winning stock in America. In short, Steve, your mega-rich friend, Mr Robert Argonaut, could lose millions if I were to run Hot Tea and he was no good, and then I bred from him."

I said to Jonathan, "I see your point, but why didn't Robert buy the colt when it was a yearling like you did, or at least bid against you?"

Jonathan said, "Steve, you're beginning to see the light. Due to an amazing blunder by those Hooray Henry prats that work for him, they had broken down on their way to the sales. BT were doing repairs at the time, and the phones were not working in the auctioneer's office, so they could not even bid on the telephone; not one of them even had a mobile. I was just in the right place at the right time, and Argonaut, that golden bollocks, thinks he can buy me off with £50,000!"

I said, "Jonathan, just tell me one more thing. Why did you knock my tea out of my hands in the canteen?"

Jonathan started laughing, and then he said, "I think it's my lucky day."

I said, "You don't, do you?"

He said, "Yes, I do."

I said, "Let me have another look at your colt."

Jonathan could not stop laughing. I've never ever seen him smile before, let alone laugh, and there we were at Goodwood, and he believed he was going to win a stakes listed race with a horse that had never run before, a race that had a prize of £45,000 to the winner.

We were both standing, looking over the stable door at Hot Tea, when Robert Argonaut's chauffeur appeared, with a security man in attendance. He had with him a letter addressed to Jonathan Ridger.

I had met the chauffeur, Vernon Poole, a few years before. An ex-SAS man, Vernon was always immaculately dressed in his smart grey uniform and cap. He had been with Robert Argonaut ever since he leaving the army in the mid-1980s.

"I am instructed to hand you this letter and wait for a reply, Mr Ridger," said Vernon. He looked at me as if I shouldn't be there, and then he said, "Good afternoon, Mr Hurst."

I exchanged pleasantries with Vernon, and then hinted to the security man that we should withdraw from earshot, which Vernon gratefully acknowledged.

Jonathan read the letter, and then, half laughing and half shouting, said, "Seventy-five thousand pounds! Is that all your boss, Golden Bollocks, wants to give me, Vernon? After my horse wins the three o'clock race, tell your boss it will cost him £150,000 to buy him, and the price will go up by £25,000 every week thereafter."

With no sign of any feelings whatsoever, Vernon Poole repeated what Jonathan had said, writing down his comments word for word, as raindrops dripped from his peaked cap onto the shoulders of his immaculate grey chauffeur's uniform.

He dismissed himself by thanking Jonathan Ridger for his time, nodding to me, and saying, "Good day, Mr Hurst."

"Vernon, please tell Mr Argonaut that I'll be back shortly," I said.

"Are you sure, Jonathan?" I said.

"Come here, Steve," he said.

Once again, we looked again over Hot Tea's door, and for the first time, I noticed Jonathan's gaze fall on his colt's feet.

"He's got his mother's feet, and I've been working him over 6 furlongs," Jonathan said. "Today's race is 5 furlongs, in bottomless going."

I must admit, they were the biggest feet I'd ever seen on a 2 -year-old, and to some extent, I could understand Jonathan's excitement. I could also see Robert's concern, and I hoped that somehow my clients would reach an agreement between themselves, in their own way. They were both gentlemen of honour but from very different backgrounds. For one, it was a full-time job making the work pay; for the other, it was just a game to play, without getting your hands dirty. As far as Jonathan was concerned, though, he had done the graft: he'd got the horse fit and ready, much to everybody's amazement – and win, lose, or draw, Robert would pay.

Jonathan winked at me. "There's only five runners now," he said. "Go and have £50 on. He'll be a big price, coming from my yard. I'm off to the saddling boxes to get ready. Steve, do me a favour," he added. "Would you tell Robert not to let the bloodline stray again?"

I said, "Sure, but I think Robert's already got the message."

Jonathan said, "He's a bloody fool if he hasn't. Oh, Steve, ring me tomorrow, would you? There is another job I need doing by someone I can trust."

I said I'd call, and then I left and went to the bookies to put my £50 on Hot Tea. I was staggered to see that Hot Tea was the rag, at 100 to 1 on all boards. I quickly worked out that £50 won me £5,000. I placed my bet and went back to join my guests.

I had only been gone some twenty-five minutes, and the favourite had flopped in the first race at two o'clock, trailing in last. The horses were going down for the second as I entered the Richmond Rooms, where my guests seemed to have doubled in number since I'd left. I managed to get myself another cup of warm tea, and then Vernon Poole saw me and asked if I would accompany him to Robert's private box, now in the sanctuary of the covered Richmond enclosure. Vernon was now hatless.

I finished my tea and followed Vernon to Robert's private box. Robert was sitting in the box alone, with what looked like a large brandy in front of him.

"Sit down, Steve," Robert said as I entered. "Vernon," he added in a more authoritative tone, "don't let anyone in until we've finished."

"Yes, sir," Vernon replied.

"Now then," said Robert in a more business-like manner. "You know my problem, Steve. What can I do about it?"

I instinctively said, "Buy the horse off him after it wins today."

Robert had started drinking his brandy whilst waiting for me to reply, and when I did, he nearly choked, spraying me with the liquid where I sat, directly opposite him. Half the contents of the glass must've hit me.

"What?" he said. "*What?!*" The second *what* was several decibels louder than the first.

I told Robert what Jonathan had told me, explaining all about the bloodlines and that Hot Tea only acted in desperate underfoot conditions. I then told him about Hot Tea's unusually big feet, and how Jonathan had been working the horse over 6 furlongs and not 5. "Hot Tea will probably win today, but unless given the same conditions as today, he'll never win another race," I added.

I had never seen Robert Argonaut in such deep concentration. He did not even hear the crowd cheering when the second race favourite got turned over by the outsider, Dark Skies.

Finally, he said, "Of course, Steve. You're right. Would you act for me in the purchase of Hot Tea?"

I said, "Of course I will."

"Very well," said Robert. "Now tell me what you think."

"Does that matter?"

"Yes, Steve, it does. I'm a client of yours, and so is Jonathan Ridger. I'm sure we both, to a great extent, value your opinion, as we have both valued the work you've carried out for us on occasions."

"Very well, Robert," I said. "Jonathan has convinced me sufficiently that his horse will win today; his odds are 100 to 1. I have £50 on Hot

Tea. You could afford to have £1,000 on him. That would eradicate your problem, would it not?"

Robert frowned, stood up, and said, "I don't gamble, Steve."

"In that case," I said, "pay up or shut up." I looked at my watch and informed Robert that I had to go. "I have other clients to entertain."

"Yes, of course," said Robert, still staring out the patio doors overlooking the racecourse, sucking on a cigar, and in deep thought.

"Steve, when you see Vernon, please tell him that I have a job for him. And would you call me tomorrow morning to conclude this?"

"Yes, of course, Robert," I said, and then I left to get back to my own party. As I left, I told Vernon that the boss wanted him, and then I headed to the lift to get back down to the ground floor.

Vernon followed me, walking up to the lift, and as we got in, he said, "Have you taught my boss how to gamble?" (He was probably earwigging at the door, listening to our conversation.)

I said, "Do you trust your boss?"

To which Vernon said, "Of course I do."

I said, "Well, put £50 on Hot Tea for yourself, Vernon. Robert wants you in his box right away to place a bet for him."

And without any further ado, I joined my guests.

The horses were down at the start for the three o'clock race, which was Hot Tea's race, and although there was some money in the ring for Hot Tea, there was no significant gamble, only tens, twenties, and the odd fifty. I guessed that Vernon had spread his bets into small amounts, so as not to alert the bookies that the 100 to 1 on offer would stand. Indeed, at the off Hot Tea was still the complete outsider, although, his odds had dramatically dropped to 25 to 1. I was about to tear up my ticket. *Why on earth do I listen to these people?* I thought. Hot Tea was about 10 lengths behind the other four runners, but not going any farther back. But then, with 2 furlongs to go, the complexion of the race changed: only 6 lengths behind, but, more importantly, the favourite and second-favourite were being scrubbed along and going nowhere. One of the other two had wandered off to the far rail, and suddenly I thought, *Hello.* At the furlong marker, Hot Tea had not changed gear and was just going at the same speed as when he started. But the favourite and second-favourite tired badly, and Hot Tea came through to win by 4 lengths going away.

There were 6 lengths between second and third, with the other two almost tailed off, which in a 5-furlong race was unheard of.

I never showed any sign of jubilation, just continued to drink tea and chat to guests and clients until the last race. That was when Jane joined me, after spending most of the afternoon in the Dunne's private box. (The Dunnes were big in the showjumping world; in fact, they owned the international showjumping arena just down the road from where I lived in Sayers Common.) I told her about my win, and we decided to dine in Brighton on the way home that evening.

Jane went to the ladies' room, and I went to collect my winnings: £5,000 for £50. I safely tucked the money away in my jacket pocket. Robert spotted me returning to the Richmond Rooms whilst getting out of the lift with a woman I guessed to be his wife, Suzi. He gave me the indication that he wanted to speak to me but did not want to say anything in front of Suzi – however, he did introduce me to her. I had never met Suzi, so we exchanged pleasantries, and then Robert asked me if I would call him early in the morning.

I said, "Yes, of course, Robert."

The Argonauts and I said goodbye.

When Jane returned, some of her friends were with her – she had bumped into them earlier, whilst with the Dunnes. We casually walked to the car park, laughing and joking. Jane suggested her friends join us to finish off the day by dining in Brighton on the way home. I was quite hungry by that point, and so were Jane's friends, so Brighton it was.

As I said, they called it Glorious Goodwood; I, for one, was most certainly not complaining.

CHAPTER 2

I never liked drinking alcohol whilst I was working, either at the races or elsewhere. Hence all the cups of tea. Goodwood, with 40,000 people in attendance, did not give me the inspiration to indulge anyway. Another one of my "funnies", as Jane always called them, was the fact that I never drank alcohol midweek. It was Wednesday, as midweek as could be. So I told Jane and the others – Mark and Julie, who were really her friends, not mine – to order whatever they wanted, and the meal was on me.

Jane quickly let Mark and Julie know about my win on the horses – a truncated form, thank God! I ordered two halves of lager for Mark and Julie, a Cinzano and soda for Jane, and a Perrier water and lime for myself. The Greek restaurant that we chose was one of my favourites, although we had not been there since Christmas.

It was weekends that we usually attended, about once a month, and always in a party of twelve or fourteen people. The waiters were friendly, the Greek music was pleasant, and if Jane could get enough drink inside me, on these occasions, I couldn't resist getting up and doing a rendition of Frank Sinatra hits. Wednesday night was a lot quieter, however, and although the place was half full, it seemed more subdued. I thought, perhaps, it would be best in future to leave Zorba the Greek to our usual monthly visits (or whenever Jane fancied going again).

Jane ordered what I always had (another one of my so-called funnies): grilled king prawns with a garlic dip, lamb kleftiko, which is a small joint of lamb slowly cooked on the bone in a clay oven, new potatoes, and a salad. Mark and Julie both ordered sea bass for the main course, and a selection of dips to start with; Jane ordered dips as starters as well. The dips were the usual for a Greek restaurant: hummus and taramasalata, served with hot pitta bread.

Following the small talk over supper and the usual Irish coffees, Jane and I exchanged goodbyes with Mark and Julie. Jane came out with the classic "we must do it again soon"; everybody agreed, and then we went our separate ways.

Mark and Julie managed to get a cab within a few seconds. They lived locally in Brighton. We waved goodbye as their taxi sped past us a few yards down the road, and then continued walking to the NCP car park, which was on five floors nearby to the Metropole Hotel. As we neared my run-of-the-mill Rover diesel saloon on the third floor, a car suddenly exploded into life and shot towards us from about 30 yards away. Luckily for us, there was a gap between cars where we were standing, and I pulled Jane towards me. She seemed mesmerised by the headlights, and the shoulder strap on her bag somehow managed to hook itself onto the offside-door mirror of the offending car as it sped past, pulling her right shoulder back round to the speeding car. Jane screamed as her right shoulder joint dislocated from its socket. As the leather strap broke, I fell onto Jane and the bonnet of the Sierra next to my Rover. Jane was screaming and crying. I was shaken but at the same time baffled as to why someone should try to run us over in a car park.

Jane cried out repeatedly, "They tried to kill us! They tried to kill us!"

The car that had tried to kill us was a Golf GTI. A white one, with big tyres, and what sounded like a straight through bore exhaust.

As we slipped off the bonnet of the Ford Sierra, I noticed it was a J registration. I did not have a mobile phone on me, but I knew Jane had one. I looked for her bag and then noticed my £5,000 winnings strewn across level 3 of the car park. A hairbrush was on the bonnet next car down from the Sierra. An old little mini car, which also had a J registration, but it had the J at the end of the registration number, not like the Golf GTI, which had it at the beginning. The rest of Jane's bag – nail file, tissues, diary, purse, lipstick, and phone – were intermingled with my money all over level 3. Jane's mobile phone was perched upon one of my £50 notes, wedged up against the tyre of an Audi. After paying the restaurant bill, I had given Jane the money to put in her bag for safe keeping.

Jane was still screaming with pain as a car-park attendant, who could not have been a day under 60, came hopping over, saying, "Now then, now then, what's going on?" By the time he reached me, I had already got through to the emergency services and asked them to send an ambulance as soon as possible to the car park nearby to the Metropole.

To his credit Hopalong (the car-park attendant) managed to grab the gist of what had happened. "Was it the white Golf GTI?" he asked.

I said, "Yes."

His eyes then focused on all the money lying around, and I told him he could keep every penny over £4,600 that he managed to find. He agreed with a nod of his head, and I attended Jane, who was sitting up by now, cradling her right arm, and sobbing. I collected the contents of her bag and tied a knot into the broken strap.

About five minutes later, the sound of the ambulance siren could be heard quite clearly, and Hopalong indicated to me that he had found £4,650; I had a £50 note in my pocket that I picked up with the phone; the Greek cost me £100, so there was still £200 missing. I gave him £100 and informed him that there was still £200 missing and that if he found it he could keep it, as long as I could come and see him the following evening to try to get some more details out of him about the Golf GTI.

"My name is Henry," he said. "I finish at 9 p.m."

I said "Thanks, Henry."

It was 9.15 p.m. when the ambulance arrived. I told Henry I was going to the hospital with my fiancée, and I gave him a business card with my name and address on it: Discreet Intelligence Reports and Technical Services, Mr Steven Hurst, White Horse Farm, Sayers Common, East Sussex, followed by the telephone and fax number 121238, and then the code for the Brighton area in brackets (01273).

Henry read the card and said, "Right."

Before I left, I told Henry that I would gladly pay for any other information he could get about the white Golf GTI, and then I gave him the keys to my Rover and asked him if he would follow me to the hospital, not realising when I asked him that I didn't even know if he could drive or not.

Henry said, "No problem. I live near the hospital anyway."

The hospital was only 2 miles away, in Eastern Road, Brighton, and we were there well before 9.30 p.m. Henry parked the car in the A&E car park, which was overlooked by the block of flats where he lived, and left the keys for me at reception.

Dr Philip Thomas put Jane's shoulder back into its socket. You could not fail to know who he was by the size of the nameplate on the lapel of his doctor's white coat. Jane was much more herself by now, and back in control. Dr Thomas indicated to Jane that the shoulder would feel very sore for a few days, and she should allow a few more days for the bruising to come out. He then put the arm in a sling, telling her not to use the arm for a few days. We both thanked Dr Thomas and left the hospital at about 10.30 p.m. It was only a thirty-minute drive to Hickstead, so at least we could get to bed before midnight – or so I thought.

The entrance off the old A23 to White Horse Farm is 200 yards before the old service station. When I moved in some five years ago, I had had two brick piers with oak wooden gates installed. The gates were electronically operated, and the piers and gates faced the A23. There would be no need to use the remote control tonight, though, as both gates were burning bright orange, a plume of smoke spiralling upwards towards the clear dark-blue midnight sky.

Wedged between the doors was a horsebox, which was also well ablaze and certainly not going to be carrying any more horses anywhere. This box had made its final journey, and my front gates were its resting place. A tarmac drive ran from the now-blazing gates to the front door of the farmhouse, some 50 yards away. On both sides of the drive were grazing paddocks where I occasionally turned out horses.

It wasn't until I got out of the car and walked round to the other side that I noticed a policeman there, as well as a police motorcycle with its blue light flashing. He told me he had summoned reinforcements and alerted the fire brigade.

"What about an ambulance for the injured?" I asked.

He said, "There's no one here."

The officer was not wearing his crash helmet, and I said to him, "Are you telling me someone's done this on purpose?"

He said, "It would appear so, sir."

I checked to make sure that Jane was still asleep in the car; she was. The sedative which Dr Thomas had given her had obviously worked. When I returned to the police officer, I could smell diesel fumes in the air, and we both retreated another 25 yards or so from the blazing horsebox. My car, with Jane in it, was some 40 yards before the horsebox, parked in a lay-by and well away from the raging blaze. Standing there looking at the box, it suddenly dawned on me that it was the same box I had hired to transport Trying Times to Brighton from Jonathan Ridger's yard. It was the same box I'd parked outside Stu Ward's Konkordski Bar. As I looked at the box, I could just make out the words "White's Horse"; the rest was a raging mess of orange, red, and blue flames. The full wording was "White's Horsebox Hire, Daily Rates". Chris Collins had been in the village for years and used to run the garage. His family had run the business for over forty years, but the new dual carriageway which replaced the old A23 turned Sayers Common into a ghost village. It suited me, as I enjoyed the quietness, and my business was mainly concerned with the immediate surrounding area. I had purchased White Horse Farm from Chris five years before, and he carried on, doing his horsebox services from a flat above the garage, which suited him.

I turned round to the policeman and said, "That's my neighbour's box." As I said "neighbours," the diesel fuel tanks exploded; the blast sent us both crashing to the ground.

Thankfully, we were only stunned but not physically hurt, which was more than can be said for the policeman's motorcycle. It would not be carrying anybody about anymore. Embedded in my post-and-rail fence, it blazed away merrily.

Jane was still asleep, thankfully, when the services arrived. I informed the plain-clothes policeman who had taken charge that I lived in the farmhouse and that I thought the horsebox belonged to Chris Collins, who lived at the garage just down the road. I also explained briefly about the "accident", as I called it, at the car park in Brighton, and then I said that I had to get my fiancée inside.

The plain-clothes officer, Detective Chief Inspector Heyes of the Sussex Police Constabulary, said he would have to take a statement from me. "Could I do it tomorrow?" he asked.

I said, "Yes, of course."

He told me that the firemen would be there all night damping down and that forensics would be here at 7 a.m. It was now 12.30 a.m. Hopefully, I might get five or six hours' sleep tonight. The inspector saw Jane in the car, still asleep, with her arm in the sling, and I assumed he must have believed me.

I started the car up and drove past the blazing horsebox, some 50 yards to another entrance off the road to my stables, which my staff, together with all and sundry, used. This entrance was the main entrance (which I would have driven up earlier anyway) to the rear of the farmhouse, the stables, car park, and ménage; it was also the main entrance for horseboxes. I drove up to the back door of the farmhouse. The security light, which reacted to body heat, came on when I got out of the car. I opened the passenger door and got Jane out of the car as tenderly as I could, trying not to move her right arm. I didn't realise how heavy Jane actually was. I'd picked her up before in bouts of horseplay, and quite often, in the summer, would put her over my shoulder and take her to the hay barn, deposit her in the hay, and then have my wicked way with her, but it seemed to me that dead weight – or in Jane's case, comatose weight – was much heavier. Anyway, I managed to get her upstairs to the bedroom, placed her gently on the bed, and took her shoes off. It was quite a warm night, so I just put a sheet over her, and I slept in one of the other bedrooms.

I was mentally making a note of who had asked me to ring them tomorrow when I dozed off. I obviously needed the sleep. I did not remember more than two names before I fell asleep: North Star and Hot Tea.

I woke to the sound of ringing bells but was not sure as to whether I was dreaming or not, as the ringing was incessant. *Tubular Bells* was one of my all-time favourite albums, but my senses began to tell me reassuringly that it was indeed not a dream; obviously, if it was not a dream, then it was neither *Tubular Bells* nor the ambulance taking Jane and me to the hospital. Further ringing confirmed to my senses that someone had a finger pressed firmly on my front doorbell and was not going to let go until the door was answered.

Wearily I got up and made my way to the front door; the nearer I got to the door, the louder the ringing became. I shouted out to the ringer, "All right, all right! I'm coming!" To my great relief, the ringing ceased immediately. I opened the front door to be greeted by a very upset Chris Collins, the owner of the burned-out horsebox, the remains of which were still smouldering between the two piers that had held my two front oak gates. A damping-down crew was still attending what was left of Chris's horsebox. I beckoned to Chris to come in and go into the kitchen, towards the back of the house, before he could say anything.

I said, "Tea or coffee?"

Chris muttered, "Coffee."

It seemed to me he said it out of astonishment.

Before he regained his composure, I informed him, "Someone tried to kill Jane and me in Brighton last night. Jane's upstairs sleeping, but she has a dislocated shoulder. The doctor didn't put it back until late last night at Brighton General."

By this time, the kettle had boiled, and as I couldn't wait to make the percolated coffee, I quickly made two instant cups. I gestured to Chris to sit down. The upset in his face was now replaced by the look of concern.

"Who on earth would want to kill you and Jane?" Chris said. "What happened in Brighton? How did Jane get a dislocated shoulder? What time did you get back?"

"Steady on, Chris! Hold on a minute."

When Chris had calmed down, I slowly told him all that happened yesterday, from winning the £5,000 on Hot Tea at Goodwood, right through to when I carried Jane upstairs and then finally managed to get some sleep myself. I then reminded myself: *Ring Argonaut later this morning. And Jonathan Ridger too.*

I could see in Chris's face that he wanted to bring up the subject of his horsebox; he must have been wondering if I thought the theft of the horsebox had anything to do with what had happened to Jane and me in Brighton.

Before he could ask me, I told Chris, "I don't know if the two incidents could be linked." I then enquired as to whether DCI Heyes had contacted him.

Chris showed me a card with the chief inspector's name and telephone number on it. "This was put through my letter box," he said. The message on the back of the card asked Chris to ring the chief inspector 9 a.m.

It was now 7.30 a.m., as my kitchen clock informed me. I asked Chris to put the kettle back on for more coffee and also to make some toast. He was more than pleased to assist. As I was about to leave the kitchen to check on Jane, the front doorbell rang for a second time. As the front door was closer, I checked on that first.

"Steven Hurst, are you?" said this man at my front door, dressed in a white overall, Country Casual shirt, and loud bow tie. Even before he showed me his identity card, I knew he just had to be forensics. "Miles Valentine," he said, holding out his hand. I assumed he wanted me to shake it, so I obliged. "Just a few questions, old boy, before I start work. Have you a few minutes?" He enquired. I told him that I was just making some more coffee and suggested we go into the kitchen. I introduced him to Chris Collins, explaining that Chris was there at that hour because he was the owner of what was left of the horsebox.

Miles took his instant coffee black, with half a spoon of sugar. Chris and I both had white coffee, one sugar. We also tucked into some thick toast with plenty of butter.

Miles asked me if I minded Chris being there, but, as it was Chris's horsebox, I believed he had every right to be there, and told Miles such.

"Fine," said Miles. "That makes it so much easier for me."

Miles then told us what he hoped to find in the remains of the burned-out horsebox, and in the next twenty minutes, a synopsis of the world of forensics unfolded. Chris was utterly amazed and so focused on Miles's speech that he totally forgot about his coffee. I thanked Miles for his informal speech, which concluded with him asking for our fingerprints – solely for elimination purposes, he hastened to add. Chris could not wait to help. I informed Miles that I just wanted to check on Jane upstairs and would only be a few minutes. Chris gave Miles his fingerprints whilst I went upstairs.

Jane was still asleep, so I put another sheet over her and opened a window. I then went into the bathroom, where I showered and shaved. I felt so much better afterwards. I was dressed and back in the kitchen some twenty minutes later, just as Miles was finishing with Chris.

"My turn?" I enquired.

"Yes," said Miles.

I must have had steadier hands than Chris, because my turn only took ten minutes.

Miles thanked us very much for our cooperation and the coffee, and then he went about his business. He said he would inform DCI Heyes if he found any evidence, and the chief inspector, in turn, would inform Chris and me.

As Miles proceeded down the front path towards the burned-out horsebox, I asked Chris to come back into the kitchen. I asked him what he was going to do for some income now that his box was no longer in existence. He told me that, as he was to have left early this morning to pick some horses up from a stud near Chepstow for a local trainer, he had filled the horsebox up last night with diesel and left the garage gates open. He went to bed at ten o'clock last night and set his alarm for five o'clock this morning in order to leave at six. Also, he said that although the horsebox was insured for fire and theft, he did not have it insured fully comprehensive, as he could not afford to.

Much to my surprise – and to Chris's – I gave him £4,600 I had left from my winnings the previous day. I told him to get some transport until the insurers sorted out the claim, as he would obviously be out of business otherwise, knowing how long insurers take to settle.

Miles had said earlier that jealousy, vengeance, and joyriding were the commonest reasons for stealing a vehicle, especially a car. "Ninety per cent of cars are taken by joyriders. It is very rare for a commercial vehicle, especially a horsebox, to be taken by joyriders," he had informed us. He had told us this at the express request of DCI Heyes, who regarded this act of theft and vandalism as an act of vengeance or maybe a very stern warning, which was not to go unheeded.

As of now, I took it very seriously, as did the chief inspector. I had earlier disregarded him, but I now had a lot more respect for the man.

After giving Chris the money, I decided it was time to start sorting some things out. I then went to my office at the back of the house. The office door opened out onto the yard. I opened the door a little, retrieved the newspapers delivered earlier by the paperboy, put them on one of the office desks.

Chris followed me through to the office, thanked me profusely, and then went home with my money, seeking to find some suitable transport to carry on his business. I could see in Chris's eyes that he wanted me to help him, so as he left I suggested that he give Ginger Martin a ring at Edenbridge.

Ginger had been selling and hiring out horseboxes for years, ever since he bought his daughter a pony when she was 11 years old and had a heck of a job arranging transport to get the pony back to his farm from the Ascot Sales. He had gone to the sales with a friend who was part owner of an old Hunter chaser called the Dunk & Duck. In his time, he was a fair old three-mile chaser, having won at Cheltenham with his amateur co-owner on board, Rick "Row" Wilson. Rick looked like he was rowing a boat in a finish, and as fate would have it, his very first Hunter chase was at Windsor. Not only did he take the wrong course on the figure-eight track, he ended up in the River Thames, which ran alongside the track. To his credit, Rick Wilson saw the funny side, and to this day, he believed his nickname came about from that very first ride, although he won many, many amateur races over the years. He would never watch himself in a replay of a finish if given the chance by the television companies. Yes, he was one of the original *Hooray Henrys*, but he worked hard in the city and really enjoyed his chosen, if not dangerous, sport of being an amateur steeplechase jockey.

Retired Army Captain Pete Parker had bought the Dunk & Duck in partnership with Rick Wilson at the same Ascot Sale, some four years earlier; now he was back there to see the old fellow go through the ring. He would make an excellent schoolmaster for an up-and-coming young jockey. The Dunk & Duck was now 12 years old and had surprisingly very few miles on the clock; he was a 6-year-old before he'd had his first race.

The Duck made 2,000 guineas on the fall of the hammer that day, and Ginger brought the next lot: Number 121, a 13-hand 9-year-old pony whose rider had sadly outgrown the pony; easy to box, shoe, and clip; no vices, according to the catalogue. Ginger only made one bid, the final one. He eyed the two interested parties, and whilst they were bidding against each other, manoeuvred his way over to stand behind the bidder he believed would outbid the other. Georgie McCawley was standing by the door to the auction ring, the pony being led round in front of him. The auctioneer called for 300 guineas at the door – for the first, for the second– and then Ginger said, "'Scuse me," to Georgie, making him turn round. "Have you got a light, mate?" The auctioneer saw Ginger's arm go up, holding the catalogue, just as he was about to say third and last time. Ginger offered Georgie a cigarette. Georgie, not knowing that Ginger still had his arm stretched out with his catalogue in it to acknowledge to the auctioneer as he once again said third and last time, and then brought the gavel down with a bang to conclude the sale at 310 guineas. Both Georgie and Ginger were now facing the auctioneer, and both acknowledged him when he said sold by the door.

Ginger hurried to the auctioneer's clerk and paid her in readies (cash), and then he went to the office for his receipt and to pick up the pony's paperwork. Georgie had an account and never found out he had not bought the pony for 300 guineas until some hours later. By that time, Ginger was at home with his feet up. Ginger had dropped off Captain Parker a half an hour earlier at his home near Shere in Surrey, where he trained his pointers.

Ginger knew all about auctions. After all, he was a car dealer, and he reasoned that car auctions and horse sales were the same: Suss out the people in the know, watch what they buy, use their experience, only buy what they would buy; you may pay a bit more, but you can be sure you've got yourself a bargain.

The old adage always worked, and the cigarette trick never failed.

Ginger was just about to go to collect his daughter (then 11 years old) from school when Chris Collins arrived in the yard with his pony from the Ascot Sales.

They put the pony in one of the garages for the time being, and Ginger paid Chris £120 for the transportation, which he considered to be daylight robbery.

If Chris told me that story once, he must have told it to me a hundred times. Anna Martin, Ginger's daughter, was now 23 and an international showjumper. Since that day, Ginger had moved into the world of buying, selling, and hiring horses and horseboxes – as well as selling cars.

Yes, I was sure Ginger would be able to help Chris out, but at a price.

I dusted the cobwebs from my recollecting. Clearly, DIRTS had some work to do, and the sooner the better!

Just after ten o'clock, I was still sitting at my desk. Jane appeared in the doorway to the office, looking more worse for wear than if she'd been on an all-night bender. "Was I dreaming, Steve, or did someone try to kill us last night?" she said, followed by a loud shriek as she tried to move her right arm.

"I'm afraid it was no dream, Jane," I replied. I beckoned for her to follow me into the kitchen, where I made more coffee and toast. I then proceeded to bring Jane up to date in regard to the previous evening's events, culminating with Chris's horsebox buried into my front gates and then purposefully set ablaze, based on what I had gathered from the police.

Jane could not believe what she was hearing. However, the message finally got through that this indeed was reality when the chief inspector called to take a statement.

The doorbell rang yet again. Jane went and opened it whilst I finished off buttering the toast. DCI John Heyes was standing at the door, accompanied by forensics expert, Miles Valentine. Although surprised at the door being opened by Jane, the chief inspector did not let it show. He casually asked Jane how she was feeling this morning. "Steve is expecting me," he added quickly. "Can we come in?"

Though surprised by their presence, Jane replied, "Oh yes! Straight through the hallway to the kitchen."

The chief inspector and Miles thoughtfully wiped their feet on the doormat, and then they proceeded through the hallway to the kitchen.

After formal introductions, for which there had been no time the night before, I offered coffee to my guests, and once again the events of the previous night were discussed.

Jane was physically shaken by the chief inspector's synopsis of events. I'd made everything seem easy to handle – or perhaps in a way Jane was aware of my capabilities and therefore felt confident in them and in my ability to handle difficult situations. This was "real vicious thuggery", as the chief inspector put it, and as far as he was concerned, it was a direct warning from desperate criminals conveying a message. That message was abundantly clear, in his opinion: It was a warning to me of some form or other, not so much for something I had done, but probably for some existing investigation I was instructed in at the moment; perhaps I was getting too close.

The rest of the morning was taken up with Miles returning to the scene of the crime at the front gates – or what was now two badly burned piers and the badly burned brass and steel furniture of the front gates, which were now lying in ashes by the burned-out shell of the horsebox. He was trying to obtain more forensic evidence to help solve this crime and find the perpetrators. Meanwhile, Jane and I gave DCI Heyes a complete account of the previous day's activities, as well as what happened that night.

Having satisfied himself as to the amount of detail he had obtained, DCI John Heyes, as usual, pointed out that he might have to contact us again should we be needed for further enquiries, and then he extricated himself back to the police station. I then returned to my office at the back of the house, as I had phone calls to make and a team to assemble. Jane decided the best place for her was bed. Once again, she was soon fast asleep and in total oblivion – aware of neither her painful right arm nor the previous twenty-four hours.

I was in my office contemplating whether Argonaut would be in his office or at home so that I could determine which number to try first. Just as I was about to pick up the phone, it rang. I answered by reciting my number to the caller.

"Is that Steve Hurst?" said the caller, to which I replied, "Yes."

"I've found another £100," said the voice on the other end of the phone.

I quickly determined that it must be Hopalong from the car park in Brighton. I replied, "I told you that you could keep it."

"I know," said Hopalong. "And thank you, but I thought you might like to know that I found a broken door mirror not far from where your lady friend got hurt in the car park. I went down to the car park early this morning to see if I could find the rest of the money, and the mirror was lying next to a concrete post. I saw it had some white paint on it, and I thought that maybe that Golf hit it on the way out."

I took Hopalong's number and told him I would get back to him. I did not know whether to inform DCI Heyes or drive down to Brighton to see for myself what Hopalong had found. After I told Hopalong that I would, of course, ring him back, I asked if he would he put some of the paint scrapings in a small plastic bag right away and save them for me, along with the broken mirror. "Please do this at once, just in case the Golf driver comes back," I said.

Hopalong promised to obey my instructions and said he'd wait for me to contact him.

After again contemplating which number call to contact Robert Argonaut, in the end, Robert rang me, from his mobile phone. Vernon Poole was driving Robert from his London home down the M4 to Wiltshire, where he had a state-of-the-art training centre, not far from Marlborough.

Robert was unaware of my situation, and I didn't volunteer any information to him during our phone conversation; it was purely business, which mainly centred around my purchasing Hot Tea for him from Jonathan Ridger "as soon as possible", in Robert's words. I did not like to mention to Robert that maybe now Jonathan might not wish to sell his stakes winner, or indeed if Jonathan did agree to sell, who was to say whether he might have upped the price.

I promised Robert that I would act for him in the proposed purchase and that such business would be carried out as discreetly as possible. Robert positively wanted no publicity, and I was to inform Jonathan Ridger that if such conditions were not met to the letter, then Robert would not be interested at any price. Those instructions were Robert's final words as we finished our telephone conversation.

Robert continued his journey to his training complex, where he had recently installed John Gosling as his trainer. Gosling's father had trained horses near to the old racecourse at Lewes in East Sussex, many years before. In the early 1960s, Lewes was a vibrant training centre, and "Dowser", as John's father was affectionately known, got his nickname for the meticulous way he would search through the racing calendar, looking for and searching for races he knew his horses could win easily. One of Dowser's jockeys, after he had won the Derby at Epsom and came in to the winner's enclosure, encountered a scribe who asked him, "When did you know you had the race won?" In his native Aussie accent, Scobe (that was the jockey's nickname) replied, "Four months ago, when Dowser entered him!"

John was now a top-class trainer like his father was in the Swinging Sixties, and also as astute. He could place his horses equally as well as his highly regarded father had in his heyday. John Gosling had recommended to Robert that he should pull his horse out at Goodwood the previous day; it would not have been a good introduction for the horse to racing. That was the comment in the racing paper which I was idly reading.

Whilst talking to Robert, I could understand the reason behind the withdrawal, as Robert had already informed me yesterday; however, he had not told me that he pulled him out on his trainer's recommendation. I could also understand just how fortunate Jonathan Ridger had been. I reached for my phone book to get Jonathan's number to ring next, but I decided I needed another coffee first. Jonathan could wait another ten minutes or so.

Returning to my office with my coffee, I eventually got round to ringing Jonathan Ridger at about 12.15 p.m., which was about the time that exercise finished. Jonathan was in his office checking his entries as we spoke on the phone, whilst his twin daughters and staff finished off yard duties and swept up. The girls had been squabbling all morning as to who would ride Hot Tea in his work from now on, according to Jonathan. He also had the press on about the rumour going round that Robert Argonaut wanted to buy Hot Tea.

I thanked Jonathan for the tip, but made it clear to him that if he still wanted me to broker the deal for the sale of the horse, it would have to be in the strictest confidence, with no press releases whatsoever should a price be agreed to.

Jonathan, as I had previously thought, now felt himself to be in a position of power. He conceived he was pulling the strings. Referring to Argonaut, Jonathan said, "Tell Golden Bollocks that I want £250,000 for Hot Tea, take it or leave it."

I told Jonathan about my conversation yesterday at Goodwood with Argonaut's chauffeur. Vernon had delivered an offer at the boxes of £75,000, and I reminded Jonathan of his comments that it would cost Robert £150,000 when he won the three o'clock race. Jonathan, however, was fully wrapped up in his own smugness, not realising who actually held the purse strings. I informed Jonathan that I would tell Robert Argonaut that the colt was being offered at an unreasonable price, and I suggested that he, Jonathan, should ring me that evening, when, hopefully, the reality of the situation would again prevail.

Jonathan was going to milk the day for what it was worth, "for he who pays the ferryman calls the tune"; I wondered, though, as to whether Jonathan had enough money to pay him every week, so to speak. Robert Argonaut, after all, owned the ferryman, who worked for a wage, and Jonathan would surely ring me back that evening. Ferrymen never missed the boat, but would Jonathan miss his through greed?

No, not Jonathan, I mused. *He's too cute. Let him have his day, though.*

CHAPTER 3

I spent most of Thursday afternoon at home. I arranged for the burned-out horsebox to be taken away, after Miles had videoed and photographed it from every possible angle, and then I organised a bricklayer for a few weeks' time, as my gate piers needed to be rebuilt. I spoke to my insurers, DCI Heyes, Jane's parents, and goodness knows who else. Charlie Rogers, my secretary, would normally do all this for me, but Charlie (God bless her, she's a girl! Real name Charlotte) always had the last Thursday of the month off. It was a ritual thing for her, and we'd agreed when I first employed her some four years prior that the ritual could continue.

Charlie's education ended at Roedean when she was 19 (as I later found out, prior to employing her). Whilst playing cricket for the English Ladies under 20s, she had carried her bat through her team's innings after opening with her pal and best friend, Laura Hallett, who made 32 before being given "out caught behind", although Laura at first did not want to walk. (She could not believe the umpire's decision.) Begrudgingly, she eventually did, and at lunch, England was 122 for 4, and Charlie had just reached her 50. The umpires, one English and one Australian (England was playing against Australia), were competent but "passed it", as Charlie put it later whilst reminiscing. Laura, still seething at her dismissal, went with Charlie during lunch to question the Aussie umpire as to why she was given "out caught" when her bat, arms, and hands, were miles away as the ball passed through. "There was not even an appeal!" said Laura in a raised voice.

The Aussie umpire refused to comment, apart from telling Laura to "act like a young lady".

"Certainly," said Laura, "and you act like one too, without the young, and try to stay awake this afternoon; you might just make some right decisions!"

Charlie and Laura both walked away, giggling, and returned to the England dressing room.

When the umpires called time after lunch to resume play, all they could here from the England changing room were the girls singing, "Dozy Matilda, Dozy Matilda, Dozy Matilda's sleeping again." The English umpire couldn't help laughing. Rachel Flint said to her Aussie counterpart, "Come on, Mattie, think nothing of it. They're only teenagers. Girls just want to have fun, and so they should; we were young once, remember?"

Matilda was in a boiling rage. She was most definitely going to have her own back later that day.

England progressed to 216 for 9 with 2 overs left. Charlie needing just one run for her first century for England, in this limited 50 over one day international. Matilda had made some more dubious decisions in giving England's "tail out", but the third ball of the penultimate over was the pièce de résistance – a short delivery was timely despatched to third man (a cricketing fielding position), for an easy single. Although the ball was hit in the air, all the world and their mothers, apart from Matilda, knew that the ball bounced first, then into the hands of the fielder who threw in to the wicketkeeper, as the crowd applauded their appreciation of Charlie's 100. Matilda, seeing Charlie in the middle of the wicket, gave her "out caught". Mayhem then followed, with Charlie using her bat to whack Matilda across the backside, sending her sprawling across the wicket, bails and stumps going in every direction.

When play resumed after returning to the clubhouse, the England girls came out to field, minus Charlie and Laura, who were stood down for disciplinary reasons. England went on to bowl out Australia for 140, off just 36 overs. None of the wickets that fell were given by Matilda, though.

I never told Charlie I knew about her ritual. Laura, who also worked for me, had told me all about it at our office Christmas party a few years before, when she was completely blotto. I do not think Laura remembered telling me anyway. The ritual was that the England team, or as many of them as possible, always met on the last Wednesday of each month to party and give a rendition of "Dozy Matilda" to whoever was listening.

"We English are so funny. We're a nation of eccentrics," Laura insisted.

I smiled to myself, thinking of the girls now. As for Charlie, I could always rely on her; she would be in tomorrow. Laura was reliable too. She looked after the yard and any horses I had in my care for various reasons. She would be back tomorrow as well.

The last Thursday of the month was also the quietest day of the month at White Horse Farm, which allowed me to sort out the monthly pay cheques for my various employees. This was the only office work I physically had anything to do with, and I must say it worked a treat. Charlie Rogers had the office sorted to perfection.

Charlie had a list of expenses for each employee, which I checked every month without fail, together with worksheets and comments. I would sign all wage cheques on Thursdays, and Charlie would prepare the wage packets to be picked up the following Friday at lunchtime. My employees preferred this method to electronic accounting. My team consisted of eight employees, including Charlie and Laura. They were all ex-army or -navy, much like myself. In their spare time over the years since they had been with me, Charlie and Laura had both aspired to black belts in judo, and each made two stripes in the Territorial Army. I had a first-class team, and tomorrow (Friday), we would plan out strategy to get to the bottom of these crimes I now seemed surrounded by. I read all the monthly worksheets and reports to bring me up to date for tomorrow's briefing.

Chris rang me at about 5.30 p.m. to tell me he had hired a horsebox from Ginger Martin, for £300 per week. He thought it was a bit steep, but he'd taken it for one month. Also, he wanted to know if I wanted the rest of my money back. I told him to return £3,000 but to keep the rest in case of emergencies; it was the least I could do, as I felt guilty for his loss, believing it was partly my fault. I toyed with the idea of offering the £3,000 as a reward for any information leading to a conviction of the perpetrators of the horsebox crime, easy money if in fact it was joyriders, and our strategy meeting tomorrow would be the most eventful for ages. But first I had to ring up Hopalong Henry to see what he had for me with regard to the Volkswagen Golf GTI broken door mirror that he had found in the car park.

I rang Hopalong at his work, as I knew he would not be finished until 9 p.m., and at the moment, it was just before 6 p.m. I must have got through to a central office, as the girl on the end of the line said, "Car Park Main Office. What level, please?"

I said, "I cannot remember what level, but I wanted to speak to the attendant with a bad leg. He's called Henry."

"Could you wait a second?" she said.

A few seconds later, a man's voice said, "Who's calling?"

"Henry, it's Steve Hurst. I spoke to you this morning when you rang me."

The voice replied, "Oh, Mr Hurst is it?"

The penny dropped. I knew the voice, but it wasn't Henry; it was DCI John Heyes. "What are you doing ringing here?" he enquired.

I told him that Henry had rung me this morning to say he had some information for me. The chief inspector gave me the news I was dreading. Hopalong was dead. He was splattered across the pavement outside the car park, apparently having fallen from one of the levels.

"Mr Hurst," said DCI Heyes, "I don't like what I smell because what I smell stinks. Be at my office at Brighton Police Station at ten o'clock tomorrow morning. There are some questions I want to ask you further to your statement I took this morning."

I wanted to ask the chief inspector if he knew whether Hopalong had on him any packages with my name, but I thought better of it. I was just going to have to be at the police station at ten o'clock tomorrow morning, to pool our resources with the chief inspector's. At the moment, though, he did not exactly fill me with any confidence.

Jane burst into tears when I told her what had happened. We both sat there dumbstruck. We knew it was no accident. We knew Hopalong Henry had been murdered. It occurred to me in hindsight, however, that the chief inspector should be made aware of the evidence that Hopalong had found for me this morning and that I should ring him back straight away. If I read it correctly, the GTI man had returned for his property – the door mirror. Hopalong would have denied that he had it unless threatened. If he had been threatened, he must have been on his own. If the mirror was not in his office or on him, it must be in his locker. Miles Valentine suddenly appeared in my thoughts, the secret world of forensics, fingerprints, and so on. I could not dial the chief inspector's number quickly enough. Whilst the phone was ringing, Jane mentioned something about Hopalong's flat in Eastern Avenue, suggesting that maybe the broken door mirror was there.

"Come on, Chief Inspector, answer the phone," I muttered. It was obvious after the eleventh ring that he was not going to answer. Next came the words we all now know so well: "Your call cannot be answered at the moment; please try later. Your call can—" I put the phone down.

I tried the car park again, but the chief inspector had left; so had the body and forensics. Damn Miles Valentine! This time, I rang the reception number for Brighton Police Station and got through on the tenth ring. "Brighton Police Station. Front Desk. How can I help you?"

"I need to speak to DCI Heyes or Miles Valentine. Urgently," I said.

"I'm sorry," replied the curt lady on the other end of the phone. "Neither is here at the moment." "Have you a mobile number I can contact them on?" I asked.

"I'm sorry we cannot divulge such information. Would you like to leave a message?"

I knew I was talking to a robot, so I said, "I believe DCI Heyes was earlier at the Metropole Car Park at the scene of a death. Are you aware?"

"Yes," she replied. "It is logged in my desk diary in front of me."

"Fine. Well, I did it. Shall I call back later?"

Madam was probably for the first time in her life stuck for words. "I think I had better get the desk sergeant," she replied.

"Yes," I said. "That would be a good idea." I sarcastically added, "Can you do it today?"

There was a pause on the other end of the line, and then a male voice said, "This is Sgt Wilson. "To whom am I speaking?" His voice was so sympathetic. If it had not been for the seriousness of the situation I would have quipped as to when he had left Dad's Army.

"It's Steve Hurst from Sayers Common, near Hickstead," I replied. "I urgently need to speak to DCI Heyes or Miles Valentine. Can you help me?"

The sergeant seemed to instantly surmise that I needed to speak to someone in authority, and quickly. "Is it about the horsebox incident, sir?"

"Partly," I replied. "But, more importantly, it's about the murder this afternoon at the car park in Brighton."

Without hesitation Sgt Wilson gave me DCI Heyes's mobile number and informed me that he was still out making enquiries.

I told the sergeant, "Please contact somebody from forensics. Get the locker room sealed off at the car park, post a constable or patrolman, and do it immediately. Hopalong was killed because he had some incriminating evidence. I do not believe the killers found it. Do I make myself clear, Sergeant?"

"Yes," said Sgt Wilson. "I will put the wheels in motion. Please ask DCI Heyes to contact the Brighton Police Station front desk when you have finished your conversation with him, Mr Hurst."

I said I would do, offered my gratitude, and then rang the chief inspector's mobile.

To my surprise, DCI Heyes was at Hopalong's flat. "Mr Hurst, you have some information for me?"

I explained Jane's and my thoughts to the chief inspector, irrespective of the fact that he was there already. DCI Heyes clearly knew his job. In the next few minutes, he convinced me he was the real thing. Inspector Clouseau, definitely not.

A van with a hidden camera was strategically placed opposite the locker room in the car park, and a microphone was placed in Hopalong's locker. It was locked, so it would have to be forced open.

"I must admit," DCI Heyes said to me, "I first found your story a bit far-fetched. However, when I attended the scene of the crime at the car park, I insisted that Miles do the forensics on this one as well. I questioned staff at the main office. It was just when you rang that one of the office girls gave me a package with your name on it. I took the liberty of opening it, and inside was a broken door mirror and some paint scrapings. For the most part, this corroborated your statement of earlier today, Steve."

First name terms now, I thought but said nothing.

The chief inspector continued. "Hopalong left an important clue, even in his death, which I now believe was murder. If only for one thing, that being he had two £50 notes in his hand when he died, or was thrown off level 3 of the car park. The murderers must have been severely pissed off with Henry to kill him without getting the incriminating evidence. I do not believe they will bother after tonight, unless they are extremely hard up. I fully expect the Golf GTI to be found burned out somewhere by the morning. No one has been here. I am convinced this is the work of novices."

I interjected, "Novices maybe, but killers all the same."

"Yes," said the chief inspector. "I assume you will look after yourself from now on?"

I assured him there was no need to worry about me; I would see him at ten o'clock the next morning.

Jane followed me into the kitchen. We did not fancy anything to eat. We boiled the kettle, made two cups of coffee, and just sat there without talking. We did not even drink the coffee; it got cold. When the phone rang it brought us back to our senses. Jane went to bed. It was 9.30 p.m. We had sat in the kitchen for hours.

When I answered the phone, it was Jonathan Ridger on the other end. "Yes, Jonathan, what can I do for you?"

"Robert Argonaut will not talk to me."

"Can you blame him?" I exclaimed.

"Okay," said Jonathan. "Look, I know I was a bit full of myself this morning. Tell Robert I'll take the £150,000 for Hot Tea. He can pick the horse up from Newbury on Friday week. I've entered him for a race there. I'll withdraw him the morning of the race, so long as I'm paid by then. And just one other thing: I think I deserve a bit of publicity, and I want it in Saturday's *Racing Post* that Robert has bought a 50 per cent share of Hot Tea, for an undisclosed sum; otherwise, no deal, and I mean it."

"Okay, Jonathan," I said. "I'll agree to that."

"Why?" Jonathan said in surprise. "Don't you have to get Golden Bollocks to agree to it first?"

"No," I replied. "And the proviso is Golden Bollocks will only be referred to from now on when you're in my company as Robert or Mr Argonaut. Agreed, Jonathan?"

There was a long pause, but, eventually, Jonathan agreed. "I'm not paying you anything either, Steve," he added. "You know that, don't you?"

"Yes," I replied. I then wished Jonathan well, thinking that at least he would now get some peace. The girls would no longer be squabbling over who was riding Hot Tea in his work.

I went to bed after we rang off. It was past ten o'clock, and it had been an eventful day. I leant over and kissed Jane on the cheek; she was fast asleep. Within minutes, I was also.

My slumber lasted barely three hours, though. The phone was ringing incessantly. I fumbled around the bedside table, half-asleep, and eventually found the phone and placed it next to my ear. "Steve? Is that Steve Hurst?" an agitated male voice on the other end of the line enquired.

"Yes, who is it? Do you know what the time is?" I exclaimed.

It was Sgt Wilson. "I have a message for you from DCI Heyes," he said. There's been a development regarding the white Golf GTI. A petrol station in Eastern Road, Brighton, has reported that a white Golf filled up with petrol, and the driver filled up two cans as well. He placed them in the Golf's boot. The driver drove off without paying. The garage reported the vehicle's index number from the CCTV to us, and it matches the description of the one that tried to run you down in the car park, sir." I asked the obvious question of whether the CCTV managed to get a good view of the driver. "Unfortunately not, sir. The driver had a hooded coat on, and sunglasses. The only evidence appears to be that the driver is about 6 feet tall and of slim build. The chief inspector would ask you to be extra vigilant tonight, sir. He is expecting further developments. We have an unmarked patrol car situated between your house and Chris Collins's garage, but please ring in should anything reasonably suspicious takes place, sir."

I thanked the sergeant, put down the phone, and looked over at Jane. The lucky so-and-so was still fast asleep. If there was such a thing as a sleep championship, she would sleep for England. I got up and went round the house, checking all the locks and windows. Satisfied, I went into the lounge and settled down on the couch. I must have fallen asleep, because the next thing I knew, I was partially waking up to the sound of Tubular Bloody Bells.

My consciousness soon returned. As my eyes slowly opened, I saw the sunshine proudly shining through my big bow front windows, and the bells, the bells. It wasn't Mike Oldfield's; the front doorbell was ringing furiously. It was eight o'clock, Friday morning. Reality returned when I looked out from my bow windows and noticed my oak gates and piers were missing. I opened the front door. It was Charlie.

"Why is the office door bolted from the inside, Steve? And who's to blame for your front gates being missing?" enquired Charlie as she made her way to the kitchen. "A long story, Charlie," I replied. "I'll make the coffee then," said Charlie. "You go and get yourself showered and changed, then you can tell me all about it. By the way, Steve, Laura won't be in until ten o'clock."

"Hangover from last night?" I said sarcastically. "You know Laura," Charlie replied. "When Laura has a drink, she has a drink big time." Thankfully, and all credit to Laura, this only happened on girls' night out or on special occasions.

I showered, shaved, and dressed, and was back in the kitchen by 8.30. Two cups of coffee and three slices of toast later, I had brought Charlie up to date with the previous forty-eight hours.

I told Charlie that I wanted everybody in the office for a meeting at 1.30 p.m., and then informed her that I had to be at Brighton Police Station at 10 a.m. to see DCI Heyes.

Charlie said, "Leave everything to me, Steve".

I usually did., so I just smiled at her.

"I'll organise everything here," she said. "You'd better get off or you'll will be late."

Charlie was too advanced for her tender 23 years of age. Sometimes she treated me like a son, so to speak, perhaps because I was 37, unmarried, and had no children. I subconsciously liked that. I admired Charlie for her powers of concentration and ability to get a job done. Charlie was my right-hand man, even though she was a girl.

I got to the police station at 9.55 a.m., and was shown through to the chief inspector's office by Sgt Wilson, who whilst walking down the corridor said, "Quiet night, sir?"

I replied, "Yes, thank you, Sergeant. Any news on the Golf?"

"The chief inspector will bring you up to date, sir."

Sgt Wilson opened the door to the office, and I walked in. DCI Heyes, Miles Valentine, and four other people were in the room. There was a projectionist (I gathered we were going to review some slides or similar), a secretary (for taking notes), Miles's assistant (for the forensic evidence), and the chief inspector's second in command, DS Sidney Harman, who was the only one of the four the chief inspector formally introduced.

We all sat down, and then the chief inspector passed me a sheet of paper with an agenda for this morning's meeting. The items were as follows:

1. Possible attempted murder of Steve Hurst and Jane Coe, Metropole Car Park, Golf GTI white
2. Horsebox arson White Horse Farm, Sayers Common, near Hickstead
3. Chris Collins, horsebox owner
4. Murder of Henry Hall, Metropole Car Park
5. Theft of petrol, Sussex Square Garage, Eastern Road; Golf GTI; thief, 6 feet tall, slim build, possibly left-handed

"We will deal with item 5 on the agenda," said DCI Heyes, and speaking to us all, he informed us that we were going to see a selection of slides.

The slides were stills of the videotape from the garage, showing the Golf GTI, its number plate, and the man obtaining petrol. The chief inspector told us the obvious, and then explained how he had come to his conclusions. The man took the pump out of its holster with his left hand; he transferred the pump to his right hand; he took the petrol cap off with his left hand; he transferred the pump back from his right hand to his left hand; he filled the tank up with petrol; he transferred the pump back again to his right hand; he replaced the petrol cap with his left hand; and so on with the boot lid and the filling up of the petrol cans. He wore sunglasses, and it was just possible to see a watch on his right wrist. The chief inspector further informed us that the height off the ground of the petrol pumps was 5 feet, and by dividing one-fifth of length of the petrol pump into the length that the man equalled and then multiplying by 5 would give us within a fraction of an inch the height of the GTI man; 1 foot of the petrol pump equalled 1.5 inches of the GTI man. Allowing half an inch for his shoe had put his height at 6 feet.

I thought about building societies and banks; near to the doors in and out of these establishments you will find strategically situated a light switch, a picture, an open-and-closed sign. On some other focal point within the view of the CCTV such items are placed at 5 feet, 6 inches; 6 feet; and 6 feet 6 inches. Any prospective robbers therefore had better beware when entering such premises.

I asked the chief inspector about the registration number and whether he'd found time to do a vehicle check.

"Yes, Steve," he said. "It was the first thing Sgt Wilson did when the theft of the petrol was reported. The registration number is a false one. The false number relates to an ex-British Telecom Maestro Van. DVLA (Driver and Vehicle Licensing Agency) could not, or would not, give us any more information. What I am about to tell you goes no further than this room. I have been requested to ring an official of the Home Office this lunchtime after our request regarding this registration to the DVLA. My belief is that this registration number is possibly that of a vehicle used by MI5 or MI6." Once again, the chief inspector impressed upon us all not to divulge any information.

When the next slide appeared, I asked the chief inspector if we could take it as for certain that this indeed was in fact the same car, without doubt, that had tried to run Jane and me down in the car park. I further pointed to the fact of the car picture on the screen, which clearly showed that the GTI most certainly had no driver's door mirror and appeared to be missing some trim from its offside, as if it had been slightly scraped by a post – or, as I thought for certain, a pillar in the car park. The chief inspector was, as he put it, 99 per cent certain but not 100 per cent. I asked if it were possible to check with the DVLA as to how many white Golf GTIs were registered in the immediate area.

"Once again, Steve," DCI Heyes said, "this particular Golf model was, from the evidence, manufactured between March 1988 and August 1991. We have requested such information from the DVLA at Swansea, but one thing we don't know is whether this car was once another colour, or in fact, whether it is what the badge on the back actually says. It has sports wheels, which were standard for this model in March 1988, but as you are possibly aware, it could be a lookalike with a GTI badge. Of course, we will carry out a check when we get the information requested. However, I am still 99 per cent sure we are going to find this car burned out somewhere. Henry's death makes it a given that the killer – or killers – now know it is vitally important that we do not find this car intact; if we did, we could trace ownership and the real registration number from the chassis number."

Sgt Wilson appeared at the door with a tray of coffee; it was eleven o'clock. We helped ourselves to the coffee.

"Right," said the chief inspector. "That deals with item 5, and also item 1. What I need from you, Steve, is a motive or reason. Why does somebody, or some people, want you and/or your fiancée dead? This is a question you seriously need to address. This leads me to question why Henry was killed. For one of two reasons, I believe he was killed because he knew the GTI man. Not inasmuch as he actually *knew* him, but more than likely he was a local face that Henry knew but did not associate with the Golf GTI; indeed, he would have recognised the face from the immediate surrounding area. Henry, for instance, might have bought a paper locally on his way into work, and this man might have served him; maybe he worked at a local bar. I will, of course, question staff at the car park as to whether they knew where Henry went or what he did. Was Henry a man of habit?"

I thought about the Konkordski Bar, which was only 200 yards away, and wondered whether Henry popped in for a pint on the way home some evenings. I asked the chief inspector if Henry's locker was still under surveillance.

He replied, "Yes, until we find the Golf GTI."

The chief inspector then said, "Lastly, that leaves items 2 and 3: the horsebox fire and Chris Collins."

Again, I thought of the Konkordski Bar: Had I insulted Stu Ward too much? Was this payback time? I did not mention my confrontation with Stu Ward to the chief inspector; however, this was too coincidental for my liking. There were too many pointers to Mr Stu Ward and his Konkordski Bar. Were the three incidents connected: the horsebox fire, the attempt on my life and Jane's, and Henry's death? My brain was buzzing.

DCI Heyes called upon Miles Valentine to offer some information he had obtained from his forensic investigation.

Miles finished his coffee, cleared his throat, and said, "The chief inspector and I did not believe these incidents were connected, however, there is overwhelming evidence which we consider to link these incidents. Firstly, Steve, you are a common denominator, and so is Jane; you both tie these cases together. Steve, you bought your farm off Chris Collins. Chris Collins's horsebox was stolen, crashed into your farm gates, and set on fire. What I found in the horsebox cab was most intriguing, though. Steve, do you know if Chris Collins smokes dope? For example, does he roll joints? Lebanese, Gold, Paki black, cocaine, heroin?"

I was gobsmacked. "Chris?" I said. "I've never seen him with a cigarette. I'm sure he doesn't smoke."

Miles said he found the stub of a joint which had wedged itself behind the throttle pedal. Although charred, the roach (which was usually a piece of cigarette packet cardboard) was glossy dark blue in colour, and had gold letters just about readable. Miles then said that "o-l-e" were the letters on the roach, which acts like a filter tip as on a tipped cigarette, but obviously this was handmade.

"We believe 'o-l-e' is part of the word 'Metropole'," Miles said, producing from his pocket a small pack of matches he had earlier picked up from the hotel. "As you can see," he continued, "forensics put beyond doubt that our conclusions are unquestionable. Our horsebox thief uses drugs; more importantly, hard drugs. In this particular joint, we found traces of powdered cocaine. I feel sure our man is a habitual user, probably into cocaine and heroin."

"Miles," I said, "that's incredible!"

"However, we've been unable to raise any fingerprints," Miles said.

DCI Heyes got to his feet just as the projectionist got to the last slide, which was a picture of the burned-out horsebox. Just as the projectionist removed the last slide from the projector and filed it, the chief inspector said, "Now then, it's 12.15. Steve, would you be available to meet me here at 1 p.m. on Monday?"

I replied, "Weekend off, then?"

I soon found out that DCI Heyes had a very dry sense of humour when he asked me if I'd gone to bed last night. I said that I had, and then the chief inspector said, "Remind me what it's like, Steve, when I get time to ask you again." That certainly put me in my place!

Sgt Wilson came in. "Chief Inspector, sir," he said. "The white Golf GTI looks like it's been burned out in Lewes, next to the tennis and hockey club in Cockshut Road. It was reported at 11.15 a.m., by club members. Fire engine, which attended, could not get to it because of a low bridge. When the fire was eventually put out, the firemen found a body in the driver's seat. Do you want to attend?"

"Yes," replied the chief inspector. "Come on, Miles. See you on Monday, Steve. Don't lose any sleep." DCI Heyes uttered those last four words with as much sarcasm as he could muster, and then he exited the police station to the police car park. Miles followed one step behind.

I drove back to Sayers Common, full of admiration for Chief Inspector John Fitzwilliam Heyes, and forensics expert Miles Valentine. They knew their stuff. Perhaps the chief inspector had a sense of humour after all, I mused, whilst heading back to White Horse Farm, with all its dramas and unsolved mysteries, which seemed to be increasing by the hour.

The chief inspector had been so right about the white Golf GTI. I wondered what he and Miles might find from yet another killing. This one, though, was premeditated and had all the hallmarks of a planned professional murder.

CHAPTER 4

I took the stable entrance into White Horse Farm, as I usually did, and parked the Rover next to Laura's MGB Roadster. This was her pride and joy: a chrome bumper model, pre-1968, in teal blue, with a dark-blue soft top and tonneau cover, black leather seats, and chrome wire wheels. The only part of the car which was state of the art was the stereo system – £2,000 worth of CD and tape player, with twin speakers fitted into the boot lid so as to enable her to listen to her sounds whilst working in the yard. I said I would buy a little stereo system for the yard, but Laura liked her sounds so much that she never gave me the chance. As I switched the engine off in the Rover, I could hear bass speakers performing admirably. Laura's beloved reggae music blasted loud and clear. Jane's Escort Cabriolet and Charlie's Suzuki Vitara were the other cars parked in the enclosed courtyard, which was in the form of a rectangle. The yard was originally a fourteen-box yard, with four boxes opposite each other on the larger sides of the rectangle, and three boxes opposite each other on the shorter sides.

The offices at the back of the house directly faced one of the longer four box sides of the rectangle. I'd immediately demolished three of the boxes when I bought the farm from Chris, in order to provide parking for four cars, along with a fairly substantial patio and barbecue area. This purpose-built courtyard had an enormous up-and-over garage door that was remotely controlled from the office. At the flick of a switch, the courtyard could be completely secluded, which was ideal when we had barbecues because I could literally shut the wind out if it were a bit blustery. To the left of the big garage door, next to the stable block, was a tarmac with a post-and-railed area which held ten cars; a quick check revealed that everybody was here. I turned the stereo off in the MGB, but not before

Jimmy Cliff had finished singing "Wonderful World, Beautiful People", and for the first time in my life, I realised that my lifestyle would probably be envied by many people. I had to find out what I had done, or what one of my operatives had unknowingly uncovered, which had resulted in the devastating effect of two deaths in the last twenty-four hours.

Laura yelled, "Who's turned my stereo off?"

I changed direction, and instead of going into the office, I went into the first box on the left. The door of the box was open, and Laura was grooming one of Jane's showjumpers, Red Regent.

"How's the headache?" I enquired.

Laura laughed, tossed her head back, and looked over her left shoulder to the door where I was standing. She pursed her lips together, closed her eyes, and said, "Quickly!"

I walked over to Laura and kissed her.

Laura opened her eyes and said, "I've just made a wish."

"Are you going to tell me about it?"

"No," Laura said in a more serious voice. She said that Charlie had filled her in with what I'd told Charlie that morning.

I told Laura that matters had taken a turn for the worse.

She removed the head collar from Red, came over to the door put, her grooming kit and the head collar down, put her arms around my neck, and kissed me. Laura was a few inches shorter than I, about 5 foot 6, and she stood on her toes to reach my lips. I put my arms round Laura without thought; I felt her tongue in my mouth, seeking for mine. I partly withdrew and moved my lips to kiss Laura on the cheek, as she did the same to me.

Laura whispered in my ear, "Steve, I'm frightened."

I felt a tear roll down my cheek, then two or three, as Laura sobbed. I moved my head down to Laura's lips, returning my lips to hers, as our tongues feverishly searched for each other's. My hands slipped down lower and settled on Laura's small firm buttocks. As I slowly took her weight, I felt her long legs move up my body, and I instinctively turned her round so her back was against the stable wall; Laura entwined her legs together behind my back and squeezed me closer. Laura knew I wanted her, and I knew Laura wanted me. We both knew it; we could both feel it. Laura's vital statistics were the same as Jane's to a degree, though Laura was slimmer around the hips, and an inch or two shorter.

I whispered to Laura, "I think it would be better if you and Charlie stay here for the next few days."

As I gazed into Laura's bright blue eyes, I told her that I loved her and Charlie too much to let anything happen to them. I felt my hands tighten around Laura's backside, and our mouths and tongues danced in and out of each other's. I felt Laura's legs tighten up, squeezing me against her nubile young firm body.

"Laura, Laura, you're squeezing the breath out of me!" I exclaimed in a laughing voice.

Laura giggled and said, "Don't keep me waiting too long, Steve."

I just said, "Not a word to anyone, not even Charlie. The office in ten minutes."

I walked round the yard for five minutes before I was able to go into the office without being embarrassed. I walked passed Laura, who was in fits of laughter.

"I think you better go round again, big boy," she said.

By the time I returned, Laura was in hysterics. Charlie came out of the office to see what all the laughing was about. I told Charlie that Red had tried to mount Laura while she was bending down.

Charlie burst out laughing too. "I thought Red had better taste!" she quipped.

I joined in the laughter with Charlie and Laura, and the three of us walked back to the office together for the meeting.

Charlie had once again excelled; of the three cases we were involved in at the moment that were live, there were up-to-date reports, together with a list of operatives involved in those cases.

Case 1. The Tote, was experiencing an unusually large amount of return tickets whenever the machines were operated at Kempton. Return tickets were tickets issued by error that should be entered back into the Tote machines to cancel them. If these tickets were losers and not paid for, then the Tote take would be down; if they were winners, they could be purchased by the Tote operators, who could then cash them in for the winnings.

It was only a small scam, but at every meeting the Tote was losing about £1,000. Forty meetings a year, though, was £40,000. When the same trend was recognised some two months ago at Ascot, DIRTS was called in.

It was a week before the Whitsun Bank Holiday when we got involved. I had two teams of two on this; Billy and Allan at Kempton; Ricky and Bob at Ascot. They were all undercover, being employed by the Tote, and methodically worked their way through different Tote outlets on different meeting days at the respective tracks when meetings occurred.

I now asked Billy to give the meeting an update. Billy informed us that he and Allan had pinpointed most of the lost revenue down to the 5- and 6-furlong races. The loss to the Tote being greater in handicaps of sixteen or more runners, where the favourite finished in the frame at odds of up to 6 to 1.

"Have you come to any conclusions, Billy?" I enquired.

"Yes," Billy replied. "Allan has a list of races for the last month that resulted in loss of income."

There was a distinct pattern, according to Allan's chart. All the horses in question paid less than their starting price on the Tote; for instance, if a horse started at 8 to 1 and was placed in more than a sixteen -runner handicap, the return would be a quarter of the odds. That is 2 to 1, so a £1 place for that horse would return a dividend of £3 – £2 plus £1 at the starting price. The Tote dividend, though, does not work on starting prices. The Tote's computer considers all horses in all races to have equal chances. The betting public decides the Tote odds. The more the public backs one horse, the shorter the price; market forces thus dictate a racehorse's price. This was the reason why the scam was so difficult to directly trace.

Allan then explained that the Tote was not being ripped off by some clever format or mathematical formula, but, rather, by simply placing bets that were the most popular with the general public.

The system was so brilliant in its concept. Allan believed there were many people interested and involved. Allan also believed there were four Tote operators operating the scam, but in this very clever and well-thought-out scam, he also hinted that some trainers might be involved as well, certainly people with inside knowledge. We did not know if there was a group of people involved, or, indeed, a syndicate.

I posed the obvious question to Allan: "How does the winning tickets get passed out for collection and paid for by the Tote operator?"

Allan's reply was fascinating. The races targeted, sprints took between sixty and eighty seconds to run, and all astute operators could square up their tills in seconds, and then balance the money out to the tickets sold, in keeping the winning tickets and putting in the correct amount of money before their supervisors did the after-race check for unsold tickets and the dividends were announced.

When the dividends were announced the Tote windows were opened again to pay out, but as Allan added, more importantly, the tickets for other races and at other tracks could be purchased also. Winning tickets could then be passed over the counter for cashing at other windows. The beauty of the scam was the flexibility it offered.

"What about suspects, Allan?" I enquired.

"We are fairly sure, as I said earlier, that there are four operatives involved working for the Tote," Allan said. "We are setting up surveillance cameras at the suspect outlet windows, with the cooperation of the Tote managers and supervisors. We would estimate another two weeks before we have enough evidence to result in a conviction."

"That's brilliant, Allan," I said. "And you too, Billy. Well done. Turning to two of my other operatives, I said, "Ricky, Bob, what's the story at Ascot?"

Bob stood up. "Much the same as Kempton, Boss. We have liaised with Allan and Billy on this one. We need to set up surveillance equipment also, but we all had a chat about it this morning, and to be absolutely certain, Boss, we would recommend that we cover the meetings at Sandown and Newbury as well."

"Why?" I asked Bob.

He replied that most of the Tote's employees came from a pool coached to and from racetracks. "We want to fit the coaches with cameras to see who sits next to who," he said. "It may just give us the edge in concluding this more quickly. We too have our suspects, but we need the proof."

"Fine," I said. "Well done. Ricky, Bob, go for it. Let's seal this one in the next two weeks then."

It was 2.30 by that point. Jane came into the office-cum-conference room and exclaimed, "Coffee time!"

Charlie switched off the cassette recorder taping our meeting, Laura made excuses that she had to go to the loo, and John and Gary (my other two employees) nipped outside for a cigarette break.

Jane told me that Robert Argonaut had rung and asked if I would ring him back. Charlie said that the wage cheques were all ready and then went to the kitchen to get the coffee. Jane's right arm was still in a sling, and whilst there was no one in the office, I informed her of the Golf GTI man's death earlier that day. Jane looked at me, and in her eyes I could see she was emotionally drained and needed an out from this environment. The chief inspector had told me to keep my back covered this morning when I saw him, and also to increase security around here.

Jane sat down, putting her left hand on her forehead, supported by her elbow on the desk. In an emotional voice, she stated she was leaving to go to her parents' house and planned to stay there until her arm was better.

As Jane stood up, I put my arms round her and asked her if she wanted me to drive her to Irons Bottom, just outside Reigate, where her parents ran a successful riding school. This was also where Jane kept her showjumpers. (The only reason I had Red in my yard was because he had caught a virus at the South of England Show whilst competing back in May, and Jane did not want to take a chance of it spreading.)

Jane said, "No. I'll be all right, Steve. You carry on with the meeting and get this matter sorted out."

As I kissed Jane, Laura walked back in. "Where's the coffee then?" she asked.

Charlie walked back into the office simultaneously, and in a raised voice stated, "Coffee, chaps!"

The six lads marched back into the office. Bob had gone outside to his van to get his sunglasses; Ricky, Allan, and Billy were on their mobiles in the courtyard. John and Gary had finished their cigarettes.

We each took a mug of coffee, and those who wanted sugar helped themselves. We all returned to our seats.

"Let's carry on then," I proclaimed. "Charlie?"

"You've got it!" she replied as she switched on the cassette recorder once again.

"Case 2. A Newmarket racehorse trainer rang me a few weeks ago. He thinks his young wife is being unfaithful." I looked at Jane standing by the doorway. When I mentioned the unfaithful bit, her eyes met mine before she turned away and walked into the lounge. "Have you got any information either way I can report back to him on, Gary?"

"Well, Boss", Gary replied, "the chief suspect I've been tailing for over a week now has not been near her."

The trainer in question strongly suspected his stable jockey, Ron Kallon, who was one of the top three jockeys currently in the country at the moment. Noel Henry, the trainer, had ditched his wife of twenty years and replaced her with a younger model, eighteen years younger to be precise, although they had been officially married now for five or six years.

47

The gossip in Newmarket was that the trainer could no longer keep up with the servicing demands being made on him. Noel was now 48, overweight, and unfit. He was the adopted son of the late, great Newmarket trainer Merlin Henry, a legend of the 1950s, '60s, and '70s, and although a superb trainer, Noel had a job keeping his young wife, Natalie, under control and happy – especially in the bed department. Noel was also a very pompous man, sometimes to an excruciatingly nauseating degree. He genuinely believed that the amount of classic winners he had trained over the years outweighed his pomposity; however, he was still a client.

Ron Kallon was a class act. At 32, he was in the prime of his life, was married to an Irish girl who was his childhood sweetheart. On the face of it, Noel had probably fingered the wrong person, though I was not the one who should question his judgement.

Gary had spied on Ron Kallon on the gallops in Noel's yard, followed him to his home, to the races, and to parties. The only times Ron Kallon was in Natalie's company was when her husband, Noel, was with her. "No way it's Ron Kallon," Gary insisted.

"Thoughts, anyone?" I asked.

Laura suggested that maybe Noel had put the finger on Ron because the racing newspapers were at the moment focusing their attention on an imminent rift between trainer and jockey. Some of the trainer's owners were less than pleased with the stable jockey.

"Good point, Laura," I said.

Charlie suggested we tail Natalie from now on, quoting that "the cat always found the cream".

Ricky asked Charlie if she was speaking from experience, and a wave of spontaneous giggling erupted from the meeting.

Charlie chose her moment like a seasoned professional comedienne. As the laughter died down, she turned to face Ricky, licked her lips, and purred. The office erupted into fits of laughter, apart from Ricky, whose cheeks were rose red by now, flushed with embarrassment.

When the hysterics had again died down, I put it to Gary that the suggestion was our best course of action. Gary suggested he go back to Newmarket that night to begin his surveillance of Natalie. This was agreed, as it was Friday and the start of the weekend.

"Right, then. That leaves you, John, and Case 3, our stipendiary steward, Dicky Head."

In his time, Dicky had been an army man who just about had enough brains to make captain before he had done the twelve years for which he'd signed up. On leaving the army, he worked as an assistant trainer in Lambourn for four years before setting up on his own. Three years further on, he resigned himself to the fact that he was not very good at that either. Having trained just four winners in three years, he sold up on the Jockey Club's order, and bought a small farm on the outskirts of Lambourn where his wife and daughter bought and sold a few horses, mostly showjumpers, whilst he, Dicky, applied to the Jockey Club for the post of steward's clerk and assistant.

Ten years later, he was a stipendiary steward of the Jockey Club. Dicky Head knew hardly anything about the intricacies of horse racing. He was, however, a good talker who knew the right things to say about the right people. More importantly, though, he knew when and where to make his voice heard.

So what was DIRTS doing investigating Dicky Head? A fellow Jockey Club member, Tim Holland, and his wife, Holly – who, incidentally, had employed us – were of the opinion that Dicky was responsible for their son being beaten up in London some six months ago, round about Christmastime. I had told Tim and Holly, who by trade were farmers with 2,000 acres between Cheltenham and Gloucester, that an opinion or hunch was not enough to launch an investigation.

Holly had suggested I take Jane up to the Cotswolds some months before (at Easter) and stay for the weekend. Holly could show Jane around, while Tim and I could explore whether there were reasonable grounds to cast Dicky Head under investigation for their son Giles's beating. Giles was beaten so severely that he was unable to ride this year in Hunter chases and point-to-points. His injuries included a broken nose, collarbone, and right arm. Now, six months later, he still woke up at night, screaming, "Stop it! Stop it!" This was the result of the nightmares he was having.

Giles was 29 now, but at the age of 16, he went to work for Dicky at the Cove Stables in Upper Lambourn, as an assistant pupil, and Tim had bought Giles a point-to-pointer for Giles to have some fun on at weekends whilst learning how to be a competent jockey.

Every Sunday however, when Giles was at home with his parents, the topic would be the same over breakfast. "Dicky Head is so ... well, Father, he has not got a clue about horse racing whatsoever," Giles would say.

Tim would correct his son and ask him not to speak of Dicky like that.

"But it's true, Father," Giles would protest, to no avail.

Giles then decided to keep a diary, which he updated daily when he got home; after Giles had persisted for six months with the daily diary entries, he then confronted his father with the evidence. By this time, Giles's pointer had broken down badly and had to be destroyed, whilst the promising young hurdler Tim had sent Dicky to train for him had been returned with "a leg" and needed a year off. ("A leg", as Tim pointed out, was a term usually connected with a tendon injury, where time would be the healer.)

According to Giles's diary, during the previous six months, seventeen out of the thirty horses in training with Dicky at the time had been retired, destroyed, or sent back to their owners with leg problems; the figures did not lie.

Tim had no choice but to investigate his son's claim, and having done so, reported his findings to the Jockey Club, of which he was a senior steward.

The evidence was overwhelming to such an extent that many of the owners threatened to sue Dicky for incompetence, and also to sue the Jockey Club for incompetence by issuing a trainer's licence to an incompetent person.

The Jockey Club did not want to take Dicky's licence away, so the club made him a gentleman's offer: the club would lend him the money, interest free, to settle up with his owners out of court, if he promised to relinquish his licence. The club even offered to find him a job in racing once he had sold Cove Stables and settled his family; however, Dicky was not to be involved in the purchase, sale, or training of racehorses – or, indeed, any other equestrian sport, ever again.

Much to his disgust, Dicky had to pay me 30,000 guineas for the horse he ruined and 3,000 guineas for Giles's point-to-pointer. He was a gentleman about it, though – or so I thought at the time. He sold his stables in no time at all, for £350,000; he owed £100,000 on the mortgage, which left him with £250,000. His farm cost him £100,000, and the other £150,000 he had to pay to the Jockey Club for bailing him out.

"Needless to say, Steve, this is off the record, never to be repeated," Tim said at the time.

"Of course, Tim," I replied.

Tim went on with the story.

The Jockey Club duly appointed Dicky to the post of steward's clerk, gave him a company car, and started him on £15,000 a year.

"We came in contact a lot through our jobs, and although I could see that Dicky resented me, he never actually said anything untoward," Tim told me. "That is, until the Gait won the Gold Cup at Royal Ascot a few years

back. *I was one of the acting stewards that day, and we disqualified him for intentional interference and careless and dangerous riding. He may have won by 7 lengths, but we took the view that the jockey was grossly irresponsible in his riding, to an unacceptable level.*

"*Dicky had said to me on the way in to the enquiry, 'The jockey should be banned, not the horse.' I told Dicky that was for the enquiry to decide. After the decision was announced that the winner was disqualified, Dicky was enraged. He caught hold of my arm and vowed to get his own back for costing him the best part of £40,000. The last thing he said to me that day was '£30,000, that's how much you owe me, Tim.' He was of course referring to the horse money he paid me when he was forced to pack up training all those years ago, or so I thought. When I saw Giles a while later, he informed me that Dicky had told him, 'It's all your fault! You and your secret diary, spying on me instead of working for me. You are going to get the severest beating of your life one day, I promise you.'*

"*I could not report it to anyone, because Dicky's record as a steward's clerk was unblemished in the eyes of the Jockey Club. He was a gentleman in the way he had conducted himself over the years, and was in line for promotion to a fully-fledged steward. To say or speak against him at the time might have been sour grapes in some people's eyes, so I resigned myself to saying nothing, and he got his promotion. In the last three years, I have sat on five steward's enquiries with him, three of which have gone against the principles of the law.*"

I asked Tim to explain.

"*Well, since the Gait affair, the Jockey Club changed the rules, so the jockey would be punished only if the horse won on merit. In other words, the jockey would be fined or suspended or both.*"

My sources some months after the Gait affair confirmed Dicky had £4,000 on the Gait, though I never told him I knew of his bet.

I'd been suspicious of him ever since, so I asked Tim to leave it with me. Dicky warranted an investigation, in my opinion. I informed Tim I would be most discreet, and we left it there.

John had made no headway on Case 3; nothing new to report.

By that point, it was 4.30, and I wanted to let the lads off as early as possible. Gary and John both had two-hour trips, to Newmarket and Lambourn, respectively; Billy, Allan, Ricky, and Bob each had an hour's drive to Langley near Slough in Berkshire, which was midway between Kempton and Ascot; the Datchet Mead Motel was ideally situated for them to base their surveillance operations from. Windsor, a few miles away, was where we hired our high-tech equipment: CCTV, infrared cameras, night glasses – all the state-of-the-art gadgets, and combat equipment also. We got it all at a shop called Wharr's, which mainly had outdoor and camping equipment on display, but out the back, for the professionals, it was a different matter. We got all our outdoor equipment there. Wharr's invoiced me monthly. My invoices just said "Equipment Hire". Any film processing they would do overnight, to be picked up early the next morning.

Jane was in the lounge, reading the *Horse & Hound.* She hadn't yet left for her parents' place. Charlie finished off in the office, handing out wage packets as the troops left for various parts of the country. Laura finished off in the yard, and apart from feeding Red, fed her own horse, Fred, and the three in the paddocks, which belonged to Cyril Night, who lived a few miles down the road and dealt in showjumpers. He would periodically use me as his overflow yard. These three were easy to handle, though, and never proved a problem to Laura.

She had been sports mad since she was 8 – cricket, football, tennis, horseback riding, showjumping, swimming. Laura had won medals in them all. She passed her BHSAI (British Horse Society Approved Instructor) six months after her eighteenth birthday.

In the summertime, though, she loved the horses and the freedom. Laura got on really well with Jane – or so I thought – and they would often go out on a hack together for hours.

I went into the lounge now. "I'm just going to call Robert," I said to Jane. "And then I'll be with you."

Jane did not acknowledge me.

In the office I searched for my phone book, and after a few minutes, I eventually found it under the coffee tray.

I dialled Robert's mobile number, and he answered on the third ring. I informed him of the deal I had done on his behalf for Hot Tea, and that it was going to cost him £150,000. I also informed Robert of the Newbury arrangements and the agreement to the press release, and then I waited for him to explode. To my surprise, he thanked me and asked me to personally make the necessary arrangements to finalise the deal. It was normal for Robert to use a third party in this sort of transaction. No one could ever claim they had sold Mr Argonaut a racehorse for far more than what it was worth.

I asked Robert if he had ever had any dealings with Dicky Head, and whilst Robert told me he thought the man a fool, I saw Jane get in her automatic Escort Cabriolet. I said to Robert, "I'm sorry. I've got to go."

As I put the phone down and dashed through the office door, Jane reversed out of the courtyard and into the ten-car post-and-rail car park, putting the car into drive. She saw me and sped off. I was standing under the big open garage door. *Women,* I thought.

Back in the office, Charlie had seen what had happened. "Problems?" she enquired, putting the kettle on. I asked Charlie to make three coffees and join me in the lounge. "Bring Laura with you," I said.

As I walked from the office to the lounge, I wondered if I had made the right decision by not involving my team in the horsebox fire and the two deaths. I could see the inquisitive looks all afternoon after Ricky asked, "Who burned the gates down, Boss?" I'd just replied, "That's my problem, not yours. I'll deal with it." That night, it would be just Laura, Charlie, and me at home.

In the lounge, on top of the *Horse & Hound,* was an envelope with one word on it – STEVE – in big bold letters. I guessed the engagement was off. I was not surprised inwardly. I saw Jane walk away earlier in the afternoon; her eyes left first. Noel Henry believed his wife, Natalie, was being unfaithful. As far as Jane was concerned, I did not have to think. I knew. Jane had just driven out of my life for good. Incidentals like Red, her horse in my yard – her tack and clothes – could be picked up later, no doubt.

So Robert Argonaut thought Dicky Head was a fool. Tim Holland, a senior steward of the Jockey Club, did not trust him. Dicky was a gambler for big stakes, and a failed racehorse trainer who had suffered serious embarrassment and believed Tim Holland and his son were to blame. Certainly, if nothing else, the motive was there, as far as I was concerned.

CHAPTER 5

I knew the contents of Jane's letter even before I opened it. My present problems were perhaps giving Jane the ammunition to end our relationship – and our engagement – a tad earlier than she might have otherwise. In any case, I expected the truth was that our relationship had gone stale; its ending was inevitable.

It had been an effort, a real struggle, to get Jane to come to the Hollands with me for the Easter weekend in April, just a few months ago. She had been a real bitch all that weekend, from the moment we arrived on the morning of Easter Saturday, right up until we left the morning of Easter Monday. Jane had never stopped moaning or complaining; nevertheless, Dicky Head would be investigated.

Jane wanted to hold a showjumping clinic at her parents' riding school at Irons Bottom – or so she'd said. It was to be for six up-and-coming prospects and their grade A showjumpers, which were the star attractions at the county and international shows the previous year. The Easter weekend was generally regarded as the crossover time from indoor to outdoor showjumping. Jane insisted we leave the Hollands at seven in the morning. All the way home, she never stopped talking about her chances of making the Nation's Cup team this year, and the fact that she would have to dedicate more time to her showjumping career in the future.

It was my nature to let people keep talking if they wanted to; I had always reasoned that there was an undeniably strong motive for people to act in this manner. My experience over the years, combined with the professional opinion of an eminent barrister who had once acted for my company had caused me to reach the conclusion that two things lay at the root of this behaviour in people: firstly, guilt; and, secondly, the overwhelming desire to be believed.

In short, Jane wanted to be believed, so I let her spout on.

As we entered the front gates of the riding school, all became clear. Emblazoned across a six-horse Lambourn turbo diesel horsebox barely a year old were the words "Cobb's for Classic Footwear". Chris Cobb, the 26-year-old sensation of last year's showjumping circuit, was here. He was 6 feet tall, blonde, with blue eyes – and sponsored by his father's business to the tune of £500,000 over the next three years. Since the flotation of the business in February, the family had raised £9 million pounds by selling 49 per cent of the shares. The family, in one shape or another, retained the other 51 per cent to hold overall control. Chris Cobb was in the fast lane of the showjumping circuit, and obviously going places. I had never spoken to him but knew of him. There was not a week that went by without one article or another on or about him in the Horse & Hound *magazine.*

His fame had begun at Christmastime, when he appeared at the last show of the year in London, the Horse of the Year Show Christmas Extravaganza, and then in the Fancy Dress Stakes when he entered the ring as Adonis (which, of course, he won the class) and afterwards was mobbed by screaming adoring female fans. The Horse & Hound *reported that they had never before witnessed such a frenzy of popularity in the showjumping world.*

Seeing Chris's horsebox at Jane's parents' riding school brought back memories of the first outdoor show of the year at Stocklands, near Petersfield in Hampshire, a few weeks earlier. That show was a weekend show, with showjumping on Saturday afternoon and all day Sunday. The first class Jane entered for was at one o'clock, and I had arranged with her that I would see her at noon and stay down until after her class had finished. We had planned to go out afterwards for an early pub supper; as events turned out, though, that didn't happen.

I had a cancelled appointment Saturday morning, so I left White Horse Farm earlier than expected. Jane went to Stocklands in her horsebox on the preceding Friday night, along with her three horses and her groom, Sally. Jane's horsebox was for four horses, but it also had living accommodation that slept two people. Jane wanted to spend the Saturday morning working her three horses in for the show. (Working horses in was similar to footballers warming up before a football match.)

Before I left at eight o'clock on Saturday morning, I had pre-packed a basket, a champagne breakfast – with smoked salmon, caviar, and brown wholemeal bread. I thought it would be a surprise and could easily make it in an hour before nine o'clock. I left in one of the DIRTS company vans, which were dark blue in colour, unmarked, and with no signs. (In my business it paid not to advertise. People hired my services on recommendation or word of mouth.) As I entered the show area, I could see the rows of horseboxes behind the clubhouse and the indoor arena, which was used in the winter. Some of the sponsors' names on the boxes were familiar, including that of Cobb's for Classic Footwear, Northampton plc, which was parked next to a box I immediately recognised as Jane's because of its colour: cream and regency red. The other side was Cyril Night's box, which proudly proclaimed, "Nights for horse feed, 24 hours a day", followed by a Brighton telephone number.

I was parked about 20 yards away from the boxes, which were immediately on my right. On my immediate left were the roped-off arenas, 1 and 2, which was where the showjumping would take place later in the morning.

As I put the handbrake on and turned the engine off, the radio announced: "Here is the nine o'clock news and sports." I decided to listen to the sports headlines before I surprised Jane. I saw Sally get out of Chris Cobb's horsebox, and instantly thought that Adonis Chris wasn't too choosy. Sally was, well, plain; about 5 foot 4, thirtyish, and blind as a bat without her glasses. She had put on weight since I'd last seen her (at Christmas). Sally had short, spiky, blonde hair, and sported an earring, nose ring, and lip ring. Not exactly what I expected would be Chris's type; however, every man to his own. Sally walked round to Jane's box, up the two steps to the side door, and entered.

Arsenal would be without their international goalkeeper, David Seaman, for today's game, according to the radio. As the report proceeded to give the reasons why, Chris Cobb emerged from Jane's box. He took the two steps to ground level, just as Sally had taken them up, two minutes before. "Now, at four minutes past nine, here is a weather update—" I turned the radio off. Jane had followed Chris down the steps, and their conversation was crystal clear.

"I've always fancied you, Chris, ever since the Christmas Show in London," said Jane.

Chris replied, "We've got to do it again."

Jane said, "You know I'm engaged, don't you, Chris?" She then turned around to go back up the stairs. (To digress for a moment, let me briefly describe Jane and our history. Jane was about 5 foot 8 and slim, with short black hair and piercing dark eyes. She was one of those lucky people who, as a result of her parents' genes, possessed the appearance of having a year-round suntan. Her 36B-24-34 figure was the envy of the female showjumping jockettes, and there was not one show that went by without Jane being propositioned by the showjumping male fraternity and the odd butch female "minger", *much to Jane's disgust. We had been together since the Christmas of the year before, and got on so well both in and out of bed that after a year of going out together, we decided to get married. I'd been a guest at the Horse of the Year show the previous year, and that was how I had met Jane, who was competing there at the riders' bar. We hit it off as soon as we met. We announced our engagement the following Christmas, after our year-long romance. Since our engagement, though, the sparkle had seemed to leave our relationship. What I was witnessing, therefore, was not such a surprise.)*

In the next instant, Chris grabbed Jane round the waist with his left arm and pulled her towards him from where she stood on the first step, about to open the door of the horsebox. Jane let go of the handle as Chris lifted her off the step and began to kiss her neck.

"Chris," Jane said, raising her hands and entwining her fingers into Chris's golden locks of hair. Chris responded by setting her down and moving his left arm from her waist. He began to caress her breasts with his left hand; his right hand by this time had moved from her right hip to massage her crotch. Jane was loving every moment of it. "Oh, Chris! Oh, Chris!" she moaned.

I slowly let the handbrake off the car and turned the ignition on to release the steering lock, the slight decline of the hill I was parked on allowed me to roll the 150 yards to the end of the one-way system around the showground. I started the engine and drove back to White Horse Farm. After about half an hour, having been deep in thought, my eyes slowly began welling up with tears, and I felt absolutely gutted. I stopped at Boxhill, just outside Dorking, which was on the way back, and went for a long walk. When I had got it out of my system, I went to the gentlemen's toilet next to the coffee and burger bar, and filled a washbasin up with water. I threw a few handfuls of water into my face and over my hair. I exited the toilet, bought a coffee, and went back to the van.

An elderly couple pulled up next to the van. The gentleman got out first, went round to the other side, and helped the lady out of the car. When he saw me looking at him, he said, "Arthritis."

I replied, "We're not getting any younger."

It was about 10.30 a.m., and it looked like we were in for a lovely day.

"She had to have a replacement hip last year," said the man. "We've been married fifty years this month. I'm 78, you know."

I nonchalantly said, "Oh really?" I never understood why people, upon reaching a certain age, are then proud to tell other people how old they are. I instinctively reached into my van, got out my basket of goodies, presented it to the golden-anniversary couple, and wished them well. As the saying goes, "such is life".

I got in my van and continued on the rest of my journey to White Horse Farm. I felt a lot better after my good deed, and I rang Jane on her mobile phone at about 11.30 a.m. to tell her I was too busy and wouldn't be able to make it after all.

Jane said, "Oh how sad. I was really looking forward to you staying down tonight. I'll see you on Monday then?"

"Yes," I said.

She finished the conversation with "must go now", and I never let on to what I'd witnessed.

Three months later, and no "nookie"; we drifted apart.

Now, Jane had left. When people wanted to talk, I let them. I was not heartbroken. I felt no guilt, especially over Laura, even if I was fourteen years older than she. It was time to move on.

"Charlie!" I shouted. "Where's that coffee?"

Jane was now old news. As far as Jane was concerned, if she wanted the other man's grass because she thought it was greener, then good luck to her.

I had the envelope in my hand, unopened, when Charlie walked in. I was sitting on the four-seater settee where I had fallen asleep after Sgt Wilson's phone call in the middle of the previous night.

Charlie put the coffee down on the coffee table in front of the settee. Laura had made some sandwiches, and she followed Charlie in. Laura sat down to my left, Charlie to my right. Simultaneously they said, "Jane left you then?"

For some unknown reason, I brought both my arms up, put them round Bambi and Thumper's shoulders, and said, "Looks like it."

We drank our coffee.

To clarify, Bambi and Thumper were characters out of a James Bond film, *Diamonds Are Forever*. They were personal bodyguards of a supposed character portrayal of the legendary Howard Hughes. The person they were guarding in the film, however, was called Willard Whyte. It was Ricky's favourite Bond film, and it wasn't unusual when Ricky was at White Horse Farm for us all, like Ricky, to refer to Laura as Bambi and to Charlie as Thumper. I could easily see and understand Ricky's logic.

Charlie and Laura would not let me throw the letter away without reading it. No matter how much I protested, they were adamant that I could not discard the best part of an eighteen-month relationship which so nearly ended up in marriage without knowing why it had ended.

"Okay, okay. I know when I'm beat," I protested as I picked up my coffee and a cheese sandwich from the coffee table. I got to my feet and said, "Before I read it, there's some home truths you should know about." I proceeded to march from the stereo system directly in front of Laura, across the fireplace, to the television some 12 feet away, and back again. The coffee table was separating me from the girls on the settee. They had both by now settled into the two corners of the settee, raising their legs to cross them on the settee and then cradling their coffees.

Laura said, "Before you say anything, Steve, Charlie and I are both aware of the problems we've got at the moment." I looked at Laura and thought of the word *we've*; we have a problem shared. These two 23-year-olds were well in advance mentally of their tender ages. Laura went on, "We are a team, and we will deal with this together, as a team. Of course we're frightened, Steve, but we'll get through this together."

Four years ago, I had advertised for two agents: "Both must be good at sports; one able to ride horses to a high standard; the other to be able to take shorthand, type well, be computer literate, and make coffee at an instant when required." In other words, I wanted a stable person for the yard and a secretary for my business, as I could no longer cope on my own. When Laura and Charlie rang me up from Laura's house, they had just got back from the disciplinary meeting held to investigate their behaviour whilst representing their country at Roedean. When England had played Australia, they had been suspended pending an inquiry by the Cricket Board, and they were both found guilty of unsporting behaviour. Laura was banned for three months initially, and Charlie for a year. The decision was final, with no appeal. The meeting took place in London at the home of Cricket, Lords. After sentence, Laura told the disciplinary committee she thought they were a bunch of old farts and they should retire before they brought cricket in this country down to its knees. For that remark, she was given another three months, making six in all; Laura, still not happy and with no respect for the committee, informed them she would do the six months standing on her head. The committee chairman suggested to his committee that perhaps Laura should have another six months then to help her back on her feet again, which was unanimously agreed.

Both the girls left then, with a year's ban each.

That evening when Laura rang me, they were both 19. Laura also informed me then that they both were good at sports and had full driving licences. As I had not had any other replies, I suggested they call in to see me the following morning, which was a Saturday.

59

When Laura put the phone down, Charlie said, "How could you tell him we're good at sports when we've just been banned for a year each for unsporting behaviour?"

"Charlie," Laura said, "we've been staying at my mum's for three months now. We are not going to be playing cricket for England or anyone else anymore. Let's make use of what we do have: my BHSAI and your secretarial skills. We need jobs, big time. It's the end of the summer, and let's face it, our prospects are not looking that good."

Charlie and Laura had met at college a few years earlier. Charlie was doing her secretarial course, Laura a sports instructor's course. Both were for two years. It was at college that they had taken up cricket. They were naturals. The match against Australia at Roedean was the third consecutive international they had won; the other two easily as well, against New Zealand and Zimbabwe, respectively.

They arrived five minutes before the prearranged interview time of eleven o'clock. They were dressed in jeans, trainers, and white Team England cricket T-shirts. I, at the time, was none the wiser. If looks could be deceiving, these two certainly were. I asked them what sports they were good at. Laura said, "Cricket"; Charlie added, "Cricket." Laura said, "One-day cricket"; Charlie said, "Limited over cricket". Laura added, "And horseback riding." Charlie said, "Yes, she's very good at that." Laura finished off with "And Charlie's the best typist in the South of England."

I said, "Charlie, Laura, hang on. Just hang on a minute." We were in the office, so I said, "Charlie, kitchen through there, coffee. Laura, through that door to the yard. First box on the left, there's a horse in there. The tack room is the third box on the left. Get tacked up and bring the horse to the front paddock."

I rang up Cyril Night and asked him if it was all right to ride his horse for ten minutes before one of his stable staff turned up to turn him out in a paddock. This had happened for the last two weeks since he left him here. Eleven o'clock out in the paddock; five o'clock, the stable lad would come back and put him back in the stable.

Cyril said, "Don't let anybody ride that horse, he's mad. He won't let anybody sit on him."

As I made my way out of the office, there was Laura next to the big open garage door, proudly sitting on Forward Fred. (I didn't' know the horse's name at the time, but Cyril informed me the next day, when I bought the horse.)

"What do you want me to do then?" Laura asked. "I have to warm him up first. He feels like he hasn't been sat on for ages. Keep out of the way, because he'll probably buck and kick for a few minutes."

I let them into a paddock and closed the gate. I told Cyril I would turn the horse out for him today. Laura was right. Fred bucked and kicked, dropped a shoulder, reared up, did everything he could to unship Laura.

Charlie shouted from the kitchen, "Ride him, cowboy!" And then she came out to watch.

After fifteen minutes, Fred was in Laura's control: walk, trot, canter, rising trot, sitting trot – Laura had him.

I was impressed. "Okay," I said, "I've seen enough."

Laura said, "Do you mind if I ride him for another fifteen minutes while you're drinking your coffee?"

I said, "Okay, sure. Come on, Charlie, let's have a look at your typing."

We went into the office, and Charlie set herself up in front of a PC.

I told her, "It's all ready for you. Type me a synopsis of the last three cricket matches you and Laura have played in."

"How do you want the synopsis to read?" asked Charlie.

I said, "In the form of a match report." It was twenty-five minutes past eleven. I said to Charlie, "Twelve hundred words, and I want it before 12.30."

"No problem," said Charlie.

I went outside.

Laura leant down to undo the gate, walked Fred out of the paddock, and leant down again to push the gate closed. She walked him up and down the pathway for five minutes and loosened his girth. Laura dismounted him by the garage gate, crossed her irons over the saddle so they would not bang into the horse's side, and led him back to the stables. "Have you a grooming kit?" Laura asked. "He could do with a brush."

"There are some in the tack room," I said. I got a kit for her and took it round to the horse's stable.

"Tell Charlie I'll be twenty minutes," Laura informed me. "And if this is your horse, you're wasting him. He's got a big jump in him. He just needs some attention and some confidence."

"No, it's not my horse, Laura. It belongs to a dealer friend of mine, and I suppose it's been left here because nobody can ride it."

Laura looked at me and said, "Is that right?"

I couldn't lie. "Yes." I said. "That's about the gist of it."

Laura closed the stable door, took off her riding hat, and put the tack away. As she approached me this time, the forefinger of her left hand was pointing at me, as if to give me a ticking off. "You tell whoever owns that horse how lucky they are! Three hours a day for a month, and that horse will be winning newcomer showjumping classes."

I said, "Let's see how Charlie's doing."

Charlie was doing fine. It was 12.15, and Charlie had finished.

We went into the lounge. The girls sat on the settee. I stood between the stereo and television, facing them.

Both girls asked me simultaneously, "Are you married?"

I said, "No." I then gave them a brief outline of what I did for a living and finished with "It's a pity you're not a bit older. I would employ you straight away."

Both girls protested at once. "Age discrimination! We are both 19. We don't exactly need our parents' consent."

So I gave them the benefit of the doubt.

Laura said, "Can I come over tomorrow and ride the horse for a few hours?"

Charlie said she would come round as well, to get used to the computer and organise the office, which was, I must admit, in a bit of a mess.

The next day, I agreed their wages with them: Charlie £10,000 per annum, and Laura £8,000 per annum. That was when they told me they needed the last Thursday of every month off, for a ritual, which I agreed to, as I thought it was hilarious – I found it even funnier later on, when Laura told me the whole story.

The rest, as they say, is history.

Laura was, of course, right about Fred. Within the next two months, he had won four newcomer's classes and a foxhunter. Laura had schooled Fred every day and rode him in his classes. I bought him from Cyril that Sunday, the day after Laura had ridden him for the first time, for £500. Three months later, I sold him to a member of the Irish Showjumping Team, Charles Paul, for £10,000. He had him for a few weeks and showed him off at the Christmas Show, before the New Year; he was in Germany a few weeks later.

My friend, Charles Paul had doubled his money, and he then sold Fred straight on for £20,000. (I knew Charles from when he dated my niece for near on a year, some time ago.) From the £10,000, I replaced Fred with another novice, once again bought from Cyril Night. Fred II cost me £1,000. I gave Fred II to Laura. He was a four-year-old gelding from Irish stock, and

Laura would never part with him. That was Christmas four years ago. The girls had by then been with me three months by that time, and they'd settled in nicely. I gave Charlie £1,000, as Laura had the horse, and that Christmas/ New Year, Laura and Charlie rented a flat in nearby Burgess Hill, about ten minutes from White Horse Farm. I told the girls it was a bonus.

That left £8,000 from the sale, and I gave it the girls as a form of loan. They used it to buy their cars: Laura the MGB Roadster, and Charlie the Suzuki Vitara. With Charlie's £1,000, the girls kitted out their flat. I didn't charge them interest; they just repaid me the £8,000 at £20 a week, each.

Charlie said, "That will take us four years!"

That was four years ago now. Four years ago, I stuck by them; four years later, they were sticking by me.

Laura's little speech gave me a lump in my throat. I was going to tell the girls about Chris Cobb and Jane, what had happened at Stocklands a few months ago. But I decided not to. I opened the letter and read it to the girls.

It started off "Dear Steve", and went on to say she was sorry that our affair had broken down. The reasons she gave were nothing to do with Chris Cobb. He never got a mention. It was all my fault – "my obsession with Laura and Charlie", Jane called it.

It was never a problem at first; in fact, Jane loved it, though she never ever gave Laura credit for sorting out some of the problems with the showjumpers that Jane had failed to recognise. Red was a pure example. Jane could not understand why Red would always knock one of the last three jumps down in competition. It was March, and the indoor circuit had one big show left: Mill Lodge in Cambridgeshire. If Jane could win another £300 with Red, he would have won enough prize money to be classified as a grade A, which a horse had to be to jump for the really big prize money. The weekend before the show, Jane came over to White Horse Farm, with Red and one of her other showjumpers that was already a grade A, Red Light, called Light for short. (Showjumpers were graded by ability – grade A was the tops.) We went into the office, and Jane produced a videocassette tape with a recording of the last three rounds she had jumped on Red. We went through to the lounge, and as Jane and Laura sat down, I turned the television on and placed the tape into the VCR, pressing Play. After studying the tape for fifteen minutes, including about four rewinds and four slow motions of the last four jumps of each round, Laura delivered her assessment of Jane's riding. Not so much as it being Red's problem. Laura delivered her criticism in such a way that Jane recognised her riding problem, which was due mainly to the anticipation of success and loss of concentration at the most vital part of the round. This was what set the truly great international riders apart from the rest.

Laura asked Jane to explain how she felt when she set off.

Jane replied, "Composed and quiet. I just let Red jump out of my hands."

"What about the middle part?"

Jane said, "Still composed, but apprehensive."

"In other words," Laura said, "would it be right to say, you were asking yourself questions in your head about your involvement?"

Jane replied, "It's about this time you have to start helping your horse over the jumps, Laura."

Jane had found her Achilles heel; she was not going to admit to a lesser person like Laura, though. Laura did not press the issue; instead, she let Jane talk herself through the last five jumps of the umpteenth rewind. Now it was pointed out, I could see Laura's point: Jane was trying to pull Red over the jumps, had shortened her reigns, and by doing so had tucked Red's head back into his chest. Red was unable to stretch his neck and lost his concentration; fighting the bit in his mouth so that he could once again stretch his neck, he had become unbalanced.

We went outside, and Sally had saddled Red and Light up. Sally was sitting on Light. Laura was unmoved and suggested to Jane, "If you want to work your horses in, I will go and put some jumps up in the outdoor ménage next to the ten-car park."

As they walked off, I said to Laura, "I thought you were going to ride one."

Laura replied, "So did I. Discretion is the best part of valour, though, Steve. I don't need or seek glory. You forget I've already been an England International. I have my job. Charlie and I are so happy, thanks to you. I'll sort your fiancée out for you, but I've got a feeling Jane's not too fond of me anymore."

We walked into the ménage and constructed four jumps: two singles down one side, and a double down the other. Jane and Sally jumped a few singles, then both singles in the line. We slowly put the jumps up over the next fifteen minutes, from 3 feet to 4 feet, going up a cup at a time. (The cups held the poles the horses jumped.)

Red was jumping better than Light, never touching a pole; that was until we reached 4 feet, 6 inches. Jane tried to pull him over the fence, and she pulled his neck into his chest, at which point Red decided enough was enough, downed tools, and instead of taking off, took another stride and dug his front feet in a foot from the base of the jump. Jane went over the jump; Red didn't. Luckily, *there was no lasting harm done. Jane never let go of the reigns, and without so much as a word, quickly remounted.*

Laura suggested to me, "Would you go and make some coffee, Steve?" She had the same look in her eye as the day I had first met her, when she came for a job interview that Saturday morning, after the same day she had initially ridden Fred. I did not get the pointing, ticking-off finger, though I could tell in her voice that Jane was going to get a scolding, job or no job, and it was better if I did not hear.

I shouted to Jane that I had to make some phone calls and that while I was in the house I would make some coffee. As I went through the kitchen door and out of sight, I heard Laura lay into Jane. "Get off that horse before you kill him." I couldn't miss this. I bolted outside to the tack room, where the window was open. It actually opened into a corner of the ménage, where Jane and Sally had been cornered by a seething, marching Laura. "Get off that horse before you kill him!" Laura repeated. Red had blood gushing out of his mouth. Before Jane could say anything, Laura had wiped her hand over Red's mouth, and she held it up to show Jane the blood which slowly trickled down Laura's hand, landing in spots on the ground. It looked a lot worse than it was because of the amount of blood.

Laura took charge. "Sally, go to the yard and get me some warm water and a sponge, also a head collar and lead." She added, "Jane, go to my car. There is a first-aid box in the boot." No "please" or "thank you". "Also, on the back seat is a bridle, get that too."

Jane obeyed without question. I walked out of the tack room towards the office, and Sally appeared on Light. Sally quickly dismounted, put him in one of the boxes, and ran to the tack room. A minute later, Sally emerged with a bucket of water and a sponge. I went back to the tack room and listened to the conversation. The girls were having an argument.

Sally said, "It's not Jane's fault."

Jane said, "The bit must have caught him as he threw me."

Laura said nothing. She took Red's bridle off, put the head collar on, clipped the lead on, and placed it in Sally's hand. "Just hold that," Laura snapped. She washed out Red's mouth with the warm water. The corner of Red's lower lip had split where the bit had been rubbing. Red flinched when Laura touched the sore spot; it was probably bruised as well. After a few minutes, the bleeding stopped. Laura produced from her first-aid bag some spray antiseptic, and she sprayed the corner of Red's mouth. After replacing the antiseptic spray in the bag, Laura then produced a small pack of antiseptic dissolving stitches. She cut off a piece about an inch square and placed it over the cut on Red's lip. "Nothing to eat for a day," Laura said, and then she put on Red the bridle that Jane had brought from Laura's car. Both Jane and Sally stood there in awe as Laura put the bridle on.

"Who's going to give me a leg up then?" Laura said.

Jane quickly gave Laura a leg up, saying, "Thank you, thank you."

Laura walked Red around for a few minutes, then explained to a stunned audience of two, Jane and Sally, (and the hidden audience of one, me), what a hackamore was. It was in fact a bitless bridle. Laura then gave Jane a lecture on how to use it, and followed up with a demonstration over the two singles and the double. Jane and Sally hung on to Laura's every word. Red never touched a pole, and by the end of the demonstration, he was jumping 5 feet for fun. After the demonstration had finished, Laura told Sally to walk Red around for five minutes but not to let him eat any grass.

I quickly went into the house through the office and acted nonchalantly as the girls' conversation, when they came in, centred around bits and bridles. "How did you get on then?" I enquired.

"Fine," said Jane. "I think we've managed to sort out Red."

The following weekend, Red went to Mill Lodge and won the first prize of £350 for the Grade B Championship Class. In the Horse & Hound *the following week, a feature on Red showed a picture of him clearing the last fence in the jump-off. The headline said: "Jane wins with ease as Red jumps to grade A status". Jane said in the article that "as soon as I tried him in a hackamore, I knew from the feel he was a different horse and I had found the answer to him."*

Laura never said a word and let Jane take all the credit. Jane, to my disgust, never had the decency to even pay Laura for the bridle that she never, ever returned.

Whilst Jane basked in her glory, Laura never said a word out of place about Jane – or let on to me it was she who sorted out Red. I knew because I'd seen it, but no one else knew that.

At about one o'clock, Laura said. "I have to go now."

I said, "Goodbye."

As soon as Laura had left, I asked Jane to tell me what the problem was with Red.

Jane said, "Oh, you wouldn't understand, Steve. We put together a bitless bridle, put it on Red, and, bingo, that did the trick."

I just replied, "Really?"

Jane did not mind Laura helping her out with her problems, but she most certainly was not going to give Laura any credit at all.

Laura rang me the following day, Sunday, and asked me if I wanted her to come in on Monday for work. She sounded apprehensive.

"Of course, unless you're fed up working for me."

"No," said Laura. "No, not at all."

Occasionally, Jane would leave horses in the yard for Laura to sort out. Jane did not want to be upstaged again by Laura, but she relied on her to sort the horse problems out. They would speak on the phone and be pleasant to each other at the farm. Deep down, however, as the months passed by, I could feel and sense a growing resentment from Jane towards Laura, and towards Charlie also, for that matter.

When Laura came in on Monday, I went into the yard and said, "Thanks, Laura."

"What for?" said Laura.

I said, "Saturday. Helping Jane out."

Laura said, "Oh … Jane."

I said, "Yes. I was in the tack room. I saw and heard the whole conversation, including your impressive demonstration."

Laura said, "Does that mean I'm sacked then?"

I said, "Of course not."

Laura said, "I did speak to Jane a bit abruptly."

"She deserved it, and you deserve more credit than you're taking," I replied.

Laura brightened up in the knowledge her job was safe.

Jane was even more successful, thanks to Laura. Leading up to Christmas last year, her success coincided with that of Chris Cobb. However, from Christmas up to the present, Jane had forever been putting Laura and Charlie down whenever she could. Especially Laura, who was now enjoying success in the showjumping ring herself with Fred II (the name had stuck). Jane had fewer horse problems, and Laura started breaking and schooling Cyril Night's horses for him whenever there was spare time at White Horse Farm, also with much success. Jane was perhaps jealous, and now, in hindsight after reading her letter, both spiteful towards and resentful of Laura and Charlie. Since Christmas, when Jane had taken an obvious liking towards Chris Cobb, I was getting weekly abuse from her about Laura and Charlie.

One week they were "mingers"; the next week, I was accused of having affairs with them – one week it would be Charlie, the next week Laura, and sometimes both of them in the same week. Jane's ulterior motive became clear at Stocklands. It was my fault; Jane could blame me, Laura, and Charlie; her indiscretions with Chris were nothing to do with it. I forced her into another man's arms, and that was how her letter to me was written.

Dear Steve,

I am so sorry our relationship has broken down. You cannot say I did not warn you. It is not possible for me to have a relationship with you anymore because of your obsession with those lesbian lovers you employ.

You obviously value them more than our forthcoming marriage. I've tried hard to make this work, but ever since Christmas, you have not believed a word I've said about bloody Laura and that stuck-up secretary of yours, Charlie.

I've just about had enough of it all, so I'm ending the relationship. I do not understand what you've got yourself into, but I do not want any part of it. You've upset me, and no doubt someone else that has it in for you, because you won't face facts. Rid yourself of those two dogs, and you might still have a chance of holding down a loving and meaningful relationship. All the time you employ them, you are warning off anybody that may come into your love life as I did eighteen months ago.

Please don't ring me or contact me. Sally will pick up Red tomorrow. I cannot even say take care, because I don't really give a damn about you anymore. You wouldn't listen to me, and now look at the trouble you're in. Chris Cobb is staying over the weekend and is going to ride Red and Light for me while I'm still recovering from my dislocated shoulder, thanks to you. I'll pick up my belongings tomorrow when Sally picks up Red.

Jane

Laura and Charlie sat with their mouths open, absolutely speechless.

I put the letter on the coffee table, looked at them, and said, "You should have let me throw it away, unopened."

It was now seven o'clock Friday evening.

The phone rang. It was DCI Heyes.

CHAPTER 6

The chief inspector was reasonably sure that the white Golf GTI was, as he put it, "another murder". The murderer had succeeded in getting rid of the evidence at the same time; whatever the evidence was, neither DCI Heyes nor anyone else was going to get it. The only lead was Hopalong's wing mirror. "We believe," said the chief inspector, "that the 6-foot-tall, slim, left-handed man is the dead man in the white Golf GTI. My long-range view is that he had an accomplice, and I really do believe there was an accomplice with him when Henry Hall was killed at the car park. The 6-foot-tall, slim, left-handed man, was a user as well as a dealer. What I'm not sure about, Steve, is where you fit in."

I asked the chief inspector to hold on a minute, As Charlie was poking me in the ribs. I put my hand over the mouthpiece of the phone.

Charlie said, "Steak?" I nodded. "Usual?" she asked, and I nodded again. "French bread and salad?" I nodded yet again. Charlie said, "Laura's gone upstairs for a shower."

I said, "Give me ten minutes, and I'll give you a hand."

Charlie said okay and went into the kitchen.

Taking my hand off the mouthpiece, I said into the phone, "Sorry, Chief Inspector. You were saying?"

The chief inspector repeated the crux of our previous conversation, and then reiterated, "I'm just not sure where you fit in, Steve." He then asked me if I had made a list of possible disgruntled clients.

I told him we'd had a company meeting that afternoon, with all my staff present. "We discussed all our live cases. I don't believe, Chief Inspector, that any of my cases could have anything to do with these murders or the arson of the horsebox."

"Let me decide that, Steve," said the chief inspector.

I told him that my clients expected and received complete confidentiality; I could not and would not divulge any information about them. The chief inspector reminded me that two people were dead, and I was involved.

There was silence on both ends of the phone.

After about ten seconds, I relented. "All right. I'll replace names with letters. The case reports will be ready for you on Monday at 10 a.m. How's that, Chief Inspector?"

"It will be sufficient," said DCI Heyes. "By the way, how's Jane?"

"Don't ask," I replied. I did not involve anybody else. I just told him that Jane said she'd had enough. I informed him that she was an international showjumper and needed to get back on the circuit. I continued to make excuses as to why Jane had left me until the chief inspector said, "That's official then, is it, Steve?" I said that it was.

DCI Heyes started laughing. It was that sort of laugh which said, "You've tried the bullshit, now tell me the truth."

When he stopped laughing, I said, "What's the joke?"

He said, "If you don't tell me the truth, I'm not going to get to the bottom of this."

I protested my innocence but was no match for John the Chief Inspector; he was different gravy.

"Listen, Steve," he said. "You are thirty-seven, and single; your farm is paid for, no mortgage; you have a thriving business, with eight staff, nine company vehicles, and business turnover in excess of a million; your pre-tax profits were £650,000 last financial year, and £500,000 the year before that; you were offered £4 million for your company at Royal Ascot just a few weeks ago; you were a guest of the Jockey Club in a private box with Jane Coe, your fiancée; you did not sell your business because you love it, because you love your lifestyle. Your business is going to make you enemies; there are some people who are going to be envious of you, and some people who are going to be jealous of you. Added to that, if you accept a client's case, you are accepting his or her problem. If there is someone who doesn't like a client of yours, you will inherit that dislike as well. "Now, Steve, please tell me what the name is of Jane's new wallet."

I was now sitting down in the office, my mouth wide open.

Charlie popped her head round the corner. "Supper's ready. What's the matter with you?"

I said, "Chris Cobb."

"Thank you, Steve," said the chief inspector.

"Chris Cobb?" said Charlie.

"Sorry, Charlie, I'm still speaking to the chief inspector," I said to her. "Sorry, Chief Inspector," I said into the phone. "Yes, it's Chris Cobb. He's a showjumper as well."

"Do you know much about him?" the chief inspector asked.

"Jane's adored him since Christmas."

"That's interesting," said the chief inspector.

I asked the chief inspector if he had heard from Miles at forensics.

"No, nothing yet," replied the chief inspector.

I asked him if he would have a car patrolling tonight.

He said, "Do you think you need one?"

I explained about my two employees staying over tonight.

"Are you expecting any trouble from your ex then, Steve?"

I told him about Jane's letter and the fact that she apparently hated Laura and Charlie and blamed them for our break-up.

"A smokescreen, Steve, by the sound of it, for what she really wanted. I hope I have not hurt you by saying that."

"No, not at all, John." I decided, by that point, that I was on first name terms with the chief inspector.

"Jane did say she would pick up her things in the morning. Chris Cobb is staying at her place tonight."

The chief inspector finished the conversation by telling me that the patrol car would be out tonight, but because of cutbacks, there would be no chance over the weekend.

I thanked him, put the phone down, and went into the kitchen to eat. It had been a long day, and I was no nearer to finding my stormy petrel.

It was now 8.30 p.m., and our steaks were on the table. Laura and Charlie sat opposite each other at the pine bench-type table, which sat six. I asked Laura to move up and sat next to her. Laura just had two towels on: one around her hair; the other around her body, just below her arms. We ate our steaks. Charlie had opened a bottle of Nuit St George and filled up our glasses. I had started drinking alcohol midweek, much to my dismay, and I liked it! We finished off the French bread and salad.

When I got up to do the washing up, Charlie said, "Sit down."

Charlie looked at Laura. Laura looked at Charlie, and then both burst out laughing.

I said to them, "Come on then, what's the joke?" I finished my wine.

Charlie quipped, "When Laura and I make love, Steve, we, we, we … make a hell of a racket."

They both burst out laughing again.

I said, "Charlie, you make as much noise as you like, but just go and get another bottle of Nuit first."

The wine rack was by the office door. I asked Charlie to lock the office door, bolt it, and press the electric button to close the garage door outside.

Laura put her left hand on my right thigh and winked at me. She moved her hand further over my right thigh until she could feel what she was after, and then she leant towards me. I instinctively slid my right hand behind Laura's left arm, put it on her left thigh, and kissed her. Laura offered me her tongue as she squeezed me with her left hand.

"Charlie!" I shouted. "Where's that wine?"

Laura left her left hand where it was and licked her lips.

Charlie came into the kitchen, carrying the wine, and took her seat at the table. She picked up the corkscrew, took the cork out of the bottle of wine, and let it breathe for a few minutes before pouring. Charlie said, "Why don't you two go upstairs?"

Laura laughed and squeezed me with her left hand again!

I said to Charlie, "There's plenty of time, and in any case, we've got another bottle of wine to get through yet."

Charlie filled our glasses back up again, looked at Laura, and said, "Laura, I think it's about time we changed our ways. We've never let a man come between us, have we?"

Laura said, "Of course not."

They both looked at me. I'd seen that look before.

Charlie said, "Well, if you're going to come between us, Steve," Charlie said, looking at me with a straight face, as did Laura, "I suppose then, from now on," she said, turning her gaze towards Laura as both burst out laughing again, "I suppose we had better get a bigger bed."

Laura laughed so much, the towel wrapped around her body fell down. She made no an attempt to retrieve her towel, and we sat there talking mostly about Jane's departure and the fact of how well the girls believed I'd taken it.

I thought Jane's letter was over the top, and I told them so. I told them about what had happened at Stocklands some months before. I said, "Don't even think for one second that our break-up was to do with either of you.

You provided a convenient excuse, or as the chief inspector called it, 'a smokescreen', for what she really wanted to do, and that was to be with Chris Cobb." My eyes never left Laura's beautiful body.

I could see the girls were relieved at what I had told them. We finished off the second bottle of Nuit. As I put my glass down, Charlie's right hand was on the table. I picked it up with my left hand and kissed her fingers.

Laura's left hand had not yet let go of me, and it was now 11.30!

"Come on," I said. "Time for bed."

The girls' eyes lit up at the thought. Charlie got up first and dashed to the loo. I lifted my right leg over the bench seat from under the table. Laura did the same with her left leg, and we pulled ourselves together and embraced each other, wrapping our arms around each other's backs, kissing and cuddling. The towel fell from Laura's light brown, blonde-streaked hair, and her damp long hair dropped lazily down her back. Laura forced her tongue into my mouth, making sounds of delirious desire as my hands caressed every part of her beautiful body.

Charlie shouted out, "Goodnight." I heard her go up the stairs to bed.

Laura did not seem to hear. She wrapped her long legs round my back. Laura wouldn't let go, so I got up, with Laura still wrapped around me, and I headed for the lounge. And then slowly, tenderly, I lowered Laura onto the settee. Now without both her towels, she looked up at me from the settee as she undid the buttons on my shirt.

The phone rang.

I said to Laura jokingly, "You expecting a call from your mum?"

Laura giggled as I picked up the phone.

"Steve?" said the familiar voice on the other end of the line.

"Yes, John," I said abruptly to the chief inspector, obviously not wanting to be disturbed.

"Some bad news, I'm afraid. Your two employees staying over tonight?"

"Yes?" I said enquiringly, now sitting up, concerned. "What's wrong?"

"Their flat's just been firebombed. My patrol car which was outside your house has attended. The fire brigade is in attendance. I thought you should be made aware."

"Yes, thank you, John," I replied.

Laura sat up as I put the phone down. "What's the matter, Steve?" Laura said, looking concerned.

I put my arms round her and said, "You'd better get dressed. Your flat's just been firebombed."

Laura ran upstairs to inform Charlie what had happened and to put some clothes on. I went into the kitchen, put some water in the electric kettle, and switched it on to make some strong coffee. My first instinct was to drive to the girls' flat and assess the damage. However, on second thought, the chief inspector would be able to do that – after all, he was only a phone call away. I made three coffees and then shouted up the stairs to the girls to ask them if they had their army camouflage jackets with them. The reply was a joint affirmative. Charlie appeared at the top of the stairs, buttoning up her combat jacket, which was coloured dark green and brown. I told Charlie I had made some coffee and was going to ring back the chief inspector back.

Charlie said, "Fine. We'll be down in a minute."

On the third ring, the chief inspector answered his mobile. I instinctively enquired about the fire damage. He informed me he was not at the scene yet; it would take him another five minutes or so to reach the girls' flat.

"Ring me, please, John, as soon as you have assessed the damage."

I informed John of what my immediate intentions were. He told me not to take any chances and said that should an intruder pay us a visit, I was to inform him immediately on his mobile. As I put the phone down in the lounge, Charlie and Laura appeared. Charlie was carrying a tray with the coffees on it. Laura asked why we could not leave straight away for the flat and why I wanted them to put camouflage jackets on.

I took a coffee off the tray, took a sip, and paused before I answered either question. "We are not going to the flat. The chief inspector will be there shortly, and he will assess the situation and inform me on his mobile." I explained to the girls that our mutual natural reaction was to get to the flat as soon as possible. Perhaps somebody, or some people, were hoping that would happen. We will not disappoint them if that was the case, and I explained what I had in mind. I asked the girls to check all the doors and windows, and to secure the farm. I went into the office and switched on all the exterior security lights.

They went back upstairs. Charlie shouted down the stairs to me. "Steve, shall we put all the lights on upstairs?"

I shouted back, "Yes!"

Happy that the farmhouse was as secure as it could possibly be, we all met back in the lounge and finished our coffees. We then briefly covered what our options were. We could defend the farm from a possible arson attack from within the farm's perimeters; or, if, as I suspected, we were being watched, we could give our watcher the idea that we were racing off to the girls' flat in Burgess Hill. I explained my plan that we would leave in a hurry; we would use Charlie's Vitara and drive to the convent about half a mile away, and then make our way back across country to three different positions, behind and both sides of White Horse Farm.

Laura suggested that a pig-sticker she had in the MGB might come in handy. The pig-sticker was an electrical gadget used for prodding cattle, sheep, pigs, etc. in an effort to get them to move along. It produced a short, sharp electric shock; one use was usually enough encouragement to man or beast. Laura asked Charlie if she had her army boots in her vehicle, which was affirmative. The girls went into the office, out of the rear door, and into the courtyard, where they changed their footwear. Charlie had two pairs of boots in the Vitara, and Laura and Charlie both took the same size.

In one of the office cabinets I kept an array of electronic gadgets which had been used in previous surveillance operations. Although a bit dated in terms of technology, I still felt some of it would come in useful one day. There were two pairs of field glasses, basically long-range binoculars, which I put on one of the desks; a navy-blue shell suit and balaclava, which I changed into; also a pair of black trainers which I put on. When the girls came back into the office, Laura put the pig-sticker on the desk, next to the binoculars.

I asked Charlie if she could think of anything else that would come in useful. She said we needed some form of communications. I told her there were some old walkie-talkies in the office cupboard. Charlie gave me one of those old-fashioned-type looks, and then she said, "Anything?" I asked her what she had recently purchased from Wharr's. Charlie said, "Steve, it's about time you had a new mobile phone. In fact, it's about time every employee had new mobile phones. These arrived yesterday." Charlie leant under her desk in the office, retrieved a box about the size of a shoebox, and took the lid off. Inside there were ten of what looked like mobile phones.

I asked Charlie, "Why so many?"

She said "These are not just mobile phones, Steve, these are liquid crystal display and text phones that use satellite-navigated messaging. "I have preset them so we can text message each other easily and effortlessly in silence," she went on. "Every employee can now speak to each other securely through Mother. The mobile phone number for each phone is exactly the same. All messages sent are recorded on this base terminal which is called Mother. Mother will automatically send the same message out to all the other mobile phones that are operational, unless the person sending the message presses a singular number for a message to a specific operative. For instance, if one of these mobile phones wanted just to text message mobile phone number 4, the sender would just press number 4 after completing his message, and then pressing the Send button. Mother will then store the message in its computer, with date and time of message, and relay that message accordingly."

When it came to electronics, Charlie an exceedingly bright girl. She handed Laura a mobile, and another to me, and then she told us both to log in to Mother. Charlie gave us the phone number to log in, and all three of us obeyed the liquid crystals which flashed "login, login, login" on each of our phones. The phones then simultaneously flashed "access code, access code, access code".

I asked Charlie what we were to do now.

Charlie typed in a few lines on Mother's keyboard, and then she told me to press 01 and Laura to press 02. Charlie pressed her mobile number, 03. "Now press Send," she said. Laura and I carried out Charlie's instructions. Charlie said, "Mother will now keep us in contact with each other. All you have to do is press the On button, type out your message, and press Send. For whomever you want to send the message to, simply press that operative's number after you have typed your message. For instance, Steve, press 02 for Laura, or 03 for me. If you do not press a number, Mother will send the message to all operative mobiles."

Laura and I both nodded that we understood.

I used the mobile straight away to call the chief inspector, who was, as he informed me, now at the scene of the fire. I gave the mobile phone number of Mother, which would route his call to me if he pressed the digits 01, after keying in my number on his phone to call me. Charlie nodded her head in agreement.

The chief inspector then told me that the fire had not managed to get a hold, mainly due to the fire doors holding the fire back. Although there would be a lot of smoke damage, he was of the opinion that a lot of the girls' belongings would be retrievable. I passed the good news on to the girls. It was now thirty minutes since the chief inspector had informed me of the arson attack. I rang off with him, and then said to the girls, "Right. Let's go and do the business."

Charlie picked up a pair of the binoculars from the desk, got her Vitara keys off the wall next to the rear door, and walked over to the Vitara in the courtyard.

Laura picked up the pig-sticker from the desk with her right hand, and with her left hand she placed her mobile in her jacket's right breast pocket.

I looked at the pig-sticker and then into Laura's eyes. "I won't keep you waiting too long, Laura," I said, and then I walked out the rear office door into the courtyard towards the Vitara.

Laura closed the office door securely and then jabbed the pig-sticker up my backside. I let out a cry of pain at the sudden shock.

Charlie looked over from the Vitara and said to Laura, "The pig-sticker sounds as if it's working okay!"

Laura replied, "Shockingly well."

As she pressed the electronically operated garage-door button on the wall near to the rear office door, Laura jumped into the back seat of the Vitara and put the pig-sticker onto the spare seat next to her, where Charlie and I had put our binoculars.

I told Charlie to put her foot down as if we were in a hurry. On the way out, I took off the balaclava as we turned left onto the old A23. I could see that the garage door had closed and the security lights were doing their job perfectly, covering the whole area of farm buildings, office, stables, and house in a blaze of electric light. I asked Charlie to drive past the convent and the Hickstead Showground, to the Castle Pub and Restaurant, and then double back and turn right into the convent, all of which Charlie did without question. Charlie parked as far away from the convent as possible, in the furthermost part of the car park.

We all got out of the Vitara. Laura handed me a pair of the binoculars as Charlie centrally locked up the Vitara. Once it was locked, Laura gave Charlie the other pair of binoculars. Laura told us to follow her, as she knew the area well, having ridden over the local bridle paths on countless occasions with and without Jane. It only took us about five minutes before we had the farm in our sights. I asked Charlie to cover the west side of the farm. This was the side nearest to the convent. I told her on no account to go near the old A23, which was where the entrances to the farm were the northern-most point. There were some private houses and a small copse between the convent and the farm; Charlie suggested she could use the copse for cover. I told Charlie to use the mobile from now on for messages, and not to take any chances whatsoever. Laura and I proceeded to the back of the farm, where the rear of the stables were overshadowed by a few large oak trees and a ditch.

"Laura," I whispered.

"Yes, Steve?" Laura whispered in reply.

"How do you fancy climbing that oak tree? You can direct Charlie and me from that vantage point. If you take my binoculars, you can see practically everything that may happen."

Laura agreed, and swapped her pig-sticker for my binoculars. As the first branch of the oak tree was about 9 feet from the ground, Laura asked me to help her up to the first branch. She put the binoculars in her jacket pocket and, with her arms above her head outstretched, reached for the branch.

"Bend down, Steve," she said. "Put your head between my legs, and lift me up on your shoulders."

I didn't need to be told twice!

I could hardly see Laura up the tree. She tapped me on the head with her foot as she sat astride the branch. I looked up and put my hand on her left boot.

Laura said, "How long for, Steve?"

I said, "Until I give you the all-clear. Check in with Mother every fifteen minutes, or straight away if you are uncertain about anything. Do not take any chances whatsoever. Text Charlie, Laura; tell her to do the same: Mother every fifteen minutes, or straight away in an emergency. I'm going round to the east side behind the vehicle parking area and ménage. That's the west side, south side, and east side all covered," I said to Laura. "From now on, you direct operations via the text messaging through Mother."

Laura said, "Leave it to me, Steve," and she climbed high into the branches of the oak tree.

Unseen by the naked eye, I made my way round to the back of the car park, which had a few the company's blue vans parked within its post-and-rail fencing. This would offer sufficient cover for me, as I did not want to be too far away from any would-be arsonists. I reassured myself that the binoculars would at least keep the girls a safe distance away. I crawled under one of the vans. I pulled the balaclava over my head, so my eyes were the only visible part of my head (through the balaclava).

I had my mobile in the pocket of my shell suit, and I made my first transmission to Mother. My text message read: "Nothing to report 01, 2,

02, 03." I understood it; I only hoped Mother did. After a few seconds, Mother showed me "message received" on the LCD, followed by "02, 03 informed". A few seconds later, the LCD lit up again with "Incoming message, 02, 2, 01, 03, ditto." Then another message: "03, 2, 02, 01, ditto." Within a minute, we had all reported to each other through Mother.

I spent the next fifteen minutes thinking about Laura and Charlie, and the fact that I had put them in an awful lot of danger. I thought about calling one of my teams back.

My LCD read, "Incoming message, 02, 2, 03, 01, AQNTR", which meant "02 to 03 and 01, all quiet, nothing to report". A further incoming message read "03, 2, 01, 02, ditto".

I transmitted my message to the girls: "01, 2, 02, 03, ditto".

Mother reported "message received".

I got back to my thoughts as to whether I should recall one of my teams. I did know, after all, the lengths to which these people after me would go; and, of course, I also knew that they were capable of murder. What I did not know was what they wanted, or what they needed to achieve or accomplish, before my employees, my friends, their property, and I would be safe again. Half an hour had now passed, which made it just over seventy minutes since the chief inspector had interrupted my night of passion – before it had even begun.

Almost to the second, Mother vibrated in my top pocket. I took the mobile phone out. It was the usual: the girls each reporting in through Mother. I received their text messages and transmitted the same, finishing with "AQNTR".

I then rang the chief inspector on his mobile.

He was still in Burgess Hill, at the girls' flat. "How is your situation, Steve?" he enquired.

Without thinking, I said, "AQNTR."

The chief inspector said, "All quiet, nothing to report."

I said, "Perhaps I've overreacted."

"Not in the least. It's in your interest to protect all that you feel needs protecting in whatever way you feel is appropriate," he said.

I explained my situation to him, including where the girls were, and, of course, that we were contacting each other by text messaging every fifteen minutes.

The chief inspector enquired as to whether Laura and Charlie would be able to stick it out until dawn.

I said, "Without doubt. They are both Territorial Army Reservists and have spent many a weekend on the Brecon Beacons."

"Fine then," he said. "It's now just after 12.30 a.m., early Saturday morning. Leave them where they are, and stick it out. I feel sure you have taken the best possible action. Your arsonists, and I'm sure there's more than one, want to burn your farmhouse down. I believe that the driver of the horsebox, who crashed into your gates, was so high on drugs that he misjudged the turn. He botched the job. I believe he's the same man who tried to run you over in the car park at the Metropole. I also believe he's the same man we found dead in the burned-out Golf. Stick with it, Steve. We have all but finished here. Miles will be round in the morning. I am keeping my two constables here for the rest of the night, so I cannot give you any surveillance until the morning." He finished by asking if he could call by tomorrow afternoon. He wanted to speak to the girls and also to review the truncated case reports that Charlie was preparing from our ongoing cases. (Charlie would replace names with letters to protect my clients' identities, as I'd told the chief inspector, and omit the clients' addresses, just leaving the town name and post code to identify the whereabouts of our clients.)

I felt the chief inspector was being too pushy, so I told him, "No chance, John. The earliest would be between 10 a.m. and 1 p.m. Monday."

"Monday it will have to be then," John said. He was not happy but appreciated the timescale and the amount of work involved in preparing the cases.

Once agreed that Monday would have to do, the call ended; we would no doubt speak later.

It was time to check in with the girls through Mother. I transmitted my usual message to Mother, and it was passed on to the girls: "AQNTR", and then I duly received the same message back seconds later from each of them. It was now 12.45 a.m. I put the mobile in my top pocket, and slowly and quietly moved my way out sideways. I got to my feet between both vans, left the pig-sticker by the rear wheel, and slowly reached down to unzip my flies. I was bursting for a pee. Whilst relieving myself, I looked over to the A23. I saw what was left of my two piers and the tarmac drive, with oak post-and-rail fencing that had been treated, and the posts then set in concrete, sturdy and strong, that would last for years.

I then remembered the words of the person who had put the fencing up for me: "You would need a lorry to knock those posts down." It suddenly

80

dawned on me, would the posts stop a lorry going straight into the front door of my converted barn farmhouse, which was 90 per cent wood? I had not realised until the chief inspector said, "Tall, thin man, high on drugs; probably misjudged the entrance." Now, as I viewed the completely open floodlit runway to my front door, the difference was not how, but when. I had given them an open invitation.

The horsebox had cleared the path for a second offensive, planned or not. I texted Laura and Charlie through Mother: "Expecting arson attack from north A23. Imminent. Target: front door of the farmhouse. Will try to block with van."

I ran to the large garage door from the ten-car park, pressing Send on the mobile. As I ran, the door opened, and my mobile showed "message received". I got my keys out of my pocket and quickly opened the office door. I took both sets of van keys and dashed back to the vans. I noticed that Charlie's spare set of Vitara keys was missing. I struck lucky first time with the right keys; the door opened, and I put the key in the ignition. I got lucky again as the engine started the first time. I purposely left the lights off on the van, quickly put the van into gear, and set off to place the van between my front door and where my gates used to be. My mobile, I could feel, was pulsating in my pocket. Laura and Charlie needed to speak to me. I was now on the A23. Coming towards me, with main beams blazing, were two vehicles abreast on both sides of the road. I put my foot down on the throttle, turned my headlights on, and crossed my fingers. Would I get to the entrance first? It was going to be close, very close. I could feel my heart pounding. My mobile was still pulsating against my chest, whether it was the adrenaline or just pure devilment I did not know. I knew, though, there and then, I was not stopping, for some unknown reason. I accepted this challenge. I wanted to know who it was that I was up against. I needed to know more about my enemies.

I knew a smash was imminent. Just before it happened, my whole life flashed before me. I thought, *What's Charlie doing crashing into me?* It was the bull bars that were mounted on the front of her Vitara that I recognised a split second before all my lights went out, amidst the sound of breaking glass and tearing metal.

CHAPTER 7

It must have been the very last split second that I turned the steering wheel hard left, and instead of a head-on, the right-hand side of the bull bars (the offside in front of the driver of Charlie's Vitara) made contact with my driver's door. The motion of the van meant that the bull bars tore the side of the van out, but at the time I did not know that. The impact sent me into the van's passenger seat. Had I fastened my seat belt, I would have not been alive to tell the tale. The bull bars never stopped at the driver's door, but continued, devouring all, taking out the back of the driver's seat and everything in their, path including the right-hand rear door.

I lay there – either unconscious or severely concussed, mainly through my head making contact with the roof of the van as I involuntarily changed seats. My head was in the floor well, where a passenger's feet would normally be when travelling in a van; my legs were either side of the passenger seat's headrest. I felt at ease as I lay there but could not understand why the van had no side. I could not feel my body; my mind, my unconscious state, had me floating on a soft, white, puffy cloud that was ascending. It was warm.

This blissful existence was shattered by a loud *bang* some minutes later. My left leg fell from the side of the passenger's headrest and wedged itself between the gearstick and the handbrake. *Bang!* That second bang did the trick, as it brought me out of my unconscious state for a few moments. As I came round, I coughed, covering the back of the passenger seat with a splattering of blood. I coughed again, gasping for air; I was choking on my own blood. I had to get up and regain my senses. *Bang!* Someone was ramming the van from the rear. I saw Charlie's bull bars coming towards me once again as I managed to get my head and body up off the floor well by pushing down with my left hand and arm. The white bull bars of Charlie's Vitara. My eyes were level with the handbrake, and where the side of the van had been taken out, I could just make out what was happening. *Bang!* My left arm slipped, and I was back to my original position. I was helpless; I couldn't move. I felt myself slipping away again. I desperately wanted to get back to that lovely, soft, warm, white cloud. I wanted them to hurry up; a few more bangs to the van would do the trick. I was being pushed up my drive to the front door of the farmhouse. I would be wedged up against my front door, perhaps doused with a gallon of petrol – another bang, and then it would all be over.

I felt prepared for the finality; however, I didn't hear or feel another bang. It seemed to have stopped. I was beginning to feel warm; every second, it felt a tiny bit warmer. I had to regain my senses quickly. I tried to lift myself up again and just about managed to get my left arm under my back to lever myself up, only to see flames slowly engulfing the van. I coughed once more into the foul-smelling air, once again spraying the grey passenger seat with specks of blood. Using my right hand, I managed to pull the balaclava off my head. My face must have looked a real mess: the bottom part of the balaclava was saturated, leaving great streaks of warm, wet, sticky blood from my neck to my forehead.

Charlie had run over from the copse. I saw her pressing the immobiliser on her key ring as she got within range. The Vitara cut out, and the occupant then got out and ran back to the main road, where a getaway vehicle was ready and waiting, with its engine running.

There was diesel fuel all over the drive where the van's diesel tank had ruptured from impact and being rammed; the van's electrical system had provided the flame that ignited the diesel; the main battery lead that ran under the van to the back of the van fed a booster battery for when extra power was needed for tools or lighting – this was what caused the fire, much to the arsonist's delight no doubt.

My saving grace was Laura, who had descended her tree perch to run across the paddock in front of the house, hose in hand. The reel of hose unwound itself as she ran, and spots of water were hitting the roof of the van. The security lights from the house were still blazing away, and as I looked directly upwards I could see the colours of the rainbow. The tiny droplets of water acted as prisms, refracting the light into beautiful rainbow colours. The darkness of the night provided a magnificent backdrop.

Laura gave the hose to Charlie and told her to soak her with the hose. Flames were now under the van, and the passenger seat was beginning to smoulder. Laura managed to free my left leg, which was wedged between the gearstick and the handbrake; I held my right arm up, and Laura grabbed it, pulling me forward with her right arm. Just as I felt I could go no further, Laura suddenly turned, and instead of facing me, had her back to me. She pulled my right arm over her right shoulder, bending down at the same time. I felt her left arm move inside my legs and wrap round my left leg, and then she dragged me out on her back. After a few steps, we reached the post-and-rail fence and turned left towards my front door, which I so defiantly wanted to defend. I felt cold, beautiful water on my legs. I did not know if I was burning or steaming; however, I could smell and taste the fresh air once again, and I gasped for more, in between bouts of coughing up blood.

Slowly, my head began to clear, and I realised I felt cold. Charlie still had the hose turned on, as I did not realise that Laura's camouflage jacket and my right leg were still smouldering and smoking. Laura staggered another few steps and then buckled under my weight and the drenching. I fell on top of Laura and rolled to one side. We both lay there, breathing heavily. Charlie turned the hose completely onto the van, and soon she had the fire under control. I sat up, breathing much easier now. I looked up to the clear dark-blue sky littered with glittering silver stars, and thanked them.

Laura groaned next to me. I put my right hand underneath Laura's face, and with my left hand leant over and pulled at Laura's camouflage jacket so that she was now lying on her back, facing me, with my right hand now cupping the back of her head and keeping it off the ground. Laura must have hit her head on the ground; her forehead was grazed and bleeding. I held her left hand tightly, and after a few seconds, her hand tightened around mine. When Laura opened her eyes, she said, "Steve, you look absolutely dreadful."

I replied, "You can talk!"

Charlie came over and said much the same. "You two look in a right state. I'll ring for an ambulance."

I said, "No, no, Charlie. Ring the chief inspector first, please. Other car, other car."

Charlie said, "It wasn't a car, Steve. It was a grey van."

"Yes, that's right!" exclaimed Laura. "It was a grey van."

"Quickly then, tell the chief inspector." I gave Charlie the chief inspector's number, and she got through to him immediately.

Charlie said, "He wants to speak to you, Steve."

Laura was now more like her old self, and I moved to one of the fence posts, still sitting on the ground, and leant against it. Laura followed me and sat in between my legs, with her head resting on my chest. Charlie gave me her phone, and I quickly let the chief inspector know what had happened. I then asked Charlie to make some coffee.

The chief inspector said he would send DS Harman, over right away, also a fire engine and an ambulance. "Are you injured, Steve?" DCI Heyes asked.

I said, "Apart from a headache and possibly a broken nose, I don't think so. It's Laura I'm worried about."

Laura protested, "I'm perfectly okay." She tried to grip the phone but missed by a mile.

"Concussion," I said to the chief inspector.

"Right then," he said. "I'll send that ambulance right away."

Laura and I slowly rose to our feet, holding each other up.

I said to the chief inspector, "I'll see you Monday lunchtime. The other vehicle that was part of the attack tonight was a van."

"What type van?" he asked.

"Was the van a big van or a small van?" I asked Laura.

She said, "It was BT size."

I told the chief inspector what Laura had just said, and then I rang off.

Laura and I then slowly walked round to the back of the house, through the big garage door, and into the office.

On walking into the kitchen, I could smell that Charlie had the coffee on, and I saw she had some warm water in the sink. I told Charlie to take Laura upstairs and get her out of her wet clothes and into something warm. She was going to hospital because she had concussion.

Laura protested that she did not have concussion. "Look," she said as she made her third attempt to pick up her mug of coffee, again missing by a wide margin.

Charlie said, "Come on, Laura."

I bathed my face as they went upstairs, and then I looked in the mirror. My nose was indeed broken, and my left eye was going to be a real shiner in the morning. My left knee would need some stitches, I realised on inspection, but apart from that, I felt not too bad. The coffee did its job wonderfully well.

Charlie brought Laura back down. Charlie had bandaged Laura's forehead and changed her into jogging bottoms and a sweater. I took a bandage and strapped my left knee, which was still bleeding.

The ambulance arrived to take us to hospital. Before we left, I gave Charlie an almighty cuddle. "Will you be all right for a few hours?" I asked her. "DS Harman will be here shortly."

Charlie gave me one of those looks. "And you're asking me if I will be all right?" she said. "Look at the state of you two when I leave you alone for two minutes. Now just go and spend the night together in hospital. I'll drive down at ten in the morning and pick you up if you are well enough. Now off with you! Leave everything to me."

I knew any further protest would fall on deaf ears. The ambulance took us to Brighton General Hospital in Eastern Road; this was becoming a habit I could well do without.

DS Harman passed us in the drive as we left for the hospital. I noticed he had a constable with him, which made me feel a lot better. I turned towards Laura to tell her – the paramedic had asked Laura to lie down, but she had flatly refused; she wanted to sit next to me.

Laura had got her way, but only for a few seconds as it turned out. Blood was running down from her forehead bandage, which had become saturated very quickly, it seemed to me. Laura had passed out, her head lying limp on my left shoulder.

The paramedic acted quickly, and within seconds had her lying down on the ambulance bed opposite. He checked her breathing and made sure her airways were not blocked; he took her pulse, whilst at the same time covering her up in a blanket. He then turned to me and said, "Don't worry, she's fine, mate, just exhausted. I'm going to monitor her condition with the aid of this machine, mate, so don't be alarmed at the wires."

I mentioned the blood-saturated head bandage.

"Oh, don't worry about that, cobber," said the paramedic.

I said, "I'm Steve Hurst, and thanks for attending so quickly."

The driver shouted, "ETA seven minutes, Aussie!"

He replied, "Both stable, no rush."

The driver switched off the flashing blue light which had been on since we left the farm.

Aussie turned round and said, "Are you the same Steve Hurst, ex-British Army, two tours of duty, stationed Belfast 1984–86?"

I nodded, but I could not recollect Aussie from my army past.

Aussie Osbourne then formally introduced himself. There were no handshakes; he had his medical mittens on anyway.

As we pulled into A&E, Aussie said, "I finish at 8 a.m. I'll pop in and see you when you've been patched up, and we can have a coffee."

I repeated, "Many thanks."

Laura was taken into Emergency. I walked in and obeyed the nurse's instructions as she ushered me into a cubical. There was a bed which I sat on. My bandaged left knee was covered in blood; I leant back against a pillow and just wanted to close my eyes for a second, I let my head lay on the pillow and immediately found my soft white cloud once again, without any trouble, oblivious to the attention I had received during the night, from the staff of the A&E Department.

My next memory of reality came at about 8.15 a.m. with the feeling of "thirsty, thirsty". I slowly opened my eyes to be greeted by Aussie, who upon seeing me enter the world of the living, said, "Drink your coffee, Steve. Do you want me to get some tucker?"

As my eyes focused, first on the plaster covering my nose, and then on Aussie, I said just three words: "Who are you?"

Aussie still had on his green paramedic uniform, which was the common denominator between my brain and reality. As I tried to elevate myself to a sitting up position, Aussie said, "Let me give you a hand, mate." He grabbed another pillow from an empty adjoining bed, puffed it up, and placed it behind my back. "There you go. Just lean back, mate."

I said, "Cheers. I must have closed my eyes for a few seconds. Could you ask the nurse when they will be able to patch me up? And could you get me two aspirins? I seem to have a terrible headache." As I said the words, I put my hand up to my face and felt the plaster across the bridge of my nose.

"Here, Steve," said Aussie. "Drink this." He passed me a cup of coffee. From his breast pocket Aussie produced two aspirins, which he handed them to me.

I swallowed the pills and drank the coffee, which was warm and sweet. Slowly, very slowly, my memory returned.

Aussie said nothing; he just sat there waiting for me – my brain, my logic, my memory – to slowly unravel the previous eight hours.

Some five minutes later, after I had finished the coffee, I put the cup down on the bedside table and said to Aussie, "Belfast, 1985, Falls Road. You treated me for a bomb-blast wound. A piece of shrapnel caught my right arm when our barracks were attacked."

"You attended me? Strewth, Steve!" said Aussie. "There's nothing wrong with your memory."

"Aussie, I want to know how Laura is. Could you find out?"

"No sweat, mate. She's fine, still asleep. Got a fair dinkum wound on her right temple; though, luckily, its above her hairline. Doctor said it needed eight stitches. Had to shave her temple slightly to be able to put the stitches in properly. Few scratches on her forehead, but she's fine, Steve. Don't worry."

"What time is it, Aussie?" I asked.

"It's 8.30 in the morning," Aussie replied, adding, "Saturday morning."

I tried to bend my left leg to get out of bed but found my movement was severely restricted.

Aussie said, "Ten stitches, just above your patella. Doctor taped it. Four stitches, right eye; broken nose, all fixed up; don't do anything for a week. Don't look in the mirror for two weeks."

I remembered how Aussie never used two words if one would do. As if by instinct, my left hand found the shrapnel scar on my right arm. As I felt the scar, I remembered the pain. The pain I went through, my comrades went through – those who were lucky to survive the blast, that is.

Aussie read my mind. "Laura was out for the count when the doctor put the stitches in. Anyway, in your case back in 1985, it was an emergency situation. No anaesthetic, just a needle and cotton. You were one of many that day, Steve."

I said, "Yes, I know."

I remembered the guilt of survival, where many of my platoon were cut to pieces by the bomb placed in a van driven into our barracks by an innocent civilian whose family was being held hostage. The van drove straight through the barrack gates, the driver jumping clear just before the van ran down a guard at the security checkpoint. The van, by then in the barrack square, was detonated by remote control. Forty pounds of Semtex packed into an oil drum filled with pitch and nails; left an awful mess. Aussie was in the medical corps, and like me, on his second tour of duty. I was a regular in the Duke of Edinburgh Corps. Having made sergeant in a comparatively short time, I helped Aussie as best I could that day. My captain and major both had suffered fatal wounds, and I just automatically took control. There were about four medical corps attached to our barracks who initially tended the wounded and covered the dead. Within minutes, a fleet of ambulances arrived from the Belfast Royal Infirmary, together with vehicles from the RUC (Royal Ulster Constabulary, the local police). The situation was under control. I informed headquarters, cordoned off a 200-yard perimeter around the barracks, and despatched snipers to cover the barracks and immediate area. After a hasty inspection, I informed HQ we had no roadworthy vehicles. I was informed vehicles from other barracks were on their way. Also a CO (commissioned officer) was on his way to take charge. I was 22 and had been in the army a year. I had seen the action, and I knew the pain; the van driver lay dead in the road, with a piece of the van's exhaust pipe embedded in his back and protruding through and out of his stomach.

"Steve, Steve," Aussie said now.

"Oh, sorry, Aussie. I was just thinking of the day the bomb went off in the barracks."

"Do you want another coffee, mate, or some tucker?"

"Some more coffee would be great, Aussie."

"Right," he said. "I'll be two ticks."

When Aussie got back, I quickly gave him a résumé of my activities. I had reached captain, and after nine years, left the army, in 1993. I told him about DIRTS, explaining that I'd set up the company up in 1994 and then describing exactly what my team and I did. I told him that Laura was my employee, and so was Charlie, who would be visiting me later in the morning, at around ten. I finished by telling Aussie how brave Laura had been the night before. I probably owed her my life.

I actually felt a lot better by that point, which was a little after nine. I asked Aussie if he could stay until ten.

"No sweat, mate," he replied.

"Tell me how you ended up a paramedic in the Sussex Ambulance Service then, Aussie."

"Well, mate, it was like this," he started off, and then he launched into his tale. "I had done my nine years by 1990, and I did not fancy Desert Storm, so when I left the army, I went on a walkabout which lasted six years. I found myself in London during Euro '96. Just off Sloane Square was a real good pub called The Australian. Well, I met this sheila; four years later, married, two dustbin lids (kids) mortgage, needed a secure job. Been a paramedic now for four years."

Aussie told me he lived at Haywards Heath, his wife's name was Karen, and the two kids were Joey (age 3) and Jenny (age 1). Aussie was always direct, just the facts. I persuaded him to give me more than just the bare details. America, Canada, Russia, Finland, Sweden, Norway – in fact, most of Europe – Aussie visited on his walkabout.

"And you ended up in London in 1996, and met your match in Karen?"

"Yep," said Aussie. "But what a girl, Steve. London, born and bred; blonde, blue eyes, tall, slim, and a real good-looker." Aussie got his wallet out to show me a picture of his wife and the kids.

I assured Aussie what a lucky man he was, and wrote my telephone number down on some notepaper, which was on the bedside table. I gave the number to Aussie and asked him if he would ring me sometime next week. It was just before ten, and I wanted to wash and tidy myself up before Charlie arrived. I was in a four-bed ward on my own.

As Aussie left, a nurse looked in and said, "Oh, Mr Hurst. Did you want some breakfast?" I asked for some coffee and toast. "I'm Becky, by the way, your ward nurse".

I asked Becky if I could get up for a wash, and she asked me if I needed any crutches. I said I would manage. I just had my pants on, and Becky passed me a nightgown. I thanked her and hobbled to the bathroom. To my surprise, I found a disposable shaver, shaving cream, soap, towels, etc. I undressed, showered, shaved, and felt much better than I looked. Aussie was right, though, when he told me not to look in a mirror for two weeks. My face looked a mess. On my way back to the ward, walking became easier. My step was "more sprightly", according to Becky. Actually, it did feel better. Becky told me that Laura was still asleep, and just then, Charlie walked in.

I beckoned for Charlie to join me for coffee and toast, and she then filled me in on the details since the arrival, earlier that morning, of DS Harman, who was still at the farm. "Forensics arrived at 7 a.m.," Charlie reported. "I've recalled Ricky and Allan from the Tote enquiries at Kempton and Ascot. I think we can make do with one operative on each case, for the moment. We are obviously short of manpower, but not so short that we cannot manage."

I asked Charlie when the lads were due to arrive.

Charlie said, "They are here already, ever since 3 a.m."

"Excellent," I told her.

We finished off the coffee and toast.

Charlie said, "Can we go and see Laura?"

I asked Becky if it was all right, and she took us to Laura's ward. It was a four-bed ward, like mine. As we entered the ward, a nurse informed us Laura had just woken up and was sitting up in bed, drinking tea.

As we walked to her bed, Laura asked Charlie if she had brought any of her tapes, meaning her reggae tapes.

"Of course," said Charlie, and out of her backpack produced half a dozen tapes and a cassette player.

Laura's eyes lit up. I knew she was all right, straight away. Whilst Charlie was plugging in the cassette player, I leant over the bed and kissed Laura on the lips.

Laura said, "I hope you feel better than you look."

I assured her I did. "What about you?" I replied.

Laura said she had a bit of a headache but wanted to go back to the farm at Sayers Common. I said I would ask the doctor. Leaving Charlie to chat to Laura, I went to find the doctor, telling the girls I would be back in ten minutes.

The ward nurse, Alice, told me the A&E doctor that treated Laura insisted that she be kept in for at least twenty-four hours, for observation. I asked the nurse if I could see him, and she corrected me: Laura's doctor was a she, Dr Amy Goble. I spoke to her, with the help of Nurse Alice, who contacted the doctor on the internal telephone. After initial introductions between ward nurse and doctor, the phone was passed to me.

"Good morning, Dr Goble. It's Steve Hurst here."

"Good morning, Mr Hurst. How are you feeling this morning?" was the doctor's reply.

I thought to myself, *Right. That's the pleasantries over with. I'll try the Aussie way: to the point.* "Can Laura Hallett and I go home now?"

Without pause the doctor said, "Positively, no! Both of you are to stay until Sunday morning."

I said, "That's out of the question."

The doctor replied, "You and Laura are not fit to drive; you both have concussion, which is my concern."

After another five minutes of consultation and arbitration, we agreed that we would review the situation in the evening, and Laura and I would stay in hospital until then.

When I returned to Laura's ward, the girls were chatting away merrily to each other. Mungo Gerry provided the background music – after all, it was "In the Summertime".

I walked up to the bed. "The good news, girls, is that we can leave today; the bad news, not until 5 p.m." It was now 11 a.m.

Charlie said, "In that case, I'll get back to the farm and come back at 4.30."

Laura said, "Could you bring me some decent clothes?"

Those were my thoughts exactly.

Charlie said, "I'm using your Rover, Steve. The forensic team is all over what's left of my Vitara."

I told Charlie to run things and said that we would see about vehicles this evening.

Charlie kissed Laura and me each on the cheek. "See you later, 4.30," she said.

I gave Charlie a cuddle. "Thanks," I said.

I sat down next to Laura's bed, and we talked about the previous night. After about fifteen minutes, Laura dozed off. I went back to my ward and got back into bed. Another four hours' sleep certainly would not go amiss … for both of us.

Whilst Laura and I were in hospital, much went on at White Horse Farm, as I would later learn from Charlie. Miles Valentine and his forensic team had been sifting through the carnage since seven o'clock that morning, slowly looking for clues – clues that would piece together this whole case. DS Harman cordoned off the drive with blue and white police tape. Charlie's badly damaged Vitara was in the drive to the front door, in between where the piers had once been. The remains of my Astra van were there too; it would not be making any more trips, business or private. The constable DS Harman had brought with him was guarding the wreckage. Charlie had sent Ricky up the drive to keep the constable company, and also to write down the registration numbers of any grey vans that might pass, rubbernecking.

Charlie then told Allan to get his head down on the couch for a few hours. "Take over at 6 a.m.," she said, adding that she would grab a few hours' sleep upstairs and asking Allan to wake her just before 6 a.m.

Allan and Ricky had headed for the farm as soon as they got Charlie's call, arriving by 3 a.m., just as she'd had told me.

DS Harman remained in the kitchen, making notes and keeping his constable and Ricky well supplied with coffee on the hour, right until six o'clock, when Allan woke Charlie, who insisted on cooking bacon and eggs for everybody.

DS Harman and Allan eagerly ate their bacon and eggs, served with toast and coffee, and once full, took over guard duty from PC Hoad and Ricky.

Ricky introduced PC Hoad to Charlie. "This is Marcus, Charlie," said Ricky.

Marcus removed his helmet and thanked Charlie in advance for his unexpected breakfast feast of bacon and eggs. Ricky made the coffee, and this time, Charlie sat down and ate breakfast as well. The small talk centred around Marcus, who had been in the force two years. He loved clubbing in Brighton, the horses – gambling types, that is – and at 21, reckoned he was a bit of a ladies' man. Charlie sure was good at getting information from people without them knowing it. DS Harman, from previous breakfast conversation, was 48, married, lived in Lewes on the Nevill, which was a pretty tidy and respectable middle-of-the-road housing estate; he and his wife had two teenage boys. Sidney Harman had been a budding young footballer as a teenager, until he broke his leg badly, which ruined a professional career. He battled on in County League football, and at the age of 28, joined the police force and started pounding the beat. A few years later, he got married. The mortgage and kids obviously followed.

After breakfast, Ricky got his head down on the couch for a few hours. Marcus offered to do the washing up, and Charlie went upstairs to shower and freshen up.

Miles Valentine and his team were still hard at work, looking for clues, when Charlie left to go to the hospital at 9.30. After doing the washing up, Marcus joined up with his sergeant, for more guard duty. Allan returned to the office at the back of the farmhouse to catch up with some paperwork, as he was not now needed at the entrance. Ricky had woken up and offered to return. When Charlie returned at about 11.30, she parked the Rover in its usual place, next to the stable yard, and walked up to the ménage gate, which was still open from the night before. Laura had taken this route, hose reel in hand, to put out the van fire. Charlie asked Miles if it was okay to rewind the hose reel. Miles told Charlie that the hose reel could be rewound, and also said that her Vitara would be a write-off, as a result of the amount of damage it had sustained. Miles asked Charlie if there was anything in the Vitara that she wanted to retrieve, as it would very shortly be taken away to the police garage in Brighton for a further, more detailed forensic inspection. Charlie rewound the hose and collected a large bag from the office in which to put her bits and pieces out of the Vitara. It was also Miles's intention to find out if there was anything in the Vitara that didn't belong to her. Much to Miles's disappointment, there was nothing amongst the collection of tapes and hairbrushes that was not either Laura's or Charlie's. As Charlie walked back to the farmhouse, Miles instructed Marcus to carry the petrol can that was in the back of the Vitara back to the farm. The petrol can was one of those large metal ones that could hold the best part of 5 gallons, the equivalent of about 25 litres. Charlie turned round and informed Miles that she didn't own a petrol can. Miles insisted it must belong to the company, as it had "DIRTS" written on the side of the can in capital letters. Charlie said that only the company vans carried cans, but they were always green and gallon-size. Miles quickly told Marcus to leave the can alone, as it could be the break they were looking for. There must be a very good chance of lifting some fingerprints from it.

Charlie took her bag of bits and pieces back to the farmhouse and asked Allan to put the kettle on for some coffee as she passed through the office. She then took her bag of bits and pieces upstairs and left it in the bedroom she was sharing with Laura. When Charlie came back down, she called Ricky back from guard duty at the front gate.

Ricky joined Charlie and Allan in the kitchen for coffee. The conversation centred around the previous night's action and the horsebox fire earlier in the week. Charlie had not wanted to complicate matters by filling in Ricky and Allan with all the details of the two incidents, so she'd just told them they were needed for security reasons back at White Horse Farm. Charlie had worked out a cross-reference system for amalgamating information, and she asked Ricky and Allan for their thoughts. In the office on some of the walls were operatives' noticeboards in which messages were left. What Charlie had in mind was to use these boards to collate information. Ricky and Allan both agreed it was a good idea. Charlie called it "Open Plan Thinking". If each operative kept his board up to date with facts and names, Charlie reasoned there might be a chance that one of us would see a common denominator or a fact we would not otherwise have noticed. In other words, we could all look to see if we had missed something that at first might have not been obvious, or that we each singularly might not have thought was important.

Allan and Ricky set about the task straight away. Charlie got the two files out of the filing cabinet; there were simply marked "Ascot" and "Kempton". Over the next three hours, names, dates, and places were written onto the boards. As the information was placed on the boards, Charlie loaded up the computer with all the details and facts as they were put on the boards. Mother, as we all now affectionately called the computer, was going to be used to good effect. Billy, Bob, John, and Gary – the four other operatives – would be summoned to do the same tomorrow, Sunday. Charlie made a mental note to ring them in the evening.

After they had finished, both Ricky and Allan could not believe the amount of information that was on the boards. Charlie explained that Mother, would cross-reference all the information from all the current cases once the other operatives had completed their boards with case information tomorrow.

"Coffee, chaps?" said Charlie.

Both answers being affirmative, Charlie went to the kitchen to put the kettle on. The front doorbell rang, and Charlie went to see who was there. It was Miles. "Coffee?" said Charlie.

"Oh yes, please," Miles replied, following Charlie into the kitchen and sitting down next to the pine table.

Charlie took the boys' coffee through to the office and then returned to the kitchen to talk to Miles.

Miles told Charlie that both vehicles – her Vitara and the Astra van – had now been removed to the police garage for further inspection. The driveway had been swept clean. All the debris from the crashed vehicles had been boxed and taken away; once again, for further inspection. Miles told Charlie to inform the company's insurance agents. Furthermore, after a brief examination, he discovered there were no fingerprints on the 5-gallon petrol can.

Miles finished by asking, "How are Steve and Laura?"

Charlie said, "Oh gosh! I've got to go and pick them up. What's the time, Miles, please?"

Miles said it was a little before four o'clock.

Charlie said, "It's cuts and bruises, mostly. Sorry, Miles, but I must hurry. I have to pick them up at 4.30."

Miles said, "No problem. We have finished. My team's left, and also DS Harman, but PC Hoad will be here until five o'clock, after which he will be off duty." Miles informed Charlie, on DCI Heyes's instruction, that he was to park the police panda car in the front drive, next to the entrance. "Perhaps you could inform Steve when you see him," Miles added.

Charlie said, "That's fine, Miles. Tell the chief inspector the information he earlier requested regarding existing cases will be ready for him Monday morning."

Charlie then said goodbye to Miles, went into the office, and said to Allan and Ricky, "Would you chaps prepare some vegetables whilst I go to collect Laura and Steve from hospital?"

The lads agreed.

Charlie picked up the pre-packed bag of clothes she had left in the office earlier, told Allan and Ricky she would be about an hour and a half, and left for the hospital.

CHAPTER 8

I woke up about 3.50 p.m., and immediately reached for the water jug on my bedside table. I felt very parched.

As I filled the glass up for a second time, Nurse Becky came over to the bed and enquired as to whether I'd had a good sleep. "Yes, thank you. The headache's gone, and I feel much more alert." Nurse Becky asked if I wanted some tea. I replied, "Yes, and some biscuits, if you have any."

Becky got me some tea and biscuits from the orderly doing the afternoon tea run round the wards. She set the tea and biscuits down on my bedside table.

"Becky," I said. "Do you know what happened to my clothes?"

"Your shell suit, if that's what you're referring to – what's left of it, that is – is in a plastic bag under your bed. Your mobile phone is in your bedside-table drawer."

I looked in the drawer, and sure enough, the phone was there. Much to my surprise, I was able to get a fairly strong signal. I wanted to talk to DCI Heyes. I dialled his mobile number, and pressed Send.

"The mobile number you have dialled may be switched off, please try later. The mobile number—" That again. I cancelled the call and tried Brighton Police Station. The call was answered on the fourth ring. "Brighton Police Station, how can I help?" I asked if I could speak to DCI Heyes. "Sorry, sir" was the reply. "He's off until 10 a.m. on Monday." I asked if I could leave a message. "Of course, sir" was the reply. "Would you ask DCI Heyes to ring Steve Hurst when it's convenient? I will be at the farm from 6 p.m., and for the rest of the weekend." I could do with speaking with the chief inspector before Monday. "Certainly, sir," said the man's voice on the other end of the phone. "Excuse me, Mr Hurst. DS

Harman would like a quick word with you," the man added. "Okay," I replied.

"Hello, Mr Hurst. DS Harman, here. I've just come back to the station from your farm. I hope you and the young lady are all right."

I replied, "Thank you, Sergeant. Yes, a few cuts and bruises, but okay."

"Just to update the situation, sir, there is a constable on duty at the girls' flat at Burgess Hill. Every four hours, the guard will be changed until Monday lunchtime. As a precaution, we have parked a panda car in your front driveway. Once again, the car is to remain there until Monday lunchtime. DCI Heyes has asked me to inform you that he is off duty from now until Monday morning. For obvious reasons, he has not contacted you today, and tomorrow he's unavailable all day. He would, however, like to see you Monday lunchtime." The sergeant continued, "Also, would you make sure you have up-to-date case-file copies on your existing enquiries available for him at that time?"

I informed the sergeant that Charlie had it all in hand, even though I was unaware how far Charlie had got.

"Very good, then," said DS Harman.

When I put the phone down, it was 4.20 p.m. I finished my tea and biscuits, got out of bed, put on my gown, went to the bathroom, showered, and brushed my teeth. I really did feel a lot better, apart from the aches caused by the stitches, which two painkillers, taken with my tea, cured. When I returned to my bed, Dr Amy Goble was talking to Nurse Becky. Dr Goble also had one of those big lapel-type badges on her white coat.

"Well, Mr Hurst!" exclaimed Dr Goble. "You certainly look well enough to leave."

I was not limping at all. I had taken the restrictive plaster bandage off my left knee and replaced it with a large flexible elastoplast. Nurse Becky had earlier obtained this for me and left it on my bedside table.

"Lie on the bed then, Mr Hurst," said Dr Goble. I obeyed without question. Dr Goble produced one of those eye-searching silver-coloured battery lights from her pocket, and after a quick inspection, gave me the all-clear to go home.

I asked if Laura could go home also, and just then, Charlie walked in. It was 4.40 p.m. Charlie had brought me some jeans and a T-shirt, also a fleece jacket, trainers, pants, and socks. Dr Goble said she would go and see if Laura was well enough to leave. Charlie escorted the doctor to Laura's ward whilst I quickly changed into my clothes. I thanked Nurse Becky, retrieved my old shell suit from under the bed, and joined Charlie and the doctor at Laura's bedside.

Dr Goble was inspecting Laura's eyes as she had earlier done to mine. Laura was still suffering from concussion, and the doctor wanted to keep Laura in for another twenty-four hours. After five minutes of protests from Laura, and Charlie remonstrating as well, Dr Goble said, "Okay, okay. You can go home on one condition, and one condition only: No work for a week. Stay in bed until Monday, when I want to see you here as an outpatient at 12.30."

Laura said, "Agreed." She put her hand out to shake the doctor's hand. Laura thanked the doctor, and then she said to Charlie, "Did you bring me some clobber?"

Charlie replied, "Jeans, T-shirt, jumper, and your blue Nike trainers.

Laura said, "Excellent. I'll be five minutes."

Whilst Laura was changing, I spoke to Dr Goble and Nurse Alice, who both asked me what had happened the night before. I briefly explained the "accident", as I called it, and how Laura had pulled me out of the van. Dr Goble could not believe how Laura could have had the strength to pull an 11-stone man out of a burning van, using a fireman's lift. Nurse Alice gave me a plastic bag with the remains of Laura's combat gear, which had been burned and singed beyond repair.

Dr Goble commented on how very lucky we both had been not to have received any burns to any degree. "Your shell suit bottoms had virtually melted," she commented.

Laura was now ready. Charlie had brought her large bag with her, into which she deposited Laura's tape player, tapes, and other bits and pieces.

As we left the ward, thanking the staff once again, Charlie commented, "You can drive, Steve. I've parked next to the flower stall at the main entrance."

Laura said, "I'm really hungry."

As we walked out the main entrance, the clock on the wall said five to six. I bought the local *Argus* newspaper from the kiosk next to the flower stall, and on the back page in large letters it stated: "'Golden Guinea' wins the Steward's Cup, at 33 to1. Aussie jockey Spencer James is top jockey at Goodwood".

As I opened the door of the Rover, I could not help thinking, What happened since Wednesday? On Wednesday, I did not have a care in the world when I went to Goodwood with my then fiancée, Jane. Three days later, my life had totally changed.

As I drove back, Charlie said, "I've got Allan and Ricky preparing some vegetables. Shall I grill some steaks when we get home?"

Laura said, "That sure sounds good to me, Steve!"

I agreed a good home-cooked supper would do us all good.

The drive back took us no longer than twenty minutes. The earlier traffic that Charlie had trouble getting through had now passed. We drove through and parked next to the stables. Charlie pressed the button for the up-and-over garage door into the yard to close, and the three of us went indoors through the office. I could not help noticing the boards in the office, and Charlie said she would update me over supper.

Allan and Ricky were in the kitchen.

"Vegetables prepared!" said Ricky to Charlie.

Allan added, "I've made five coffees. I did potatoes, broccoli, and carrots."

"Charlie?" said Ricky.

Charlie got five fillet steaks from the fridge and asked Allan and Ricky how they liked them; both said medium rare.

I asked Allan to take our coffees into the office, but leave Charlie's and Laura's in the kitchen. I wanted to talk to Allan and Ricky and give them some idea of what the problem was.

Charlie poked her head through the office door. "Supper twenty minutes then?"

"That's fine, Charlie," I replied.

Laura sat down on the pine bench next to the table in the kitchen, she had her coffee and the biscuit tin in front of her, and she sat nattering to Charlie, who prepared and cooked the steaks and checked the vegetables.

In the meantime, I informed Ricky and Allan of the horsebox crash; the death of Henry Hall; the death of the tall, slim, left-handed man in the VW Golf fire; the girls' flat being firebombed; and, of course, the crash of the Astra combi van and Charlie's Vitara. I explained that there was now no reason not to believe these incidents were in fact linked. I explained to the lads about how Jane had suffered a dislocated shoulder in the car park on Wednesday night, and the sequence of events thereafter. Both Allan and Ricky were stuck for words. The look of disbelief at what they had just heard was very apparent on the face of it. It really did sound an incredible story; however, the facts were there.

"Oh, and by the way," I added. "Jane has left me, and to avoid gossip and speculation, Charlie and Laura are staying with me until this matter is sorted."

Laura came into the office to let us know supper was ready. She stood behind me and put her left hand on my left shoulder.

I said to Allan and Ricky that they could regard Laura and me as "an item" from now on. As I said it, I turned round to look at Laura and put my right hand on top of Laura's left hand, which was still on my shoulder. Laura leant down and kissed me on the left cheek.

Ricky commented that we looked a great couple, considering all the stitches and plaster we had around our heads. We laughed at our misfortune and went into the kitchen for some "tucker", as Aussie called it.

Hardly a word was spoken as we all ate our supper. It was a good job; Ricky had prepared plenty of vegetables. After supper, we had some cheese and what was left of the biscuits after Laura had earlier been at them. Ricky made some more coffee, and the conversation centred around the message boards in the office. It was decided that I should have a message board as well, and my problems should also be displayed for all to see. I objected at first; I was at a disadvantage and easily outnumbered. My first job Sunday, though, would be to update my own board from previous files or present cases.

As it neared 9.30 p.m., I asked Allan and Ricky if they could do a watch each that night. I wanted someone awake and alert all through the night. The lights would be left on outside, the house secured.

"I'll take 10 p.m. to 3 a.m.," Ricky volunteered.

Allan said, "I'll do 3 a.m. to 8 a.m."

I wanted a good night's sleep. Charlie was by now dead on her feet. And Laura, well, I had to keep my promise to Dr Goble. I ordered Laura straight to bed, telling her to stay in bed all the following day.

Laura said, "Yes, Boss," and followed Charlie up the wooden hill.

I gave Ricky a pair of binoculars and suggested we kept the lights off downstairs. Allan slept on the couch in the sitting room, and I retired upstairs to my bed.

Concussion does make you tired. As I opened my bedroom door, I yawned out loud and headed for the en suite bathroom, without noticing Laura in my bed.

I heard a voice say, "I hope you're not too tired."

I wondered if Dr Goble was wrong about Laura's concussion.

The mind was willing; the body was not. The two painkillers I had taken earlier with my four o'clock cup of tea had worn off. The aches had returned; my knee was aching like crazy, and my body felt like a punchbag. The obvious effects of changing seats involuntarily and much too quickly when I last drove the van. I took two painkillers with some water, brushed my teeth, and returned to the bedroom.

As I pulled back the duvet cover, I said to Laura, "You are not serious!" There was no reply. Laura was sound asleep.

I got comfortable very quickly and was soon off into a deep sleep. When I reached the dreaming period of sleep, I was driving a van in a demolition derby – a blue van – all the other vehicles were Vitaras with white bull bars, and all the drivers looked the same. I weaved my way through all of them, round and round. There was no start or finish. I just kept going round and round. Occasionally at first, and then more frequently, I would be rammed up the back of the van. The Vitaras were ganging up on me, in front and behind. I could not get through anymore. *Bang! Bang!* The Vitaras were taking it in turns to ram me. Suddenly the back doors of the van fell off. I could see all the white bull bars; all the drivers looked the same: red jackets, white shirts. They all wore neat white ties. They were going to crush me; satin collars; nights in white satin, with white bull bars. Just as I was about to meet my maker, Laura woke me up.

"Steve, Steve, Steve," she said.

I slowly woke up from my dream, my nightmare. She said I had been saying, "Stop it, stop it, stop in, sto, sto, pin, pin, satin pin, stop, tie, tie, satin, van, satin, the van, can't move."

When, eventually, I came round, Laura said she had been trying to wake me up for five minutes. Laura repeated what I had been saying. I said I could not make it out. Laura insisted I write it down. It was eight o'clock in the morning on Sunday. Laura got the notepad and pen from the bedside drawer, and she wrote down what I had said.

I told Laura I needed to shower. I could feel the sweat dripping off me. After showering, shaving, and brushing my teeth, I felt much better; no aches, no pains.

Laura was still in bed. She said, "You must have been having a nightmare about the smash."

I agreed and asked Laura if she felt like getting up. She said she would stay in bed. "Could you ask Charlie for some toast, marmalade, and tea?"

I said, "Twenty minutes, and you can have the Sunday papers as well."

Laura said, "Great, I'll get up and have a shower then."

In the meantime, I went downstairs and into the kitchen.

Charlie had made coffee. Allan and Ricky were already seated at the pine table in the kitchen, eagerly awaiting a breakfast feast. Charlie had butcher's sausages in the oven, bacon under the grill, and mushrooms in the frying pan; the toaster was doing overtime. The fat in the other frying pan was just beginning to spit, ready for the eggs. I sat down opposite the lads and thought of Aussie: tucker was about to be served. I passed on Laura's message to Charlie about the tea and toast, and asked everybody present to be available in the office at 10.30.

Charlie said, "Oh sugar! I forgot to call the rest of the team."

I told Charlie not to worry. I would call them after breakfast and arrange with them to be at the farm for an afternoon meeting. "You can teach them how to get the information for Mother," I told her. Ricky and Allan had filled me in the night before with regard to Charlie's brilliant idea.

We ate a wonderful fried breakfast, with toast and marmalade.

Charlie took Laura up some toast, marmalade, and tea, along with the Sunday papers. When Charlie returned, the lads were in the office preparing for our meeting. I finished off my coffee and asked Charlie to sit down. Charlie sat down opposite me. I looked into Charlie's eyes and picked up her right hand, holding it between both of mine. "I don't know what I would have done without you these last few days. You've been absolutely wonderful. Ricky is going to chauffeur you about tomorrow. First things first. Go round and have a look at your flat, sort out what you need or what you can salvage, and then would you mind doing the supermarket run for me?"

Charlie said, "Steve, I really do not have a problem, and I certainly do not mind seven-day weeks. Do believe it, Steve. You will win in the end."

I squeezed Charlie's hand and said, "I knew I could rely on you."

Charlie leant over the table to kiss me on the cheek.

"Perhaps tomorrow you could also take Laura to the hospital for her outpatient appointment. Take my Rover. If you fancy a bit of lunch in Brighton, do it; give yourselves a bit of a break."

Charlie said, "What about yourself, Steve? Is there anything I can get for you? Razor blades?"

I said, "Yes, I need some razor blades and some shaving foam."

Charlie said, "If you think of anything else, add it to this kitchen list I've already made up."

Charlie showed me the list, which she had already started with a view to restocking the fridge tomorrow: steaks, bacon, eggs, milk, bread, butter. Wine had a question mark next to it. I crossed out the question mark and put, "Nuit St George, usual wine merchant, one case". (I was really getting used to this midweek drinking!) I wrote down "razor blades" and "shaving foam", "toiletries" and "biscuits".

"Don't forget the biscuits, Charlie," I said. "In fact, as there are now five of us here, double up on everything you buy." I gave Charlie my debit card and number to pay for the shopping.

Charlie gave me a big cuddle, and I made my way to the office.

Once again, not for the first time, Charlie gave the kitchen a good clean and tidy-up.

There was a lot of soul-searching to carry out today, and plenty to discuss. We needed a break desperately.

CHAPTER 9

We gathered in the office shortly after 10.30, and for the next hour, I completed my board with names. Names of clients, friends, and acquaintances connected with my business. Ricky contacted the other operatives, and between us, we decided upon 4 p.m. for our case-review meeting. That gave them plenty of time to get back to the farm, complete their work boards if necessary, and have Charlie instruct them on using Mother.

My board was so full of names that Charlie put a second board up. I was astonished at the amount of people I had spoken to or met in the last ninety-six hours. On Wednesday at Goodwood races, I had spoken to Robert Argonaut, Jonathan Ridger, Vernon Poole, and Robert's wife, Suzi. Jonathan's twin daughters, Rachel and Rebecca, had been mentioned in conversation, as well as the trainer, Jamie Bolton, and Jonathan's ex-owner Stu Ward, the bar proprietor on Brighton seafront. On Wednesday evening, there was Mark and Julie, Jane's and my Greek dinner guests; the ill-fated Henry Hopalong Hall from the car park; Dr Phil Thomas from the hospital; DCI John Heyes from the police; the list went on and on. Thursday included Chris Collins, my neighbour and provider of horsebox transport; Miles Valentine from forensics; Ginger Martin, who hired Chris a horsebox. For good measure, and not to leave any stone unturned, I included some names of bygone eras that were mentioned in recent conversations and anecdotes. They included horse owners, trainers, jockeys, showjumpers, car dealers, and horse dealers. I never missed anybody out – or so I thought.

Charlie entered the office with a tray of coffees at just after 11.30, and I said to her, with great satisfaction, "I doubt if you will be able to add to that list."

Charlie put the coffees down, paused briefly, sat down, crossed her legs, and leant back against her chair, clutching a mug of coffee with both hands. She said, "I can add two."

I said, "And who might they be?"

Charlie said, "Your ex and her new wallet."

I had completely forgotten about Jane. Jane had never even crossed my mind. I was going to protest that Jane should not be on the list. However, I bit my lip, so to speak, and picked up a coffee. No one round the table said a word.

I broke the silence. "You're right, Charlie. Jane should be on the list, and, of course, so should Chris Cobb, her new wallet."

Charlie spent the next hour on her computer, typing away at her keyboard, storing information from Allan's board, Ricky's board, and my board – all names to cross-reference at a later date. It would be a long painstaking process, but everyone agreed it was a job that needed to be done if we were to find a lead or clue to a breakthrough, which we so desperately needed.

At the back of my mind, I was aware of an ever-increasing accumulation of tasks that needed to be concluded. Charlie would have to work until late this evening to be able to give DCI Heyes what he had requested in time for tomorrow lunchtime's meeting. I went into the kitchen and prepared some cheese sandwiches for the four of us: Allan, Ricky, Charlie, and myself. (Laura was asleep upstairs.) The rest of the team were not due to arrive for another two hours or so.

I made four rounds of cheese sandwiches, cut them into halves and then again into quarters. I took the sandwiches into the office, collected the mugs, went back into the kitchen, and made some more coffee. I took the tray of four coffees into the office and handed them out. After a sandwich and a sip of my coffee, I asked Charlie when she contemplated doing a board of her own, and perhaps one for Laura as well.

Charlie replied, "I've already spoken to Laura about that. She's going to do a list today when she wakes up, probably this afternoon. I don't want to wake her. I will compile a list myself later," Charlie added. "The case files the chief inspector requested of our present investigations will be ready at about eleven tomorrow morning. Clients' names, of course, will have been omitted. What I'm doing, Steve, is replacing our clients' names with their respective professions; I've omitted addresses, obviously, but included towns and post codes, slightly different from what we previously agreed, but I believe it's nearer the mark."

I replied, "That's fine, Charlie."

Ricky and Allan had by this time polished off the cheese sandwiches; their coffees, though, were untouched.

Before he could say a word, I said to Ricky, "Bring me back a six pack of Foster's." (That was my favourite brand of Australian lager.) Stocks were beginning to run low with this midweek drinking.

Ricky replied, "No problem."

He and Allan left to go down to the Castle for a few pints. This had become somewhat of a ritual if they were at the farm on a Sunday. I did not mind, though.

Charlie shouted out, "And six Bacardi Breezers!" Charlie turned her gaze back to my direction. "For this evening, Steve," she said.

"My thoughts entirely, Charlie," I replied.

We drank the spare cups of coffee.

Charlie said, "I'm going to be at least another hour, Steve."

It was about 1.30. I said, "I'll go and see how Laura is."

Laura was in the shower, so I shouted to her, "How are you feeling?"

She replied, "Horny."

I did not need prompting. I wasn't even thinking about concussion – Laura's or mine. I quickly undressed and joined Laura in the shower. We could not keep our hands off each other. We adopted the same position as we had a few days earlier in Red's stable. This time, though, with no inhibitive clothes on. Various parts of our bodies showed clear signs of how pleased we were to finally succumb to our feelings for each other. We made love in the shower, there and then. Laura had her back against the shower tiles and her legs wrapped around my hips. The shower water cascaded down onto the pair of us. Laura was sucking my tongue in and out of her mouth in exactly the same rhythm as our lovemaking. Her legs tightened around my hips, her tongue increasing the tempo of our lovemaking. Laura was moaning with cries of delight. Screams of indescribable pleasure as she had her second orgasm – this time, I exploded inside of her.

I turned off the shower, and, with Laura still wrapped around me, we made it to the bed. Laura was on top, straddling me. I had my hands on her hips as she slowly moved up and down, forwards and backwards.

It wasn't long before Laura had climaxed again. Her screams of delight I found pleasing and comforting. Laura leant down, and our tongues danced merrily in and out of each other's mouths. We stroked each other, caressed each other, and when we got our breath back, made love once again.

Time and tide wait for no man, especially when you are having fun. I looked at the bedside clock: it was almost three. I told Laura I loved her very much. We showered again, dried ourselves off, and quickly changed into jeans and shirts. Laura put a cap on so no one could see her stitches and where her head was partly shaved to allow the doctor to put the eight stitches into the wound on her temple.

I replaced the plaster on my nose with a new strip, though I could not do much with the two shiners I now was sporting. I also put a new strip of plaster on my knee, which felt surprisingly easy and painless; even the stiffness had seemed to disappear.

Laura said she felt much better and asked if she could attend the meeting scheduled for four o'clock.

I put my arms around her. "If you feel you're up to it, then why not?" I said.

Laura replied, "Well, Steve, I think I've just passed my fitness test."

We both burst out laughing simultaneously as we left the bedroom and walked down the stairs.

It was approximately 3.30, and as we entered the kitchen, we could see through the kitchen window that the lads were arriving for our 4 p.m. meeting. They parked in the ten-vehicle post-and-rail parking area next to the stables.

Charlie came into the kitchen from the office. She knew what we had been up to. She said to Laura, "You're looking more your usual self. Has Steve given you something to perk you up?"

Laura said in reply, "Yes, Charlie. I suppose you could call it that." Laura looked at me, and with a broad grin on her face, exclaimed, "Another course of treatment tonight, and I'll be right as rain by the morning."

Charlie's quick retort was spot on. She said to Laura, "If you make as much noise when you get the main course tonight as you just have getting through your hors d'oeuvres, you will keep the whole house awake."

Laura's cheeks went bright red with embarrassment. As Charlie went back into the office, with a can of Coke obtained from the fridge, she turned her head and said, "It sounded as if you enjoyed it immensely." She added, "Both of you."

The lads were now entering the office, and Charlie was organising some boards for the operatives to fill in. (That is, for those who had not already done so. This also applied to Laura.) I got a board and marker from the office, gave them to Laura, and explained what I wanted her to do.

Laura said, "Charlie told me about this. I'll do it upstairs in the bedroom." She made herself a coffee, and took it, the board, and marker pen upstairs with her to complete her board of names.

I went into the office to greet my operatives.

"Put the drinks you brought back from the Castle into the fridge, would you?" I asked Ricky.

It was just before four o'clock when Ricky returned from the kitchen. I explained and outlined the recent situations that had arisen for us, and then I asked those operatives who had not yet completed a board to do so immediately. Ricky made everybody a coffee.

Charlie was updating Mother from the information on the boards, inputting only the relevant information. She said to me, "Oh by the way, Steve, Robert Argonaut and Jonathan Ridger both telephoned you this afternoon."

There were certain items that needed my immediate attention. Robert Argonaut and Jonathan Ridger were two of them. Whilst the lads were finishing off their boards, I went into the lounge and telephoned the both of them. I mentioned about my accident in the van outside my house, and that I had been in hospital for a large part of the weekend. They were sympathetic to my situation. I convinced them both I was still ahead of the Hot Tea deal, and they agreed to wait until I was in a position to conclude the deal.

My first priority in the morning, though, was to write a list of jobs, in order of importance. I would review the situation this evening, after this afternoon's meeting, and then draw up a rough list needing attention. From this list we would draw up a further list prioritising the items that required attention immediately.

I felt really happy inside. My exterior profile did not match my inner feelings, though, as I looked in the mirror in the hallway going back from the lounge into the office.

Once I entered the office, our meeting began.

The main priorities were for the operatives to complete their boards, so as to allow Charlie to input the information into Mother. In her way, Mother would then compute the information, and maybe, just maybe, steer us in the right direction – we so desperately needed a lead, a clue, anything to give us a breakthrough.

I looked up at all the boards, and for the love of horses, all I could see was corruption and death, love and adultery, thuggery and drug abuse, arson and attempted murder, jealousy and greed. Someone – or some people – up there on one of those boards required total vengeance. I was their target, and as the penny dropped, I felt the hairs stand up on the back of my neck and a cold shiver ran down my back.

I needed some space, some fresh air. Charlie was busy on Mother's keyboard; my operatives had their case files in front of them and were busy writing names on their respective boards. I let Charlie know I was just going out into the stable yard for ten minutes. I wanted to just walk around and think.

On the third or fourth time around the rectangular yard, my dream – no, my nightmare – returned. I could again see the white bull bars banging into the back of my van, the knights in white satin. I thought of the song "Nights in White Satin", the rest of the lyrics filling my mind "never meaning to send, letters are written, is it death in the end". ...

I ran back to the house, through the office, into the hallway, and up the stairs to my bedroom. I retrieved the notes Laura had written down earlier. This morning, after waking me from my nightmare, she had written exactly what I'd said in my sleep: nights, white satin, white bull bars, and so on. I had been thinking of it as *nights,* and it had made sense, and that must have been why the song lyrics suddenly filled my mind. But suddenly I put the *k* on it, making it *knights,* and everything clicked.

Laura had finished off her board, and she could see that maybe I was on to something.

"Laura," I said. "Get Charlie to input the details of your board onto Mother. Quickly."

Laura went downstairs to the office, and ten minutes later, we were ready to reveal some raised-eyebrow possibilities, some of which were so near to home that the possible consequences were simply shocking.

The office was deadly silent now. All eyes were fixed on the VDUs (video display units) as Mother cross-referenced the information gathered from the operatives, and once processed, reported its alarming possibilities, which we itemised and allocated to each respective case that we were investigating at the moment. These updated case files were for the operatives only; Charlie spent most of Sunday evening and the early hours of Monday morning replacing my clients' names in the files with towns, post codes, and professions to protect their identities – as Charlie had explained, and I agreed, this was the easiest way, and the safest way to ensure my clients' confidentiality.

We were all aware that the seriousness of Mother's revelations meant that we could not exactly rule out the possibility of further violence – against any one of us, or anyone involved in the cases we were working on.

Case 4 was the most violent of them all. This was our newest case – my case – murder and attempted murder had already taken place.

Ricky got some lagers out of the fridge, and Laura made some more sandwiches; it was going to be a long evening. We had to prioritise our cases, and list the possible leads.

Allan had made up some extra beds in the lounge earlier in the afternoon, with the help of Charlie, who knew where the camp beds and sleeping bags were tucked away in the tack room. None of my operatives would be going home tonight. I wanted total protection, and everybody had to be present and available should the chief inspector wish to question anyone during our prearranged meeting. We would continue working until the early hours of Monday morning, if necessary; no stone was to be left unturned.

Charlie had simply stated the obvious when suggesting that I add Jane and Chris Cobb to my board. What had not been obvious was the fact that Jane was and had been privy to all our case files, and she knew exactly how my operation was run, how it worked, and who the operatives were. Jane knew 90 per cent of my clients; she also knew how to source every conceivable piece of information, if she so required, of any part of my organisation, including my employees' names, addresses, and current assignments and locations. In short, Jane knew it all.

Was it Jane who had the girls' flat in Burgess Hill firebombed?

Regardless, Jane was the common denominator, according to Mother (our computer). Jane, along with me, was the link that joined everything up together. (Needless to say, our ongoing cases, and those Charlie was preparing for DCI Heyes, were none the wiser of what we were looking for, or why.)

We broke off the case-review meeting at 8 p.m. Laura had cooked an enormous fish pie which we all eagerly tucked into with some French bread. They say an army marches on its stomach, and my team of employees were well up for it, should there be any further trouble tonight. The thought of

Jane being a spy of some description made me feel sick inside. Could she really hate them so much that she – or others – would firebomb their flat in the hope they were inside? My anger was turning to a rage, burning up inside me, which I knew I had to control. I wanted to be upstairs with Laura, in the peace and tranquillity of my bedroom. *Our* bedroom.

Some of the team carried on with the case-file reviews in the office, whilst keeping Charlie company as well. The lads had also devised a rota for guarding the farm throughout the night, so we were for all intents as secure as we possibly could be. Charlie, with the help of the Bacardi Breezers, was still working on Mother when Laura beckoned me to call it a day and go to bed. It was a little after 11 p.m. when we said goodnight to Charlie, who indicated she would be at least another hour or so. Charlie asked us to keep the noise down. Fat lot of chance that happening! Laura was not kidding earlier: she wanted her main course, and she was damned well going to get it – whether I was tired or not.

Laura was naked on top of the bed. It was so peaceful; the moon, so bright in the sky, cast shadows across the bedroom. Sade's *Diamond Life* was in the CD player, so I turned it on. I took a swig from Laura's bottle of strawberry cider – her favourite – which was on the bedside table, and then I sat on the bed, gazing into her eyes. I leant down to kiss her, whispering in her ear, "This is going to be the most amazing for you, the most sensuous massage you have ever experienced." I went to the bathroom, got the baby oil from the bathroom cabinet, came back into the bedroom, and turned the music up a notch.

Laura had turned over on her belly. I slowly worked the oil into her back and shoulders, using both my hands, as I sat straddled across her hips, moving my hands slowly to the melodic rhythm of the music. I massaged her neck, then her arms and upper back, and her lower back and hips. I turned round and then proceeded to massage her lovely long legs, and then her ankles, feet, and toes. I did not want to miss any part of her beautifully toned body. Laura would squeal with excitement when I found one of her erogenous zones, so I teased her by kissing them and running my tongue over them. By the time Laura turned over onto her back, she was clearly in the middle of the most sensuous experience of her young life. I used the baby oil more liberally on her chest, ribs, and breasts, giving her whole body a beautiful, lovingly caring massage. Laura was now reaching the stage of ecstasy as I kissed and licked her inner thighs; my tongue had found her most pleasurable erogenous zone.

Laura then positioned herself on top of me as the track "Your Love Is King" came on. She gently swayed to the tempo as she sat astride me, and she knew all the words to the song: "Your love is king, the ruler of my heart, your love is king, I'm crying out for more, your love is king, kissing the very soul of me, giving me everything, your love is king." She put her hands on the bed and arched her back for ultimate penetration during our lovemaking.

As the track ended, Laura sipped her cider. "Wow!" she exclaimed. "When someone really loves you, that must be when your life begins. When we can do it again?"

I finished off her bottle of cider, and we snuggled up under the duvet, our arms and legs entwined. I never realised until that moment just how much I loved Laura. She was probably right: when someone really loved you, that was when your life began. I never felt that intense with Jane; I never wanted to be that intense with her. Perhaps tonight had changed a few future destinies for sure.

"Soon," I said to Laura, in response to her question. "Very soon."

And then we drifted off to sleep.

The lads would take it in turn to guard the house during the night, according to the rota they'd prepared. Eagle-eyed Ricky had the shift between 4 a.m. and 6 a.m. Whilst looking out one of the big bay windows, with the aid of binoculars, he spotted a grey van passing the farm, on not one but two occasions: at 4.15 a.m. and 5.30 a.m. Ricky noted the van slowing down considerably each time it passed the panda car that was strategically parked in the main drive, between the two burned-down piers.

Before we went to bed on Sunday night, I'd asked everybody to be on parade for 9 a.m. in the office on Monday, with the exception of Charlie, who was on Mother until 3 a.m. Ricky offered to do the breakfasts at 8 a.m.; it consisted mainly of toast and coffee.

At precisely 9 a.m., we started on the agenda that Charlie had clearly written down, in order, on one of the whiteboards, before she eventually went to bed. Item 1 on the agenda was the racehorse trainer from Newmarket, Noel Henry, and his unfaithful wife, Natalie; item 4 just said "Steve Hurst: murder, attempted murder, arson, drug dealing"; once again, I felt the hair stand up on the back of my neck at the thought of the revelations that later would be revealed.

Gary was my operative dealing with Noel Henry's problems, and I did not expect any results in the short time since we had last spoken on the subject. Gary had only a few names on his whiteboard: Noel Henry; his wife, Natalie; his head lad, Taffy Stevens; jockey Ron Kallon; and Noel's ex-wife, Julia, who had set up training herself in Newmarket since the split and the messy divorce, which for many months afterwards had resulted in a lot of bad-mouthing, especially after Noel's new younger model of wife (Natalie) moved in. Gary was fairly sure, since our previous meeting, that he was now on the right track. After tracking the "naughty-but-nice Natalie", as Gary put it, he had established she definitely was seeing somebody else, especially after observing her antics in a pub car park in nearby Cheveley: the springs of the little Daihatsu Hijet van were not going up and down on their own. According to Gary, Natalie had met an unknown person in the bar, and they had drinks and sandwiches before leaving the pub together and getting in the back of the van, where they had the main course, which lasted about half an hour.

Charlie, Laura, and acting chauffeur Ricky left at about 10.30 a.m. Ricky had been looking forward to taking Bambi and Thumper to lunch. Simon from Sporty Cars at Ditchling had left a message on the answerphone that a white Vitara had become unexpectedly available, and he thought it was sure to be an ideal replacement for Charlie's old one, which was now in a police compound awaiting further forensic tests.

Charlie said she would do the shopping first. The wine merchants would be next on the list, followed by Laura's outpatient appointment at the hospital with Dr Amy Goble. Lunch would follow that.

As they left, I asked Charlie to fill up the Rover with fuel whilst at the supermarket. I pulled Ricky to one side and quietly told him to be aware at all times. Ricky pulled his jacket slightly open to reveal a truncheon in his inside pocket. "Marcus – PC Hoad – lent it to me. He said he had a spare one." Ricky added, "Collarbones and knees."

I looked at Ricky oddly. "Collarbones and knees?"

Ricky said, "Marcus said if I need to use it, aim for collarbones and knees."

I nodded in agreement. "Deactivate the limbs."

As they left the office, the phone rang. It was DCI Heyes.

"Morning, Steve," he said.

I replied with the usual pleasantries.

He asked if Charlie had finished the files for our meeting, as it was now fast approaching 11 a.m. I told him that the final touches would take about another hour.

"Steve, I would like to start the meeting at 2 p.m., not at the police station, but at your farm, and I'd like Miles Valentine to attend as well." He further stated that he would also update our meeting with his four crimes. Evidently, the chief inspector did not regard the attempted hit and run in the car park, which had dislocated Jane's shoulder, as a crime.

"We can start the meeting at three o'clock, John," I said.

He agreed immediately, informing me that he could now have a lunch break.

As we would later discover during the meeting, the chief inspector's four crimes were: –(1) the horsebox fire; –(2) the murder of Henry Hopalong Hall at the car park; (3) the arson of the girls' flat in Burgess Hill; and –(4) the attempt on my life.

When I rang off with the chief inspector, I informed the lads that I wanted to move on rapidly; we only had four hours to finish off the files. We moved on to cases 2 and 3: the organised Tote scam going on at Sandown, Ascot, Kempton and Newbury, and the Dicky Head investigation; once again, I did not expect too much movement since our previous meeting and agreed action. The secret cameras, however, were fitted into the coach carrying the Tote staff; also, microphones had been fitted to record some of the conversations that would take place on the way to the races from the various pickup points along the way.

This was not a priority case at the moment, considering all that had happened in the last five days. However, we did give the problems equal consideration as the more serious cases which were haunting me in the back of my mind.

The Tote scam was exceedingly clever, conducted by brains, not brawn; logic was telling me that it would be time and careful collection of evidence that would trap the people responsible. We would take our time and be extremely tactful. We would uncover those who conspired to rob; even if it were purely a white-collar crime, we would get there in the end.

Billy, Allan, Bob, and Ricky were my operatives responsible for this ongoing enquiry. As Ricky was otherwise engaged in the capacity of chauffeur to Bambi and Thumper, it was up to Billy, Allan, and Bob to further update us from our last meeting on Friday. We knew the cameras were installed into the coach, together with microphones to perhaps pick up some loose talk. So I asked the lads if there was anything else they could offer to further the enquiry. The data cross-reference by Mother did not throw up anything new on these cases; nor indeed was there anything cross-referenced relative to Noel Henry and his naughty wife, Natalie.

Billy got up from the desk in front of him. "Coffee?" he asked.

We all said, "Yes."

The phone rang. It was Jane. When I answered, all she said was, "I'll be over at three this afternoon to pick up Red and my belongings."

"What happened Saturday morning?" I said.

Jane just replied, "We were too busy, and Sally decided to have Saturday off at short notice."

I replied, "You could have at least called me."

Jane reckoned she did on Friday evening.

I did not see the point of pushing it, so I just informed her, "I stayed in on Friday and decided to go out and get a Chinese takeaway at about 8 p.m."

Jane took the bait. "I phoned at about 8.30 p.m."

"I forgot to switch the answerphone on," I said.

Jane replied, "Yes, I know. I would have left a message, so it's not my fault. I went round to see the Dunne's at Hickstead after I rang you, and did not get back until the early hours of the morning, so I never rang you back. Saturday I was out all day.

I remembered my eminent barrister friend, and chuckled down the phone.

Jane just said, "I'll see you later then?"

"No," I said to Jane. "It is inconvenient for you to call later today. Could you call tomorrow morning, about eleven?"

Jane asked, "Why?"

"The chief inspector's calling this afternoon," I told her. "He thinks he knows who killed Hopalong."

He didn't, but Jane didn't know that. I did not want Jane to see me in the battered state I was in. It was not vanity, it was just, well … I wasn't sure exactly. The bit about Hopalong was something I'd said on the spur of the moment. Perhaps an inner sense was activated; it just seemed the right thing to do at the time.

Jane just said, "About eleven tomorrow morning then?"

I said, "Yes. All your belongings will be in two boxes in the stable tack room. Red's been well looked after, and if I'm not in, just help yourself.

All my operatives are here this week, so if you need a hand, just ask. Oh, and by the way, Jane, the two mingers had their flat firebombed on Friday night. They have had to stay with me as well." I put the phone down and drank my coffee, feeling just a little bit smug.

Some of the lads were still outside in the courtyard, having a cigarette, so I took the opportunity to ring both Jonathan Ridger and Robert Argonaut; it was now a few minutes past noon, and I thought I would catch Jonathan at his office. The phone only rang twice before Jonathan answered.

"Hello. It's Steve!" I said.

Jonathan replied, "I wondered when I would hear from you."

I told Jonathan he would be paid on Friday of this week, by an interbank transfer from my bank to his. I already had his bank details on file. Just as a precaution, I asked Jonathan to make sure he declared Hot Tea to run at Newbury on this coming Friday, adding, "It is Robert's wish that you declare him."

Jonathan said, "Does that mean Mr Argonaut wants me to train for him, Steve?"

I just replied, "That is his wish."

Jonathan sounded surprisingly happy. "Are you going to Newbury on Friday, Steve?" he enquired.

Not knowing whether I was or wasn't, I replied, "Yes, of course."

"I'll see you Friday then," said Jonathan. "And thank you, Steve, for your help."

I put the phone down, finished off my coffee, and rang Robert Argonaut. I rang his mobile number, and after the fourth ring, he answered.

"Steve!" Robert exclaimed.

"Hello, Robert," I replied. "I've arranged for the funds to purchase Hot Tea to be in your account on Wednesday of this week."

"That's fine," Robert said.

"Robert, what about delivery of the horse?"

Robert informed me he wanted the horse to stay at Mr Ridger's yard until the day of the races at Newbury. I told Robert that I would pay Mr Ridger on Thursday this week, and that I'd told Mr Ridger that it was Robert's expressed wish that he (Mr Ridger) declared his horse for Friday's race.

Robert replied, "Fine, Steve. I will speak to you later this week to discuss the finer details of my purchase."

He further informed me he had arranged for a vet to check Hot Tea's wind, eyes, heart, and action on Wednesday morning at ten. This was the norm, according to Robert, when purchasing a racehorse. I did not disagree; it was his money after all. Robert told me to pass the information onto Mr Ridger, which on finishing my conversation with Robert, I did straight away.

Jonathan was still in his office when I relayed Robert's message about the vetting of Hot Tea. Jonathan just said, "That's to be expected, Steve." He added, "However, in this case, I cannot understand why."

I told Jonathan, "Mr Argonaut could not be seen to be had over, so to speak; and as the buyer, it is his prerogative. Furthermore, as you know, Jonathan, he would need a vet's certificate for insurance purposes."

Jonathan agreed, half-heartedly at first, saying, "I suppose you're right, Steve. As it happens, when I bought him at the sales, I had him vetted. I was looking for the dodge, but there was nothing wrong with the horse. That could not be said for some of the idiots that work for Robert Argonaut though, Steve."

Jonathan was happy with the arrangements.

Once again, I put the phone down.

The lads had now finished their coffees and cigarettes, and were all back in the office. It was time now to move on.

"Right, lads! Case number 4!" I proclaimed.

The office was as quiet as a morgue; to say you could have heard a pin drop was an understatement.

Before we started on case 4, John, the operative on the Dicky Head investigation (case 3), informed the meeting that Dicky had not been sighted at home or at the races since before the weekend. When we had our meeting on Friday, John had informed us that he had made no further progress; the story was still the same, with nothing new to report. Somehow I had a feeling that it was soon about to change.

We then set about case 4 – my case, that is.

It was just after 1 p.m. when Ricky, Charlie, and Laura got back to the farm, with all the shopping now completed. Laura had managed to get an earlier appointment with Dr Goble, who had given her the all-clear. Laura, Charlie, and Ricky joined us as we set about case 4; they did not want to miss the bombshell that was about to be dropped.

Jane Coe, my ex, was our number 1 suspect, along with her new wallet, Chris Cobb, the dope-smoking, junkie showjumper. My operatives just sat there in stunned silence, in utter disbelief, as I further elaborated with regard to my ex-fiancée and my recurring nightmare of knights in white satin.

Chris Cobb was driving the grey van when Charlie's Vitara was stolen and they tried to kill me with it. I believed he was involved in some sort of drugs organisation, based probably in Brighton. I further believed we had stumbled on their clients or territory by accident. I believed they had a delivery network somehow linked to either the horse-racing industry or the showjumping fraternity, or even both.

Once again, you could have heard a pin drop.

"Right," I said. "Let's prepare for the chief inspector. I'm sure he wants to speculate on his four cases."

It was getting on for 2 p.m. by that point.

CHAPTER 10

DCI John Heyes and forensics expert Miles Valentine arrived at 2.30. After introductions and coffee, we set about the immediate case files my teams were currently investigating.

Case file number 1 was the Tote scam, of which Billy and Allan, and now Bob and Ricky, were my operatives. This was now an expanding investigation, to cover five racecourses: Ascot, Kempton Park, Newbury, Sandown, and Windsor. (Ascot and Windsor were added at Mother's direction, and I explained to John and Miles that Mother was the name we'd given to our computer.)

The chief inspector questioned Billy, Allan, Ricky, and Bob, all at length. DCI Heyes was extremely thorough, and with the help of Mother – and, of course, Charlie's computing skills – we had churned out some exciting leads for the lads to follow up. The police were not active or that much interested in this investigation, and in any case, our report, when completed, would be for your eyes only, and those eyes belonged to Lord Oakley of the Jockey Club, no one else; my reputation was based on discretion, after all.

At this point, DCI Heyes offered us a golden opportunity that we couldn't turn down or remotely consider refusing: if we had a list of the fifty-six employees of the Tote that were regular travellers on the coach, as well as being the ones who worked at these racecourses, the chief inspector offered to run these names through the police computer to see if any of the employees had a police record. The four lads working the investigation were all for it; should it prove fruitful, it would certainly save us a lot of time, and perhaps expense, should a few names be thrown up by the police computer. With the access code inserted, thanks to the chief inspector,

Charlie sat at Mother's keyboard, inputting the names, addresses, and dates of birth. Within minutes, we had a list of six names. Our individual boards, which we had each worked on over the weekend, were beginning to pay dividends.

The chief inspector's offer was most surprising to me, as I knew he had a very dry sense of humour and it was not his nature to volunteer such a favour. Perhaps I was being cynical, but nonetheless I knew I owed him a favour: the six suspects all had criminal convictions, either for fraud or drugs. I was now very eager to close this investigation down and wrap it up as soon as possible. I was so sure we at last were on the right track. I wanted the chance of having extra staff on hand at the farm later in the week; I was beginning to get extremely concerned over the safety and security issues we would soon be facing. We gambled on a change of tactic, and my four operatives agreed that CCTV strategically placed on both sides of the Tote ticket windows, where the six would be working, would tell us all what we needed to know. We would set up the operation tomorrow for Wednesday, and with the help of the Ascot security department, I would let them chose the most suitable different locations. So as to not give the game away, we would keep our suspects apart, and only one suspect in the same block of Tote window ticket outlets.

Ascot was a grade 1 track, and on this coming Wednesday, they had a really good card of racing, so a big crowd would be expected. We would implement as soon as the chief inspector's meeting was over later today. This really concluded our case file number 1; our previous ideas and intentions had been superseded by the chief inspector's intervention.

Case 2 was the case file regarding the Newmarket trainer, Noel Henry, and his suspected un-faithful wife, Natalie. The trainer had asked us to carry out a surveillance procedure for an unspecified amount of time, listing who she met, where, and for how long. The trainer suspected his stable jockey, Ron Kallon, was giving a "Halifax" – a little bit extra outside of marriage. So far, our enquiries could not put the jockey in the frame; however Natalie was most certainly getting a little bit extra, without her husband's knowledge. Charlie, of course, had concealed their identities; however, the chief inspector had not the slightest interest in our case file number 2.

It was a different story with case file number 3. Mr X (Dicky Head), as Charlie had listed him, was a stipendiary steward of the Jockey Club, and he lived in the Lambourn area, near Newbury racecourse. Charlie had called Dicky Head Mr X because in her mind he was the most mysterious.

DCI Heyes had a damn good memory as well; he informed us he knew who our Mr X was straight away. The chief inspector had been a CID officer with the Berkshire force some time ago, and was assigned to the case of Giles Holland, the victim of a vicious assault. GBH was the term the police used for grievous bodily harm of a nature likely to cause serious bodily damage.

"Dicky Head's name was in the frame at the time," said the chief inspector. "I had to visit him to take a statement. We couldn't pin anything on him, but he was so smug at the time, I just knew he had something to do with it." DCI Heyes looked at Charlie. "No point calling him Mr X, Charlie. I know exactly who you are talking about."

I suggested, "In that case, Chief Inspector, if you want to dig a bit deeper, I will clear it with Mr and Mrs Holland if you wish to reopen the inquiry. I take it nobody was ever charged regarding this incident."

"No," said the chief inspector. "We never charged anyone. Let's see what you investigation turns up in the next forty-eight hours. I will then decide whether to reopen this particular case."

My involvement was to carry out and produce a report on Dicky Head, mainly to see if he was breaking any Jockey Club rules whilst working for them. Deep down, I believed my company was being used by Mr Holland to see if there was a way for the Jockey Club to get rid of Dicky Head.

John, my employee on this investigation, at this point said, "Don't forget, Boss, Dicky Head has been missing since Friday."

Charlie would contact the Jockey Club for an address for Dicky Head, and then let the chief inspector know.

Despite his reaction, I assumed the chief inspector was again interested in Mr Dicky Head. Very interested indeed.

It was now nearly four o'clock. Time was getting on, so we stopped for a coffee break. Charlie had located an address for the chief inspector regarding Dicky Head: he was indeed still registered as living in the Lambourn area.

During coffee, I made a quick call to the local locksmith to come and change the locks on all the doors; he said he could fit us in tomorrow afternoon, which was excellent news. "Thank you, Tom," I said. "See you Tuesday afternoon then." I turned off my mobile.

I had not figured yet out how Charlie's spare Vitara key had got into the hands of my would-be assassin. Was it Chris Cobb? I had no proof, so this was in-house, not yet for the chief inspector's ears; no matter how clever he was, I couldn't prove anything whatsoever, and Miles could find no forensic evidence from what was left of Charlie's Vitara.

Coffee break over, it was time to hear what the chief inspector had to say over the horsebox fire, my attempted murder, Henry Hopalong Hall's murder, and the arson attack on the girls' flat in Burgess Hill.

DCI Heyes had segregated his murder inquiry into four components parts:

1. Horsebox fire
2. Henry Hall's murder
3. Arson attack at Burgess Hill
4. Attempted murder of Steven Hurst

"Let's start then with item 1, the horsebox fire," the chief inspector said. He drank the last of his coffee before he continued. "Forensics strongly suspects that the target for the horsebox was indeed the front door of your farm, Steve," he stated. "The tonnage of unladen weight of this particular horsebox was 7.5 tonne; it was one of the older type horseboxes, a Bedford TK diesel. This box was quite capable of taking out the oak doors on the piers if driven straight at them, and on to the front door, of which the whole farmhouse would have gone up being mostly made out of wood; that, is if the driver was in control of his senses. From the evidence obtained from the floor of where the driver would put his feet whilst driving in this horsebox, we strongly suspect that the driver was under the influence of drugs, the type that are smoked."

Miles interjected that there was a small amount of DNA found on the roach (the discarded end of a joint that had been smoked); this mostly matched the DNA of the deceased body in the burned-out Golf GTI found in Lewes, near the hockey club. "Therefore," he said, "it is a distinct probability they were one and the same person."

Laura asked, "Then, to put a percentage on it, Miles, how sure are you?" Miles said he was 95 per cent sure. Laura said, "That will do for me. I'm convinced; in fact, I think we all are."

The second component of the chief inspector's case was the murder of Henry Hopalong Hall. As previously suggested, DCI Heyes and Miles

Valentine were fully of the belief that the Golf GTI driver and the horsebox driver were one and the same person; we were all now of a similar opinion.

"He was a local man, probably Brighton central or the Kemp Town area, who knew the local drug scene and was or had been part of it for a good few years now," the chief inspector said. "The DNA on the roach, if you remember, suggested the cardboard used for the roach came from the Metropole Hotel, or even the Midnight Blues Nightclub adjacent, which used same safety matches. He was a heavy user of drugs, and every day to him was just a question of where he would get his next fix from. He was probably in debt to his supplier, who had complete control over him; he had reached the stage where he would simply kill for a fix. Such is the curse of drugs. We believe last Wednesday evening, Steve, in the NCP car park, you were the target, and you were meant to be injured – cuts and bruises, maybe; a broken leg would do – you were getting too close to someone who had to stop you, or at least slow you down. However, he, the Golf GTI driver, misjudged his target and collided with your fiancée, catching the strap of her handbag and dislocating her shoulder. The driver panicked, and upon leaving the car park, scraped his car on a pillar and smashed his door mirror off the car. Henry Hall found and saved the mirror for you. We believe the Golf GTI driver left Brighton and travelled up the A23, towards Hickstead, where he intended to meet someone – probably this would be his controller or handler; he was then given another job and another fix, a joint. His controller would have been present at the NCP car park and very pleased to have heard the siren of the ambulance called in the emergency; now, with you out the way, he could burn down your farmhouse and business, or so he thought. The Golf GTI man's next job was to ram your front door with the horsebox and then watch the whole lot go up in flames," the chief inspector said, adding, "It will only be a matter of hours, Steve, before we have the name of our junkie. This junkie was on borrowed time; he was killing or trying to kill people for fixes on a daily basis. Rest assured his handler or controller murdered him. You all need to be on maximum alert at all times."

Most of us had been affected already by the harsh reality of it all; we knew the chief inspector was deadly serious. I thought of Laura, sobbing on my arm in Red's box a few days earlier. "I am frightened, Steve," she'd said. Inwardly, I was as well, but I wasn't letting on.

"What was left of the Golf driver's payment, the roach end of the joint, was our lucky break," the chief inspector continued. "We believe the junkie parked the white Golf GTI at the Castle Pub, and either walked or was given a lift by his handler to Chris Collins's garage. The old Bedford TKs are easy to break into and steal; they just got lucky that Chris Collins had filled the tanks up with diesel for an early start the next morning. The only problem was, the junkie was unable to deliver the horsebox into your front door; he must have been so high on drugs that he completely misjudged the turn. His handler must have been very angry with him, and, furthermore, in our opinion, the fix stashed behind the driver's door mirror was probably payment for the NCP car-park job where your ex was injured, unbeknown at the time to the junkie's handler. The handler must have told the junkie it was his own stupid fault and not the handler's problem; he probably further told the junkie to go and retrieve the broken mirror after he finished his next job: the intended horsebox fire and arson of your farmhouse, which is also the place where you operate your business. Stupid junkie. It would seem was very stupid indeed, and he must have known Henry Hall as an acquaintance – perhaps from a local bar – and was not able to put the facts together. Henry would have been aware, wanting to save the mirror for you, Steve. Henry knew who the driver was, and that's what got him killed; even if Henry had given the junkie the mirror, he would probably have still killed him, Steve, so don't have it on your conscience."

"Oh really," I replied. I did still have it on my conscience, and I could not discard it as easily as the chief inspector wanted me to.

"The junkie is a known face in the Brighton drug scene," DCI Heyes repeated. "I can assure you all he will be missed, and that will help us to learn who he is. We will then be able to at least clear up the horsebox fire, Henry Hall's death, and perhaps your lucky escape in the NCP car park, Steve."

Lucky? I thought. *Maybe.*

The chief inspector slowly carried on with his synopsis. "This now leaves the arson attack in Burgess Hill, as well as your attempted murder, Steve. All these crimes we now believe are, without any doubt, linked in some form or other. However, apart from drugs, we cannot see a motive."

DCI Heyes wanted to elaborate more on my individual case, my attempted murder, but he dealt with the arson attack on the girls' flat first, as he'd indicated he would do.

"We have no leads whatsoever!" the chief inspector exclaimed. "That is, nothing other than the fact that the fire brigade believes that petrol or some other highly inflammable liquid was used. Poured into the flat through the letter box to start the blaze. It's a ground-floor flat of a converted semi-detached house, with a community-type passage for entry to both flats; the smoke alarm in the hallway would have sounded the alarm within seconds of smoke detection. It was very lucky that Charlie and Laura's neighbour upstairs was in at the time and called the fire brigade instantly before leaving the building; otherwise, there could have been another fatality. Alternatively, if this was a warning, it was of the most serious kind. We are dealing with a ruthless gang of drug dealers, in the very least."

DCI Heyes paused to let his comments sink in, and then he turned towards me.

"I am beginning to fear for your employees' safety, Steve, especially your young ladies," he said, stressing the last part in a more dignified manner than the rest of his speech. "Until this is all over," he added, "I would suggest, for the time being anyway, that the two young ladies should remain at this farmhouse, and that at least two of your other employees remain also. I am now starting to take these incidents even more seriously than before, Steve. We don't take to kindly to madmen running around our neck of the woods in Brighton, and there have been two killings too many in the last few days. It's not for my liking, and I don't want any more. Don't give them a chance, and sod the cuts. I'm leaving a panda car at the burned-out piers, with an officer on duty round the clock until this is all over. This is now a major incident, as far as the Sussex Police Constabulary is concerned," he finished.

Miles concluded, "Due to lack of forensic evidence, my department has been of little or no use here; however, the fire brigade is sure that it was a deliberate arson attack, and that will be in their reports to the insurers and the police."

At this point, we took another break; it was just after five.

The chief inspector had a call from Brighton Police Station in Edward Street, after which he informed everyone in the office, "We have now identified the horsebox driver was also the Golf GTI driver; they are indeed one and the same person."

Everybody in the office paused, as if they were on CCTV and the film had stopped. DCI Heyes had everyone's attention. All eyes were focused on the chief inspector, and everyone was doubtless thinking the same thing: *Come on out with it then!*

Laura was the only one who carried on with what she was doing, as both kettles were filled up in the kitchen to make eleven cups of coffee – one each for my eight employees, Miles Valentine, DCI Heyes, and me.

The chief inspector kept us in suspense; he was still in deep conversation on his mobile. "Yes, yes … I've got that … yes, okay, very interesting indeed … yes, I wondered where he had been; he was off our radar for ages … yes, we thought he was Mr Big in Lewes for a while in the 1990s; we nicked him for a few minor offences, but nothing we could or were allowed to keep a record of, just on-the-spot fines, mainly for possession of drugs, we got him into court once for supplying class A drugs, but the prosecution couldn't make it stick – that's how he got the nickname "Jammy" … yes, okay … yep, got that; we had a feeling he had moved into Brighton territory, more chimney pots, more customers, more profit; the last we heard, he had a string of prostitutes working Kemp Town for him … yes, that's right … no, I think he probably became heavily addicted himself, and then, instead of being a supplier, he became a heavy user … yes, many thanks for the information … yes, I agree that does seem to be the case … yes, thank you … so he died from a lethal injection – an overdose, self-inflicted – correct? He was murdered before the car was set ablaze, right? Yes … I will inform Miles." DCI Heyes rang off, putting the mobile in his pocket. "Is that coffee ready?" he called to Laura as he beckoned Miles to join him on the other side of the office.

The two of them were in deep conversation for about five minutes. Laura gave them their coffees. Meanwhile, my employees were chattering amongst themselves; the office was simply buzzing with speculation as to who, what, where, and why.

At last, the chief inspector said, "Okay, the dead junkie is—" And then his mobile rang. He retrieved it from his pocket and answered it straight away. "Yes," he said, repeating it four or five times. Yes," he said again. "Thank you." He replaced the phone in his jacket pocket. He turned back towards us and said, "The dead junkie was known to us as a supplier, a major supplier some years ago; however, we could never fathom out how the drugs were coming in and who actually supplied him. In recent years, he had become a heavy user and not a supplier; a habitual user only interested in his next fix."

We were all on tenterhooks by this point.

"Come on, Chief Inspector!" I exclaimed. "Who the fuck was he? What's his fucking name?" I was not accustomed to swearing; it just came out.

"Mr Hurst," said the chief inspector, "I was about to give you his name. It is Jay Penfold. We had a tip-off about thirty minutes ago; someone had grassed him up to us from a call box in Brighton. We know him as Jammy Penfold – at least, that's how he used to be known to us – we gave him that nickname because we could not get a major crime to stick on him. He peddled death, and death got him too in the end. No doubt he has ruined many a young life in his time, and taken a few as well; he was murdered though a syringe which was still embedded in his arm, so we think he *was* lethally overdosed before the Golf GTI was set ablaze."

Charlie said, "Well, that sort of fits in with your synopsis doesn't it, Chief Inspector!"

"Yes, Charlie, exactly," said DCI Heyes. "But where are the ringleaders? Where is this all leading to, and why?" The chief inspector was indeed deeply perplexed and concerned about this state of affairs which so far had resulted in two murders.

"And now, component number 4," the chief inspector said. "The attempted murder of Steve Hurst." He explained his theory with regard to the need of putting me out of business, adding that the arson attempt on the girls' flat was a distraction designed to take us off the scent. The real intent was to gain access to your farmhouse, to destroy it all – everything. We need a reason, Steve, a motive. Can you think of any minute possibility as to why someone might want you dead or out the way?"

I could, but I wasn't telling the chief inspector just yet. His name was my nightmare, the knight in white satin, Mr Chris Cobb. "No," I said to the chief inspector. "Off the top of my head, I cannot think of anyone. We've shared our current investigations – the Tote scam, the unfaithful wife, and Tim Holland asking me to make some discreet inquiries into Dicky Head – they are not exactly what I would call major investigations, are they?!"

"Well," said the chief inspector, "be it upon yourself if you are holding back any information, but I am definitely getting a whiff of horse manure here. I'm going to be honest with you, Steve, I do believe your ex, Jane Coe, is involved, and possibly her new wallet, Chris Cobb. And yes, we have put these names through our police computer, and they both have had not so much as a parking ticket. And yes, I am also aware that there is a possibility that Jane took the spare set of keys with her when she walked out on you – have you thought about that?"

I felt as if I had just been given a good enough reason to throw up. I was not ready to own up to the fact that this was a distinct possibility, but then it sunk in that Chris Cobb had been at Jane's this past weekend. I sat down, feeling ill, and slightly nauseated, I thought the colour must be draining from my cheeks. Laura brought me over some coffee, and I took a few mouthfuls of the lovely sweet liquid that I thrived on. After I regained my composure, I said to DCI Heyes, "Yes, I am fully aware of the probability that my ex could be involved; I am just taking a bit of time in coming to terms with the probability that my ex is involved with a bunch of drug dealers and murderers."

The chief inspector then speculated on the incident that nearly killed me – and they would have succeeded if it were not for Laura. "Late last Friday night and in the early hours of Saturday morning, persons unknown again tried to set fire to White Horse Farm, this time by ramming the front door with a stolen vehicle belonging to one of Steve's employees, Charlotte – Charlie – Rogers," he said. "Charlie's Vitara was to be used as a battering ram against the front door, doused in petrol, and set ablaze; this, I believe, is what they had in mind. They used two vehicles: the Vitara to crash, and the grey van to get away. At this time, the drivers remain unknown, but at least two people were certainly involved, though I would suspect three as a getaway if they got into complications."

He continued, "The first thing that springs to mind is that you have now been attacked twice with vehicles, both times with the intention of creating a massive fire. They are very desperate, vile people, and they want to burn down your farm and offices, Steve. And they don't care if people are in the house. However, because of the farm's unique layout – which these people are aware of – an assault from the rear would be useless, with the loose boxes in the rectangle being adjacent to the main house, and the offices in between and forming part of the house, the large kitchen next to the office giving easy access to the yard and horses, and, of course, the garage door sealing the rear off completely.

"These evil people are fully aware of the layout of White Horse Farm. This is another indicator, Steve, I'm sorry to say, of your ex, Jane, being someway involved. As I said earlier, all roads seem to lead to horse manure. It stinks to high heaven, and again, I have to say that somewhere along the line, the horseback-riding fraternity is involved.

"These people have been thwarted now on two occasions, and let's not forget, they have even murdered one of their own when he became a threat and a liability. Clearly, these people believe that you are a threat to their organisation and set-up; this is the stark reality of the situation. You, Steve, possess knowledge – knowingly or unwittingly – that can perhaps harm or seriously damage their business, or possibly even destroy their organisation. It is my job to find that knowledge which you possess, and to act on it as quickly as possible to prevent any more loss of life. I need to put these disgusting people behind bars as quickly as possible. Do I make myself clear?!"

He paused to let that sink in before continuing. "Once again, I say, Steve, thanks to young Laura here, you are still alive. So is there anything you can tell me about your ex or Chris Cobb that would give us a break as to where this is all leading to? We cannot – and by 'we', I mean none of us in this room – hold back the slightest detail or any secrets, because, literally, it may cost someone's life. Someone sitting in this room here and now, and I am certain none of you would want that on your conscience for the rest of your life."

The chief inspector got through to me, hitting the rawest of nerve ends. "No, Chief Inspector," I said. "Henry Hall is one too many on my conscience already. The only lead I can give you at the moment, albeit without a shred of evidence, is that the night of the attack with Charlie's Vitara, a split second before the inevitable collision, I would swear I saw Chris Cobb driving the grey van, and I am absolutely certain he had on a white shirt with a white tie, similar to what the showjumping riders wear in the main ring of a competition. As far as Charlie's Vitara is concerned, all I can remember of the driver is that he – or she – had two giant staring eyes. It looked as if they were not part of the driver's body." Although it was all had happened in only a split second, I had seen those images clearly. In that instant, I dearly wanted to know who was trying to kill me. I wasn't bothered about why, just who, and all I could see was Chris Cobb, his white shirt and tie, and those fucking horrible eyes.

"At last!" said the chief inspector. "Now we are getting somewhere. This Chris Cobb, where does he live, or where does he come from, Steve?"

I said, "The Cobb family business is based in Northampton. The family is in the shoe business." I then added, "But if you did a CRB check (criminal records bureau) on Chris Cobb, you would know that, and you would know where he lives!"

The chief inspector replied, "Not necessarily. As you know, because of his profession, he could be away from his home for months at a time. International showjumpers compete on a circuit, don't they, Steve?"

"Yes, you're right, Chief Inspector. From April to September, they are all over the country and abroad, from week to week." I added, "It's just like a travelling circus. Jane's rarely at her parents' house during these months, always travelling or competing. All the top showjumpers have enormous horseboxes capable of holding six big jumpers, with living accommodation and a kitchen, and they travel from show to show."

"Right," the chief inspector said. "Nearly finished now?"

It hit me like a bolt from the blue. Embarrassed, I said, "The next big showjumping event is on at Hickstead this week, with the big competitions on Friday, Saturday, and Sunday. The outer rings are used on Tuesday, Wednesday, and Thursday, for qualifying."

"And when do the top international riders start turning up?" asked the chief inspector.

I replied, "Most of them should already be here to prepare and school the youngsters." I added, "Doug Dunne, the owner, always lets them use the showground from Monday onwards to prepare for the big classes."

"Very well," said the chief inspector. "This revelation certainly throws a new light on this matter. And yes, a lot of what we have discussed is circumstantial, but in my world, too many pieces conveniently fit the jigsaw, and I never overlook the obvious when it's staring me in the face." He added, "In light of what we've just heard, I would suggest strongly a complete lockdown of White Horse Farm, Steve – immediately – until we gather more information and know exactly what we are up against, and exactly what you have that they want to totally destroy or kill for."

I nodded my agreement.

"Very well," said DCI Heyes. "Let's call It a day. It's well past 6.30. I think we have made a lot of headway this afternoon, ladies and gentlemen, and I thank you for your time and patience."

I showed DCI Heyes and Miles Valentine to the door, and asked the chief inspector if I could call in at the station on Thursday morning. He asked me to arrange it with the duty desk sergeant at the station, and to call in by phone to let them know what time. I thanked them once again as they left.

My whole team had a serious amount of thinking to do this evening. Charlie had baked an enormous cottage pie and cauliflower cheese, both of which were due out of the oven in twenty minutes – just enough time to shower, shave, and change the plasters on my knee and nose. Most of the lads wanted to change and brush up as well. There were two bathrooms downstairs: one was used mainly for staff working in the yard, and the other for overnight guests. We had three bathrooms upstairs, of which two were en suite, so we had no problem with us all getting brushed up for our evening meal.

Laura and I were deep in thought as we went into our bedroom.

As soon as I shut the door, she burst in to tears. "Oh Steve!" she said. "I am so scared, and I don't want to lose you."

I said, "I feel the same about you, Laura. And Charlie too."

We just stood there holding each other until we were both sure we were back in control of our emotions and feelings. After we showered together, our confidence returned, and we went downstairs to a very quiet kitchen.

"For God's sake, someone get some bloody beers out the fridge," said Charlie.

And then, at last, normality returned to White Horse Farm.

After supper, the four lads working on the Tote scam – Billy, Allan, Ricky, and Bob – got to work on their computers, organising Wednesday's operation. Ascot security was alerted, and also Lord Oakley at the Jockey Club, of what our planned operation would entail on the day: we would vet and scan every single customer they individually served throughout the day's racing; Lord Oakley would e-mail my office with a password for the operation later that evening, and he would also inform the Ascot security team and the local police of this undercover operation; Billy and Allan would leave the farm first thing in the morning, when the officer in the panda car at my front gate would finish his shift and be replaced by another officer (this would happen at 6 a.m.); I wanted Bob and Ricky to remain at the farm for added security. That meant I just had to sort out our ongoing procedures for the week ahead concerning Gary's case of the unfaithful wife, Natalie, and the mysterious Mr X, as Charlie had labelled him – now where had he disappeared to, the elusive Dicky Head?

I informed Allan and Billy I wanted them to stay over at Ascot Tuesday night and Wednesday night, and to contact Wharr's in Windsor to expect the VT (videotape) from the CCTV surveillance cameras at around 8 p.m. Wednesday; Wharr's operatives would work through the night, if need be, to establish any sort of pattern of which we could tie the six suspects to fraud. In the back of my mind, however, was this nagging sixth sense: this wasn't just a scam, but a distribution outlet for drugs; my gut feeling was that these six suspects were passing on "wraps" to customers – just enough for a fix, and if you got caught, well, the way the law was in this country, you would be let off with a warning or an on-the-spot fine,

Wharr's of Windsor was not on the radar. They were a retail outlet for camping gear and outward-bound adventure seekers; they were suppliers of clothing and equipment, but, as I've said, out the back, for the very special customers, it was a completely different story. Once through security clearance, it was definitely James Bond gadgetry: all up-to-date, highly technical equipment, and they had developed with funding from the Home Office a highly sophisticated technique of facial recognition by using magnetic resonance imaging (MRI). Hospitals now use MRI – known to the public as MRI scanners – and this technique is the most thorough forensic examination and evaluation available, the VT would be MRI-scanned, and we would have the results the next morning. On Thursday morning then, the lads – Billy and Allan – would report the findings back to me at the farm.

The six suspects, we'd found out earlier, thanks to DCI Heyes, all had police records for either fraud or drug violations, and they were all in their thirties or forties. There were three men and three women, surprisingly – well, to me anyway – they were all single or divorced; two of the men came from Slough, and the other man came from Datchet, near Windsor, which was really now a very large village of which the River Thames passed through on its way to London; two of the women resided in Taplow, again a rather large village now, near Maidenhead, and the other woman lived in Wokingham, which wasn't that far from Ascot. However, the coach had a set pattern and routine, where all Tote operatives were transported to and from set points and delivered to the race tracks as a unit; the day's racing details could be delivered by their supervisor thus en route, and afterwards, they would be delivered back to their pickup points.

At about 8.30 p.m., I had the chief inspector on the phone.

"Why the bloody hell could you not give me this information earlier?" he protested as he shouted at me over the phone.

I was stuck for words for a few seconds, as this reaction was completely unexpected. "Sorry, Chief Inspector," I replied as I subconsciously searched for an excuse. "What with the concussion and trauma, and the general mayhem, I just have not had enough time to recover and gather my thoughts.

DCI Heyes never apologised; he wasn't buying it. He just said, "You've been through worse than this, Steve, and you need to pull yourself together. Those girls are relying on you to pull them through this ordeal. We could be dealing with anything, literally, because of the drug abuse; mentally unstable madmen with no respect for human life. Let's have no doubt about this, Steve."

"Yes, Chief Inspector, without any shadow of doubt," I replied.

"Now," said the chief inspector, "what are your plans for tomorrow? I want to know your movements and if are you expecting any visitors."

I replied, "Well, Tom the locksmith is coming over in the afternoon to replace all the locks on all the doors, and – oh shit – Jane's probably over in the morning – late morning, around eleven – to pick up her horse, Red, some tack, and the rest of her belongings."

The chief inspector took a few seconds before replying. "Good job I rang you then, Steve! I think it's about time we turned the tables somewhat."

"How do you mean, Chief Inspector?

The chief inspector stated that he wanted to bug Jane's transport tomorrow, whatever vehicle she or her groom, Sally, turned up in. I told him Jane would probably use her Range Rover and trailer, as it was just the one horse.

"Good," said the chief inspector. "We will bug them both. One of my spooks will be over at 9 a.m. They only take seconds to attach. You will just need to hold their attention for a few seconds, Steve. Whoever turns up, just try to get her attention away from the transport, and my phantom will do the rest."

"I don't really want to see Jane, let alone speak to her," I told the chief inspector.

"You need to, Steve," he said. "Let her see the damage she may have caused, and be calm; you know her better than any of us, so look for any physical reaction that is out of the ordinary of what you would expect. Just be casual, as if life goes on as usual. And tell her the chief inspector running the investigation expects to make three arrests within the next seventy-two hours. Tell her I know who killed Henry Hall, and then drop this one on her: tell her I know who killed junkie Jay Penfold. Oh, and by the way, Steve, the officer in the panda car at the front of your farm by the burned-out piers is a specially trained firearms officer, and he is well tooled up! Goodnight, Steve. I will call you again at nine in the morning for an update."

134

I replied, "Thank you. Thank you, Chief Inspector, for everything."

It was now just after nine in the evening at White Horse Farm, and all the lads were in the lounge, either playing cards or watching television; both the girls had tidied up the kitchen after supper, and I joined them for a drink. I had a lager, Charlie had a Bacardi Breezer, and Laura a bottle of cider. I told the girls I had just had the chief inspector on the phone. Although I never went into specifics – for instance, I never told them we had a special firearms officer now guarding the front gates – I did inform them of the chief inspector's strategy for dealing with Jane tomorrow. Surprisingly to me, both the girls agreed wholeheartedly with the chief inspector's cunning plan. We would all put on a brave face, as if we had not been perturbed by the recent events that had affected our lives greatly over the last six days; however, Laura was adamant she did not want to meet my ex ever again.

"Then why don't you have a lazy morning?" I suggested.

"Yes," said Laura, "that sounds good to me, and when she's gone, I will catch up on the laundry." Laura added, "Don't forget, you guys, I'm jumping Fred II in the Grade C Championship at Hickstead in the main ring on Friday." She had prequalified Fred at the Guildford show earlier in the year. "I'm going to concentrate on positivity, and give Fred all my attention from Wednesday on. I want to win on Friday, you two."

I agreed. "What could be more normal than that?" Though, inwardly, I was petrified. Talk about walking into the lion's den! The chief inspector would have to help me out with this one. Boy, did I respect Laura's courage, though.

I asked Charlie if she had any plans for the coming week.

"Yep," she replied. "I'm going to be Laura's groom at Hickstead. We will get there about one, just after lunch. We will win, and be back home at five. Fred II is exciting – a fast, accurate jumper. I can't really see him being beaten, although it will go to a jump-off," said Charlie.

"Right," said Laura. "I'm ready for bed. Steve, do you want to come and tuck me in?"

Charlie said, "I'm off to bed as well." This was followed by "I think Ricky fancies me!"

"He always has," said Laura.

"Steve, could Ricky come to Hickstead as well?" Charlie asked hopefully.

"Yes, of course. It was always in my mind to have Ricky here all week anyway. I'm just going over the lads' objectives for the week, and I'll be up in a few minutes," I said to Laura as the girls went to bed.

I checked with the lads in the lounge, and they had again devised a rota system where two of them would be awake all night. They had the two-way phones that operated through Mother to keep in contact with the officer at the gate throughout the night. Bob went down to check in with the officer and gave him one of the phones, telling him there would be two of us awake all night if he needed us. The officer agreed. I didn't tell my lads that he was a specially trained firearms officer, but I did tell the lads we would meet in the office at eight in the morning, with the exception of Billy and Allan, who would be leaving earlier.

I went over this week's schedule, really hoping we would have a peaceful night.

Laura was already in bed as I got undressed. I went to the bathroom to brush my teeth, and there was a little stick-on note on the mirror – one of those yellow ones – it simply said, "I love u so much!" I closed the bathroom door and turned the light out. The moon was once again casting shadows across the bedroom. It was a clear August night, and the stars had come out to play as they dazzled and sparkled against the midnight-blue backdrop that was the night sky. I knew Laura would be naked too as I got into bed. I leant over and kissed her as our arms and legs embraced each other.

I whispered in her ear, "You know, Laura, you're right: When someone really loves you, that's when your life begins."

We fell asleep in each other's arms.

CHAPTER 11

We woke up to a bright and beautiful Tuesday morning. Lord Oakley had duly sent me an e-mail with the operation password late yesterday evening. It was to be known as "Operation Mousetrap"; that really did put a smile on my face. All we needed now was for the six suspects to perhaps take the bait without ever realising we were on to them! I did indeed feel a lot better when I got up this morning. Laura was still sound asleep. I guess I felt invigorated; today was going to be the first day of the rest of my life. Whether it was the chief inspector's lecture from last night or the deep true love I had been feeling for Laura ever since I awoke, I did not know; probably a mixture of both. I kept telling myself that what I knew for sure was that the next week or so was going to have a major influence on the rest of our lives – my life, and the life of every single one of my employees, especially Charlie and Laura. The chief inspector was right of course: both the girls would be looking to me to pull them through this ordeal, and there was absolutely no way that I would let either of them down. The lads were big enough and strong enough to look after themselves in any situation; such was the faith I had in them.

I went downstairs for some breakfast at about 7.30. To my surprise, Ricky had already prepared coffee and toast for me. I asked him if there was anything to report.

"No," said Ricky. "All quiet on the western front."

"That's an odd comment to make," I said.

Ricky replied, "That was the title of the old war film I watched last night on the telly. It was a First World War film about trench warfare and a sniper who eventually got sniped himself."

Ricky could be very informative at times.

The rest of the lads were slowly gathering for our eight o 'clock briefing, and as usual, the toaster was working overtime to keep up with the appetites of my hungry employees. Ricky had nominated himself chef this morning as he busily prepared more fried eggs and bacon to go with the toast. When I went upstairs to put some fresh plasters on my now slowly disappearing wounds, Charlie asked me if she could have some breakfast in bed.

"Of course," I replied. "I will ask Ricky to come up and take your order."

Charlie smiled. "I knew you were going to say that!" she replied, adding, "Be best if Ricky knows right now then that I have a big appetite."

I reiterated to Charlie that I would be keeping Ricky at the farm all this week, and that I would sort out the replacement Vitara for her later today.

"Whoopee!" she replied. "Double celebrations then! I'm really hungry now."

I went back down the stairs to the kitchen, finished my toast and coffee, and let Ricky know about the request for room service from Charlie. "Could you go upstairs to take her order?" I asked. I didn't have to ask him twice.

At eight o'clock we gathered in the office for the team briefing. Ricky was a little late joining us because of his breakfast preparations earlier. Billy and Allan had already left for Ascot. I texted Allan the operation password (mousetrap), which he texted me back to confirm; they had arrived at Ascot racecourse, as had the Wharr's technicians and operatives (there were two of each). Allan was designated to be in charge of the operation, and he hastily gathered the team and Ascot security staff (of which there were four) to be briefed on the operation now officially recognised as Operation Mousetrap. This was to be a ten-man operation. The police were informed of the operation but would not be involved in it; however, the police would provide backup should that be necessary. Lord Oakley, having learnt from past experiences, did not want a press leak, and he knew the police public relations office was very good at providing such leaks – without realising the consequences – no, they would be backup only. My orders were to keep it strictly in-house at all times. I really did want to deliver on this one, and I felt in a strange way that cracking this case might deliver some answers to our other cases on file, which were live and ongoing but at such a laboriously slow pace.

I briefed the rest of the team on what Allan had relayed to me. Those of my operatives present in the office this fine August morning were John, who was in charge of the Dicky Head case file; Gary, who had the unfaithful wife case file; and Bob and Ricky, who would both be retained at the farm all of this coming week as field support – and added security.

I asked John to return to Lambourn. "Flash around your Jockey Club security badge," I told him. "Check all the betting offices and pubs; show them a recent picture of Mr Dicky Head. Scour Newbury as well, and do the same there. Let's see if we can flush him out if he has indeed gone on the missing list."

I wanted to show the chief inspector just how good my team really was; this week, the lads would bloody well prove it.

As John left the office, I told him to stay down in the area all week. I also informed him that I was meant to meet Robert Argonaut at Newbury races on Friday, and to meet me there for an update on the search for Dicky Head, if we had not located him by then. "Find the bastard," I said to John as he shut the office door behind him.

Ricky was the first of my team to notice the change in my general demeanour and attitude.

"Hey, Boss!" he shouted across the office. "You've changed. I noticed it this morning when you came downstairs for breakfast."

I looked at Ricky, with my newly found confidence, and nonchalantly said, "Oh really?"

"Yeah," he replied. "When I took Charlie up her breakfast this morning, she kissed me and asked if I could help her shower. Sorry, Boss, that's why I was a bit late for the briefing," he explained, then added, "Well, I couldn't refuse, could I, Boss? Anyway, after the shower, when I came back downstairs, I think I was changed too. I felt like a new man. I know how you feel, Boss: I have someone I love to fight for too."

Charlie and Ricky had definitely bonded, it seemed.

"Good," I said to Ricky. Inwardly, I was so pleased for Charlie; it sort of put my mind at ease and balanced things up a bit.

Ricky was about 5 foot 10, weighed about 12 stone, and was 30 years old. He'd joined the army at 18 and served as a Royal Marine for about eight years. He was a strong, fit lad who had been with me now for four years. He was also a keen rugby player and was a regular for Richmond Rugby Club in West London. Ricky was well into his recovery from cruciate ligament surgery on his left knee. He had the operation in March, some five months ago, but the surgeon had said no competitive sport for a year. The knee was fine and not remotely giving him any problems. He had some weights in one of the stables where he would, if time allowed, work out and do some specific knee-strengthening exercises.

Bob was Bob: reliable and efficient. Bob was about 6 feet tall, weighed about 13 stone, and was 40 years old. Also an ex-army man, he was married (unlike the still-single Ricky) and had two teenage boys; the family home was in Hove, near the seafront. When he had any time off, he would take his boys to watch his beloved Albion – Bob loved his football, and was a season ticket holder at Brighton and Hove Albion. He was the quiet man of the group, really; kept himself to himself, but he was a superb operative nonetheless.

Gary, on the other hand, was a bundle of laughs: "Hey, Boss, have you heard this one? What's got a hazelnut in every bite?" "I don't know, Gary, what's got a hazelnut in every bite?" "Squirrel shit! Ha, ha, ha, ha!" Gary always laughed at his own jokes. The squirrel bit was last week's; we had not had one so far this week, though. Gary was single, though living with his partner Hugh – yes, Gary was gay; he and Hugh had been together for six years. They lived in Crawley, near to Gatwick Airport. Hugh was a pilot for British Airways, mainly long haul. On the odd occasion, such as Christmas parties or social events, I had met Hugh. When Hugh and Gary were together, you could see the special love they shared, the deep feelings they had for each other. I was not at all affected by their relationship, and I was glad Gary was so open about it. I had employed Gary for three years now, and he was an excellent operative. He was about 5 foot 8, weighed about 11 stone, and was 34 years old. Gary was ex-Royal Navy; he had served for eleven years on the same aircraft carrier, and when it was mothballed and decommissioned, he wouldn't serve on another ship, so he left the service.

Gary's case file was that of the "naughty-but-nice Natalie", to use Gary's term, the unfaithful wife of racehorse trainer Noel Henry. Noel Henry had instructed us to carry out surveillance on Natalie, and we had been doing so for a few weeks now, as we had relayed to the chief inspector. We had to put together a dossier of everyone she met, where, and when, so as to gather any evidence regarding sexual activity (and if so with whom). As discussed with the chief inspector, Gary had already obtained evidence of sexual activity outside the marriage, so it was probably now a question of how many other men was she seeing behind her husband's back. Gary was the ideal operative for this assignment: he had joined the navy to see the world; women didn't interest him at all. Gary said that the file would be ready at the weekend, so I instructed him to return to Newmarket and carry on the surveillance until Friday evening.

"Return to the farm on Saturday to complete his report for me to give to Noel Henry," I told Gary. It would be up to the trainer to confront his wife and sort out their matrimonial problems; we would just supply the evidence.

We finished our briefing at about 8.50, and I asked Ricky if he would make some coffee. Gary drove off in one of the company's diesel vans, headed for Newmarket. The chief inspector's spook was due to arrive at nine o'clock.

I rang Simon up at Sporty Cars in Ditchling to check on the replacement Vitara for Charlie, which we urgently need. Simon informed me it was currently being serviced and would be ready about two in the afternoon. I asked if he could deliver the vehicle to us at Sayers Common, and he said it would not be a problem. He then gave me the registration number so that Charlie could arrange her insurance. Simon further informed me that the Vitara was already taxed to the end of the year, and it was a top-of-the-range model in white, with full leather black trim, sports alloy wheels, and air conditioning; it also had electric windows and mirrors. The vehicle was only three years old, so I agreed the price of £6,000 over the phone with Simon – it was the least I could do for Charlie; she was a lovely girl, and the love I had for her was akin to the way a brother would love a cherished younger sister. I think Charlie knew that as well. I really was hoping that her newly found romance with Ricky would flourish and eventually blossom. Charlie now had her own personal bodyguard. I doubted that she would realise this; however, for me it was a great relief, especially at this time. Ricky would guard Charlie with his life if he had to; I knew that from our conversation this morning.

It was now nine o'clock. Bob was sorting out John's accommodation in Newbury. After making the coffee, Ricky had gone into the yard to feed Red, Jane's showjumper, and also Laura's jumper, Fred II. The spook had arrived, and he was mucking out the two horses as they ate their breakfast. He blended in perfectly! I told Ricky he was an undercover police officer from the mounted police unit in Sussex; I did not want to cause any undue alarm. However, the chief inspector's spook really was licensed to kill. He was a trained killer, pure and simple. His transport was a grey van – the type British Telecom use – and DCI Heyes told me I had him for a week. I had a trained marksman at my front door, and a trained killer – a spook – at my back door. I was still hoping, though, that Jane was not mixed up in this and was just a dumb innocent. However, before the end of the day, I would know the painful truth.

DCI Heyes told me never to speak to the spook, and if I ever had to – for instance, when Jane turned up later in the morning – to address him only as Mickey. His name was Mickey Smith, according to the chief inspector. (*Yeah, I'm gonna believe that!* I thought when he told me.) I instructed both Bob and Ricky never to speak to the spook, but if they ever had to, to address him only as Mickey – just as the chief inspector had instructed me to do.

It was fast approaching ten o'clock; both the girls had now decided to honour us with their presence in the kitchen. They had been having a girlie chat upstairs in Charlie's bedroom. Charlie had shared her breakfast with Laura – and after Ricky had performed his manly duties, with distinction, according to Charlie, as Laura was to inform me later with distinction. Ricky was now eager to get back in the house; he wanted to see Charlie, which was obvious, as it had been two whole hours since he served her breakfast, with an extra-special helping. Charlie had a great deal of office work to catch up with, and Ricky's main function this morning was to track the operation going down at Ascot. He was pleased to know Charlie would be in the office for the rest of the morning; later on, no doubt, he would find out that his performance rating was more than adequate.

I was now beginning to feel even more confident, not just about today but in general, and I let Ricky tell Charlie about her new set of wheels being delivered at two o'clock. I also gave Ricky the registration number to give to Charlie to arrange her insurance at lunchtime. It was also time to start getting Jane's gear together for when she arrived in about an hour's time to pick up Red and the rest of her belongings. I would get Jane to check out Red's shins, saying I thought they were a bit sore and that there seemed to be some heat in them. Mickey Smith would then have all the time in the world to fit bugging devices to whatever transport Jane arrived in.

I put all her grooming and riding equipment into two large cardboard boxes, whilst Laura cleared out all of Jane's clothes from the bedroom wardrobe. Laura hated doing it, but at the same time, she insisted she had to do it. So she just tipped anything that belonged to Jane into plastic bin liners – jodhpurs, dresses shoes, riding boots, smalls – Laura didn't care.

She filled up two sacks, brought them downstairs, and dumped them next to the cardboard boxes filled up with riding equipment from the tack room.

Jane arrived at exactly eleven, in her Range Rover and trailer, just as I expected she would. Sally, her groom, was doing the driving; Jane was in the passenger seat. Jane got out of the car first and made her way directly to where Red was boxed; she still had her arm in a sling. I was waiting in Red's box, and I opened the half door as Jane approached.

Upon seeing me, her first words were "You fucking idiot! Look at the state of you! I tried to warn you—"

I interrupted her. "I think Red's got some heat in his front legs," I said. "I think he's suffering from sore shins."

She replied, "I would not be at all surprised with that fucking lesbian slut looking after him."

I gathered from that comment it was not the case that Jane simply did not like Laura at all; she loathed and absolutely hated her. I saw a side of Jane I had never seen before: pure hatred that I never thought could possibly exist. When she held her arm out to check Red's shins, I noticed some needle-puncture marks on the inside of her elbow, and some bruising that was mauve and yellow. Jane had started, so it would seem, injecting herself with drugs. I was shocked but showed no visible signs of my inward reaction.

"That was lucky," Jane said. "Lesbian Laura hasn't fucked him up."

Jane's comments could not be any further from the truth, of course. I knew that from my very recent pleasurable experiences with Laura, light years from Jane's conclusions. Meanwhile, I focused on the present situation, where I deduced that Jane seemed intent on taking a nosedive into a cliff, perhaps. If in fact she was now abusing hard drugs, that was exactly where she was headed – straight into a cliff.

Sally also checked Red's legs. "Yes," she said. "Very lucky indeed." She seemed intent on hammering home the point Jane had made.

In the background, Mickey gave me the thumbs up.

Good, I thought. *Now both the vehicles have been bugged.*

Looking straight at Jane, I nonchalantly said, "Why don't you two scumbag fuck-pigs load up your stuff and fuck off! Just load it up and fuck off!" After repeating myself, I added, "Oh, and by the way, DCI Heyes knows for sure who killed the car park attendant, Henry Hall. He also knows who killed the junkie Jay Penfold." When I mentioned Jay Penfold, for a split second, both the fuck-pigs looked at each other; I knew then they knew him, or at least knew of him. I continued, "The chief inspector will be making three arrests before the weekend: two for murder and one for drug dealing."

Jane was physically shocked by my statement. Again she said, "You just don't know, do you, what trouble you've got yourself in!" She added, "You fucking idiot."

"Just fuck off, the pair of you," I replied.

As they drove off, Ricky came out. "You were brilliant, Boss! Got it all on VT."

We joined the girls in the kitchen for a celebration cup of coffee. It was now about 11.30; we were having a good day so far.

Simon confirmed by text that he would be at the farm at two with Charlie's Vitara.

Shortly afterwards, DCI Heyes rang me on the mobile for an update. I got up from the kitchen table, where we were sitting, and walked out into the yard. Only Fred II was in the yard now, probably wondering where his mate had gone, but Red was gone for good. Laura followed me outside, and we went and sat down in the tack room whilst I spoke to the chief inspector. We put our coffees down instinctively and held hands, not for reassurance but for the deep love and affection we knew we shared for each other. I continued my conversation with the chief inspector; I never missed anything out and brought him completely up to speed with the events of Tuesday morning, adding that, as a bonus, Ricky had secretly filmed with audio my encounter with Jane this morning. The chief inspector wanted to see the VT immediately, and I informed him that Ricky would deliver it this afternoon to the police station in Edward Street, Brighton. Mickey had already informed the chief inspector that the bugging of the Range Rover and trailer had been completed; the range to eavesdrop was 50 miles, so if, as we believed, the Range Rover or trailer were going to be used in the vicinity of Hickstead, every word spoken would be listened to and recorded with date time technology, as the bugs were voice activated.

Ricky had produced an audio recording of this morning's conversation between Jane and me, and we played it back to DCI Heyes over the phone. When the audio recording had played through, he had only one question for me: "Is Jane doing drugs? Is she injecting herself with hard drugs?!"

I instinctively replied, "I have absolutely no idea, Chief Inspector." That was in fact true until this morning.

"Think, Steve," said the chief inspector. "When was the last time you actually saw Jane's arms in a short-sleeved shirt or blouse, or even in bed?"

My answer told me I never actually knew Jane that well at all. "Whenever Jane was in the yard doing her horses at any given time, she always wore a long-sleeved sweater, and since Easter this year, she always wore a silk pyjama top in bed. In hindsight, I cannot remember the last time I saw her arms, Chief Inspector, apart from the one I saw this morning – probably four or five months ago, to the best of my recollection."

Laura was still holding my hand, and her grip was a hell of a lot tighter; she now was holding my hand in both of hers, and she seemed to be gripping for dear life. Whenever Jane's name was mentioned, Laura seemed to grip my hand even tighter. She was visibly shaken and upset when she heard the audiotape. I told the chief inspector I would call him back a little bit later in the afternoon. By this point, Laura was in floods of tears; all that pent-up emotion and anger came flooding out in torrents upon torrents of tears.

I just held her and let her cry on my shoulder. "Just release it, Laura; let it all out," I said to her.

After about five minutes, the crying subsided. We both stood up and just embraced each other; we wrapped our arms around each other as tightly as we could. I could feel Laura's tears running down my cheek. I had tears in my eyes too, not tears of sadness but tears of joy – I loved Laura so much, I just had never realised it until about a week ago.

After the tears had completely subsided, Laura said, "The cow! The fucking liar!" I was surprised; Laura rarely swore – at least not in my hearing. "Steve, she told me she was a diabetic. She said it was an insulin injection. Jane told me she was a diabetic, and she didn't want you to know, Steve," Laura reiterated. She was furious; anger had now replaced the tears. "It was just before you went to Gloucester at Easter, I think, Steve; right here in this tack room. The fucking cow was shooting herself up!"

So Jane had been injecting herself for at least four months then. It all began to fall into place; in the last four months, Jane was certainly having mood swings, and, yes, objectively speaking, lately they had become more apparent. Perhaps recently Jane had become more drug dependent. What probably started off as recreational use had turned into dependency and abuse. Was it really up to me, though, to try to save Jane from herself?

I looked at Laura and quickly answered my own question inwardly, of course. To Laura, I said, "When someone really loves you, that's when your life begins."

Jane was history.

Laura and I shared a long, lingering, sensual, passionate kiss. As we released the tightness of our grip on each other, we eventually started laughing. We must have walked round the yard five or six times before walking back into the tack room. We discovered our coffees were now cold, so we went into the kitchen to make some more, still giggling and laughing.

Ricky, Charlie, and Bob were all in the office at their respective computers, working away. Laura wanted to do a proper roast for us tonight, just the four of us, so I gave Bob the afternoon and evening off, and tomorrow morning as well. I knew Brighton was at home to Charlton Athletic tonight, and he would be overjoyed if he could take his boys to the game. Out of courtesy, I invited the spook and marksman to dine with us, knowing both would refuse.

Mickey did ask me if he could bed down in the tack room, though.

I replied, "Yes, of course," and added, "The old sofa pulls out to a bed, and there are plenty of blankets in the chest of drawers next to the sofa. There's also a sink with running water, and some mugs on the shelf underneath, power points, and a kettle. Help yourself."

Mickey just said, "Thanks."

In the house, Laura had started to prepare the veg we were going to have with our slow-roast supper, and Simon was just about due to deliver Charlie's Vitara.

I had just enough time to contact Robert Argonaut and complete the finer details of the intended purchase of the racehorse Hot Tea. After the third ring, Robert answered his phone, and once we had exchanged pleasantries, we got down to the finer details. Robert said he would deliver the funds for the purchase to my bank tomorrow by electronic transfer; the horse would not run at Newbury on Friday, although it was still entered up to run. Robert said he had other plans for Hot Tea, although he wasn't telling me at the moment. He did ask me to book up my neighbour Chris Collins, though, to pick the horse up for him from Jonathan Ridger's yard in Guildford at eight o'clock in the morning on Friday. He then asked me for Chris's mobile number, and for me to give Chris his mobile number, for instructions on Friday morning when the horse had been picked up and was safely on board; he would then telephone Chris himself to tell him where to take the horse. That was to be the arrangement, and I was also to pay Chris for his services and put it on Robert's account. I asked Robert if he still required me to be at Newbury this coming Friday; no was the reply. I was hoping he would say no, as now I might just be able to see Laura ride at Hickstead on Friday.

Robert elaborated, "That will not be necessary now, Steve, and thank you for all your help in this matter. It is much appreciated."

I said goodbye to Robert. As I turned off my mobile, though, I couldn't help wondering what indeed he was up to.

Good, I thought as I looked out the window. *Simon is here with Charlie's car.*

Simon came into the office to do the paperwork. Charlie had arranged her insurance. Both the girls and Ricky went to inspect Charlie's new set of wheels, and within a few minutes, all the paperwork was complete. I gave Simon his cheque for the purchase, and as we left the office, I told Charlie and Ricky to take the rest of the afternoon off and share some quality time together. They said they would go down to Brighton for a few hours, so I asked Ricky to drop off the copy of the VT for DCI Heyes at Brighton Police Station, in Edward Street. Ricky said, "No problem, Boss." I thought it was the least I could do, given the mayhem the last week or so, and the fact that things seemed to have settled down considerably. It was a lot quieter now than it had been, so at last we could all get our breath back.

As they left, Laura shouted out, "Supper at six! Would you stop by at the supermarket, Charlie, and get me some of my favourite cider?"

"Yep," was the reply. "I will get some Bacardi Breezers as well. I feel like a drink tonight, if that's all right with you, Steve." Charlie came over and gave me a great big kiss. "You know what that's for," she said.

Yes, I did, and I felt elated that we had found some happiness for Charlie as well. "Yes, we will have drinks tonight," I said in response to Charlie. "Some Foster's lager for Ricky and me." I was really getting to like this midweek drinking; obviously, I hadn't realised what I was missing.

Tom the locksmith texted me that he would not be able to make it until 5.30 p.m.

Good! I thought. "How do you fancy one of my special massages?" I asked Laura.

"I think we could work up a really good appetite in three hours," she replied.

We ran up the stairs together, but Laura got to the bathroom first and quickly grabbed the baby oil. "My turn this time, Steve," she insisted. "Get stripped off and on this bed now!"

I obeyed without question. We discovered that men do not have as many erogenous zones as women do. Laura knew exactly where mine were, though, and they didn't take a lot of working out with her intensive hands-on approach. We loved each other truly, madly, deeply, and neither of us had any inhibitions about our bodies – we just used them to please each other. By the time five o'clock came round, we had got to page 19 of the Kama Sutra.

"Eighty-one pages to go! Laura said. She was a great learner, and very adventurous by nature. We both had an appetite by now, and the roast to follow wasn't bad either. "Come on, Steve," she said. "One more page for luck! Let's do page 19 before we stop."

I looked on the bright side: at least we would be out the teens! I laughed at that. "All right, Laura, just eighty more pages to go."

We showered together – obviously, we were going to do *everything* together from now on – we put on jeans and T-shirts, and went downstairs. Laura put on the veg and attended the slow-roasting lamb. Tom the locksmith had just arrived to change the locks on the front, kitchen, and office doors. Perhaps we had turned the corner after all.

Charlie and Ricky returned to the farm just before six, and both immediately went to their bedroom for a quick shower and to change their clothes before supper. I had confided in Ricky before they set out to go to Brighton this afternoon that he could sort of move in with Charlie if that was what she wanted; even though they were employees, there was a sort of empathy inside me telling me this was the right course to take. I mostly always went with gut feelings anyway. Charlie never got on with her parents; she never even spoke to them on the phone, as far as I knew. In the four years I had known Charlie now, never once had she even spoken to or about her parents in any form of conversation. Some three years ago, Laura had said it was a taboo subject and to leave well alone. Obviously, time had not healed this rift, circumstances had brought Ricky and Charlie together – circumstances beyond my control – and I for one was not going to keep them apart now that they had found each other. I also wanted to keep a happy house where we would all look out for each other, should we come under yet another attack – heaven forbid.

I helped Laura with the roast. She was still giggling about position number 19 in the Kama Sutra. I think Charlie had purchased the book in a shop near the hospital and given it to Laura to cheer her up during our enforced stay a few days ago. It was the doggy-fashion position. Laura had decided she quite liked that one.

"When we have some quality time again, Steve, let's do that one again before we move forward to position 20."

Charlie and Ricky had now changed and were coming down the stairs to join us for supper. We laid the table, and Ricky sorted out a few Foster's lagers for us lads. Charlie had a Breezer and Laura had her favourite strawberry cider. We kept the beers in a separate fridge in the kitchen, one of those shelf fridges with a glass door that just chilled the bottled or canned drinks; we always kept it well stocked up.

The slow-roast lamb was delicious. We had it with broccoli, carrots, and mangetout. Laura made some mint gravy to finish the roast off; her mum had passed on the secret recipe of the mint gravy when Laura was about 12, she confided in us as we sat round the table talking, laughing, and, of course, drinking.

We never bothered with desserts; however, we did get the biscuits and cheeseboard out for nibbles as the evening passed on. We talked for hours, and come ten o'clock, we were all quite tired. Laura was even getting a little sleepy. (*I wonder why!* I thought to myself, with a grin.) Ricky and I did the dishes and checked both the main doors to the house: they were bolted and secure.

The girls had both gone to bed. On entering our bedroom, I found Laura fast asleep; I expected Ricky found Charlie the same. I went into the bathroom, brushed my teeth, and got into bed. I cuddled up to Laura and straight away fell into a deep sleep.

It had been a highly productive but exhausting day; however, I wouldn't have changed it for the world.

When I woke up, Laura was already up, showered, and in her riding gear.

I quipped, "What's position 20 then, fancy dress? Ha, ha, ha!" I did have a sense of humour after all.

Laura laughed too, and then added, "Don't forget when we get back to the KS – as she now called it – we start on position 19."

"Okay," I replied.

"It's Fred II's day today, Steve. I need to school him so he'll be ready for Friday at Hickstead."

We had planned for Laura to hack him over to Hickstead, but the recent turn of events in the last week or so meant a change of plan. Given the present situation, I would get Chris Collins to box Fred II over to the showground when he got back from the Hot Tea transport job for my client Robert Argonaut. I was still none the wiser of Robert's plan for Hot Tea.

Laura agreed. "Better to be safe than sorry," she said.

Laura and Charlie would travel in the horsebox also, whilst Ricky and I would travel over in one of the company vans, following the horsebox over to the showground.

When Charlie and Ricky were up and about, just after eight, we let them know our plans.

Laura went out into the yard. Mickey had already mucked out and fed Fred II, but was nowhere to be seen; he really was a spook. Our front-door marksman was less of a spook, and could clearly be seen from the farmhouse front windows. His shift replacement had just turned up for the day shift, driving a new white Mercedes estate car. "Police" was emblazoned on both sides of the vehicle, which also stated, "Tactical Firearms Response Vehicle". The chief inspector was really putting it in the face of our drug-dealing murderers.

Mickey suddenly appeared out of nowhere. "I want to show you someone," he said to me. "Come with me."

I followed him. We went into the yard. Laura was grooming Fred II, oblivious to our presence. Mickey took me over to one of the boxes, as far away from the tack room as possible; next to the big garage door, there was a man expertly tied up, looking worse for wear. Mickey whipped the tape off his mouth. The man shrieked, "You bastard!" Mickey whacked him with the back of his hand.

Mickey said to me, "Do you know him?"

"No, absolutely not," I replied.

Mickey said, "He tried to get into the yard last night. He had a syringe on him, full of heroin. I think he was after the horse, Laura's horse. What do you want me to do with him?" Mickey asked, adding, "I can kill him and dump him out the back on the scrubland, if you like. I've already dug a hole; nobody will find him. The way that Mickey said it sounded like he had already done it many times before.

"Yeah," I said. "Why not waste him?"

I have never seen so much fear in a man's face before. The man tried to scream as Mickey got the syringe out of his coat pocket. He tested it to see if it was working okay by squirting some of the liquid in the man's face; he then pushed the needle through the lobe of the man's right ear; he seemed to feel the prick but didn't know the needle had gone all the way through his ear. The man by now was a quivering wreck; the smell suggested he had literally shit himself. Whatever he did know, he told us. A man who had paid him £500 to kill Laura's horse; the money had been given to him in an Epsom pub on Monday night, and the man he described fully fitted the description of Dicky fucking Head.

I went to the office to get a recent image of Dicky Head, returned to the box, and showed the man the image.

"Yes, that's him," said the man. "Without doubt, absolutely, that's him."

It was definitely Dicky Head who had paid someone to kill Laura's horse by filling him up with the syringe of heroin.

We hosed the man off, and I got him some old clothes from the tack room. The laundry van had arrived that Mickey had previously ordered to take away the shit arse. I had used Ricky's video camera to video the confession, minus the syringe of heroin being stuck in the man's ear. MI5 had their own secure unit at Gatwick; no doubt he would be taken away for further interrogation. MI5 had a different way of doing things that brought instant results! Mickey sure was a professional, and, boy, was I glad he was on my side.

I never mentioned a word of this to Charlie, Laura, or Ricky. Laura was still grooming Fred II, whilst Charlie and Ricky were in the office gazing into each other eyes, oblivious to what had just gone on in the yard. And I planned to keep it that way until after the show on Friday.

CHAPTER 12

It was a beautiful Wednesday morning in August. It was going to be busy, and thanks to Mickey, we had already landed the catch of the day. I went into the kitchen and put the kettle on. I made four coffees: two were for Laura and me, and two were for Charlie and Ricky, who were both busily beavering away in the office on their computers.

Ricky was also on the phone to his colleague Allan, who was in charge of the Ascot operation – Operation Mousetrap – that was about to go down. The office clock was fast approaching 10 a.m., and all ten of the team at Ascot were in the field and fully operational. We always gave great attention to detail; that was how my company functioned best. We respected our clients, and above all, their right to privacy; however, breaking the law by premeditated criminal actions of murder meant that my company would have to at some stage decide the balance between privacy and justice. In my mind, justice was going to be the rightful winner.

Robert Argonaut texted me to say that the funds for the purchase of Hot Tea had now been electronically transferred to my firm's client account. I in turn texted Jonathan Ridger to tell him the money transfer to his account would now take place tomorrow, Thursday, not Friday, as had been our previous envisaged arrangement. Furthermore, Chris Collins would now be picking Hot Tea up on Friday morning at eight in the morning; however, the destination was unknown, at Robert's instruction. Jonathan texted me back just before 10.30 to say that the arrangements were fine by him.

Damn, I thought. *I forgot to take Laura out her coffee.*
I made her a fresh cup and delivered it personally.

Laura had just finished grooming Fred II. We went and sat in the tack room, and in between kisses, Laura sipped her coffee.

The bruising on the right side of her temple was now a yellowy mauve colour. The eight stitches were holding firm, but Laura was sure to have a scar.

How sad for such a beautiful girl, I couldn't help thinking.

Laura read my mind. As I touched and caressed her beautiful facial features, she said, "War wounds, Steve." And then she added, "A small price to pay for the man I am so deeply and passionately in love with."

Laura then commented on my two shiners, which were going the same colour as her temple; the bruising was beginning to disappear as well. We were both on the mend.

Laura said she was going to work Fred in the ménage for an hour. She never left anything to chance with the horses, and everything had to be spot on with regard to detail.

I thought, *I've definitely taught you well, Laura.*

Laura wanted to give Fred II the best possible chance of winning on Friday, and she knew that meant putting in the hard graft and groundwork at home. She was indeed a girl who had blossomed into a beautiful young lady, and it had been an honour for me to have been part of that transformation and to witness the transition. I was in awe of her in so many ways. They say opposites attract; well, so do people who share the same characteristics. Laura and I were so similar in so many ways: we tended to love the same things, we both were ambitious, we both loved our jobs, we both were adventurous, and, most of all, we shared our ups and downs. Our bond was one of knowing our hearts were for each other. I was perhaps a bit slow to realise that. *Fate moves in mysterious ways,* I mused. Our deep love for each other, though, I believed was the greatest gift mankind had to offer to us mere mortals.

As Laura took her bridle and saddle out of the tack room to tack up Fred, she stood by the door, turned around, and with the broadest possible smile, said, "Destiny brought us together, Steve; some things in life are just meant to be. Let's go with the flow."

I replied, "Then to the Lord we are truly thankful."

Laura giggled with one of her girlie laughs – inwardly, I hoped she would never grow out of that. She said one more word as she left the tack room: *nineteen.*

"Yeah," I said, and then I started laughing too.

John, my operative on the Dicky Head case file, rang into the office to report; he brought Charlie up to date on this particular case file, the search for the elusive Mr Head. So far, in the Lambourn and Newbury area, John had drawn a blank, no sightings whatsoever. Charlie passed the message over to me, as I was now sitting in the office at one of the computer desks, with another coffee. I asked Charlie if she would give me the cordless phone so that I could speak to John directly. I then informed John that Dicky Head had most definitely been sighted in the Epsom area on Monday night; I instructed John to literally stake out Dicky Head's home just outside Lambourn, until further notice. Charlie asked me how I knew that information, and I informed her that the chief inspector had contacted Mickey much earlier – about 7 a.m. – and that they had apprehended a man in the Sussex area who'd been about to injure or perhaps kill a horse that was due to compete in the Hickstead showjumping event later this week. (I didn't say which horse, of course, and I also left out the bit about the syringe full of heroin he had on him; my clever lot would put two and two together.) I left it at that; not quite the truth, I realised, but this version of events would suffice for now.

I contacted Lord Oakley on my mobile phone. It was a for-your-ears-only type of call, to update him on the search for Dicky Head. After all, he had just been a party to an attempt to kill or seriously injure a competition horse worth thousands of pounds, which was a criminal offence. Lord Oakley was deeply shocked at this revelation. I asked him if Head still had the use of a company car.

"Yes," said Lord Oakley, and he gave me the registration number, make, and model. It was a Ford Focus Ghia estate car.

I also asked if Head had any company plastic to pay for expenses, which Lord Oakley confirmed that he did, and then gave me all the details of the account card. This was a break for us: at least we could track Head's movements and whereabouts from now on through monitoring his credit card. Lord Oakley suggested that I must notify the police immediately of this attempted criminal act. I replied that I would share this information with the chief inspector who was in charge of several other cases that could be linked to this one.

Lord Oakley now became a bit more inquisitive. "You mean there's more, Steve?"

I let him know that his other steward, Tim Holland, had contacted us about making some discreet enquiries into Dicky Head, and the fact that Mr and Mrs Holland were of the opinion that Head was responsible for their son's beating. Lord Oakley then informed me that Tim had given him some details of this event, and that he, Lord Oakley, was aware that Head's name was in the frame. The Jockey Club Head was definitely on the radar now. Lord Oakley left it to me to deal with the situation as I saw fit. I told him I would contact the chief inspector immediately.

DCI Heyes answered his mobile on the second ring. The first comment he uttered was that he intended to reopen the file on Dicky Head in regard to Giles Holland's beating, the GBH assault. Mickey had contacted the chief inspector earlier and brought him up to speed with the early morning events. The arsehole Mickey had apprehended earlier that morning was now at the MI5 holding centre at Gatwick, near the airport. The arsehole's name was Pete Gregory, and he was squealing. A low-life scumbag from the Epsom area in Surrey, he had a string of offences to his name, among them: horse theft, vehicle theft, petrol theft, robbery, drugs, and affray, including GBH. Oh, how the chief inspector wanted to get his hands on Dicky fucking Head now.

I gave the chief inspector the registration number, make, and model of the car Head was driving, and explained that it was a company car either belonging or leased to the Jockey Club.

"We'll put out an APB, Steve," said DCI Heyes, referring to an all-points bulletin, a nationwide call to track or find the elusive Mr Head. However, the chief inspector said the orders would be to observe from a distance, as he wanted to see who Head's accomplices were – and also to whom Mr Head would indeed lead us.

I informed the chief inspector that Laura would be competing at the Hickstead show on Friday afternoon at about three o'clock. He was way ahead of me: he intended to flood the showground with some police and plenty of plain-clothes detectives on Friday, Saturday, and Sunday.

"Laura will be safe," said the chief inspector. And then he added, "You don't have to worry about that, Steve. One of our friendly marksman guarding your front gate will be on point duty at a safe distance, with a telescopic high-powered rifle."

DCI Heyes was taking absolutely no chances whatsoever, which was a relief and a great comfort to know.

The gates at Ascot opened at around 11.30 a.m., with the first race scheduled for 2 p.m. The last of the six races was due off at 4.50 p.m. We were going to be looking for specific punters, with specific patterns of betting. Allan phoned in to the office at just after eleven to say the Tote employees had arrived on the coach and were now being despatched to their various positions; they had gone through the rota on the coach, which had been prearranged with the help of the Tote security. The manager on the coach would tell the employees what building they would be working at, and the supervisor of that particular building would allocate the Tote windows each employee would be operating from. This was the usual; we didn't change the way they operated. To avoid suspicion or possible lingering doubt, numbers were written down next to the operator names, and the operators would take up their positions for the afternoon's racing. Therefore, we had our six suspects right where we wanted them. Allan would further update Charlie at noon in order to keep Mother up to speed; he would then provide further updates throughout the afternoon, on the hour.

Charlie checked our client account to verify that Mr Argonaut's money had arrived for me to send on to Jonathan Ridger, so as to conclude the Hot Tea deal; this would be completed first thing in the morning. I rang Chris Collins just to make sure he was still able to do the transport job on Friday morning; furthermore, if time allowed, I asked if he could take Laura and her horse to the show at Hickstead in the early afternoon, at around one o'clock.

Chris was dead keen. "I wouldn't miss it for the world, Steve," he informed me. "Creating quite a stir in the village is your Laura, Steve!"

"My Laura!" I said in a surprised exclamation. "Chris, she's a natural with horses."

"Cyril down the road told me so, Steve," Chris replied.

I was pleased for Laura; all that hard work deserved some credit. Although Cyril Night never actually said so, he was a believer in her talents also, if judging by the times he would ring me up now with a horse problem of which he wanted Laura to sort out for him.

Aussie was next on the phone; I answered it on the second ring. Charlie and Ricky had not had a second to spare all morning, so I didn't mind.

"Hey, cobber, it's Aussie. How you feeling, sport?" he said and then added, "You said to give you a ring midweek."

There was no mistaking Aussie. "Laura and I are doing just great, Aussie," I said. I asked if he was working over the weekend.

He replied, "Yeah, sorry, sport if there was something you had in mind."

"Oh well," I said, explaining I was going to invite him to lunch at Hickstead on Friday as a sort of thank-you for the help with regard to our hospitalisation.

"You don't have to thank me; just doing my job, cobber," he said. "But as I'm working at Hickstead over the weekend, I will take you up on the tucker, sport. Do like me grub," he added.

He further informed me that there were always two emergency crews at Hickstead on standby throughout the show. The first thought that came into my head was, *Well, that's reassuring.* I told Aussie that Laura would be jumping in the all-England Grade C Final in the main ring at three o'clock, and to meet me in the members' bar at two o'clock, where we could lunch and watch the showjumping at the same time.

"Yeah, okay. No sweat," said Aussie. "Will see you Friday then, cobber."

"Thanks for ringing, Aussie. See you Friday," I said.

Good, I thought as I put the phone down. *Another loyal man on the ground, and medical backup if required.*

I wanted complete lockdown round Laura, and it had to be done without her knowing. Slowly, slowly, like a game of chess, I was manipulating the pieces, putting them in the right places. I was outsmarting the murderous bastards, whoever they might turn out to be.

Coffee time! I made three coffees. Laura was still schooling Fred, so I took the coffees into the office and handed them out. Charlie and Ricky worked even better since their coming together, and I hoped that, at long last, whatever it was that troubled Charlie so deeply would soon be released, and the burden that had troubled her for so long could be vanquished, for good.

Gary was the next of my operatives to phone in to the office. Again, I answered on the second ring.

"Hey, Boss, this might be a coincidence, but I thought you should be informed all the same," Gary said. He filled me in on the latest details regarding Naughty Natalie. Noel and Natalie Henry had just had a blazing row, right on the forecourt of a petrol station just outside Newmarket. "I followed them in, Boss, and managed to tape about five minutes of the conversation," Gary informed me. "The argument was over the fact that Natalie wants to go to the showjumping at Hickstead this coming weekend, to meet some friends; her husband doesn't want her to go, calls them 'riff-raff'. And get this, Boss, Natalie told Noel he can fuck himself from now on then! She told him she had been invited to Hickstead by the

Cobbs, those people with the shoe chain from Northampton. Evidently, they have their own private members' box at Hickstead, overlooking the main ring. She said she would do the trainer's wife bit with Noel and attend the race meeting at Newbury on Friday, as they have two runners, but she would then travel on to Hickstead, where she plans to spend the weekend."

I asked Gary if he thought that Natalie could be doing drugs, maybe recreational use.

Gary replied, "Well, she certainly likes a drink and a fuck, and I don't suppose she's that choosy. Maybe to her, any dick will do. Maybe she just doesn't get a kick anymore of being pissed and occasionally fucked, and is now looking for a more self-abusing pastime. It is a distinct possibility, Boss, though she seems to me to be the sort who would maybe prefer to snort a line of charlie (cocaine) rather than put needles in herself; coke seems to be the favourite recreational drug of the jockeys and stable lads in Newmarket at the moment. And, furthermore, Boss, there always seems to be an ample supply of cocaine in the area at the moment," Gary said. He then added that Natalie was a very attractive lady, about 27, 28; tallish, with an incredible catwalk figure.

I replied, "Thank you, Gary, this is really interesting news. Well done; excellent work! Furthermore, I want you to stay in Newmarket until Friday. Oh, and by the way, have you managed to put a name to the Daihatsu Hijet mystery man that she shagged, of which you witnessed in the back of his van?"

"No, sorry, Boss," he replied. "But, hey, if I give you the registration number of the Hi-jet, maybe you could ask your friend the chief inspector to run it through the computer for a name and address."

I informed Gary that would be my next job, and then I asked him to follow Mr and Mrs Henry when they set off to Newbury on Friday morning. "They'll probably leave by nine. You can follow them down on to the M25, and then until they branch off on to the M4, as that would be their most direct route to Newbury. I want you to then come back to Sayers Common, and I would like you back here for noon."

Gary said, "Okay, Boss."

"You have a few days left to compile more information, Gary. Try to find out if Natalie is fucking for money, or even drugs; find out if she is some sort of jockey junkie, not just fucking, but some sort of distributor in Newmarket. Find out if Noel Henry knows but hasn't exactly told me the truth. Use your Jockey Club badge; tell whoever you call on it's an official

JC investigation. Visit Noel's ex-wife Julia; she's got an axe to grind, and she's a trainer herself now. See if there is any burning resentment for some sort of retribution. I'll clear it with Lord Oakley."

"Okay, Boss," Gary said again.

I was suddenly very interested in Naughty Natalie.

"One last thing, Gary. Make sure you update Charlie every morning before 9.30, please."

"Okay, Boss. Speak to you tomorrow."

It was soon lunchtime. I made four rounds of sandwiches and put the kettle on; it was past midday.

Laura came in from the yard, planted a big juicy smacker on my cheek, and said, "Fred II schooled brilliantly."

Mickey the silent assassin never let Laura out of his vision all the time Laura was schooling Fred, though Laura never knew.

"Fred never even touched a twig," Laura said. "I put him in long to a double upright. I put him in short. He corrects me, even though I feed him the wrong message, Steve, and he just jumps his way out of trouble. I wanted to know, if I were to give him the wrong message, would he be clever enough to know how to get me out of trouble on Friday? If I put him in short on a tight turn, or went long chasing the clock in a jump-off, what would he do? I tried everything to get him to knock a pole down, but he is one smart horse."

"The person sitting on his back was smarter," I told Laura as I took the sandwiches and coffee through to the office.

We were all hands on deck at the moment, and information would be coming through from Ascot anytime now. Allan called in, telling Charlie there was nothing new to report; Operation Mousetrap had started.

I pondered what this afternoon's operation would tell us. Would we be able to crack this case?

I joined Laura in the kitchen once again, and demanded the rest of that big juicy kiss. Laura willingly obliged.

And then she said, "Steve, prior to leaving the hospital, I had a quiet word with Dr Goble and told her that I needed to get some more of … um … you know … the pill. I told her I had run out. Dr Goble asked me if you were my husband or partner, and I said we had been partners for quite a long time and that I was still working on the other bit. I hope you don't mind. Steve. After all, it was a very little white, and one for a good cause."

I laughed. "Nurse Becky asked me virtually the same question: 'Is Laura your wife or partner?' I replied, 'Well, she's my partner at the moment, and one day, probably, maybe …'"

Laura loved that remark, and she nearly choked on her sandwich as she started laughing whilst eating, giggling in that girlie giggle that I so loved. After a few seconds, she said, "I got Dr Goble to give me a prescription for a month's supply."

"Good," I said. "Just as I planned."

Laura replied, "Great minds must think alike then after all."

Laura suddenly become very serious. "I want to talk to you later, Steve," she said. "If we are an item – and I do so want to be with you, and I do love you so much – there is something I need to tell you." She took a breath. "I need to take this burden off my back that I've been carrying for far too long now. It's the issue that Charlie has, you know that taboo one that has been hurting her since she has got romantically involved for the first time. Sorry to put this on you, Steve, but a problem shared, and all that—"

I interrupted her. "Then let's have an early night."

Laura replied, Okay. Nineteen." I started laughing, and then she added, "Hundred hours."

We were going to bed at seven o'clock tonight; the return of a doggy-fashion session would have to wait a while longer.

It was fast approaching one o'clock, and Laura volunteered to man one of the computers and take over answering the phone for the rest of the day. It was going to be a hectic afternoon; however, there were now four of us in the office. The spooks were covering us front and rear. Operation Mousetrap, bring it on.

CHAPTER 13

At lunchtime, Allan was on the telephone, calling from Ascot with his one o'clock update. "Nothing unusual so far," he reported.

The betting on the Tote was light, but Allan insisted that as the hour progressed and approached two o'clock, it would become much heavier; the punters would be placing their place-pot and jackpot bets. (These bets were to forecast either all six winners, or a horse to be placed in the first six races on the card, a popular bet with small-stake punters, but with the potential for big returns. Another popular bet for small stakes was the forecast bet where you nominated the first two horses past the post in the correct order. Dividends for such bets have been known to pay thousands just for a £1 stake; however, these were not the sort of bets we were looking out for.)

We were interested in something out of the ordinary but at the same time not so unusual as to arouse suspicion – a bet most punters would wager, but a bet that was somehow different. An odd sort of bet that left very little to chance but could deliver a profit of nearly 100 per cent, thereby doubling the punter's outlay. In other words, a bet that stood very little chance of failing to deliver. Was there a special race, for instance, that would be targeted? A set amount of money that would be staked at Ascot today or maybe at some other track tomorrow or maybe at Newbury on Friday? We did not know anything for sure, so we were just looking for the unusual.

If we missed it, we had the Wharr's team to back us up with forensics and detailed powers of analysis. The Wharr's team was on standby and would use all the sophisticated equipment at headquarters in Windsor this evening, and during the early hours of Thursday if necessary, to try to find what we perceived to be a scam or some sort of money-laundering operation.

It was indeed a tall order, and whoever had developed and conceived this way of making money was a very clever person indeed.

It was now approaching two o'clock, time for the first race at Ascot. Allan telephoned in to the office with his hourly update. Charlie answered the telephone.

"Nothing new to report," said Allan. "Although there is a high volume of business now being turned over by the Tote service, which is not unusual for a grade 1 track like Ascot, with a good card, and especially a big meeting like today."

Charlie relayed Allan's comments to me, and I signalled her to ask him about the elusive Mr Head. "Allan, out of curiosity, is Dicky Head on duty today?" she asked.

Allan replied, "No, Charlie, but he is listed to be on duty at Newbury on Friday."

"Okay, that's interesting," said Charlie. "I will put that into Mother. Thank you, Allan. Hear from you again in an hour then."

John contacted the office at about 2.15 p.m., to report on the Dicky Head case. "All set up, Boss," he reported. "There are some roadworks going on outside the road where the Heads' house is situated, so I will blend in with the workmen on the job; shouldn't be a problem, and I won't look out of place. I'll stick a pair of overalls on, and a hard hat, and if anyone asks what I'm doing, I will just reply, 'Health and Safety Executive'."

I indicate to Charlie this was okay, and she relayed the same to Allan.

The favourite won the first race at Ascot, and fancied horses filled the places, so the punters were off to a good start. The second-race runners had just left the paddock and were going down to the start. The four of us in the office were able to follow the action from Ascot with the help of the big 46-inch television hanging on one of the walls in the office. This also allowed us to check on any betting patterns that were out of the ordinary. Were there any horses, for instance, being "backed off the boards". (This was a racing term for a serious amount of money following one particular horse and being back at any price the layers put up on their boards; being backed off the boards simply meant that the bookmakers would simply refuse to lay a price anymore. A similar term in racing was a "springer in the market", when an outsider suddenly, and without reason, started attracting big money in the ring, and that horse, which had originally been a 33 to 1 no-hoper suddenly just became a 10 to 1 shot; if the money kept coming, then the bookies would cut the odds to 8s, then 6s, and even 4s – and sometimes shorter still. In other words, a springer in the market was a horse that had been backed off the boards, usually surprisingly so; not quite the same as in Hot Tea's case at Goodwood, but definitely a similar pattern.)

For us, at the moment, it was a question of logging all information, no matter however trivial it might seem. This was Charlie's main task, and it was the reason why she had to spend so much time on the storage of data: we had to keep up with events as they happened.

I was inwardly beginning to feel more apprehensive. Many times today I had wondered whether I'd placed enough emphasis on cracking this case, without having had too much serious evidence to go on. Everything about this case was circumstantial, combined with my dogged belief in my own intuition.

Laura read my mind. "Whatever happens today, Steve, it will be necessary in cracking this case," she said. "We will have some evidence to show at the end of the day; we just have to decipher and recognise that evidence, and not overlook anything."

"Have you a plan B?" Charlie asked. "What have you in mind?"

Laura then stated the obvious. "Well, Newbury looks like it's going to be eventful on Friday. Maybe we should carry out today's Operation Mousetrap at Newbury as well." She added, "We could call it Operation Mousetrap, Part II!"

We all looked at each other in astonishment.

Laura will have to spend more time in the office, was the thought that immediately crossed my mind.

"Why didn't I think of that?" Charlie said. "Absolutely! Great call, Laura."

Ricky added, "Yeah, we will need a comparison, anyway, to get to the bottom of this."

I agreed wholeheartedly. "We are unanimous then?"

All four of us agreed to the proposal.

"Charlie, when Allan telephones next hour, would you inform him of our decision to set up the operation again at Newbury on Friday?"

"Yes, Steve," she said.

It was now approaching the off time for the second race at Ascot. We watched the race on the office television, and the favourite duly obliged, winning by 4 lengths. Two races down, and four to go. So far, no strange betting patterns had emerged. I thought now that I had probably overreacted to the situation; however, thanks to Laura, we had an alternate plan – Operation Mousetrap, Part II – to enhance our chances of cracking this case.

Ricky called out, "Coffees, everybody?" He received three yeses, so he went into the kitchen to make them, hotly followed by Laura, whose intent was to be first to grab the biscuit tin.

Charlie was still banging away on the keyboard when Ricky returned, after a few minutes, with the tray of coffees. Laura had her mouth full with the chocolate bourbons, which were her favourite.

Our conversation then turned to this evening's supper: Ricky and Charlie both fancied Chinese; Laura and I instantly agreed that our local pub, the Castle, just down the road, was the best around; it did a Chinese takeaway menu of which we had a copy in the office, so we could ring our order through. As it was less than a mile away, Ricky said he would go and pick it up at six. The restaurant part of the Castle Pub had recently been leased separately to the pub by a Chinese restaurant chain, and the food was superb; it had a hundred seats in the restaurant and was open seven days a week, from five to eleven every evening. A thought suddenly crossed my mind: Jane used to love our takeaways when just the two of us were at the farm. But I was going to love takeaways even more with Laura, that was for sure!

We were going to eat earlier this evening because Laura wanted to have an early night and unload some deeply troublesome baggage which both she and Charlie had been burdened with for some years now, and which Laura felt was time to get it off their backs. Laura and I informed Ricky and Charlie that we were both going to have an early night tonight; we were going to bed at seven, as Laura and I had earlier agreed. Charlie and Ricky stated that they would stay up until ten to catch any telephone calls or messages, and also to monitor the situation going down at Ascot – not to mention the CCTV footage Wharr's would be studying throughout the night from the day's racing from Ascot.

Meanwhile, the horses were going down for the third race from Ascot – the three o'clock – this was a more open contest of sixteen runners, and the favourite was at the odds of 5 to 1. There were no springers in the market, and this was the most difficult race on the card in terms of trying to predict the winner. It was no surprise, therefore, that the winner was an outsider that returned at the odds of 25 to 1, paying 33 to 1 on the Tote, eight points higher than the starting price. The second was 12 to 1, and the third and fourth were both 10 to 1. The favourite was unplaced, so it probably ruined a lot of place-pot tickets. Still, there were no unusual betting patterns.

Allan telephoned the office just after three with another "nothing further to report". Charlie informed him of my decision to continue Operation Mousetrap, Part II, at Newbury on Friday. "It will be exactly the same operation as today," Charlie informed Allan. "Use the Newbury security staff. Steve will clear it with the Jockey Club."

Meanwhile, I called Lord Oakley on his mobile at Ascot, where I knew he was attending the day's racing.

When he answered his mobile, I said, "It's Steve, here, Lord Oakley. We are going to run this operation again at Newbury on Friday. Furthermore, although we have nothing to report on today's action, we are adamant that we will gather evidence today with regard to some sort of fraudulent act or scam." I also added Ricky's earlier comment that we needed a comparison.

Lord Oakley duly obliged, saying that he would inform the Newbury security team and executive immediately to let them know to fully cooperate with DIRTS, and also the police if need be.

Good, I thought as I put the phone down I had hoped for a simple conclusion to this case; however, we were not going to get one. We were going to have to turn over every damn stone. I just couldn't help wondering where Dicky bloody Head fitted in to all this. Was he the brains behind it all? No, surely not. I believed him to be devious but not clever, so I dismissed that notion from my thoughts.

Laura came over, sat on my lap, and proffered the biscuit tin. "Can I tempt you?" she said.

I replied, "Not with a biscuit."

Charlie said, "It's not fair how Laura can eat a tin of biscuits a day and not put on any weight! I only have to look at them, and I put on a pound."

Ricky and I both laughed.

Laura had another chocolate bourbon in her mouth, as if to tease Charlie, and offered me half, of which I accepted.

The fourth race at Ascot was the three thirty. There were only six runners; once again, the favourite won easily, although at odds of even money, which meant that for every pound you put on, you got two pounds back. Yet again, no betting patterns emerging. I started wondering about the four o'clock race: a handicap sprint on the straight course, and twenty-eight runners. There was an old racing saying: "the bigger the field the bigger the certainty"; I wondered whether this was going to be the race. There was a warm 4-to-1 favourite, and it was 8 to 1 and bigger, the rest of the field. So at least the race gave us something to feed our growing frustrations and curiosity on.

Allan telephoned at least ten minutes before the race was due off.

"Hi, Allan," said Charlie.

Allan replied, "Tell Steve we have a strange betting pattern emerging."

When Charlie relayed Allan's comment, all of us in the office clicked on the loudspeaker part of the internal telephone system.

"Go on, Allan," I said. We were all ears in the office.

Allan continued, "If you were going to back a horse for a place only, most people or punters would back in denominations of £1, £2, £5, £10, or £20. But so far, on this 6-furlong sprint race, the Tote has had over fifty bets of £18, place only, on the favourite, and that's odd. If this betting pattern continues, we will have had about £2,000 placed on the favourite, in £18 single bets. That is weird, to say the least! The current price of the favourite is 4 to 1, and it is 9 to 1 and upwards the rest of the field. If the favourite finishes in the first four, the likelihood is that the scammers would have doubled their money, from £2,000 to £4,000 – a 100 per cent profit!" Allan said.

Allan went on, "The average punter is always after value and Joe Public; if they see the dividend return on the favourite is way less than normal, they will look elsewhere for a horse to back with their small bets of £1, £2, £5, and £10 wagers, which increases the return on the favourite if less people are backing him. These days, the computerised odds and possible returns are there displayed for all to see, and if the dividend looks like it will return less than even money, it will deter people from backing the favourite for a place. What the mug punter doesn't understand is that by backing another horse in the same race, he is actually keeping the dividend up on the favourite, so it's a win-win situation for the scam. And I have to say, it's all above board."

I thanked Allan for his synopsis, and he rang off.

The four of us then quickly went about our homework; we just simply couldn't see the favourite not being in the first four past the post.

We only had a few minutes, though, before the off – just enough time for me to contact Lord Oakley once again. Perhaps he could offer an alternative opinion. We had to take into account the way the scam worked and whether the scammers were actually operating within the rules of racing. Lord Oakley answered his mobile immediately, and I quickly explained the situation to him. He agreed with me that on balance, if there were perhaps fifty or a hundred people each putting £18 on a horse for a place bet, we would have to prove that they were all in a conspiracy to manipulate the odds in an open market, in which the Tote betting operated with instant odds for all to see before and after punters placed their bets; it was up to the public to decide on whether to place a bet, and indeed there was always the option to not bet at all.

I agreed with Lord Oakley's assessment, adding, "What we can do, though, is to scrutinise the winners when they pick up their winnings. Of course, should the favourite oblige and finish in the first four past the post, we could further cross-reference the winners with the CCTV footage to see if they bought their tickets from our six Tote employees who were under suspicion." This, eventually, would have to be our course of action.

At four precisely, the race was off and ran at a breakneck speed. The favourite led right to inside the final furlong up the stands rail; there was absolutely no chance he wasn't going to finish in the first four past the post. The favourite got collared right on the line and was beaten a short head in to second place by another outsider at odds of 16 to 1. The starting price of the favourite returned at 4 to 1, and the place return was an even £2. The scam had paid off, and the scammers – whoever they were – had doubled their money, turning £2,000 into £4,000.

There was something that none of the four of us could quite put our finger on, though. It just never seemed to quite stack up: so many people were involved – over a hundred people to earn just two grand – we weren't buying it. There had to be something more sinister to all this; we just couldn't see it, though, no matter how hard we tried. We all hoped that Allan and the team of operatives and security staff had better luck on the ground at Ascot.

The last race was an uneventful affair, with the heavy odds-on favourite in a seven-runner field winning by 6 lengths at the odds of 4 to 6 on.

Allan was going to telephone in at five, in some twenty minutes' time, which gave us enough time to order our takeaway for six o'clock. We eventually settled on a set meal for four, which consisted of spare ribs with salt and chilli, seaweed, sesame prawn, shredded beef, double-cooked roast pork, lemon chicken, sweet-and-sour prawn balls, and egg-fried rice. Ricky telephoned the order though, and we all suddenly became very hungry indeed. Ricky confirmed to the restaurant that he would pick up at six. Charlie was still on the computer, and Laura had gone into the yard to feed Fred II and tidy up his bed for the night. Mickey was nowhere to be seen, as usual, although his grey van was still in the ten-vehicle parking area next to the yard. The police marksman was seated in his Mercedes estate car outside where my front gates used to be. I reckoned we were making some sort of progress, but oh so boringly slowly. I told Ricky to go and have a shower and freshen up for supper, as he was going to be picking up our takeaway later. Now was a good time for us all to start getting ready for supper, since it looked like we might be quiet for an hour or so.

Allan telephoned in to the office bang on five. I told Charlie I would answer the phone. He confirmed that 112 tickets had been purchased that were £18 placed on the favourite. This was near the £2,000 estimated; however, only half of those tickets had been paid out on so far – that is, as of five o'clock – which was unusual. Furthermore, Allan pointed out that there appeared to be eight people who were repeatedly cashing the tickets in, and they appeared to have all the £18 tickets between them.

I immediately instructed Allan to use all the available staff to follow these eight people whenever they next cashed their tickets in. "See where they go and who they talk to, within the next hour, up to when the Tote windows would shut at six," I said.

Maybe, just maybe, we would get the lead we were so crying out for.

Allan did as I instructed, reporting back further that he had a word with the Tote manager at the course, and they decided that for the last forty-five minutes, they would only keep one Tote building open, with ten serving windows for ticket holders to redeem their winnings. This was normal practice, but it helped us out immensely, as we could just about cover all ten windows with our ten operatives. We also managed to get some images of all the eight people who carried on cashing in their tickets right up to six o'clock; they never went to the same window twice to cash in their tickets, and, eventually, all the winning tickets were cashed in.

We had six suspect Tote employees, and now at least eight people who were in on the scam for sure; however, as far as we could ascertain, they had not broken any rules or committed any crimes. It was the perfect scam. That said, it would be up to Wharr's to provide us with some tangible evidence if we were to be able to prove some form of conspiracy, or even fraud. Would they find something on the CCTV tapes tonight? We would have to sleep on it and wait until the morning.

"Thanks, Allan," I said at the end of his report.

"Right, Boss. I'll be back at the office tomorrow morning at ten," Allan said.

We said goodnight, and I put the phone down.

Ricky had just left to pick up the takeaway, and both Charlie and Laura were having showers and getting ready for supper. I manned the telephones in the office until Charlie reappeared back in the office at about 5.45 p.m. – just enough time for me to shower and shave before Ricky got back with our takeaway feast.

As I passed Laura on the stairs – I was going up, and she was coming down – we kissed each other. I went into our bedroom and then into the en suite bathroom. Laura had left me another little yellow stick-on message on the mirror: "I love you so much!" It was signed with two crosses as kisses.

I showered, shaved, and wondered about the hidden secrets which Laura wanted to share with me. What sort of burden had they carried between them for the last five or six years? The mirror inspection of my face was showing a distinct improvement in my appearance, and the arnica cream was working well on the bruising, with the shades of mauve and yellow just about showing signs of fading. I heard a vehicle pull up outside, which had to be Ricky. I hurriedly changed and went downstairs to join everybody in the kitchen.

Charlie and Laura had laid the table, Ricky and I had been designated Foster's lagers to drink tonight, judging by the cans on the table. Charlie had her usual Bacardi Breezer, and Laura had her favourite strawberry cider. As we tucked into our feast of Chinese delights, all talk centred around the Ascot scenario; the girls problems, burdens, and taboo subjects were not yet ready for Ricky's ears, at least not at the moment, I deduced, and so I followed and joined in the conversation.

As we chatted in between mouthfuls of delicious food, Charlie posed a question: "Steve, would it not be easier to have a Tote account, and have one big bet?"

I answered as best I could from my experience. "Good question, Charlie. Wouldn't that just make life simpler? However, would you back the favourite for a place in a race if you were only going to get £1.10 back for an outlay of £1? When you back a horse, that should at least pay a return of even money, so that you then get at least £2 back. What we saw today at Ascot is how to trickle the money into the Tote pool without arousing suspicion."

Laura indicated that it was possible that they were using the Tote pool to launder money at the same time that they were making money.

Ricky said, "There's no point in laundering your own money if it's clean in the first place."

I agreed, adding, "The double-cooked roast pork is amazing."

Laura chimed in, "Yeah, it is, and so is the duck. You can't beat a good duck," she added before she realised what she had said.

The rest of us burst out laughing, and Laura joined in after the penny dropped with her description of the duck dish, which Ricky picked up as a freebie extra.

"Well, you know what I mean," Laura added, rather sheepishly, as Charlie refilled our glasses.

Ricky got us back to Ascot with a question. "So what if a hundred or so individuals each bought £18 tickets? How the bloody hell do just eight people suddenly own them?"

I concurred. How indeed did they all end up in the hands of just eight people? That was when the penny really did drop.

Each in our own way, we said that the same thing: the £18 tickets were being used as currency, but what for? That was another question, and we were not sure what the answer was. We just couldn't fathom that one out at the moment. How was it possible for 112 winning tickets to fall into the hands of so few people? Just eight, in fact. How could this happen? We had some serious thinking to do.

The time was now approaching seven, bedtime tonight for Laura and me. Charlie and Ricky tidied up the kitchen. Laura went to the drinks fridge and got herself a two bottles of cider. Charlie and Ricky had made themselves coffees, and they retired to the lounge to watch a film; should the telephone ring, they would answer from the lounge.

Laura and I went up to our bedroom, and after both of us visited the bathroom, brushed our teeth, and checked our rapidly improving wounds, we were ready for bed. We puffed the pillows up, Laura took the top off one of her bottles of cider, and we sort of sat up, making ourselves comfy. Laura had her head on my chest, sitting between my legs and leaning back. We were sort of both facing forward, propped up by the pillows. the Sade CD was still in the player, so we put it on as background music. I told Laura I loved her so very much, and that was when the floodgates opened. I put her bottle of cider on the bedside table and just held her as she cried her eyes out, floods upon floods of tears that just would not stop. I just kissed her and held her tightly; it was all I could do until, eventually, the tears subsided. Laura then released the traumatic secrets that she and Charlie had endured during their latter teenage years, and how they first met each other in Ringmer village, near Lewes, some six years ago.

Laura started telling me her life story, as well as Charlie's, from their late adolescent years.

"I met Charlie on the 28 bus into Lewes from Ringmer. Charlie had recently moved into the village and was staying with her aunt, her mother's sister. Charlie's parents lived in Bourne End in Bucks near Maidenhead. Charlie's dad was a Member of Parliament (MP), and her mother was a doctor at Wexham Park Hospital near Slough. Charlie's mother had fallen ill and was admitted to the hospital where she worked. She had a bowel problem, and she had to spend two weeks in hospital. And that's when it all kicked off for Charlie. We were both 16 at the time. Charlie had no brothers or sisters, and nobody to turn to. She was in the house alone with her dad, and she was always scared of her him because he would touch her up at every opportunity when her mum was out – ever since Charlie was 14."

Laura took a breath. "Steve, Charlie only told me this after we had become firm friends and had known each other for about four months and she wholly trusted me. Charlie and I became very close when we were past our eighteenth birthdays, Steve. Probably *too* close, if you understand what I mean, but we only had each other. I wasn't that close to my parents either. Yeah, they were all right, but always arguing. I spent most of my childhood in my room with earphones on. The cricket was a great outlet for Charlie and me. It took our minds off a lot of unpleasant things that had happened to us, but we even managed to fuck that up as well. That was a few months before we met you after applying to you for a job. We did sixth form and college, but our life experiences really shattered our egos, dreams, and ambitions.

"I don't know how to say this, Steve, but Charlie's dad raped her, when her mum was in hospital. The only saving grace for Charlie was that he was really drunk at the time, and the rape attack didn't last long. After a minute or so, Charlie managed to get her father off her and out of her – he had her pinned down. Once she was free, Charlie bit her father's penis so hard that she almost severed it in two. He called her a 'fucking little prick teaser'. He had to call an ambulance and was in hospital for five days. Charlie fled the house that night. She rang her aunt up in Ringmer, and she ordered Charlie to get a taxi to Sussex straight away. 'Just pack a few things that you treasure to bring with you,' she told Charlie. She arrived at her aunt's house at two in the morning, with just the clothes she stood up in and a bag of bits and pieces.

"The next day, her aunt rang Charlie's father up on his mobile; he was in hospital and had just had his penis stitched back together. Charlie's aunt told him never to contact his daughter again, ever. When Charlie's mother found out what had happened after she was released from hospital, she went ballistic; she never went back to the family home in Bourne End. She moved to London, divorced her husband within months, and that was it. Charlie's mum has never been to visit her daughter or her sister since then; she was too embarrassed at not believing Charlie for years, when Charlie had told her mum what her father had been doing to her. However, Charlie's mum did send a cheque without fail to her sister (Charlie's aunt) for Charlie's well-being: £500 every month. Charlie called it 'conscience money', although it stopped when Charlie was 19. Through Charlie's aunt, her mum knew that Charlie was in regular employment from then onwards – that was when we started work for you, Steve. Charlie would never forgive her father, though, for taking away her virginity; that made Charlie freak out more than anything. That's why she tried to bite her father's dick off!"

I told Laura to come up for some air, and we both drank some of her cider. Laura was more controlled now as she continued to tell me about their teenage trials and tribulations.

Laura continued, "Charlie had managed to get into the sixth form and college at Lewes Tertiary, in Mountfield Road, Lewes. She was doing a secretarial course, and also a design and photography course. I was doing my BHSAI at Plumpton College at the time, which was three days a week; the other two days, I enrolled into Charlie's photography course, and I also enrolled for a business studies course to keep Charlie company."

Laura paused. "Everything was fine for the first year, what with the cricket. We were both 18 by then, and looking forward to September later in the year when we would be 19. And then we would be proper adults. We were both enjoying our courses we were on. The only trouble with me was that I was still a virgin, and I think Charlie sort of thought that as well. We stayed behind at college one early evening to do a photography shoot in one of the college studios, with two of the boys on the same course. Charlie and I had these flimsy silk shirts and scarves on, and nothing else. We were prancing around the studio whilst the boys were taking hundreds of photos in loads of different poses. We got a bit carried away, and Charlie and I became a bit more daring, so the shirts came off, and we danced around and became more provocative in our poses; we even started kissing each other and fondling each other. We were really turned on. It was all a bit lesbian, really, but as we started stroking each other's nipples, they started standing to attention, and Charlie and I started kissing each other more deeply. The two lads got turned on as well, and they stripped off and joined kissing us. They were quite nice boys, and I thought, 'Oh well, why not?' After all the fore play, I was wet and ready. Mike, the one I liked was, about 6 feet tall and skinny, but quite good-looking, and I knew he fancied me like crazy. Charlie would be okay with Hugh, or so I thought. Mike couldn't wait to have sex. As he fumbled in his jean pockets to get his condoms out, he was erect but having trouble opening the condom packet. I was lying on the studio floor on some cushions, with my legs open, and I couldn't stop giggling as Mike eventually got the condom packet open and then proceeded to come all over me with a premature ejaculation. He literally shot his lot all over me; he was so embarrassed. He finally got the condom on, but after a minute or two inside me, he went all limp and couldn't do it. 'What a way to lose your virginity!' I thought. Meanwhile, I could hear Charlie crying. Hugh was protesting he hadn't touched Charlie, and I believed him. Charlie was still suffering trauma from the experiences with her dad – that was clear to see. We got tidied up and decided to go home, but that wasn't the end of our bad experiences.

"After a week or so, the two boys started spreading rumours around the college that Charlie and I were lesbians. I think Mike sort of got in first because of his lack of performance and his total embarrassment about it. I explained to Hugh about Charlie's trauma, how she had been sexually abused not that long ago before, and he sort of understood. Hugh was nice; Mike was a shit.

"During the next few months, Charlie and I did become close, as I said before, Steve. We bought some girlie sex toys to play with. By that point, Charlie was virtually living with me at my mum's house. Anyway, we experimented and we played with each other; however, deep down, we both knew we were not cut out to be lesbians – we both knew that, eventually, we would want our meat and two veg. Charlie was prepared to wait for the right one to walk into her life; I was still after some experience. I really fancied this gym instructor at Lewes Leisure Centre. I had been there to work out a few times, and I knew he was clearly interested. I had arranged to meet him at the centre, and because I was so excited, I got there half an hour early. I thought I would go into the steam room for twenty minutes, and I caught him with a young girl still in her school uniform. She didn't look a day over 15. When he saw me, I just said that I had called in to tell him I wanted a man, not a boy. And then I just walked out and left it at that."

Laura paused for a breath, and then continued. "My final encounter was at Plumpton College, Steve. I was nearing the end of my course. My instructor was about 35, but he was in great shape and very good-looking. He asked me if I would help him tidy up the tack room one early evening after college had finished at four, and I said okay. When everybody had gone, he told me he really liked me. He held me in his arms and kissed me. I thought to myself, 'A real man at last!' I responded by saying I liked him too. He told me he was divorced and living alone, but would really like to make love to me. We arranged for that following Friday, which was in a few days away. After college that day, we went to the local pub, the Half Moon, where we had something to eat and drank a bottle of wine between us. He lived at Plumpton Green, near the station, so we went back to his place. We made love, and he was so gentle with me – and he got through his packet of three condoms that evening. I really enjoyed it this time, and although I was still quite naive, I had learnt a valuable lesson: boys, girls, and slappers fuck; educated men and women make love. I knew now what I wanted, and that was to make love. I wanted to grow up, and I wanted love. I did not want to be a statistic or ever to be demeaned or treated like a piece of meat. I wanted pure love.

"The council estates up and down the country were full of young girls who wanted to fuck and throw their futures away, getting banged up with two or three kids, with no husbands and no futures, living in council flats on state benefits. That wasn't for me; no way at all. It was a great experience with John (my instructor); I slept with him that night and got the train back in the morning to Lewes. I told my mum a friend at college had a riding accident and that I was staying the night with her. John told me he really liked me, and if I wanted to, we could do the same next Wednesday. I agreed without hesitation."

We sipped some more of the cider, and Laura continued, "I was really looking forward to Wednesday, and when it came, I was once again very excited. We went straight back to John's house this time, dispensing with the food and drink; we both couldn't wait for it as we stripped off, though I had to be back at my mum's house by seven that evening. Once again, John used all three condoms in the two hours we had. Before we made love this time, he played with my nipples and clitoris, using his fingers to sexually arouse me. I had two orgasms before we actually made love. This was another first for me, and it underlined my earlier thoughts: men made love; boys just fucked, without a clue of what women really want. John was a good lover."

Laura paused again. "And then, suddenly, that same evening, my whole world fell apart. His wife walked in, with their two children; they had come back from holiday two days earlier than planned. John looked like he had seen a ghost when she burst in the bedroom door. I just said, 'Who are you?' And then she started on me: 'Who's this one then, another one of your fucking whores from the college? Not bad, this one; quite tall, lovely tits, and a good-looker. You've excelled yourself this time, John. I bet she fucks like a rattlesnake, and you've told her you love her.' She looked at me and said, 'Get out this house, you fucking whore!' All I could say was, 'I am really sorry. He told me he was divorced.' She said, 'Men are born liars if there is some spare pussy going about. Did he buy you dinner the first time?' Looking for some credibility, I said, 'Yes, he did.' 'Oh,' she said, 'he must have really liked you then. The last girl he took out twice got banged up the second time, and the silly little cow thought he loved her, so she decided to have his baby. You better have a pregnancy test soon, because his party trick is to not use a condom at some time on the second date.' I looked at his packet of three, and sure enough, there was one unused. I looked at him and said, 'You bastard.' His wife called me a 'silly fucking whore' again and told me to get out of the house.

"I put my clothes on, crying at the same time because of my stupidity, and then I ran as fast as I could to the train station. I even contemplated throwing myself in front of a train, Steve. I felt unclean, used, cheap – what use was I to anyone now? I felt like everything that I did not want to be, a cheap slut and no better than a slapper. When I eventually got home, I told my mum I had been thrown from a horse at the college. I told Charlie the truth when my mum went out, though. I washed and washed myself – three or four times every day for three weeks – but I never felt clean. I was

175

so ashamed. I went to the doctor's the next day and told him I had sex with my boyfriend the previous night and the condom had split; I thought I might be pregnant. He gave me some morning-after pills, and I took them both to make doubly sure I would not end up pregnant. I was naive and really stupid, Steve, and I had absolutely nobody to turn to – that is, until our paths crossed, and even then, I didn't know exactly what I wanted. I was just too young, and I couldn't grow up quick enough.

"John wrote me a letter to apologise for his actions towards me, and he sent me my approved instructor pass certificate for which I was studying; he told me not to bother coming back to the college. He said I was the best student he had ever seen, and that I had a natural talent with my understanding of horses; he said I was a natural horsewomen and should seek a career with training young horses.

"So as you can see, Steve, I have had some bad experiences and some near misses – also some disasters. I have been called a lesbian and a whore. I've at times acted like a lesbian and a whore, because I trusted people. I cannot believe how naive I was in my teens. Charlie was raped by her father; we are not exactly the type of girls you would want to take home to meet your parents, now are we, Steve?!" Laura exclaimed.

"Laura, my lovely Laura," I said. "I would love to take you home to meet my mum and dad. You've just been a bit unlucky, but certainly not a disaster. We all have to grow up, and sometimes it is not easy. The most important thing is that you and Charlie found each other when you both needed a friend and confidante, and that in itself is a blessing. Everything else is the sort of thing that happens at college. Charlie's rape, though, should have been reported to the police; that is tragically sad," I said. "Although I'm sure the family took the logical step, rather than tearing the whole family apart. I'm sure Charlie's aunt is a woman not to fool around with, so let's look on the bright side: if the events of Charlie's teenage years had not occurred, you would in all probability never have met me."

"Steve," Laura said, "you have a knack of saying the right thing at the right time. I never thought of it like that, but one single life-changing event can change our whole future. It changes everything, doesn't it?"

"Yes, my beautiful Laura. Simply put, if Charlie's dad had not raped his daughter that night, then Charlie would not have gone to Ringmer, and she most certainly would not have met you; you would not have played cricket together, and then the most important event of all that would never have happened is that we would never have met."

We opened up Laura's second bottle of cider. After all the trauma, we finally had something to celebrate.

Laura said, "From now on, Steve, I'm definitely going to believe in angels."

Laura turned over so that she was now lying on top of me, and she poured some cider into my mouth. She slowly let it trickle onto my chest, and lower still, meaningfully to my navel and beyond. Laura then tantalisingly licked the cider slowly, first from my chest, then lower, and lower still, until she reached what she was really after all along. Laura bathed the meat and two veg in her cider, then either licked or sucked them dry. I managed to hold out for about five minutes, but I came as Sade started singing "Smooth Operator" on the CD for the third time. Laura had completed page 20 of the Kama Sutra; I think she knew all along what page 20 was about.

The next word Laura uttered was "nineteen".

I went downstairs to get Laura another cider, and I made a round of cheese sandwiches. It was about nine o'clock. Ricky shouted out that there had been no phone calls. I thanked him, and then I went back upstairs to our bedroom.

Laura was on her hands and knees, on the bed. "Steve," she said. "I'm waiting."

We ate the sandwiches and made inroads on the new bottle of cider. I dribbled some over Laura's clitoris, and then slowly, deeply licked the sweet liquid off. I then dribbled some over Laura's breasts, and sucked on her nipples until they stood up to attention; they were without doubt the most perfectly formed breasts and nipples I had ever seen. We made love, beautiful deep passionate fulfilling love; we never fucked, we shared our deep love for each other, together, – it was, after all, our joint pleasure, our deep affection for each other, which we both knew would end up with us being together all of our lives.

I finally let Laura have her way, and we ended up in position 19 of the Kama Sutra. We had banished the skeletons, unloaded the baggage, and rid the girls of their perceived burdens which they had carried around with themselves for so long. Laura had also rid herself of guilt and finally accepted she never was a whore or a lesbian. As they say, don't knock it unless you've tried it. She was just growing up, as was Charlie. I told Laura I would have a quiet word with Charlie tomorrow; after listening to Laura's sad account of Charlie's rape ordeal, I felt it was the right thing to do. Charlie knew, of course, that Laura was going to tell me.

By now, Laura and I were both well and truly knackered. We fell asleep in each other's arms, stinking of strawberry cider.

CHAPTER 14

We woke up to the faint whiff of stale cider in the air. It was just a little after seven.

Laura said, "I really fancy some scrambled eggs on toast for breakfast, Steve."

"Good idea," I replied.

So we showered, dealt with the rest of the ablutions, and got dressed. We had a very busy day ahead, and Laura's call about a decent breakfast for a change made me feel hungry all of a sudden. However, before the breakfast, we had to change all the bed linen from our escapades the night before; only after that would it be time for breakfast.

Ricky and Charlie, much to my surprise, were up already and in the kitchen. Charlie had just finished her breakfast of toast and marmalade, with a cup of coffee or two. Ricky had made himself an egg-and-bacon sandwich of which he was making great inroads into, and he was on his second cup of coffee.

Laura said, "I will do the scrambled eggs, Steve, if you take care of the toast."

I agreed and loaded up the toaster with four slices; I would turn on the toaster just before the scrambled eggs were ready. I then sat down at the kitchen table to have my first coffee of the day.

"Charlie, any news from Wharr's?" I asked.

"Yes," she replied. "That's why we got up early. We stayed up until eleven last night, Steve, and nothing came through at all. According to the timed e-mails, since midnight, we have had a constant stream of information. Ricky and I thought we would make an early start to get all the data stored before the lads get back from Windsor."

"Thank you, Charlie," I said. "So let's start planning our day then. Charlie and Ricky, you stick with the data processing. We will have an office meeting as soon as the lads turn up at ten. I don't think Allan and Billy will be late; furthermore, I want to get them straight back out again by twelve and on their way to Newbury."

I flicked the switch on the toaster. A minute or so later, Laura pronounced the scrambled eggs were ready, as right on time the toast popped up. Laura's scrambled eggs were delicious, just eggs and a knob of butter, with some pepper-and-salt seasoning, and definitely no milk. Another coffee later, we were all ready for action.

Laura went into the yard to feed Fred II. Mickey had already mucked him out but, as usual, was nowhere to be seen. Not for the first time, I cleaned up the kitchen, and then joined Charlie and Ricky, who were now at their computers to finalise today's events in the office.

Charlie said, "Oh crikey!" Ricky and I looked up in surprise. "Sorry, Steve, it completely slipped my mind. I forgot to tell you that Bob rang in at eleven yesterday: one of his boys fell over yesterday evening at the Brighton match, and, unfortunately, broke his arm. Bob wanted to know if he could have the rest of the week off.

I replied, "Don't worry, Charlie. Bob texted me during the racing from Ascot yesterday, and I agreed that was okay. He is going to come back in on Monday."

Charlie said, "Oh thank goodness for that."

Bob was a family man, so it seemed the right thing to do to let him spend a bit of time with his family, given the circumstances.

"Charlie," I said, "at ten, would you electronically transfer the £150,000 from our client account to Jonathan Ridger's account?"

Charlie replied, "Yes, Steve, that is on my list of things to do today; ten o'clock it is then."

Laura popped her head in to the office to let us know she would be in the tack room, cleaning tack for tomorrow's big day, and if we got busy to let her know.

Wharr's certainly sent a lot of information through to us; however, I did not want to discuss it until the two operatives had returned to the office from Windsor – they had been at Wharr's until one o'clock this morning, before returning to their hotel to get some sleep. We had at least fourteen different people now with their names in the frame: the six Tote employees and the eight people who had cashed in all the £18 Tote winning tickets; notwithstanding that, there were another 112 suspects, all of whom we believed had bought the £18 tickets.

DCI Heyes rang me on my mobile, just after eight o'clock.

"Steve, would it possible for us to speak at length?"

I replied, "Yes, of course."

He then informed me that Mickey had paid Pete Gregory another visit at the Gatwick holding centre whilst he was still in custody. "Pete Gregory signed a full confession implicating Dicky Head in the firebombing of the girls' flat," said the chief inspector. "Furthermore, a special sitting of magistrates yesterday allowed us to remand him in custody for a further seven days. When Gregory saw Mickey after the court remand hearing, he also confessed to the outstanding Giles Holland case of suspected GBH. So we also have a fully signed confession for that case as well. Evidently, Dicky Head paid Gregory £500 for the GBH case and £500 for the firebombing of the girls' flat, so there are some deep implications here."

The chief inspector continued. "Jay Penfold, in my estimation, was certainly the culprit for the horsebox theft and fire, and also Henry Hall's murder. The only case I have to close now is yours, Steve – your attempted murder – when we solve that one, I believe it will solve quite a few other case files as well. So, rest assured, we will be monitoring your situation very closely indeed."

I thanked him.

"There is still no news of the whereabouts of Mr Dicky Head," said the chief inspector. "I have asked Mickey to keep leaning on Pete Gregory, as we believe he is the one who will lead us to Head. We are of the opinion that our Mr Gregory has a lot more beans to spill."

I told the chief inspector that the scam involving the Tote was almost certainly a cover for something a lot more sinister, which were also reaping the benefits as far as a cash turnover and profits were concerned. I explained how they had managed to make £2,000 at Ascot the previous day, and I also let him know about the £18 tickets which we believed were being used as a form of currency.

"Go on," said the chief inspector. "This is good, this is very good. By the way, Steve, do you know what the going rate is for a small line of coke?"

By coke, he meant cocaine, also often referred to as "charlie". "I've absolutely no idea," I informed him.

DCI Heyes said, "Between £15 and £25 would be the going rate. So wherever they are passing over the tickets is where they are scoring, and also where the drugs are being distributed." He added, "You're right, Steve, the tickets are currency; no ticket, no coke."

I then told the chief inspector that give what we had discovered during Operation Mousetrap, we would be implementing Operation Mousetrap, Part II, at Newbury tomorrow. He told me to keep him up to date with whatever we found out

"Even though some of the cases have been solved, Steve, in my opinion, your case has the biggest implications, by far," he said. "National security is involved now; you have stumbled on a nationwide operation, and I want to put the bastards behind bars for a long, long time indeed – all of them, including your ex, if need be."

I said I understood.

"I have to go now, Steve," the chief inspector said. "But I'll call you at the same time tomorrow morning, with regard to security at Hickstead. One last thing, though: we have recorded no conversations from either Jane's Range Rover or trailer, so we assume it's parked up somewhere and not being used."

"Okay," I replied. "Thanks for letting me know."

We said goodbye, and I put the phone down.

It was now almost nine; time was flying by this morning. I went into the kitchen and made the usual four coffees. Laura came in from the yard with a smile on her face, looking exuberant as ever. I gave her one of the coffees as she parked herself at the kitchen table, next to the biscuit tin. I took Charlie and Ricky's coffees into the office for them; they were still tirelessly recording and storing all the data into Mother. I then went back to the kitchen and sat with Laura.

Still beaming, Laura said, "Fred II is in great shape. I'm going to school him in half an hour. I just want to go over a few details with him, to make sure what I want of him tomorrow. I want him jumping out of my hands; I just want to guide him, not push him unless I have to. I want to make sure horse and rider are absolutely spot on for our big day, Steve. After lunch, I will get all the tack ready." Whilst munching on her second chocolate bourbon biscuit, Laura continued, "I will give Fred a thorough shampoo, a wash to tidy him up for the big day. I think I will plait his mane and part of his tail as well. I really want to show him off, big time."

We were holding hands. I said to Laura, "Yeah, that sounds good to me." I thought, *If you are going to do something, do it well, do it to the best of your ability, if you want to reap the rewards.*

Laura had indeed grown up; in the four years I had known her, I for certain now knew that girl had matured into the most beautiful of young ladies, not just physically but also mentally. I took a lot of pride in having been her mentor, and Charlie's as well. In their time with me, they had grown into charming, caring, and, most of all, determined-to-succeed people. They were lovely in every way, and you could actually feel the aura around them. It was the most beautiful transformation, and to have been part of it and to witness it was a gift. I knew Ricky felt that special presence as well, especially with regard to Charlie.

I told Laura I had just had a long chat with the chief inspector, and that he was adamant the £18 Tote tickets were indeed currency. "Allan and Billy are due to arrive in the office from Windsor in about an hour's time, and we will have an in-house discussion then until midday; then I wanted them to leave straight away for Newbury to start setting up Operation Mousetrap, Part II," I told her. I hoped we would be in a better position by then, so as to know what to look out for and then, of course, how to proceed. "We received a mountain of data from Wharr's overnight, and that it's taking a great deal of time to process the data through Mother, but I feel confident we are very much closer to putting this case to bed."

"Then I feel confident too," she said.

We finished our coffees, kissed, and parted. Laura went back out to the yard to continue her preparations for tomorrow, as always, under the watchful eyes of our resident spook, Mickey – not that Laura knew that, or even had a clue. I returned to the office.

The team would spend the next three hours dissecting the avalanche of information that had been coming through from Wharr's since midnight.

We started off with the six Tote staff on our radar, who, since the criminal-records check, had become suspects. Firstly, we went through the computerised information received from the Tote: between them, the six staff had sold a good 75 per cent of the £18 tickets at Ascot the previous day. We knew this for sure, as the Tote allocated staff with special serial numbers and added barcodes to completely stop any type of fraud; the Tote could tell which of their staff sold which ticket, at what time – even from what position or building on the course – there could be no denying the winning ticket, or, indeed, the losing tickets.

Seventy-five per cent was a far too high a figure for there to be no connection. Charlie put a board up in the office, and that was point number 1 in our favour – the percentages, that is. Next, we looked at the punters who had bought the £18 tickets. As we only covered with CCTV the six outlets where the Tote employees under suspicion were, we could only identify about 78 of the punters, out of the 112 that we knew had bought the £18 tickets. However, once again, I felt sure the percentages were in our favour. Seventy-five per cent was good enough for me. This went up on Charlie's board as point number 2.

We never had the time to carry out a facial-recognition search through the police computers, with regard to the punters' images that had been recorded, nor did Wharr's. However, as the images had been recorded, every punter would be screened and checked over the weekend. So we would indeed find out who they were and whether they had any criminal convictions. We also fully intended to cross-reference tomorrow's events at Newbury with the information obtained from the CCTV footage from Ascot.

There was a big sprint handicap on the card for Friday's meeting at Newbury, a mid-afternoon, 6 furlong race, with a declared field of twenty-four runners. Once again, there was an obvious stand-out favourite; all of us in the office were wondering if another scam was about to take place. We would certainly be fortunate if indeed this was the case, as it would positively help us no end to cross-reference the punters from Ascot with the £18 tickets, with those from Newbury tomorrow; it was a great opportunity for us, and we would discuss it in detail during our strategy later this morning.

It was now approaching ten, and Allan and Billy would be here soon. Ricky made us some coffee.

Charlie shouted over to me, "Transfer of £150,000 has now been completed, Steve. The funds are in Mr Ridger's account."

The telephone rang, and I answered. It was Chris Collins.

"Are you still able to take Laura to the show tomorrow?" I asked.

"Yes," he replied, and then said, "Steve, Mr Argonaut contacted me this morning to tell me the drop-off point for delivering Hot Tea would be in the Gatwick airport area."

I asked Chris what time he had to be at Mr Ridger's yard.

"I must be there on the dot at eight, Friday morning," Chris said. "There will also be a return journey to Mr Ridger's yard, with another delivery. Mr Argonaut told me not to say a word to anyone, even you," Chris added. "But I thought you should know, Steve."

I replied, "Don't worry, Chris, your secret is safe with me. And thank you."

Chris said he would be with us tomorrow at about noon, and I asked if he would like to have lunch with me at two. I was meeting my old friend, Aussie, and possibly Charles Paul, the international showjumper from Ireland.

Chris replied, "Thanks for the offer, Steve, but I will have my work clothes on and no time to change." He added, "I'm not really a lunchtime-eating person."

I replied, "Okay. I will see you tomorrow at twelve then." I put the phone down. Boy, though, was I intrigued at what Robert Argonaut was up to.

Allan and Billy arrived shortly after ten. Windsor to Sayers Common was little more than an hour to drive on a good day, with light traffic; however, when they left for Newbury, that would be a good two-hour drive, so time was precious. We started our in-house discussion at 10.15.

Charlie asked both Allan and Billy to check out the new board up in the office, with regard to percentages of the six Tote employees and the seventy-eight punters who had purchased the £18 winning tickets.

Ricky added, "The purpose and reason for Operation Mousetrap, Part II, is to cross-reference those faces we know with another time and another place, that being Newbury tomorrow."

Allan and Billy agreed.

The five of us in the office now had to work out our strategy for tomorrow, taking into account all the events from yesterday's meeting at Ascot. I asked Allan to lead on this, as he was my key operative with regard to Operation Mousetrap.

Allan was another ex-army man; a six-footer and about thirteen stone. He had served his time, about nine years, with the Royal Argyle and Sutherland Highlanders Regiment in Scotland. He joined my company about a year ago, after he left the army when the regiment was disbanded following government cutbacks. His wife, Ellen, was a physicist and had been offered a position at Sussex University, so they moved south. Both Allan and Ellen were 32 and had been married for four years; they had no children, and lived at Hollingbury, a residential suburb between Brighton and the university, which was situated on the A27, midway between Brighton and Lewes.

Allan brought us all up to date, with a detailed report of yesterday's events at Ascot. Thankfully, Allan was aware we were actually all up to speed with yesterday's events up to the end of the last race, so his synopsis would begin with his agreement with the Tote manager just to open the ten Tote outlets in the one building for those punters wanting to cash in their outstanding winning tickets from the day's racing for the final forty-five minutes the Tote would remain open.

Allan stated, "We had ten operatives strategically placed near to the windows where the Tote would pay out. The manager made sure the six employees under suspicion were not selected to operate at these windows; however, the operatives were selected at random from those that were left, not that the six knew anything untoward and were none the wiser.

"The operatives soon latched on to the eight people who were cashing in the £18 winning tickets, and after following them some two or three times, each was aware of who they talked to and where they came from: they were all working at food and drink retail outlets at the course. What we still didn't know was how they came by the tickets. But what was evidently clear was the fact that we need to cover these outlets tomorrow with more CCTV cameras, and they need to be installed as soon as possible at the four retail outlets at the course."

These outlets were away from the main stands; they were the trailer-type outlets that were towed in, and throughout the day, run off their own generators. They were towed around most of the fairly local racecourses. These confectionary trailers mainly sold sweets, cigarettes, and hot and cold drinks. There were usually two people who worked these trailers; there were four of these trailers at Ascot, and the same four would probably be at Newbury tomorrow.

Allan concluded by saying that we were awaiting confirmation as to whether these particular four trailers worked Windsor, Kempton, and Sandown, as well as Ascot and Newbury.

I thanked Allan and added, "Just one more question, Allan. Have you alerted the security staff at Newbury?"

"Yes, Boss."

"And have you set up a meeting today?"

Again, Allan said, "Yes, Boss, and we hope to convene between 3 p.m. and 3.30." He added, "They have also told me, Boss, that the Jockey Club had contacted them and sanctioned this further operation, and they are to give us full cooperation. So we are all set up."

"Fine then," I said to Allan. "Would you give them a call now to see if they know the exact positions these confectionary trailers will be in tomorrow at Newbury? Before we go any further, let's break for ten minutes. Ricky, could you do some coffees? And Charlie, please get me Wharr's on the telephone please."

Billy said, "Yes, Boss, cigarette break. Thanks, Boss." And out he went.

Charlie got through to Wharr's. "It's Tony, Steve," she said.

"Hey, Tony. It's Steve. Would it be possible to set up some extra CCTV cameras at Newbury tomorrow, to specifically cover the four trailer confectionary outlets?"

"Yes," said Tony. "No problem. We've been anticipating that request. Given the chance, we will try to bug them to eavesdrop as well."

"Excellent," I said. "Allan will once again lead this operation, and I believe there is a team meeting planned for after three this afternoon at the course."

"Yes," said Tony. "And I will be leading our team of four from Wharr's in the field. You know this is now a top-priority case, don't you, Steve?"

I said yes, but I actually had no knowledge of that fact. No doubt the chief inspector was trying to keep it low-key.

Tony enquired as to how we were getting on with the data that had been sent over, and I told him that the data had been very helpful and that we hoped to have this case wrapped up by early next week. Tony thought it might take a bit longer, but he said that we were heading in the right direction. I thanked Tony for all his help, and then I put the phone down.

"Okay, everybody, let's get back to it!" I shouted.

Ricky was on his way into the office, with five coffees; Billy had finished his cigarette and came back inside; Charlie had never even left her desk; Allan was just finishing his telephone conversation with the security department at Newbury racecourse.

Allan filled us in with the results of his telephone conversation. "These mobile retail outlets are strategically placed at every racecourse," he explained. "They are also contracted from season to season; if a racecourse has a jumps and flat season, then the caterers have to have two separate contracts with the racecourse to supply, as is the case with the confectionary trailers. The company that runs these four trailers is called Chris's Outside

Kiosks & Events, and the head office is in Watford, just north of London. Well, that's where they are registered anyway."

I said, "Okay, Allan, that's great."

Charlie or Ricky would do a company search later, and then we would see what we could dig up with regard to who the directors were and whether the information led us anywhere.

"So now let's concentrate on our strategy for tomorrow at Newbury," I said. "Allan and Billy, this is still your show." I further explained that I would not be attending, as Mr Argonaut's new purchase, Hot Tea, the recent Goodwood winner, would not now be running there. I also informed them that our other operative, John, was in the immediate area, trying to locate Dicky Head, and to call on him if they felt that another pair of hands would be helpful. Furthermore, I let them know that Gary would be making his way back to the office tomorrow morning, to arrive at lunchtime; he would be following the trainer Noel Henry and his naughty wife, Natalie, for part of the way as they journeyed to Newbury from Newmarket. This just about brought us up to date with our ongoing cases. I then asked Allan and Billy for their observations and strategy for tomorrow.

Allan stated that a meeting was scheduled for just after three this afternoon, when all the finer details of the operation would be discussed with Newbury's security team (of which there were five), Wharr's team of four technicians, and Allan, Billy, and maybe John; there would be eleven or twelve people on this operation, with police backup if necessary.

Slowly, very slowly, the pieces of the jigsaw were coming together. An awful lot had happened in the last eight days, including two murders and three attempted murders, arson, and vehicle thefts – not to mention the intervention of spooks from MI5.

Allan carried on. "What we were initially looking for on behalf of the Tote was the irregular large amount of tickets for non-runners. Tote operators, we believed, were running a scam; however, our investigations have led us to bigger fish to fry, which we hope to identify tomorrow. The £18-ticket scam, we agree now, is a form of currency, and the people who have cashed in these tickets appear to work for or are part of an organised crime ring fronted by a company called Chris's Outside Kiosks & Events. As far as we know, there are at least eight of these individuals, so we need to know whether these people really are employees. Or, are they foot soldiers or even the actual ringleaders? How do they deliver whatever it is they are illegally selling, and how do they accept payment? These are some of the questions we need to put answers to tomorrow."

I thanked Allan for his presentation of these facts as we were aware of them, to the best of our knowledge and ability, given the evidence we had accumulated. I then asked Billy if he had something he would like to add or recommend.

Billy was the only one of my employees never to have been in the armed forces; however, he had ridden more than 500 winners, both flat and National Hunt over the sticks. Billy was 42, and although he was five foot eight and still a trim ten stone and seven pounds. He had been married twelve years, and he and his wife had an 11-year-old son who was dead keen to follow in his father's footsteps and become a professional jockey. Billy hung up his boots and gave up race riding two years ago when he passed the 500-winner mark without too many bad falls. He decided to quit in one piece. His wife, Sue, was also 42, and had held a racehorse trainer's licence for ten years, sending out a steady flow of winners from the small string that she trained. Sue and Billy Smithson trained their horses at the Old Lewes Racecourse, just behind the prison in Lewes. They had twenty boxes and two large paddocks, and they lived there as well, in an adjacent three-bed bungalow. Billy didn't want to share in his wife's limelight, so when he packed up, he came to work for me. He was an articulate man, and it was a plus for my outfit to have an ex-professional jockey on the team.

In response to my question, Billy said, "A lot of my former riding mates and colleagues in Lambourn and Newmarket are constantly being hassled by drug dealers in the pubs and clubs of those two towns. When I spoke to John last weekend whilst he was looking for Dicky Head, he had come to the same conclusion. Judging by the comments of the people he had spoken to, the racing towns of this country seem to be awash with cocaine – not that I know anything about drugs, but where I live in Lewes, about seven or eight years ago in the mid-nineteen nineties, we had the same problem. A lot of the stable lads got hooked, and it was terrible to see those kids throwing their lives away."

DCI Heyes had touched on this when we all met him in the office. He'd told us about the drug problem in Lewes, and about Jay Penfold. Everyone agreed with Billy's conclusions.

Billy continued, "It looks to me like drugs are now being distributed through some, if not all, of our racecourses, and this could quite easily become an epidemic. I can therefore see why MI5 has become involved, and also the government, although nothing official has been said. All we know is that somehow the company we work for – your company, Steve – seems to have stirred up a hornets' nest, probably without us even knowing how. And furthermore, these people feel their network and distribution is being threatened. Whoever these people are, they are dangerous and murderous. They have obtained information, and, obviously, they know all about us. That information could only have come from two sources, I believe. Sorry to say this, Steve, but Jane would be one source, and the other source would have to be the result of loose talk at the Jockey Club."

Billy paused for a second, and then said, "We will probably find out tomorrow how their distribution system is operated. We would then have the weekend to collate the information and put a stop to this evil gang that deals in death and misery."

Wow! I thought. *That was some statement.* I knew Billy was articulate, but I hadn't realised he was so logical "Thank you, Billy, for your valued insight," I said. "Okay, everyone, let's leave it there. Coffee and sandwiches in the kitchen for lunch."

It was nearly noon. I took Charlie some coffee and sandwiches into the office; she was still firing away on keyboard, feeding into Mother the never-ending stream of data from Wharr's.

Laura joined us in the kitchen for lunch. She was talking to Billy. Laura had ridden out for Billy's wife when she was on work experience from Plumpton College, doing her instructor's course.

Billy said, "Laura is such a natural. There was not a racehorse in my wife's yard that Laura couldn't ride. She was with us every morning for three months that spring."

We finished our sandwiches and coffee at about 12.30 p.m. Allan and Billy set off for Newbury. Laura went to the tack room. Ricky and I went back into the office.

CHAPTER 15

After lunch, we spent most of the afternoon double- and triple-checking all of the data we had stored with regard to the Ascot race meeting. We had really good images of the eight suspects who were presumably the vending trailer employees and who had cashed in all the £18 winning tickets. I thought it just might be beneficial to us to send these images by e-mail as attachments to the chief inspector, who would then run them through the police computer. There was no point in taking any chances; we needed to know if these eight people were dangerous or had police criminal records. If they did have records, what were their previous crimes? They were all male, and their ages ranged from probably mid-twenties to late thirties. None of them, judging by their physiques, looked as though they had ever missed a meal in their whole lives; they all could obviously handle themselves, and we would therefore be very cautious indeed.

Ricky carried out a company-records check on Chris's Outside Kiosks & Events. "Hey, Boss," he shouted across the office. "Some interesting news on coke!" He started laughing as he read out the company's slogan: "Thing's go better with COKE. For all your outdoor events, we supply everything!"

Yeah, I thought, *you probably do.* Ricky explained that the slogan had C-O-K-E, all in capital letters, but we knew it meant coke, as in cocaine, not Coke, as in Coca-Cola. "Anything on the directors? Are there any listed?" I asked Ricky.

"Just coming up now, Boss," Ricky replied. "The company is owned by another company called Cobblestone Investments, which is based in Jersey," Ricky informed me, and then he added, "Do you want me to keep on checking?"

"Yes," I said to Ricky. "And copy in the chief inspector with any information that you consider to be relevant."

"Will do, Boss," Ricky replied.

Charlie called out, "Finished!" She threw her arms up in the air in exaltation. It was fast approaching 2 p.m., and Charlie said, "I need to stretch my legs for a bit. I think I'll go and see how Laura's getting on shampooing Fred."

"Hey," I said. "I'll join you."

Ricky manned the office whilst carrying on his company search of Cobblestone Investments.

Charlie and I walked into the yard, where Laura was hosing off Fred now. The shampooing had ceased, and he really did look magnificent.

Laura said, "In about twenty minutes I'll be finished."

I said to Charlie, "How's the new Vitara then?"

We walked over to the other side of the yard, where it was parked.

Charlie said, "It's beautiful, Steve. Thank you! I'm so pleased with my new set of wheels."

Charlie remotely unlocked the doors of the Vitara. We opened both the front doors of the Vitara and sat inside.

Charlie said, "So Laura's told you all about my rape ordeal then?"

I held Charlie' right hand and said, "Yes. Laura's told me everything, Charlie. She opened her heart out to me and cried her eyes out. She even told me that on one occasion, in a moment of deep distress, she contemplated committing suicide by throwing herself in front of a train."

"Yes," said Charlie. "I know." Charlie started to cry, and I kissed her hand. "This is the first time I've cried since my dad raped me," she said.

I replied, "Cry for as long as you like. You have moved on now, Charlie; let go of the past, and concentrate on the future."

Charlie said, "Yes, you're right Steve." She then added, "You know, Steve, Laura's been in love with you since the very first time we all met. Do you remember? She asked you if you were married; this was when we first met you for our job interview. You said we were too young, but you gave us a chance and employed us."

"Yes, Charlie, I remember that day very well."

"Just after we left you and were driving back to Laura's mum's house in Ringmer, Laura said to me, 'Right, Charlie, that's it! Fuck the boys! I need to grow up quickly. That's the man I want to spend the rest of my life with.' When you started going out with Jane and then got engaged,

Laura was absolutely devastated and heartbroken. She wanted to leave. She just cried and cried for a whole week. Eventually, we had a heart-to-heart talk to work it out. I said to Laura, 'Let's just take a step back and look at where we are now, and where we were, before we started work for Steve. Look, Laura, we have a lovely flat, lovely cars, and great jobs; your job was made in heaven for you! You're doing absolutely what you love, Laura, working with horses and teaching them how to showjump, bringing on youngsters after breaking them in and teaching them their jobs. As for me, I love my secretarial duties. Laura, we are so lucky to have what we have at our age.' And then I said, 'Laura, we are only 21. Remember all those pricks at college? We have moved on, while they're still fucking each other. We are doing professional jobs in the real world; we are surrounded by professional people. We really have grown up a lot in the last year or so. And there comes a time when you have to fight for what you want. This is your time, Laura: you can give up and walk away, or you can fight for your man. You still obviously adore Steve,' I said to her. We both trusted you, Steve, without question, straight away when we first met you. So I added, 'Someday Jane will fall out with Steve. Until such a time as this happens, look at life as a sort of courtship., Just have faith, Laura; if it is meant to be, it will happen, and you and Steve will eventually be an item. He does love you, I sort of know it.' That's what I told her.

"I think that did the trick, Steve. From that moment onwards, Laura bent over backwards to help Jane whenever she could. Jane had good horses, but Laura thought she was a shit rider, to tell you the truth, Steve. Laura sorted out no end of problems for Jane that were equine related. I think Laura wanted to prove to you at the time, Steve, that you'd simply made the wrong choice with Jane. So Laura decided to be the model of professionalism from that moment onwards; she wanted to prove to you that she, ultimately, was the one and only girl for you. She just loved you so much."

"I know, Charlie," I told her, and then I changed the subject. "But what about you? How are you now, emotionally?"

Charlie replied, "It has taken me all this time, Steve, to get over my ordeal. However, in the last year, I have finally regained some confidence. Ricky told me a year ago he loved me, and in that time, Ricky has been my rock, so supportive and caring. Although I will never tell him I was raped by my dad, I feel so safe with him. Steve, can you understand that?"

I said, "Yes, of course, Charlie. And I know he loves you dearly. He's only had eyes for you since he joined the company. He told me so." He hadn't, but I knew Ricky wouldn't deny it, and I wanted to let Charlie know there was absolutely no doubt where Ricky's heart was.

Charlie responded by saying, "I love Ricky very much, Steve. I won't be looking anywhere else. I too have found the man I love, and I want to spend the rest of my life with him."

I kissed Charlie as Laura was walking over to us. She had finished with Fred and put him back in his box. "Where's mine then?" she demanded, pursing her lips.

I got out of the Vitara, and kissed Laura. Charlie got out as well, and joined us.

Charlie said, "Thank you, Steve. From the bottom of my heart, thank you."

The three of us hugged each other, and then Charlie returned to the office.

Laura said, "I have some tidying up to do, Steve. I will be about another half an hour in the yard."

It was now 2.30 p.m. I went into the kitchen, made three coffees, and took them with me into the office.

"Any luck with the Cobblestone Investments search?" I asked Ricky.

"Not so far, Boss. We're being given the runaround. Cobblestone is owned by another company registered in the Virgin Islands. I cannot find a single name of directorship or ownership anywhere."

"Okay," I said to Ricky. "Let's approached this from another direction. Contact all the racecourses where we know they operate – for instance, Ascot, Kempton, Newbury, Sandown, and Windsor. If they are contracted, then somebody must have signed the contracts on the company's behalf. There would have to be a name and address somewhere."

Ricky said, "Right, Steve. I'm on it straight away."

"Charlie, have you sent the eight COKE employees' images off to the chief inspector?" I asked.

"Yes, Steve," said Charlie. "They went off this morning. I also asked the chief inspector to contact you no later than eight tomorrow morning to update you." I had already confirmed to Charlie that the chief inspector would be telephoning me with early morning calls from now on.

Laura came into the office from the yard. "I'm just going to have a shower. After that, I can give you a hand with some office work for the rest of the afternoon, Steve."

"Thanks, Laura," I replied.

I went outside to see if I could find our resident spook, Mickey. He was sitting in his grey van reading a paper, and I asked him if I could talk to him for a few minutes.

"What's on your mind then?" he said as he opened the passenger door for me.

"I wanted to thank you personally for the protection you have been giving to me and my team of employees," I said.

He just shrugged his shoulders and said, "It's my job."

I asked him if he really would have killed Pete Gregory if he hadn't squealed.

"Yes," he said without hesitation. "The world would have been better off with one less scumbag on the planet." And then he added, "I have not finished with Pete Gregory yet. He has more secrets to cough up. I will haunt him and not give him a moment's peace. I'll break him, and when there's nothing else to learn from him, I'll fill him up with a syringe of heroin, and then I'll dump him somewhere on Epsom Downs. I'll kill him in just as the way he wished to kill Laura's horse, and perhaps Laura as well. Some people are just not worth locking up, and in my opinion, this piece of filth known as Pete Gregory is one of them."

A cold shiver ran down my back. Just the thought of someone filling Laura up with a syringe of heroin made me feel utterly nauseated.

"That's a lovely girl you've got there, Steve," Mickey went on. "She is so passionate about her horses. She talks to them, you know, never shouts, just a kind, quiet word, a pat, and a lump of sugar or piece of carrot. I muck her horse out for her first thing in the morning, and she leaves me a packet of biscuits after she finishes evening stables."

I asked Mickey if he was coming to Hickstead tomorrow.

"Not sure yet," he replied. "DCI Heyes will give me my orders in the morning, after he has spoken to you on the telephone."

"Okay then," I said. "Well, thanks again."

"Yeah," he said. "Okay."

I then walked up to where my lovely front gates had once stood, before they were crudely burned down. I wanted to have a word with our friendly firearms officer guarding our front drive to the house. As usual, there was the white Mercedes estate car with the big black letters written on the sides pronouncing, "Police Tactical Firearms Unit". I asked him if he had anything suspicious to report.

He replied, "I'm only allowed to talk to my chief inspector, sir."

He knew I was after some information and that I wouldn't go away until I had some. I asked, "How many times had the grey van driven past in the last three days then?" This was the same grey van that Ricky had spotted previously whist guarding the house.

"That grey van has driven past your house on eighteen occasions – morning, noon, and night – in the last three days," said the firearms officer. "It has false number plates. It leaves the Hickstead showjumping arena, drives past your house, and returns from whence it came. The people driving the said vehicle always wear hats and dark glasses, so it is hard to establish some sort of facial recognition. At this stage, sir, the chief inspector is satisfied that as long as whatever people are so really interested in you remains so, we are going to be even more interested in them. Your case is now top priority, sir."

I thanked the officer for this information.

I walked down my front driveway and back to the office; it was getting on for 3.30 p.m. Laura, Charlie, and Ricky were now seated in the office, sifting through and sorting information.

I asked Ricky if he had any luck with the individual contract searches from the separate racecourses regarding our COKE suspects.

Ricky replied, "All the requests have been sent to the tracks, and I am awaiting replies, Boss."

"Thanks, Ricky," I said.

Charlie's new office board now had a third piece of information. The board stated that of the £18 ticket purchases, 112 in total, 100 per cent knew what they were buying.

I said, "Right, everybody, I want to spend the next hour on how the drug purchases are carried out. We have established that the £18 tickets are the currency, so they must purchase something from those four trailer outlets. They must hand over the £18 tickets with some money to purchase their drugs. How are the drugs wrapped up? What sort of drugs are they selling? Are we talking pills, cannabis, cocaine, heroin? What do we know? Think, everybody. Have you seen something on the television, maybe something that made you laugh? What about newspaper articles, or drug-related stories and reports, drugs in sports? We are missing something which is right under our noses; it is so close, we cannot see it."

We deliberated. We explored every angle; we threw ideas at each other. Out of sheer despair, we even contacted the cleaning contractors at Ascot, who were still cleaning up from yesterday's events, to see if there was any abnormal rubbish they had come across. We got lucky: the cleaning contractors at Ascot gave us a big, big clue. They said all the toilets, men's and women's, had lots of unopened cans of Coke in them, in the rubbish bins; also, there were lots of straws strewn all over the floors of the cubicles. This was abnormal, to say the least, and there had to be a reason for it.

It was Ricky who eventually put the right words in the right order to solve the mystery that we had struggled so despairingly to answer.

"Eureka!" said Ricky. "Steve, you said we were missing something right under our noses, and that's it! Do you remember that footballer that played for Liverpool, Robbie Fowler? He was a centre forward, and one of his goal celebrations was to pretend to snort one of the white lines on the football pitch. We know that the main racehorse training areas like Newmarket and Lambourn are at the moment being swamped with drugs, mainly cocaine. We also know the Lewes training area had the problem in the mid-1990s., These people are snorting coke– as in, cocaine – and are using straws to do so. I reckon If I went to one of those trailers tomorrow with an £18 ticket for a place on the favourite in the big handicap sprint, gave him £2, and asked for a can of Coke – as in Coca-Cola – with two straws, I would score. One of the straws has a line of coke in it; it's that simple!

The three of us clapped our hands together to show our appreciation to Ricky for solving the puzzle.

Charlie said, "I always knew you were a smart-arse, Ricky. And as Chris's Outdoor Kiosks & Events states in its slogan: "Things go better with COKE"!.

Yeah, right, cocaine, not Coca-Cola. Now, though, we had to gather the evidence. Allan would be ringing me at 5 p.m. to tell me how the meeting went with the security staff at Newbury; I would pass on the latest information to Allan then.

Laura said, "What are we doing for supper tonight?"

We all agreed on steaks and salad, followed by cheese and biscuits; then we would have another fairly early night. We had accomplished a great deal today, but all four of us knew tomorrow was a very important day, a day when all of our futures could be affected in one way or another.

Laura, having already showered and changed earlier, went into the kitchen to start preparing our supper. Ricky was chasing up the racecourses with telephone calls to the secretaries; this was with regard to his earlier requests for contractual information. Charlie informed us she was off upstairs for a nice, hot, relaxing bath.

Almost to the second, at 5 p.m., Allan telephoned the office from Newbury.

On answering, I said, "Hi, Allan. How did the meeting go?"

He replied, "Much the same as on Wednesday at Ascot, Steve. We will still target the six Tote employees that remain suspects. We've also been lucky with the four trailer retail outlets. They arrived this afternoon, and the lads from Wharr's are going to bug them tonight for audio; the CCTV has already been installed. Tony from Wharr's has had his team on the go all afternoon. The technicians got to the racecourse at 11 a.m. to make sure all the equipment was in place, in good time, and without too many eyes. Is there anything else, Steve, we should know about or that you want us to cover?"

I replied, "Yes, Allan, there is. Though this may sound a little peculiar, what I want to do is to rig up some CCTV in two of each of the men's and women's toilets to cover the individual cubicles. We actually want to see if any of the racing crowd or punters are literally snorting cocaine at the track." I explained to Allan Ricky's eureka moment. I also told Allan to make sure they got plenty of CCTV footage of the £18-ticket exchanges. Now that we had audio coverage as well, I felt so close to solving this case. I wanted as much evidence as was at all possible to make available to the Jockey Club and the police, so that large-scale arrests could be made to close this gang down completely. "Allan," I added. "I will be talking to the chief inspector tomorrow morning at eight. Please ring me at nine for any last-minute changes of plan."

Allan said, "Okay, Boss, will do."

I put the phone down.

Ricky was at last making some headway with finding out who ran Chris's Outdoor Kiosks & Events. This was after all the racecourses had reported back through either e-mails or Ricky chasing them up on the telephone. The signatory on the contract forms was a Mr Christopher T Ward-Stuart, and the address was the company's registered address in Watford. We were going to have to continue the search in earnest tomorrow morning. However, I couldn't help but wonder, is the mystery man who purportedly runs these mobile retail outlets the same man who runs the nightclub and bar in Brighton, Konkordski's? Ward-Stuart and Stu Ward – seemed too coincidental for me.

I asked Ricky to speak to all the secretaries at the racecourses that had given us the same information. "See if any of their employees were present when the contracts were signed," I said. "Can we get a description of the elusive Christopher T Ward-Stuart – or Stu Ward?"

Charlie was back in the office now, and I asked her to send an e-mail to the chief inspector asking for a criminal-records check on Mr Ward, or whatever his real name was. I also asked Charlie to try to find an image or photo of our Mr Ward to send to the chief inspector as well. For Charlie, this was a piece of cake. She just put "Konkordski Bar Brighton" in to her computer search engine, and, presto! There was a recent image of Stu Ward within seconds.

Good, I thought. *Progress.*

It was now nearing six o'clock. Ricky and I went upstairs to shave and shower and get ready for supper.

A brief facial check of my black eyes clearly showed the bruising was beginning to fade away at last.

When we had both finished, we returned to the kitchen. Charlie had laid the table, and our drinks were already on the table as well. Charlie had a Bacardi Breezer, as usual; Laura, one of her favourite ciders; Ricky, a can of Foster's lager; and Charlie had opened a bottle of my favourite red wine for me.

The steaks were just about to be served. Luckily for us, we were all medium rare, so there would be no mix-up of the steaks. They were fillet steaks, cooked perfectly. I liked French mustard with my steak, whilst Ricky preferred Coleman's; the girls just preferred some salt-and-pepper seasoning. Laura sure knew how to cook: the steaks just melted in your mouth; the salad was also superb, with tomatoes, hard-boiled eggs, onions, lettuce, olives, goat cheese, grated carrot, and a French vinaigrette dressing. We spent the best part of three hours eating, drinking, and talking, and the evening went by far too quickly.

We agreed to let the girls sleep in until 9 a.m., although Ricky and I would be up at 7 a.m. Ricky offered to feed Fred in the morning. Mickey would muck out his box, as usual. Laura had already put Mickey's packet of biscuits in the tack room before she started cooking supper.

Laura said she was really looking forward to tomorrow, and we all nodded in agreement that tomorrow could indeed be a good day.

Secretly, I was worried sick something might happen to Laura, and I definitely wanted Mickey about to protect her, there by her side, everywhere she went. Maybe I was overreacting, but what Mickey had said to me earlier about Pete Gregory, the syringe of heroin, and what Gregory was prepared to do was simply inhuman. What made people act like that! How could a fellow human being be so cruel! What had turned this man into an evil, sadistic person, prepared to kill a defenceless horse and innocent young girls, either by lethal injection or firebombing their home and burning them to death? In that moment, there and then, I began to reason like Mickey. I glanced over at Charlie, and for the first time in four years, I saw contentment and happiness. Ricky, was fast becoming a great asset to my company, what with his newly found confidence and assertiveness. And my beautiful Laura. Why would anyone want to kill such a wonderful, lovely person? Yes, Mickey was right after all: when this was all over and Pete Gregory was of no use to anyone, anymore, put the evil, filthy, bastard down – he doesn't deserve to live.

Laura was saying, "Steve, Steve!"

"Oh, sorry, Laura," I replied. "I was miles away."

"You look as if you've seen a ghost," said Ricky.

"No. I was just thinking how wonderfully well Laura has done just to qualify for tomorrow's Grade C Final at Hickstead. To me, that's a feat in itself," I said.

Laura replied, "I don't do second, Steve. The world only remembers winners."

I said okay to Laura, and added, "But just don't go putting on too much pressure on yourself."

Laura said, "Competitors thrive on pressure, Steve. It's what sorts the men out from the boys, and the women out from the girls. Tomorrow is a great opportunity for me to make an impact on the showjumping world in one of the world's best known venues: Hickstead, in the main ring, in front of a big crowd, and on television. And I am determined to seize it with Fred."

I replied, "Well I'll say cheers to that!"

We refilled our glasses and made a toast: to Laura and Fred, and to winning tomorrow's Grade C Championship at Hickstead.

We clinked glasses in the traditional way. Laura was now cosily nestled up to me, with her head on my chest. I had my arm around her. Ricky and Charlie were holding hands. We were all quite content, and oh so happy and relaxed in each other's company. We were a good team that worked really hard to achieve results; however, I could not stop thinking that was this the lull before the storm. We finished our drinks, did the washing up, dried everything, put it all away, and went to bed. It was about 10 p.m.

Laura was still excited, so we did the bathroom bit, brushed our teeth, and got into bed.

"Let's just talk for a bit, Steve."

There was not much to say about tomorrow. Laura was adamant she would win, and I was beginning to believe her as well. I did not tell Laura that Charles Paul, the international showjumper who bought her previous showjumper over three years ago, was now after Fred II. Charles had contacted me earlier in the day, and I said I would be at Hickstead tomorrow and invited Charles to lunch in the members' bar. Charles had accepted my invitation for 2 p.m., we could eat first and then watch Laura compete. Aussie, of course, would be lunching with us as well.

"So what do you want to talk about, my beautiful Laura," I asked.

Laura said, "How did you get on with Charlie, today? I sort of noticed when I was in the office this afternoon that she had sort of … changed. I know this may sound silly, but I saw love in her eyes for the first time since she and I met at college. She was at ease with herself, I guess, for want of a better expression. I think that is the best way to describe it, Steve. Whatever you said to her, it obviously worked."

I told Laura the conversation I had with Charlie, word for word; however I left out the bit that I believed Charlie had told me in confidence: this was about Laura falling in love with me the first time we met. That was a secret between the girls that I should not have known; I therefore did not want Laura to know that perhaps Charlie had betrayed a secret. If Laura wanted to tell me this, she would do it in her own good time. It was love, a declaration of love, and one very close friend confiding in her best friend her hopes and aspirations; let it stay that way. Simple logic was, if she did tell me, I would act surprised; and if she didn't, well, I knew anyway.

Laura said, "You know, Steve, I think Ricky loved Charlie from the outset, when he first laid eyes on her."

I said, "I think you're right there."

Laura added, "I just don't think Charlie was prepared to let anybody in close to her hurt. She just sort of wanted time to come to terms with herself. Ricky, bless him, was prepared to wait and be there for her. That's lovely, isn't it, Steve?"

I agreed with Laura, and then added, "And all the time, you and I had ringside seats."

"I love you so much, Steve."

"Laura," I replied, "you can love me as much as you want to tomorrow night, after you have won the Grade C Championship." And then I added, "If you win, we could invite some close friends back for a little barbecue, just eight or ten people, here, tomorrow evening."

"Hey," Laura said, "that's a great idea, and it's about time we had a bit of entertainment around the house."

We'd been talking for about a half hour. Now we kissed and cuddled, and I played with Laura's nipples. They stood up to attention instantly.

Laura said, "Any chance of a 19 before we go to sleep?" We giggled. Laura's hands were searching under the duvet for my erection.

I said, "Laura, why don't you settle for a 20 tonight? You'll get more than enough riding tomorrow during and after your win."

Laura said, "Promise?"

I said, "I promise."

Laura got to work on me. She gave the most sensuous of BJs, and within five minutes, I had come in her mouth. She swallowed, and within another five minutes, we were fast asleep, as always in each other's arms.

CHAPTER 16

On Friday morning, the sun was shining, and we were in for a beautiful day. We were into the second week of August, and according to the weather forecast, we were in for wall-to-wall sunshine all day. I had the radio on in the bedroom; the temperature from noon on was expected to be in the 70s. Laura was still sound asleep. I showered and shaved all the usual. There was no need for replacement dressings or plasters on my injuries now; they had healed relatively quickly.

I put on some jeans and a short-sleeved shirt, and then I went downstairs to the kitchen. It was just after 7 a.m. Ricky already had the kettle on for the first cup of the day. Neither of us was very much hungry, so we settled for two slices of toast each, with some marmalade. We sat down at the kitchen table. Ricky said he would continue gathering information on Stu Ward and his various aliases, and also dig a bit deeper into the company registered in the Virgin Islands, Cobblestone Investments. I told Ricky that the chief inspector would be telephoning me at 8 a.m., about an hour from now. Furthermore, I said I wanted to keep tabs on what Chris Collins would be up to this morning and where he would be taking Robert Argonaut's recent purchase, the racehorse, Hot Tea.

What is Robert Argonaut up to? I mused for a minute or two, whilst drinking my coffee.

Charlie would look after the office from nine o'clock until roundabout noon. I let Ricky know about my idea for a barbecue tonight, and he offered to go and get the meat required from the local farm shop and then to the off-licence in Burgess Hill for more liquid refreshment supplies to accommodate our guests at this informal gathering tonight, hopefully, to celebrate Laura's success on board Fred II in the Grade C Championship Final at Hickstead this afternoon.

"Who are you going to invite, Boss?" said Ricky.

I replied, "Well, obviously, the four of us; Gary will be back; maybe Aussie and his wife; certainly Charles Paul and his wife, Becky; and Chris Collins. So that would be ten at least."

"Hey, Boss," Ricky said. "Why don't we just order loads of Chinese from the Castle Pub down the road? Saves all that cooking tonight. And they do a catering service, so they will come and set it all up, keep it hot, and do all the serving and clearing up as well."

I had to admit the Chinese we had during the week was truly scrumptious. I said to Ricky, "Great idea. I will leave it to you to organise then, and get in the drink supplies."

"No problem, Boss. I will have it all sorted before we leave for Hickstead lunchtime."

So the dinner was organised. We both had our second cups of coffee, and we had finished our toast and marmalade. It was now 7.30 a.m.

Chris Collins rang me he was on his way to Jonathan Ridger's yard and about fifteen minutes from arrival. *Good,* I thought. *Better to be ten minutes early than ten minutes late when dealing with Robert Argonaut.*

I went outside to the yard. Fred was looking out into the yard from his box, probably wondering where his breakfast had got to. On cue, Ricky went to the feed room and got him his grub, which mainly consisted of bran and oats. Laura had already made his feed up for him the night before. Mickey, as usual now, had mucked out Fred, but was nowhere to be seen, although his grey van was in view. I walked round to the front drive; the white Mercedes estate car was still there, with our specially trained firearms officer showing off his submachine gun, both hands on gun, and finger of his right hand on the trigger. A strap secured the gun from his neck. He carried the gun at waist height, and his posture sort of said, "don't even think about it."

It was fast approaching 8 a.m.; time to get back into the office.

Ricky was in the office talking to the secretary at Sandown Park racecourse. "Yes," said Ricky into the phone. "So your recollection of Christopher T Ward-Stuart is the following: 6 feet tall; about 13 stone, or maybe a bit more; in his middle to late thirties; brown curly hair; and speaks with a soft often quiet voice. Okay, thank you Sue. … If you could confirm that by e-mail, and maybe also send us a copy of the signed contract as an attachment, it would be a great help in this case."

Ricky put the telephone down, I said, "Ricky, don't bother anymore with this line of enquiry. That was a great description."

We had our man: Stu Ward and Christopher T Ward-Stuart were indeed one and the same person.

At eight o'clock on the dot, the chief inspector telephoned. "Morning, Steve," he said.

I replied, "Morning, John."

"My, oh my," he said. "You have been busy. First things first, Steve. Stu Ward, Stewart Ward, Christopher Ward, Christopher Stuart, and Christopher T Ward-Stuart are all one and the same person. His proper name is Chris Stuart; that's the one he was born with. The others are all aliases. He does indeed own the Konkordski Bar and Nightclub in Brighton, and he has a police record for drugs, both owning and supplying them; running a brothel; affray, and ABH."

By ABH, the chief inspector meant "actual bodily harm". "No surprise," I said.

"So, I guess he's a bit of a shit person, really," said the chief inspector. "A man who likes to live off immoral earnings, which is probably what his life is all about. We never knew he was a director of Chris's Outdoor Kiosks & Events, though. Good work, Steve. Also, I think your team's evaluation and estimation is spot on. The question we have to decide on now is, how do we proceed from here? Do we take what's on offer, or do we spread the net a bit further and see what else we can trawl up?"

"Yes, John," I replied, adding, "I have come to the same conclusion."

The chief inspector asked me to run through our plans for today's meeting at Newbury.

"Well, much the same as Ascot on Wednesday; however, we have extra CCTV cameras in operation this time, and, furthermore, we also have audio. This way, we can listen in and record the conversations of customers and the staff working the four trailers that Chris Stuart owns. We believe firmly they are using them to supply drugs to the general public, as well as serving sweets and soft drinks."

"Useful," said the chief inspector. "Very useful indeed."

I added, "Furthermore, we have CCTV in two of both the men's and lady's toilets, to see if punters or customers are buying cocaine and taking it into the toilets to snort up their noses. Once again, the six Tote employees are CCTV covered, so we can cross-reference over the weekend. But there is another big handicap today at Newbury: over 6 furlongs, with a fairly strong favourite. We are hoping for a bigger crowd today, so turnover should be greater as well – certainly better than it was at Ascot on Wednesday."

I further explained to the chief inspector that the Henrys – Noel Henry, the trainer from Newmarket, and his naughty wife, Natalie – were travelling down to Newbury today. I told the chief inspector that they had two runners at Newbury, and also about the blazing row they had on the petrol forecourt that my operative Gary had heard and reported. "Natalie told her husband he could 'fuck himself'; she was going on to Hickstead and staying over the weekend, whether he liked it or not."

DCI Heyes replied, "Well, it looks like it's all happening this weekend then! And isn't it the Hickstead Derby on Sunday, Steve?"

"Yes," I replied.

He asked, "Do they still have a derby trial?"

I replied, "Yes, they do. It is in fact the next class after Laura's class in the main ring. It will start soon after the Grade C Championship that Laura is competing in. I would imagine at about 4.30."

I asked the chief inspector if he would like to join me for lunch this afternoon at Hickstead, in the members' bar. It was a rather tongue-in-cheek request, and I assumed he would say no. I told him the other guests I had invited.

To my surprise, DCI John Heyes said, "Yes, I would love to."

I told him to pick up a member's badge at the entrance to the members' area, to the right of the entrance to the main arena. "Just give them your name," I said. I had done the same for Aussie.

"Well, then," said the chief inspector. "I believe we have covered everything."

I said, "There is one other item. Could you let Mickey the spook go to Hickstead as Laura's personal bodyguard?" I added, "Without her knowing, of course."

"Would it put your mind at ease if I did, Steve?" he asked.

I instinctively replied, "Yes, ever so."

The chief inspector said, "All right, then. I will detail PC Hoad and DS Harman to your property today from 1 p.m. until 7 p.m. Also, there will still be an armed presence at your front drive. With regard to this afternoon, I have twelve plain-clothes detectives on the ground, four uniformed officers, myself, and a tactical firearms officer who is a trained sniper positioned in between the main ring and the stabling and horsebox area, on high ground."

I thanked the chief inspector. "I will see you at two o'clock then, in the members' bar," I said.

"Oh," said the chief inspector. "There is one other little bit of information I want to share with you, Steve. This is with regard to Mickey bugging Jane's Range Rover and trailer last Tuesday."

"Oh yes? Have you recorded some conversations?" I enquired.

"Yes," said the chief inspector. "Jane's groom, Sally, got fucked last night in the trailer by two men who gave her a line of cocaine in a straw for the pleasure, Sally said to them, 'Do you want to fuck me the same time tomorrow night, at about ten, for another two lines of charlie?' Both men agreed and said they would meet Sally in the Castle Pub."

This was situated next to the horsebox entrance to Hickstead, about 300 yards from the main entrance. It was the same pub where we get our Chinese takeaway from – and, hopefully, would be doing tonight if everything went according to plan. After the chief inspector told me about Sally, I covered the mouthpiece and spontaneously started laughing, and the word that immediately came into my head was fuckpig. That was exactly what I had called Sally to her face on Tuesday morning, when she and Jane came over to pick up Jane's horse, Red, and her clothes and tack. Sally was most certainly living up to my description of her.

The chief inspector said, "See you at two then, Steve."

"Yes, I replied. "We will eat and then watch Laura's class at three and then perhaps some of the Hickstead Derby Trial."

I knew Charles Paul had a few of his good horses entered for the derby trial – grade A's – so I thought it would make a change to just have a nice day out with friends, and then a pleasant evening with friends back at the farmhouse. After I put the phone down, I went to the kitchen and made two coffees for Ricky and me. It was now 8.30 a.m.

We sat in the office sipping our coffee, and I asked Ricky if he would compose a letter for me to send to the Hollands, the parents of Giles who had been badly beaten up. The Hollands, had asked my company to look a bit deeper into this assault, as the police had failed to bring any charges against anybody by that point. I asked Ricky to tell them about the signed confession of Pete Gregory for their son's horrific GBH attack; specifically, that he had stated in his confession that Dicky Head had put him up to it and paid him £500. I asked Ricky to keep it short and informal. My thoughts were that Dicky Head would not be in any way officiating today at Newbury, that was for sure.

Allan was on the telephone next, from Newbury. "Everything is going according to plan, Boss, Allan informed me. "John is going to join us at lunchtime, and he told me to tell you, still no sign of Dicky Head." (By John, he meant our operative, not the chief inspector!)

I said, "Thank you, Allan, and please keep us posted on the hour from eleven o'clock and for the rest of the day."

"Okay, Boss, will do."

Chris Collins was next on the telephone, at 8.45. "I have Hot Tea on board, Steve, and I am five minutes from Gatwick. I have to pull over then and telephone Mr Argonaut on his mobile for the address of where to take Hot Tea."

"Thanks, Chris, for letting me know. Please keep me informed throughout the morning."

"Yes, okay, Steve," he replied. "Will do. Speak to you later."

Laura popped her head round the office door. "Morning, guys. Charlie and I are having some boiled eggs with toasted Marmite soldiers for breakfast. Do you guys want me to do some for you?"

Ricky and I both declined but said we would love another coffee.

"Okay, will do," said Laura.

Charlie came into the office. "Any news to tell me?" she enquired.

Ricky said, "The bar owner from Brighton, Stu Ward, and Christopher T Ward-Stuart are one and the same person. He also has a few more aliases and a criminal record, our Konkordski Bar owner, mainly for drug offences," Ricky added.

Charlie said, "Well, I have to say that does not surprise me."

Laura brought our freshly made coffees into the office. "Eggs are ready, Charlie!" she exclaimed.

The girls returned to the kitchen to eat their breakfast.

Chris Collins telephoned again, just after 9 a.m. "This is odd," he said. "Mr Argonaut wants me to take the racehorse to Masnun's in Crawley. That's an abattoir, Steve! They're horse slaughterers!

So that's Robert's game, I thought. *He's going to have the horse put down.* I asked Chris if he had another horse to pick up and take back to Jonathan Ridger's yard.

"No, Steve. Mr Argonaut said to just unload Hot Tea and give it one of the staff at Masnun's."

"Well, Chris," I said. "You better do as you're told."

"All right, Steve," he replied.

I went into the kitchen to let the girls know what was going on with Hot Tea, the racehorse that Mr Argonaut had just purchased for £150,000. Both the girls thought there must be some sort of mistake; Hot Tea must surely be in transit to another yard, and Chris must have another horse to take elsewhere.

Chris was back on the telephone ten minutes later, and he could hardly speak. "They've just shot him he, Steve," said.

I replied, "Shot who, Chris?"

"The horse," he said. "Hot Tea." His voice was trembling. "A perfectly sound, nice, 2-year-old colt. They put a gun to his head, and shot him."

Both the girls stared at me, with mouths open wide in total disbelief. My mobile was on loudspeaker.

Laura was the first to speak. "Robert Argonaut's a bastard," she said. Charlie agreed.

"Are you still there, Steve?"

"Yes," I said to Chris.

"They've just given me a box to take back and deliver to Jonathan Ridger, Steve. What shall I do?"

I told Chris to do as he was told. Out of curiosity, I asked Chris how big the box was.

He said, "It's about twice the size of a shoebox."

I thought to myself, *About enough room for 5 pounds of rump horsemeat then.* I didn't say it in front of the girls, though. "Well, off you go then, Chris," I said. "Go and deliver your package."

Chris said, "Okay. I will give you another call when I am on my way to you at Sayers Common."

"Okay, Chris, you do that," I said.

He sounded as if he was on autopilot. I put the phone down and sat at the kitchen table, whilst the girls finished off their boiled eggs and Marmite soldiers.

I said to the girls, "Mr Argonaut threw away £150,000 just to prove a point."

Both the girls said, simultaneously, "What point is that, Steve?"

I replied, "That money talks; however, it is not for us to judge. We may have our opinions, as Laura has quite candidly pointed out, but whatever we think stays in-house, in the office."

I informed Laura that Chris was still on time to be here at noon. Laura said she was going to give Fred a brush off and then walk him out in the ménage. All the tack was ready in the hamper.

After Charlie finished her breakfast, washed and dried the dishes, and then tidied up the kitchen, she went into the office.

Ricky was just putting the final touches to the letter to the Hollands. At least this would clear up one of my case files, and with a satisfactory ending of which the Hollands would believe that justice had now been served for their son's beating, their thoughts having been completely justified, and once we found Dicky Head, he too would be looking at a long custodial sentence. We were wondering, though, in the office, how many more crimes we would find that he was involved in, who his contacts were, and why we, with the help of the police, had not been able to spot his car. Why had he not purchased any fuel in the last few days? Where was he holed up, and when was he going to break cover? Dicky Head now certainly had a lot of questions to answer.

It was just about 10 a.m. Laura was in the yard to walk out Fred, then twenty minutes' exercise, and when warmed up, a few jumps to finish with. Laura would be finished by 11.15.

Charlie had an idea. She was pursuing a hunch and checking out Cobblestone Investments, and also Chris's Outdoor Kiosks & Events, the company now most definitely linked to Chris Stuart – or his alias, Stu Ward – which was registered in Watford, just north of London virtually on the M11 and M25 interchange. "Steve," Charlie said. "Could we reroute Gary? He is still following Noel Henry and his naughty wife, Natalie. As they come off the M11 onto the M25, we obviously know that they're heading for Newbury. Could we send Gary to the COKE registered address in Watford, just to check it out and maybe see if anybody is in the office? Maybe Gary could call in for a few brochures, ask for some rates of hire for a food-and-drink trailer, for an whole day, for a football festival in Reigate, or something like that maybe. We might get lucky with some vehicle registration numbers. Gary is very observant, he doesn't miss a trick."

I replied, "Yes, definitely, Charlie. Great thought. Give Gary a call on his mobile, and give him the address details of COKE. We have everything to gain and nothing to lose."

Ricky said, "Your letter's ready, Boss." I checked it out on Ricky's computer. "That's fine, Ricky. Spot on, very kind and considerate but to the point." And, of course, the letter was a completely discreet report, finishing with "the police will be charging Mr Dicky Head as well, as soon as he is apprehended; furthermore, Pete Gregory is remanded in custody, awaiting trial", and so on. We obviously left it there, as it was not for Tim Holland or his wife to know that Gregory would not live to stand trial – or indeed see the back of a courtroom ever again.

Ricky pressed Print on his computer, and I signed the letter. Charlie printed me off an envelope, and it would be in the post within the hour. That case might be solved, but there still was a deranged madman out there seeking vengeance for his troubled warped mind, and we were still his main targets.

It was now 11 a.m., and Allan was updating us on his mobile from Newbury. The gates were just opening, and everything was now set up. The COKE employees had arrived and already had opened up for business. The audio bugs were working perfectly; two of the COKE employees had already tested the audio bugs for us. Allan played us a recording: "Hey, Dave," said one of the employees. "I wonder how many fucking cokeheads we'll serve today." Dave replied, "Hey, Danny. I'll have an even score with you, it's over fifty. Yeah, go on, then you fat fucker." They slapped hands, which was covered on the CCTV. The bet was struck, and by 1.30 p.m., Dave had won his bet: they had collected over sixty £18 Tote place tickets on the favourite in the big sprint race later on the card.

"We have two names. What a great start," Allan said. "Have to go now, Boss. Tony wants me."

"Okay," I said. "Thanks, Allan. Speak to you at noon."

Dave and Danny would close early; they had to leave by 2 p.m. The boss called them on Dave's mobile at 1.45. "Got a job for you at Hickstead," he said. "Give all your Tote tickets to the other employees in the other three trailers. I will call you on the mobile at three with the details." Dave said, "Yeah, okay." Dave then told Danny, "We have to leave at two."

Nothing else was said until Natalie exchanged a ticket for some cocaine a few minutes later.

Charlie had contacted Gary, and he had detoured to check out the Watford address; he let Charlie know he probably now would not make it back to the office before 12.15 to 12.30 or so.

Charlie had told him that was okay. She explained that the Watford address was only a mile off the M25, so there would be no time lost to traffic jams. Noel Henry never stopped at any of the motorway services all the way down the M11 or M25 since leaving Newmarket, so when Gary branched off at Watford, there was nothing new to report, Charlie informed me.

"Right," I said. "Coffee time." I went to the kitchen and made four cups of coffee.

Laura walked in on cue, just as the kettle had boiled. "Excellent timing," I said as she planted a smacker on my left cheek. I put the coffees on a tray with the tin of biscuits; all the chocolate bourbons had vanished, though; someone must have eaten them. I took the coffees into the office, where we could discuss the morning's events. Laura grabbed the biscuit tin, and I said, "You've eaten all the bourbons."

She opened one of the desk drawers and produced another two packets. "Always have a plan B," she said, and we all started laughing.

Ricky said, "When I finish my coffee, I'll get over to Burgess Hill to load up with drinks from the supermarket. They'll have more selection and probably cheaper than the off-licence."

Ricky had already told Charlie about my plan for tonight. Charlie said, "A dozen Bacardi Breezers, please."

Laura wanted a dozen of her favourite strawberry ciders. "And a few bottles of champagne, to celebrate my win," she added.

I asked Ricky to get three cases of Foster's lager, and some various bottles of spirits – scotch, gin, vodka – and some mixers, tonic, orange juice, and any other drinks that came to mind.

Charlie went into the kitchen to switch on the ice-making machine which was part of the fridge freezer. We would not be short of ice tonight, in what promised to be a warm and lively evening.

Ricky said he would call in at the Castle on his way back, to place our order for Chinese food for this evening. I reminded him that Hickstead was on and that the Castle was sure to be busy throughout the day. "So be discreet," I said. "Only talk to one person regarding our order, and tell whoever it is that you do not need a receipt; give no name or address, and say that you will personally pick up the order and the tables, chairs, plates, and cutlery. The staff supplied with the order can follow you back in their own transport. To set up and later serve our guests, say that you want two waitresses."

Ricky said, "Will do, Boss. I understand what you mean." He finished his coffee, and set off in one of the blue company vans to Burgess Hill.

The landlord who owned the flat that the girls leased, which had been firebombed, telephoned into the office. Charlie answered.

"Could I speak to Miss Rogers, please?" said the man's voice.

Charlie switched the loudspeaker on. "This is Miss Rogers speaking," she said.

"It's Roger. Roger Smith, your landlord."

"Hi, Roger," said Charlie.

"I'm afraid the flat is going to take about two months to repair, and your lease runs out the end of September, in about six weeks. What do you have in mind, Miss Rogers?"

Charlie was a bit stuck for words. "Just a minute, Roger," she said. "There's someone at the door."

Buying some time to think, I said to Charlie, "Tell him you've decided to buy a house with your boyfriend, and at present you are staying with him until you move into your new house on 1 October."

Laura was giggling, but all the same, Charlie repeated what I had told her to say to Roger the landlord.

Roger replied, "And what about your partner … Laura, is it?"

Charlie replied, "Oh, she's all loved up as well, so we won't be needing the flat anymore or renewing the lease." Charlie added, "Laura's boyfriend has a big house in Sayers Common, and it is where she works too. We will pay you, though, up until the end of the lease, even though at the moment it is uninhabitable due to the fire and smoke damage. No doubt, Roger, you will claim off the insurance for the damage, won't you?"

"Oh yes," replied Roger. "And thank you, Miss Rogers. My best wishes to the pair of you then. Goodbye."

Charlie said, "Goodbye, Roger."

I said to Charlie, "That was a nice gesture, paying him up on your contractual lease."

"Well," said Charlie. "It was hardly his fault we were firebombed; it seemed the right thing to do."

"Yeah," said Laura. I agree."

The telephone rang again, and I answered.

It was Gary. "Hi, Boss," he said.

"Well, did you find out anything?" I asked.

"Yes, Boss. I have three registration numbers from vehicles parked on their premises. There were two women in the office; looked like mother and daughter, the way they acted and talked to each other. So I picked up some brochures with trailer rates on them, I parked about a hundred yards down the road from the address, and when I walked to the office, I used my mobile to store the registration numbers of the vehicles. Whilst we were chatting about hire in their office, I couldn't help but notice the calendar on the wall. The August picture was of showjumping: it was a picture of the Hickstead arena with a rider coming down the derby bank. It was a Cobb's for 'Classic for Footwear calendar."

I asked Gary how long it would take him to get to Sayers Common, and he said he was just approaching Reigate Hill on the M25. "About half an hour, I would say, at the most, Boss," he added.

It was now 11.45, so Gary should arrive no later than 12.15. "Okay, Gary," I said. "See you soon." It looked like Charlie's hunch might have paid off.

Chris Collins called me on my mobile, and I immediately asked where he was and how much longer he would be. He said, "I'm about 20 miles away, on the M23. I should be with you by 12.15. You will never guess what was in the box I had to deliver back to Jonathan Ridger, Steve."

I walked into the kitchen, not wanting the girls to hear my conversation. "About 5 or 6 pounds of rump horsemeat," I said.

"Well, I never!" said Chris. "How did you know?"

I replied "A mixture of intuition and educated guessing, Chris."

"There was a note with the box from Robert Argonaut to Jonathan, Steve. It said, 'Jonathan, have a meal on me.' Signed, Robert Argonaut. With a postscript, 'Never cross my path again. Enjoy your Hot Tea pie.' Jonathan Ridger thought it was some sort of sick joke, Steve, and he stuck the box in the dustbin."

I said, "Okay, Chris. I will speak to Jonathan Ridger and Robert Argonaut early next week. But my business with them at this moment is at an end, I did tell Chris, though I thought Robert had acted in a deplorable manner towards an innocent horse. By the way, we are all ready for you. Park round the back, next to the big garage up-and-over door. You can then hose the inside of the box out before you take Fred to the show. Come into the kitchen for a coffee and a sandwich. We will all be here."

"Okay," Chris replied. "Thanks for that. I really am looking forward to this afternoon, and I'm keeping my fingers crossed Laura can win. See you shortly then!"

Allan telephoned. "Nothing new to report, Steve."

"Allan, same today as Ascot," I said. "All CCTV and audio back to Wharr's for scrutiny and evaluation. Stick with it like last time, and can you and Billy phone in to the office at 10 tomorrow?"

"Okay, will do, Boss," said Allan. "Ten tomorrow will be no problem."

I then told Allan I was having lunch with the chief inspector at Hickstead, at two this afternoon, and that he would be with me for most of the day. "So everything through Gary, please, for the rest of today," I said.

"Okay, Boss," Allan.

Gary would be holding the fort all the time we were over at Hickstead. He would collate all the information coming into the office; if he considered information to be of a serious nature, it would be up to him to then contact me on my mobile for an opinion or further action.

It was now a little after 12 p.m. Both Laura and Charlie had gone upstairs to shower and get themselves ready for the show this afternoon. Ricky was due back anytime now, so I manned the office on my own for the time being. I made myself a coffee, and then sat in the office and pondered as to what this afternoon would bring. Would it bring joy or would it bring sorrow; would we enjoy good luck or suffer bad luck? I looked outside: it was a beautiful summer day, with not a cloud in the sky. I saw Gary and Chris arrive simultaneously. It was just about 12.20. Chris set about hosing out the horsebox straight away. I went into the kitchen, put the kettle on, and then made two rounds of cheese sandwiches: one round for Chris, and the other for Gary, who was walking across the yard now to the kitchen back door. Gary joined me in the kitchen, and I made him a coffee to go with the cheese sandwich. We sat down at the kitchen table, and whilst he was eating, I gave him instructions for this afternoon and early evening.

I told Gary we would be leaving at 1 p.m., and that PC Hoad and DS Harman would be here to keep him company throughout the afternoon and early evening; most specifically, I insisted that the big up-and-over garage door must be closed all the time we were away. We would probably be back around 6.30 or 7 p.m.

Gary said, "Okay, Boss, you just leave it to me to look after the fort. I will spend the afternoon drafting my report on Noel Henry's naughty wife, Natalie, if it's quiet."

"Thanks, Gary, I replied. I then asked if he could stay the night. "We are having a little get-together, just friends and staff, with some Chinese food and drinks." I added, "You can use the downstairs bedroom."

"Yes," said Gary. "I would love to. My partner's on long haul to Sydney at the moment. Thank you, Steve."

Ricky arrived back at about 12.30 p.m. "Sorry I'm late, Boss. I got held up at the Castle … didn't realise it got so busy at lunchtime. It was packed! Mr Wong said that because we were regular takeaway customers, he would be able to accommodate us this evening, no problem. We agreed I can pick up the food at 7.30, together with four tables, twelve chairs, and serving dishes, plates, and cutlery. He said he will send his wife and daughter as waitresses, as we are only just down the road. His wife will follow me back here in her car, and we can take the chairs, tables, and crockery back tomorrow, in our own time. No hassle. I based the food order on what we had during the week, with some extra fish dishes, and I told Mr Wong we wanted crispy duck and pancakes as well, with all the trimmings for ten people. Mr Wong said, 'You have eyes bigger than belly! Enough food here for twenty, but thank you for your custom. I will give you free crackers and free fortune cookies for sweet.'"

I said, "Well done, Ricky. Now you better hurry and get ready for this afternoon."

Ricky dashed upstairs to shower and change.

Gary said, "You do the same, Boss. I can look after everything from now on."

I thanked Gary, and made my way up the stairs to shave, shower, and get dressed for Hickstead.

I was undressed as Laura came out of the shower. "Oh," I said to her. "If we only had time!"

"I'm so excited!" Laura replied.

I could see her nipples were already standing to attention, without manipulation or encouragement. I held her in my arms and gave her a slow passionate kiss, whilst caressing her breasts.

She said, "I think you better have a shower now, big boy."

I looked down, and she was right. "I will be down in fifteen minutes," I said.

Laura was giggling as she got dressed.

Chris had now hosed out the horsebox and was loading up Laura's tack. We all congregated in the kitchen at about 12.50, and we did one last check to make sure we had everything we would need. Ricky got his cosh from the drawer in his desk. I got my sunglasses from my old Rover car, and I made a mental note to replace it very soon with something more upmarket. Laura loaded Fred up as the two policemen turned up to guard our property whilst we were out.

I said, "Help yourselves to coffee or tea. Gary is in the house."

DS Harman said, "Thank you."

Chris had just finished his cheese sandwich and coffee. Returning from the kitchen, he jumped up into the driver's seat of the horsebox, and then we were on our way.

We would enter the showground from the entrance next to the Castle Pub. This entrance was for horseboxes and trailers only. We had been sent passes for two vehicles so that there would be no hassle on the gated entrance. Laura, Charlie, and Chris were in the horsebox. Ricky and I were in one of the blue company diesel vans, and Ricky was driving. Mickey the spook was already there, checking out the stable we had been allocated for Fred whilst we were at the show; we would not need it for very long, though.

It was 1.30 p.m. when we unloaded Fred, and by the time Laura went to the office to declare, register, and then collect her number, it would be nearer 2 p.m.; this was the time Laura had set to start warming Fred up for the task ahead. Forty-five minutes of warm up and some jumps to finish, fifteen minutes for the riders to walk the course, then off we'd go in the drawn order. The draw would take place as the riders were walking the course.

Charles Paul contacted me on my mobile.

"Hi, Charles," I said. "We are here. Laura's just getting Fred out to start warming him up.

"Grand," he said. "Grand." Charles was about 40, and a brilliant horseman. He had ridden for Ireland and Great Britain for sixteen years, a seasoned international, and this was his favourite course. He loved it here. "Would Laura like me to walk the course with her at 2.45, Steve?"

I replied, "I'm sure she would be thrilled! Thank you, Charles, thank you."

He would walk the course with Laura and pass on any tips that might give her an edge, especially in a jump-off.

When they walked the course, Mickey would be no more than three steps behind. He had managed to get a groom's badge. I did not ask him where from, but I let him know that Charles Paul was one of the good guys, and pointed him out to Mickey a full-colour picture was in the programme for today's competitions.

I let Laura know of Charles's offer to walk the course. She said, "Steve, that will be so helpful! Thank you."

I said, "Right then! I'm off to lunch."

Ricky and Charlie were both close at hand, and Chris was at Fred's stable, putting a lock that he'd brought with him on the door.

CHAPTER 17

I booked our table for 2 p.m., we had a great view over the course for the Grade C Championship, the last fence, was a hedge with a white pole set in cups across the top, it looked flimsy and I thought it may catch quite a few competitors out, it stood about 4 feet, 6 inches from the ground.

My guests for the day were DCI John Heyes, though today I would refer to him as a business associate; my old buddy Aussie; and Mr and Mrs Charles Paul. Laura would join us later, we all hoped, with Fred victorious on the day, and Laura proudly sporting the winner's sash.

The chief inspector was the first of my guests to turn up. I offered him an alcoholic drink, although I knew he would refuse.

"Just coffee, please," he said.

I caught the attention of the waitress for our table. "Could you get me a coffee, please?"

"Certainly, sir," she replied. After a few minutes, she returned with the chief inspector's coffee. "Call me, Rosie, sir. I am your waitress this afternoon," she added.

Aussie arrived. I shook his hand. "Glad you could make it, Aussie. What would you like to drink?"

Aussie replied, "A pint of the amber nectar."

I said to Rosie, "Did you understand that?"

"Of course, sir. That's a pint of Foster's lager then!"

"Thank you, Rosie," I said.

I introduced my guests to each other. "Aussie, meet John; John, meet Aussie. John is a business associate, Aussie. And Aussie – as you can see, John – is a paramedic." I then added, "Aussie and I did two tours of duty whilst serving in the army in Northern Ireland during the troubles of the early 1980s, and we became friends."

Aussie was not officially on duty until 4 p.m., and he was not a designated driver for today's shift. He told me this as Rosie returned, and he took his first sip.

Charles Paul was next to arrive, with his wife Becky, who I was meeting for the first time. Charles was still in his riding gear, and for a brief moment, it made me think back to my worst nightmare: knights in white satin, and Chris Cobb trying to kill me. A cold shiver ran down the back of my spine.

"Hello, Charles," I said as I greeted them to the table. We shook hands.

Charles said, "And this is my wife, Becky."

Becky and I kissed cheeks. "So nice to meet you, Becky," I enthused.

I then introduced my other guests to each other. John Heyes stood up and shook hands with Charles, as did Aussie, and they all exchanged greetings. I explained about Aussie being in his paramedic uniform, that he was on duty at 4 p.m. and that we were old buddies from our army days. I left it there, secretly saying to myself, *Aussie, don't order any more alcohol.*

I asked Charles and Becky what they would both like to drink. They both said, "A glass of white wine with soda water, please."

Rosie took our order and was back with the drinks after a few minutes. I told her we were now ready to order lunch. Rosie took the order pad out of her pocket, and with pen in hand, was ready to take our order. Becky was first to give Rosie her choice of starter, battered mushrooms with a garlic dip. Aussie followed suit, as did Charles. John (the chief inspector) went for the farmhouse pâté' with toast, which was my choice as well. We then ordered our main courses. Once again Becky ordered first: fish pie topped with cheese and chive. John opted for the fish pie as well. Aussie and Charles ordered sea bass, with a salad and new potatoes. My choice was good old cod and chips, with mushy peas.

It was now 2.15, and the afternoon was progressing well; no telephone calls from Gary, so I just tried to enjoy the day. There were plenty of people about, so I thought we would surely be safe after all. Ricky was texting me every half hour with updates.

Our starters arrived at 2.25, and the conversation then centred on the showjumping, as expected. To my surprise and amazement, John Heyes was most knowledgeable on the subject. I asked Charles what he thought his chances were with his two grade A's in the Hickstead Derby Trial, which was the next class in the main arena.

"Dublin Bay has a good chance if he decides he wants to do it, Steve," he said. "But Touch Type is a different proposition; he's scared stiff of water, and the water jump might put him off."

We continued eating our starters. Ricky texted just after 2.30 p.m.: "All quiet on the western front." I knew exactly what he meant.

Charles had now finished his starter, and said, "I will walk down, meet Laura, and walk the course with her."

I told Charles that one of her grooms, Mickey, would also be walking the course with her, but at a discreet distance.

For experience, the riders were now gathering in the tunnel into the main arena.

At 2.45 p.m., over the public-address system, the announcer said, "The riders may now go and walk the course." After about five minutes, the announcer further stated, "There are twenty-four competitors for the Grade C Final, and here is the drawn order ..."

He read off the names. Laura would be eleventh to go, and the list of riders numbers was put on the board, next to the collecting ring and the start. As the riders finished their round and left the ring, the numbers were crossed off by one of the officials.

Chris Cobb had two rides, and was drawn seventh and eighteenth; he had qualified his own horse, Classic Punch, and was also down to ride one of Jane's, Red Surprise. Red Surprise was drawn number 7, and Classic Punch was drawn number 18. The programme listed the owners' and riders' names, as well as the names of the horses in all of today's classes. The owner of Classic Punch was listed as Cobb's for Classic Footwear.

Not that I was an expert, but it looked a pretty tight circuit. When Charles returned from walking the course with Laura, I would ask him to enlighten us. Whilst they were walking the course, we could see that Charles was giving specific instructions to Laura at two particular fences: Laura was pacing the strides from the previous fence to those particular fences, and Charles was gesticulating with his hands of what he expected Laura to do should the need arise during the competition; if there was a jump-off, it would emerge later.

The riders returned to their respective mounts in the collecting ring.

Charles returned to his lunch, and after he sat down, I said, "It looks like a pretty tight circuit, Charles."

"Oh yes, it is," he said. "The course is the latter half of the Hickstead Derby Trial course; you need a bloody good horse to win this class."

Rosie brought us our main courses.

The first rider appeared in the ring, the bell sounded, and so the class began. It was a stiff course indeed, and after the first four competitors had been, the best score was eight faults, which was two fences down; the fifth and sixth riders could do no better than eight faults as well. Chris Cobb was next into the ring, with Jane's horse, Red Surprise.

Charles said, "I wonder why Jane isn't riding." He then added, "Didn't you go out with her, Steve?"

"Yes," I replied. "But it was some time ago, Charles." I knew I would have to explain to Charles in greater detail tonight, but that was sufficient for now.

John Heyes was enjoying the food, but the mention of Chris Cobb now in the ring made him pay closer attention to the showjumping.

During his round, Chris Cobb had fortune on his side: he knocked a few and rattled a few, but they stayed up, and this was the first clear round of the competition.

Aussie was talking to Becky about the hospital treatment both I and Laura had received last week, after the crash.

Thanks, Aussie, I thought. *Yeah … more explaining to do tonight.*

By the time the eighth, ninth, and tenth riders had competed, we had finished our lunches. Rosie had taken away the empty plates and replaced them with coffee cups, and cheese and biscuits. The class was now heating up, and Laura was next into the ring, on Fred II.

Laura looked immaculate, in her black leather riding boots, white breeches, navy-blue riding jacket, and matching navy-blue riding hat. Fred must have sensed the atmosphere: he was pure poetry in motion.

Charles kept saying, "Good girl, well ridden!" Nearing the end of the round, the dodge fences were coming up – the same ones that Charles had asked Laura to pay special attention too. The cheering became louder, especially from our table. "Now jump, Laura! And yes, go round the ditch. Good girl, Laura!" Charles was shouting by now, mentally jumping every fence with Laura. "Now jump the third, last, and go round the wall, Laura. Good girl! Final two fences; balance, Laura – now give him his neck … one, two, pop! Well ridden. Final fence, to the last, the hedge, and single pole that's been catching out most of the field so far … one, two, pop! Cleared it by a mile!"

The announcer said, "Well done, Laura Hallett! Our second clear round, and two seconds faster than Red Surprise."

There was a crowd of some two thousand people watching and clapping and cheering. I felt so proud and yet so humble – if that is at all possible both at the same time.

Aussie patted me on the back, commenting, "Hey, what an amazing sheila that girl is!"

Charles and Becky enthused, "Boy, can that girl ride! Where did you find her, Steve?"

I replied, "That's a long story. I found her ten days ago, but I have employed her for the last four years."

More coffee and biscuits arrived. It was about 3.35 p.m.

Allan had called in to the office from Newbury: the favourite was being backed in the big sprint, heavily, for a place; the race was due off at 3.45. Allan had also stated that the two trailer employees had closed their trailer early, at about 2 p.m., and left with a girl. Gary had texted me, rather than ringing, to relay all this. *Good thinking, Gary,* I thought. So far, the Tote had sold more than a hundred £18 tickets – 150, in fact.

Just then, John Heyes said, "Where are the toilets, Steve?

I replied, "I want to go as well. I'll show you."

On our way, he asked if there was any news from Newbury. The chief inspector had good antennae.

"Yes," I said. "One of my operatives texted me just now. They are backing the favourite in the sprint, John: more than £18 tickets sold already; 150, to be exact. Also, two trailer employees closed early and left with a girl, at about 2 p.m."

"So they're at it again," said the chief Inspector. "Damn good rider, your Laura, Steve."

"Thank you, John," I said as we returned to our table.

Ricky texted, "Jane's not using a sling on her arm any more for her dislocated shoulder, but she's red with rage after Laura went clear. Charlie and I watched her watching Laura ride; we were only a few yards away from her. She said, 'Go on, knock one down, please knock one down! Fall off then, and break your fucking neck. Oh fuck and bollocks, the cow's gone clear!' Sally, her groom, was with her. And she said oh fuck too. Just thought you'd better be aware, Boss."

I showed the chief inspector the text message, though not a word was said at the table.

The favourite duly obliged in the 3.45 at Newbury, winning the race at a price of 3 to 1.

At Hickstead, Chris Cobb was just about to enter the ring on his other mount, Classic Punch. We gathered to watch, and Rosie brought us some more coffee. Aussie was drinking his share of coffee as well. *Good,* I thought. Chris Cobb rode his own horse a lot better than Jane's Red Surprise, and went clear in a time slightly better than Laura's – by a second – so there were at least three horses that would contest the jump-off. We settled back to watch the six remaining riders jump, but none were able to go clear. The best of the last six was the last rider, who was clear to the last, but his horse dropped a hind leg and pulled off the top white pole which sat on top of the hedge: four faults.

The jump-off would be Jane's horse, Red Surprise; Chris Cobb's horse, Classic Punch; and Laura's horse, Fred II. A lot could depend on the draw for the jump-off; the course builders were busily preparing the jump-off course. Charles went down to the collecting ring to talk to Laura. As she told me later, he said, "Ideally, we want to go first or last, so we have a number of plans to go through. Now listen, Laura, and don't forget about what I said to do with the dodge fences: if you are drawn first to go, cut inside the ditch this time, don't go round it; and the same with the wall. Now, if your drawn second and Classic Punch is drawn first, watch him ride on the big screen, and see what he does with the dodge fences; if he is last to go or behind you in the draw, go for it. Don't worry about Red Surprise; he's not in it. He will knock two or three fences down when pushed. It's just you and Cobb, Laura – trust your intuition."

The course was ready, and the draw was made.

The announcer said, "And here is the draw for the jump-off: number 11, Fred II; then number 7, Red Surprise; and then number 18, Classic Punch."

Charles had joined us back at the table. "Perfect!" he said. "Just perfect! Now show them, Laura, how good you really are."

Laura rode into the ring, and the bell sounded. There were eight fences on the jump-off course, including the two dodges. Laura was already through four of them, clear and in a good time, according to Charles.

Charles took over the commentary for those in earshot of our table. "Laura, now jump the fifth fence, and cut inside the ditch. Good girl! Oh Laura, perfect! Now jump the sixth. Yes, cut inside the wall, Laura. Go, Laura, go!" Charles was now shouting his head off, as were Aussie and

Becky. Even John Heyes was transfixed. Laura cleared the second-to-last fence with ease, and met a good stride to the last, giving it a good foot of daylight. Fred never touched a twig. A clear round in an impressive 39.4 seconds. Another standing ovation for Laura – we were all clapping and cheering. The chief inspector was clearly just John Heyes at the moment, a spectator enjoying the excitement.

We settled down to watch Chris Cobb ride Jane's horse, Red Surprise. It was no surprise, though, to our resident professional analyst Charles that Chris clouted the second, for an instant four faults, eventually to be 16 in a time of 45.6 seconds. Classic Punch would be a different proposition, though. He set off well, and like Fred, was clear through the first four fences. But, crucially, half a second up on the clock, he jumped the fifth.

Charles said, "He's wrong." And he was; he had the horse on the wrong leg as he tried to cut inside the ditch, but was completely unbalanced going to the sixth, and the horse refused, throwing the rider.

Laura had won the Grade C Championship at Hickstead!

Charles asked me about tonight's plans, and I informed him that the barbecue planned for tonight had sort of morphed into a Chinese feast instead. I explained the logic and that we had waitress service throughout the evening. I told Charles, "Any time after 7.30 is fine."

Charles replied, "We will see you about eight o'clock then." He added, "I have some business I want to talk to you about, Steve."

Yes, I thought. *You want to buy Fred II!*

Charles was riding in the next class, and he had two rides, so I thought it would be safe to text Ricky to ask him and Charlie to put Fred II safely back in his box after the victory parade and lap of honour, and then to come and join us for a coffee in the members' bar with Laura.

Twenty minutes later, a victorious Laura was by my side, with Ricky and Charlie. Mickey was bringing up the rear at a discreet distance, so as to fend off any unprovoked sudden attacks. Yes, I was *that* cautious.

Ricky said, "Chris Cobb and Jane were arguing hysterically, Steve. Jane said to Chris, 'You've just made us look like fucking idiots!'

I suddenly had a thought: *Chris Collins! I've left him exposed, guarding Fred II.* I texted the chief inspector to relay my thought, along with the stable number we had previously been allocated when we arrived, and he got up and walked away from the stable. Out of sight and earshot, he summoned two of his plain-clothes detectives to immediately go to the stabling area; he gave them the number, and told them to guard the horse there until further notice. But when the detectives reached the box where Fred was stabled, they found Chris lying injured outside the stable door, with a pitchfork through his hand.

Chris was in shock. "I wouldn't give them the key. No, sir, I wouldn't give them the key," he kept repeating. "There was nobody about; they were all watching the showjumping in the main ring," Chris said. "Two of them jumped me, about five minutes ago."

It was nearly 4.30 when the chief inspector came back to the table and told me discreetly what had happened.

I asked Ricky if he had ever driven a horsebox.

"Yes," he replied. "In the army."

I said, "Chris injured his hand. Could you drive Fred back to the farm, put him in his stable, and feed him? Leave the horsebox at the farm. And Charlie, could you follow in the van, and then return back here to the show?"

Charlie and Ricky said, "Straight away, Steve." They left immediately.

I was relieved to get Fred away from Hickstead. Given the rage those two psychopaths were in, I now knew we had to cover our every step.

Laura and Becky were enjoying a coffee together. Aussie had already thanked me and said his goodbyes; he had to report for duty at 4 p.m. I wondered whether his first casualty would be Chris Collins. The chief inspector – still just John Heyes – also said his goodbyes, but he first congratulated Laura on her success. I knew where the chief inspector was going: to the stabling area. Mickey was still hovering, drinking a cup of coffee at the bar, just a few yards away. The detectives at the stabling had summoned some medical attention, and it was indeed Aussie's first job of the day. Seeing that Chris was indeed in shock, they swiftly loaded him into the ambulance and off to A&E for medical treatment to the hand which would need stitching, and the general state of his condition which would probably mean an overnight stay for observation. Chris gave the stable door key to Charlie before leaving for hospital in the ambulance.

The riders were now walking the course for the Hickstead Derby Trial. it was a little after 4.30; there were only twenty competitors, as some riders did not bother entering the trial, keeping their horses fresh for the big day on Sunday. Charles Paul was different, though, he reasoned that the three minutes in the main ring jumping the very fences that would be jumped on Sunday was an opportunity to gain valuable experience for the horse; thus, it was too good to miss, as the riders left the ring having walked the course. The draw was made public by the announcer: Charles's horses were drawn eleventh and twelfth, good draws, but this meant he would have to exchange mounts in the tunnel to the main ring from the collecting ring; a quick change would be needed. Touch Type was drawn number 11, and Dublin Bay, 12.

As soon as the draw was made, Charles was on his mobile to Becky. "Can I speak to Laura, please?" he said to his wife. Becky passed the mobile to Laura.

"Hi, Charles," said Laura.

"Hi, Laura. Could you do me a big favour?"

"Yes, of course," said Laura without hesitation. "What do you want me to do?"

Charles said, "My horses are drawn 11 and 12. Touch Type is first in the ring. Could you warm up Dublin Bay for me? Pop him over a few jumps and have him in the tunnel, ready for me to swap mounts?"

"Yes, of course," Laura said again. "Charles, I'll come down at once."

Mickey the spook would proceed to follow her everywhere.

Charles said, "My groom will bring Dublin Bay down at once from the stabling area, but she is not yet good enough to work a horse in. "She will have the horse all tacked up and ready to go."

Laura explained to me what she was going to do, as I'd only caught her end of the phone conversation. This meant that just Becky and I would watch the Hickstead Derby Trial. Charlie and Ricky had just left the farm and were returning to the show. Ricky had swapped the van for my old Rover, according to his text. That was a good idea, as there were now four of us to require transport home. Becky and I watched the first six round, but there were no clears.

The derby bank, the treble of rustic poles to the left of the judges' box, the water jump in the middle of the course, and the fences gave the most trouble to the riders, even though the weather was beautiful, with not a cloud in the sky. Of the next four riders, eight faults was the best score of the day, so far from the first ten riders. Charles Paul came into the ring on Touch Type, the bell sounded, and his round began; it looked as if Touch Type was having one of his good days, as he came down the derby bank clear, on to the rustic triple to the left of the judges' box clear, then on to the water jump. Charles was pushing, pushing, urging him on for all he was worth; Touch Type, though, could see the water. A slap down his hindquarters with the whip; kick, push; Touch Type was stopping quickly, but Charles managed to get a jump of sorts out of him. He did drop both hind legs in the water, but at least it was only four faults so far; he jumped the rest of the round perfectly, giving the last a good 6 inches of daylight. He went through the timing gun to finish the round and record his time, circled as the crowd of some three thousand cheered in appreciation of a fine effort.

The announcer said, "A fine effort there from Charles Paul, our new leader, on four faults."

As he passed the water jump to leave the ring, Touch Type spooked at the water jump, jinked, dropped a shoulder, and deposited Charles into the water. Charles was absolutely soaked. Dripping wet, he took hold of the reins of Touch Type, who was standing next to the water jump as if nothing had happened, and walked him out of the ring.

As I would later learn, Charles then told Laura that she would have to ride Dublin Bay. He checked with the judges, and they agreed that because of the extenuating circumstances, this would be in order and the correct procedure to take. They allowed the change of rider, and the loudspeaker informed the general public.

Just as the announcement was made, Ricky and Charlie were approaching the collecting, ring after parking the Rover in the stabling area. Ricky texted me.

Laura told me afterwards that the judges gave her two minutes to familiarise herself with the course. The bell sounded, and Laura was off. She had seen on television hundreds of times this course being jumped when she was growing up; now it was her time to do something special. She was on a grade A showjumper, riding in an international competition, at one of the top showjumping venues in the world – Hickstead – she was an English rider, and the home crowd of three thousand or so was going to cheer her on. Would she, could she, spring a surprise!

Laura was clear coming to the derby bank, up they went to the top of the bank, steady, down the bank, jump off the bank with some impulsion, and over the white planks which dislodged quite easily. Good, now gallop on; next problem the triple to the left of the judges' box, the rustics.

"Great stride, Laura!" said Charles, still soaking wet as he joined us once again in the members bar watching Laura's round, with a clear sight of the arena and the action. "Over the first part, two strides, pop, another two strides, pop, over the third part, and out! Beautifully ridden, Laura, now gallop on to the water jump."

Dublin, aware that Laura had let out a notch of rein, was now fighting for his head.

"Sit tight," Charles was saying. "Sit tight; give him his head three strides from the water jump."

Laura did exactly that, clearing the jump by a good foot

"Go on, Laura!" Becky was now standing at the table, willing her on. I stood up as well, also willing Laura on.

Becky said, "Four fences to go, a double, a gate, then the last, the hedge with the white pole."

That was proving a problem to the riders all afternoon, but Laura met the double on a great stride.

"Over the first part, one stride, then over the second part, now the gate, aim for the middle. Good girl, Laura!" said Charles. "And to the last, one, two, three! Great stride, Laura!" said Charles as she sailed over the last.

The crowds were cheering and applauding. The announcer over the loudspeaker said, "Our first clear round of the afternoon, Laura Hallett on Dublin Bay!"

The ovation she received as she left the ring was deafening. Charles, though absolutely wet through, greeted Laura as she left the ring and went to the collecting ring where it was quieter. The next rider was in the ring; it wasn't all over yet. Mickey followed them. He wasn't more than 4 yards away from Laura all the time she was not in the main ring, riding.

Meanwhile, Becky was wrapping her arms around me and kissing me. It was going to be some party tonight if Laura was the only clear round.

In the event nobody got even near, the best of the remaining riders had eight faults. That meant Charles had finished second on Touch Type, a one-two for the international rider. Laura had won the Hickstead Derby Trial and was now doing a television interview. The presentation was to follow. When Laura had finished the interview, she was back in the saddle aboard Dublin Bay, next to her was Charles Paul on Touch Type.

Charlie and Ricky congratulated Laura whilst keeping an eye on Jane and Chris Cobb, who were still arguing and gesticulating. Mickey had positioned himself between Laura and the argumentative Jane and Chris, just in case their obvious envy and jealously boiled over. The chief inspector, noticing now that the psychopaths were having a full-blown argument, positioned two of his detectives to tail Jane and Chris, with audio pocket recorders switched to record every piece of evidence. This was vital. Would they say anything to give the game away and incriminate themselves? All evidence, no matter how it was gathered, was vital.

Laura and Dublin Bay led out the winner's procession to collect the winner's sash and cup for the first prize, followed by Charles and the rest of the placed horses, and then a lap of honour. The crowd responded with a standing ovation all around the ground. The second lap of honour was to a Mexican wave as she passed each section of the arena. This was Laura's day; she had just lived the dream.

For Jane, though, the nightmare was just beginning, and with Chris Cobb, no less. Clearly, they both were unhinged. We all needed to be extra vigilant.

It was now just after 6 p.m. I settled up our table bill with Rosie, and gave her a big tip for her excellent service throughout the day. It was time to round up everyone and leave as a group: safety in numbers, which made sense. We congregated in the collecting ring, Laura thanked Charles and Becky for such a wonderful day, and the two grooms took the horses back to the stabling area where Charles had another two showjumpers that would be competing tomorrow.

Ricky had earlier loaded all the tack into the horsebox, including Laura's clothes, so in between Laura signing autographs, we made it to my Rover car. All four of us got in. I drove, and Laura sat next to me, still hanging on to the silver trophy she had just won. The other trophy, for the Grade C Championship, had gone home earlier in the horsebox. Ricky and Charlie sat in the back, and we made our way out of the stabling area. Ricky had thoughtfully taken the pass-out badges and stickers from the van and put them in the front of the Rover, attached to the left-hand side of the windscreen. As we joined the A23, for the first time in the afternoon, it felt safe – let's just get home and party. Mickey was following me in his grey van.

We were eventually back at the farm, not long after 6.30 p.m., as a result of some traffic hold-ups exiting the showground. We still had an hour or so, though, to get ourselves ready for tonight.

The girls went upstairs, singing.

Ricky and I joined Gary in the office for an update. Gary brought us up to speed with a synopsis of today's events since 1 p.m.

Mickey had just pulled into the yard in his grey van. He parked in the ten-vehicle car park next to the big garage up-and-over door.

I thought, *Whether he likes it or not, he will be getting more than a packet of biscuits tonight!*

Gary was overjoyed to hear of Laura's success. Cyril Night rang me to offer his congratulations, and I invited him to pop round later and join us for a drink. He asked if he could bring his wife, Betty, and I told him that of course could; they had been neighbours and friends for a good few years now, and we got all our horse feed from him.

Laura's mum also rang to offer her daughter her congratulations. This put me in a spot of bother; I had never spoken to Laura's mum before, and I guessed I had better get used to it. Her mum said she had watched it on the television. She had taken Laura many times to Hickstead to watch the showjumping – it was all Laura lived for as a child, her mum explained. I told her mum a porky.

I said, "Laura isn't back from the show yet, but I will tell her you rang."

Her mum was crying on the phone. She said, "It's Steve, isn't it? When I said yes, she said, "Thank you for all you've done for Laura, and Charlie as well. Her aunt and I have become close friends. Tell Laura we don't argue at home anymore; I divorced her father three years ago. Steve, I would very much like to be friends with my daughter again. I have taken her for granted since she was 14, in favour of my husband, and I chose wrongly. I would dearly love to see her and talk to her again."

I replied, "I will tell Laura when she gets in, and ask her to give you a call tomorrow evening."

Her mum said, "Thank you, Steve."

I then rang the chief inspector for an update. Chris Collins had been taken to Brighton General in Eastern Road. Apart from the hand injury, he had been treated for shock. He would be kept in overnight for observation. I asked the chief inspector if Chris had given him a description of his attackers.

"Yes," said DCI Heyes. "Chris was very aware and gave us very good descriptions. My detectives are looking for his assailants now; if they had any sense, they should have scarpered by now."

"Just for good measure, could I have the descriptions, Chief Inspector?"

"Yes, okay, Steve. Both are late twenties to middle thirties; the blonde one had tattoos on both hands – the usual 'love' and 'hate', with one letter tattooed on each finger; earring, left ear; about 14 stone, with a bit of a beer belly; about 6 feet tall; blue eyes. The other one was the same age group; brown hair; a bit heavier, about 15 stone, but looked fit, like he worked out a lot; again, about 6 feet tall; he had tattoos as well on his fingers – 'mill' on one hand and 'wall,' on the other."

"Well," I said. "That sounds to me like a Millwall supporter."

"Yes," said the chief inspector. "My thoughts exactly, Steve."

"Anything else, Chief Inspector?"

"Yes, we are just setting up now to catch Sally the fuck-pig, as you call her. We are setting up CCTV with some miniature cameras in the back of the trailer. Two of my detectives are wearing riding gear to blend in and not look out of place. At ten o'clock tonight, the men have planned to meet her in the Castle Pub for a drink, then to the trailer to fuck her for her two straws full of coke to snort tonight."

"What about Dicky Head? Has he surfaced yet?"

"No," said the chief inspector. "We do not have a clue where he is."

"Okay, well, I guess there's no more we can do until tomorrow then," I replied.

"Steve," said the chief inspector, "would you give Laura my regards? My daughter rode for England twenty-five years ago, though, she wasn't in the same league as your Laura."

I said to the chief inspector, "Why don't you do it yourself? We are having a few close friends around this evening, some of whom you've met already, for something to eat and drink. Why don't you join us?"

The chief inspector said, "Well, that's very kind of you Steve. I will call in between nine and ten for a coffee then, but I want to be there for the ten o'clock show staring Sally the fuck-pig."

At long last! I thought. *Chief Inspector John Heyes has a sense of humour after all.*

Ricky and I went upstairs to shower, shave, and change. It was still beautiful outside, and the sun would last well into the evening.

Laura had just come out of the shower as I was undressing. When she saw me she jumped on the bed, on her hands and knees into position 19. "Quickly, Steve!" she said. "I feel so horny."

She was after a 19 before the party even started. I obliged before I had my shower.

Laura had her first orgasm almost immediately. "Oh ... oh ... oh, Steve! I wanted that since Fred won the Grade C this afternoon. I had an orgasm doing my lap of honour. Steve ... oh ... oh ... oh, Steve! I love you so much." Laura had her second orgasm as I exploded my lot inside her.

We showered together and then got ready for our little celebration party. It was nearly 7.30 p.m.

Ricky went in one of the company vans to collect the Chinese feast he had ordered at lunchtime. Gary was now showered and changed.

PC Hoad and DS Harman were now officially off duty, and I invited them to stay if they wanted to. The sergeant had to get back to the wife, as they had planned to go out tonight, but Marcus said he would stay until his mate picked him up at 9.30 to go clubbing in Brighton.

Aussie telephoned to say he could not make it tonight, after all; he was to remain on duty until midnight.

Charles Paul was the next to telephone on my mobile. Did I mind if he were to bring along a few of his friends who were his main sponsors? I replied that I did not mind at all. They were members of the Saudi royal family, Prince Ahmed and his wife, and had sponsored Charles for the last ten years, with fantastic worldwide success.

"Thank you," said Charles. "We will be with you then about nine. And if you could let me and His Highness have about an hour of your and Laura's time, Steve, I am sure you will both find it exceedingly rewarding and of great benefit to you both for the future."

I put the phone down, sure that Laura and I both would indeed find it exactly that.

Doing a rough count of heads for tonight, that would be Laura, Charlie, Ricky, Gary, and me, which was five; plus Charles and Becky Paul and the Prince and his wife, which was another four; Marcus and the chief inspector (two); Cyril and Betty Night (another two); the two waitresses. Probably round about fifteen in all.

It was 7.45 p.m., and Ricky had returned with the food, tables chairs, and everything else required for tonight's entertainment. The two waitresses followed him back. Ricky parked inside the yard and shut the big garage door; the waitresses parked in the ten-car parking area and walked round to the house.

CHAPTER 18

The two waitresses, Mrs Wong and her daughter, Wiwi, laid out the chairs and tables, and then set out the tablecloths, cutlery, and condiments. There were four chairs per table; all in all, enough room for up to sixteen people to eat and drink. Next, they went back to Ricky's van to get the hotplates on which to put the food and keep it hot throughout the evening. Fred was looking out of his box at what was going on. It was just before 8 p.m. It was easy to enter the office or kitchen from the yard, and also easy to walk from the ten-car park into the yard through the big garage up-and-over door, or the walkway between house and yard, then through the kitchen entrance, and then into the yard. No doubt all these areas would be used tonight.

Laura had decided to wear a black cocktail dress for tonight, with white high-heeled shoes. Her hair fell over the right side of her face, covering the sight of her stitches and now fast-fading bruises. Charlie, not to be outshone, opted for a matching Prince of Wales check outfit of matching skirt and tailored jacket, with a cream silk blouse. Ricky was in a light-grey summer suit, similar to my dark-blue summer suit. We both wore white short-sleeved shirts. Gary was in a light-blue summer suit, with a dark-blue shirt. We all dressed smartly, but informally – no ties. The two girls looked stunning. In four years, it was the first time that they had both been to a function and got their stunning pins out. At 5 foot 4, Charlie was not as tall as Laura, but she had a fuller figure.

Laura had her MGB in the yard, which supplied the background music. She had recently installed a twelve-CD stack system, so there was no need to keep changing tapes or CDs. Most of us were in the kitchen, having our first drink of the evening. All the lads went for the Foster's lager. Laura and Charlie were well aware it could turn out to be a long night, so they opted for soft drinks for the time being. Charlie had a Coke, and Laura stuck to lemonade. Ricky got the spirits out, and the mixers, and set up another table next to the Chinese food for people to help themselves. Ricky then cut up some lemons and limes, and put them on a plate. Charlie filled an ice bucket up with ice, and placed it on the table, next to the lemons and limes.

Our first guests of the evening arrived: Cyril and Betty Night.

I had let our friendly police constable Marcus go upstairs to use a shower and change; he had brought with him a change of clothes. He had a smart pair of black stay-press trousers on, and a black-and-white striped shirt. He was out to impress the girls in Brighton tonight no doubt.

Laura was being the perfect hostess. She poured Betty a gin and tonic, with ice and a slice of lime. Cyril opted for a lager. Once with drinks, Laura sat at the table with them, talking showjumping. Marcus, not realising the situation, was trying to chat up Charlie. Ricky and Gary were laughing at his cheesy chat-up lines. Charlie was egging Marcus on, whilst Gary and Ricky were talking shop and listening to Marcus's corny comments, aimed at Charlie. It was quite a funny moment. I joined Gary and Ricky, and we talked and discussed the afternoon's racing from Newbury. After about ten minutes, I spotted Mickey, who was over the other side of the yard.

I excused myself, and I went over to speak to him. "Mickey, please come and join us," I emphasised the *please*. I told him this was not a party as such, but more of a business meeting. "PC Hoad is here, and DCI Heyes will be here later, at around nine." I further asked him to talk to whomever he wished, and to mix. "Please eat whatever you wish, Mickey, and if anybody should ask – which I think not – just tell them you are a groom here."

Mickey said, "Okay, thanks. I like Chinese food. I will stick to soft drinks, though; the chief inspector may need me later over at the showground."

I sat down with Cyril, Betty, and Laura; they were still talking showjumping. It was getting on for 8.30. Mickey was being served by Wiwi, with his first plate of Chinese food. Charlie was now talking to Ricky and Gary. Marcus decided on some Chinese as well, and then he and Mickey found a quiet spot, to talk shop no doubt. I offered Cyril and Betty each a refill, which they eagerly accepted. I went to get them their drinks.

Laura said, "Cyril, Betty, try some of the Chinese."

They both said, "Oh well, okay, then." They both got up, and Mrs Wong was serving now.

Laura saw me struggling with the drinks, and came over to give me a hand. "I could murder a large vodka and tonic, Steve," she said.

"No," I replied. "Not until we have talked business with Charles Paul and his sponsors; then you can have whatever you like."

Laura replied, "Promise, Steve?" She had a glint in her eyes and a huge grin on her face.

I replied, "Anything."

Laura said, "I'd better keep myself sober then!"

Betty and Cyril returned to the table with their plates of food, and you could not have got another single prawn on either of their plates.

I told Laura that her mum had telephoned earlier to congratulate her.

Laura said, "That's not like her at all."

I told Laura that her mum had said there were no more arguments in the house anymore. "Laura, she divorced your father over three years ago now. She said she had made a great mistake four years ago when you left, and she wants to see you and Charlie. Your mum and Charlie's aunt have become very good friends in recent years," I said. "I think your mum wants to make amends, Laura, I think you should see her."

Laura was adamant. "My life's here now, Steve, with you."

I said, "If you want to meet my mum and dad, I think it's only fair that I should at least meet your mum."

Laura said, "Then you'll come with me if I go to see her?"

I said, "Of course."

Laura had a smile back on her face.

We took our drinks back to Cyril and Betty's table. They were halfway through their plates of food, and we sat with them whilst they ate.

Mickey and Marcus were now queuing up for seconds. "Better to go clubbing on a full stomach," Marcus informed Mickey.

Ricky, Charlie, and Gary sat down at one of the tables to tuck into some Chinese. It was just before 9 p.m.

DCI John Heyes turned up, with Miles Valentine in tow. I excused myself from Cyril and Betty, and went to greet the chief inspector and his forensics expert.

Laura was sticking to her promise. She went to get another glass of lemonade. "Betty, another gin and tonic? Cyril, some more lager?" As Laura left, Betty called after her, "Could you make it a large one, dear?

And go easy on the tonic – no point in wasting it, and we don't want to drown the gin now, do we, dear?"

Laura replied, "Yes, okay, Betty! I'll make it a large one, all right."

I shook hands with Miles Valentine and DCI Heyes, who had called in Miles because of the drugs that might turn up tonight; it was mainly because of Sally and the two men she had arranged to fuck tonight for some cocaine. "What can I get you to drink?" Both asked for soft drinks, and settled for orange juice and soda water. We went into the kitchen, and I prepared their drinks with some ice; it was a warm evening.

Next to arrive were Charles and Becky Paul, along with their sponsors, Saudi Prince Ahmed and his wife. Their transport was a gleaming white Rolls Phantom, chauffeur driven. They certainly arrived in style!

The chief inspector noticed them through the kitchen window. "Expecting royalty tonight, Steve?" he commented.

Charles Paul obviously had high-roller contacts. I wondered how much they were going to offer Laura for Fred II. My gut instinct was £70,000. But would Laura want to sell? That was another question that was going to be answered this evening.

"So, Chief Inspector, are you expecting some fireworks after ten?" I enquired.

"Yes, Steve. I am expecting a major development tonight."

I greeted Charles and Becky, and also the Saudi Prince Ahmed and his wife. Laura had joined me at the kitchen door to greet our guests.

The chief inspector required a private word with me, and said he would wait in the yard with Miles, if I could spare him a moment.

I replied, "Okay, John, give me ten minutes."

Laura and I greeted our guests, and after the formal introductions, Laura asked them what drinks they would like. I excused myself for five minutes whilst they were chatting to Laura and offering her their congratulations. Charlie joined them, and offered to get them their drinks. Charles and Becky wanted white wine and sodas; the Prince and his wife stuck to lemonade with ice.

I beckoned for the chief inspector to join me in the office. Miles followed.

"I have just had the hospital on the phone, Steve," said the chief inspector. "Chris Collins is in a bad way. The shock and trauma have caused him to have a heart attack. They are doing all they can for him, but I have to tell you, Steve, he has been moved to the ICU (Intensive Care Unit). If he dies tonight, this could well end up another murder inquiry."

I would not be telling anybody this sad news tonight. I said, "Thank you, Chief Inspector, for letting me know. Laura and I now have to have a meeting with our four guests, but if you want or need to pop back later, then please do. Our little get-together tonight will probably go on until about 11.30 or 12. Also, I would like to know the outcome with Sally the fuck-pig before I go to bed tonight."

"Very well then, Steve," said the chief inspector. "Miles and I will pop back about 11 to 11.15, for a coffee and something to eat, and then we can update you on this evening's events."

I said, "Thank you, John," as they left by the kitchen door.

I then got back to my guests. I joined Charles, Becky, and the Prince and his wife in the yard. They were looking at Fred, over his stable door. Laura was with them, and so was Charlie. They were talking also about Laura's skills in the ring today, and the two major wins.

Charles said, "Is there anywhere, Steve, we can have a private discussion for about an hour?"

"Yes, of course, please follow me into the farmhouse."

We went through the office and into the lounge. It was quieter and less informal. We made ourselves comfortable around the coffee table, seated on the two big settees and armchairs.

Charlie came in and said, "More drinks, anybody?"

We all said, "No, thank you."

Charlie asked if it would it be okay to invite the chauffeur in for a soft drink and some food.

Prince Ahmed said, "Yes, of course. Thank you. Alex would be most grateful for your hospitality."

Charlie said, "I'll make sure you not disturbed."

Once Charlie had closed the door, Charles said, "Down to business then."

Charles stated the following: "Laura, what you have achieved today is incredible! I have been following your progress for the last three years – in fact, since you and Steve sold me Fred I. I have checked on a regular basis with Cyril Night, who is one of the main showjumping dealers in the area, and he always tells me good things about you and your techniques. He is here tonight no doubt to see what I'm here for; he knows I am very interested in you Laura."

I said, "Charles, what is it you are actually after then?"

Charles replied, looking directly at Laura, "Laura, would like to come and work for me in Ireland?"

Laura stood up and said, "Absolutely no way!" She came over to me and sat at my side. Laura held my hand with both of hers; together, we wrapped our hands around one another's.

"You're both absolutely in love with each other, aren't you?" said Charles.

"Yes, we are," said Laura. "Absolutely. Truly, madly, deeply."

Prince Ahmed's wife said to Laura, "You are the best woman rider I have seen in over twenty years. We have a team that Charles runs of over twenty grade A jumpers, and we would like you to travel and ride five of them. We will pay for everything; all you need to do is ride and school."

Laura said, "I do thank you for your offer, from the bottom of my heart. Since the age of 18, all I've ever wanted in my life is to spend the rest of it with Steve."

I thought it would come out sooner rather than later, that she would tell me in her own good time, and now was the right time for Laura. I pressed the hands I held, and smiled at her.

Laura continued, "That, and to teach young horses to be good showjumpers, by breaking them in properly, schooling them, and training them to be athletes and to perform to the highest of their ability. I have done this, as you know, for Cyril, and he pays me well for the time and effort I put in to his young horses." She paused, and then added, "I want to stay here and remain part of this unique team we have here. I could do with a few more horses, but I certainly do not want to go on the circuit. I want to continue doing local shows – in, Sussex, Surrey, and Kent – but my heart is and always will be with Steve. He is my inspiration and the man I am so deeply in love with. Charles, you have been so kind to me today, and that experience will live within me forever. I have loved every moment of today, and I would like to think that one day it will happen again. However, I want quality of life, and that quality is to be here with Steve, building his business and our futures together. I would love to help you in some way if I can, Charles, because you too understand horses and how they work, just like I do. We have unique skills, Charles; that's why I found it so easy to ride Dublin Bay today. It's all about preparation."

Prince Ahmed's wife said, "What a beautiful young lady you are, Laura. So honest, so passionate, so lovely, and so beautiful."

"I know exactly how you feel," Charles said. "Steve, could you give us ten minutes to contemplate?"

Laura and I left the lounge.

We went into the kitchen, and I said to Laura, "Well, I wasn't expecting that."

"No," said Laura. "I was expecting Charles to make me an offer for Fred II."

"Exactly," I said to Laura.

Laura replied, "I could do with a large vodka and tonic now, Steve. I need a drink."

We walked out into the yard. I picked up another lager, and Laura fixed herself a large one. Cyril and Betty were drunk; the last gin and tonic that Laura gave to Betty was a treble with very little tonic. Cyril was on the scotch now.

"Good job they had got a taxi to us tonight," said Charlie.

It was now 9.30, and Marcus was leaving; his friend was here to pick him up. Marcus and his friend offered to give Cyril and Betty a lift home, as they were going past Cyril's farm anyway. So the Nights left with Marcus and his friend. Before they left, I thanked them for coming.

Cyril said, "Don't take less than a hundred grand," as he passed Laura and me, heading for the ten-vehicle parking area.

I sat down with Laura, and had some Chinese nibbles – some sesame-toasted prawn and a spring roll.

Laura sat on my lap. "Well, I guess we will have to come up with a figure that you will take for Fred II – that is, if you want to sell him, Laura."

"Yes," said Laura. "I have to face facts: Fred will be a grade A showjumper within the next eighteen months. It would be unfair of me to keep him here and not let his true talent come to fruition. He is ready now to go on the international circuit, and I would like Charles to ride him; he will get the best out of him."

I said to Laura, "Then what figure have you in mind?"

"Steve, to me it's not the money. I want him to go to a good home. If I were forced to put a price on him, I would be happy with £75,000."

I said, "Cyril thinks he's worth more; he just told me as he left. But what do you want to do, Laura?"

"Steve, I just want to be here with you, and carry on what we are doing now. I'm happy, settled, and surrounded by lovely people. Maybe if we sell Fred, I could buy some horses and school them; perhaps sell them on later."

"Yes," I said to Laura. "But that means having to search for the horses, which is so time-consuming; you'd also have to buy a horsebox and tack, and employ people. Is that really what you want?"

Laura said, "No, you're right, Steve. Maybe it's best to see what Charles and his sponsors have in mind."

"If he has a cash offer for Fred, then Cyril said not to take less than a hundred grand, so let's say a hundred, Laura," I said.

Laura said, "Yes, okay. I'm happy with that."

We sealed it with a kiss. Laura finished off her vodka and tonic.

Gary, Mickey, and Ricky were talking about the Newmarket case, and Naughty Natalie, who was by now somewhere in the vicinity of Hickstead. Charlie had made the chauffeur a coffee and got him a plate of Chinese food. Alex was telling Charlie he had been a chauffeur for six years to the Ahmeds, and had loved every minute of it.

Charles came out of the lounge and asked if he could have two more drinks, another white wine and soda each for him and Becky. Charlie excused herself from the chauffeur, and dealt with Charles request. She told Charles she would bring them through into the lounge. Charlie also made two more lemonades for the Ahmeds. Charles then requested that Laura and I should now return to the lounge.

Becky spoke for the first time. "What you said earlier, Laura, we sensed as well. Both you and my husband have a rare and unique talent: you can both talk to horses. We want to nurture that talent. We thought it might be difficult to prise you away and get you to leave, but we had to ask. We like your small set-up here; it's nice, compact, and very workable to cope with six to eight horses. Plus, the fact you are so close to Hickstead and Gatwick is a great incentive for us." Becky paused, and then continued, "We run a stud in Ireland, breeding and rearing potential showjumpers. For us, though, the problem is that the competition is not that great. It's much better in England. We have a proposition for you and Steve to consider. You do not have to give us an answer tonight, but we would like you to give us an answer before the end of the Hickstead Derby on Sunday. We would also like you to join us for lunch on Sunday, in Prince Ahmed's private box, at 1 p.m. The derby will start at 3 p.m."

I asked Becky what she actually had in mind, and she said, "Prince Ahmed would like you to take two of their most promising youngsters every month, to school them and send them back ridden and broken in after three months. You will get two new horses every month, so the maximum number in your yard will be only six. If you have a horse which you believe is an exceptional talent, then you can keep the horse for one year, minimum, and perhaps get it to grade C level – or until we decide where the horse's future lies. We would also like you to ride the horses in local shows and all the Hickstead meetings. We will pay you £1,000 sterling – per horse, per month; calendar months, that is. We will supply all tack, and you will get an expense account card for entries, fuel, feed, and other sundries; we will also supply you with a brand-new Renault diesel horsebox for two horses."

"This is a most generous offer you have made to Laura," I said to all of them. "I am very grateful to you for offering Laura this opportunity; however, she would be working for you, wouldn't she!"

"Yes," said Becky. "We cannot deny that, but you will still be your own boss, Laura, and nothing will change or conflict in any way your relationship with Steve. We know that now, and the offer has taken the great love you both share into consideration. We intend to supply you with some of the best showjumping stock in the world; furthermore, and as a bonus, if you accept our offer, all the horses we send you that you break in, school, and train up ready for the ring, should you consider them not up to standard, or should they, in your opinion, not have the scope to make up into grade A potential, then they will be sold, and we will pay you a bonus of 10 per cent of the sale price. This would be an assessment fee payment; in the long term, it of course will save our operation a lot of time and money. Literally, Laura, we want you to run our England-based operation. We want the best showjumpers, with the best potential, and we believe in you to deliver."

Charles added, "We would also like to make you an offer for Fred II."

Laura said in reply, "Cyril has already made me an offer, Charles. Just tonight."

Charles replied, "I knew it!" He started laughing, and then he said, "I bet he never offered you £100,000 for him, though, Laura, did he?"

Laura started laughing also. "No, Charles," she said. A few seconds later, when the laughing died down, Laura said, "Actually, Charles, Cyril offered £120,000! He has a buyer for Fred in Germany who's prepared to give £150,000 for him."

Charles sipped his white wine and soda. Prince Ahmed nodded to Charles as their eyes met.

"Very well then, Laura," said Charles. "We will match the offer you have received for Fred, if you decide to accept our offer by the end of the Hickstead Derby on Sunday."

Laura said, "I can tell you now of my decision if you wish, Charles. Let me ride Dublin Bay on Sunday in the Derby, and invite my mum and my best friend, Charlie, together with her aunt, to lunch on Sunday, and you have a deal. The answer is yes."

Without hesitation or prompting, Charles said, "Done then! A handshake is all we need to conclude our business." Laura shook hands with Charles and exchanged a kiss on the cheek with Becky. Charles said, "We will give you a cheque tomorrow for Fred, and we can deal with the paperwork over the weekend. We will pick Fred up on Sunday, and I will take him back to Ireland with me when the show finishes on Sunday, after the derby."

There were smiles on everybody's faces, none more so that Laura's, though.

After Prince Ahmed, Charles, and their wives left, then the festivities really kicked in. Laura turned the reggae music up a notch. It was fast approaching 10 p.m. We put two tables together, and all got stuck in to the crispy duck, with pancake rolls, cucumber, and soya sauce. Ricky, Charlie, Gary, Mickey, and I tucked into our feast. The evening was proceeding better than I could ever have expected, and we were truly enjoying ourselves. I had a good team, and it was nice to see them having a bit of fun as well.

Ricky was turning into a real asset for my company; he had in the last few days developed a great and caring attitude. Now he plated up and delivered some Chinese food to the firearms officer guarding our front drive. I'm sure the officer was grateful; he would be there until 6 a.m., when they would change the guard.

Laura was now on her second large vodka and tonic. I stuck to the lager. Ricky returned from his good deed and sat down; he had a lager on the table. Charlie promptly sat on Ricky's lap. It was approaching 10.30, and I was wondering if Sally the fuck-pig had scored yet.

My mobile rang, and I answered.

"Steve, can we talk?" said the chief inspector. I walked into the kitchen. "The hospital has just been on to me again, Steve. Chris Collins has just had another heart attack; this time, it was fatal. Chris died at 10.12 p.m. The doctor told me the death was due to the shock and trauma brought on by this afternoon's assault. This is now officially a murder inquiry, Steve."

Solemnly I said, "Thank you, Chief Inspector, for informing me." I further enquired about Sally and the two men.

The chief inspector then related what had transpired.

They had just left the Castle Pub and were returning to the stabling area, where all the caravans and horseboxes with living accommodation were parked on-site of the horseshow.

Sally and the two men entered the back of the trailer. There was a straw bale this time, in the back of the trailer; the trailer was lit up by the bright outside security lights floodlighting the area for people staying on-site for the duration of the show. Sally dropped her jeans and panties, lay on the straw bale, and opened her legs so one of the men could fuck her.

First the body builder, the Millwall supporter, asked Sally, "If I give you two straws of coke, can I fuck you up the arse?"

Sally said yes, obliged, and turned over, with her head now dangling over the edge of the straw bale. Millwall man put on his condom, and started fucking Sally up the arse.

The blonde man, with 'hate' and 'love' tattooed across his fingers, said, "I will give you two straws as well." He grabbed Sally by the hair, lifted her head up, and knelt down. He got his prick out, and said to Sally, "Suck on this."

She opened her mouth, and started sucking; after five minutes, the men decided to change over. Semen was dripping from Sally's mouth. It was then the back of the trailer suddenly burst open. DCI Heyes was standing there, cars' headlights on full beam, shining directly into the trailer. Next to him stood a firearms officer holding a submachine gun in his hands, finger on the trigger. In all there were six detectives and two uniformed officers in attendance.

The chief inspector said, "You filthy, low-life, scumbag fuckers! I'm arresting you two men for the murder of Chris Collins earlier today. You don't have to say anything, but anything you do say may be taken down as evidence. Do you understand?"

They sealed their own fate when they said, "We only put a pitchfork through his hand. We didn't murder him."

"Oh yes, you did," said the chief inspector. "You put him in a state of shock and trauma, brought on by the injury you inflicted upon his person, which in turn led to a fatal heart attack this evening. He never recovered after your violent, unprovoked assault." He further arrested them for supplying class A drugs – namely cocaine – and dealing in drugs. "I think we can safely say we can put you two away for fifteen years."

Sally started crying as she got dressed.

"Why are you crying?" the chief inspector asked her.

She replied, "They got me drunk in the pub."

DCI Heyes asked her if she worked at the show, and she said she was a groom. So he asked who she worked for. "Jane Coe," she replied. "She's an international showjumper."

He asked if she was staying on-site and if she had a mobile phone; she answered yes to both questions.

The detectives took the two men out in handcuffs; they'll be detained at Gatwick for further questioning."

Mickey's type of questioning, no doubt, I thought as the chief inspector talked on, but I said nothing.

The chief inspector said, "I confiscated Sally's phone, and told her she may be needed in future to give evidence. We need your name and address also, your full name and address. 'It's Sally Gregory,' she said. I showed no sign of the significance of the revelation; I just carried on writing down her details, Steve. She said she had never met the men before that night. I told her, 'Okay, don't get drunk again, and let this be a lesson for you.' No doubt Sally thought she had got away with a ticking off from me, the kindly chief inspector. 'You'd better get back to where you are staying,' I said. 'Oh,' she said. 'Jane has a big horsebox, with accommodation for two.' 'Right then,' I said. 'Best you get back there. We will keep your mobile phone for now, and would you leave me the straws of coke you were given? They will be required as evidence. Lastly, Miss Gregory, how long will you be remaining at the show for? 'Until the end,' she said. 'We have a horse competing in the derby.'"

What happened next was the kicker, though.

Sally had given Jane's address at Irons Bottom, just outside Reigate, as her home address As she left the trailer, one of the detectives followed her back to Jane's horsebox, with the recorder of his audio equipment turned on. He recorded Sally giving Jane an account of what had just happened.

"Jane," she said. "I have just been caught fucking Danny and Dave in the trailer for four lines of coke!"

Jane replied, "You silly, fucking idiot! Have they been arrested then?"

"Yes, they have," Sally replied. "For murder."

I listened as the chief inspector finished his update. We said our goodbyes, and I put the phone down.

CHAPTER 19

It was now 11 p.m., and Laura was on her third large vodka and tonic. Charlie was now on the Bacardi Breezers, but Ricky had stayed with the Foster's lager. Gary was drinking tea, and Mickey was sipping a coffee. Our resident spook said he needed to stay alert in case the chief inspector needed him. Mickey had earlier shut the big garage door, locked it, and secured any open windows. Mrs Wong and Wiwi started winding down, although there was still a great deal of food to be eaten in the next hour.

DCI Heyes telephoned me on my mobile. "Steve, could I feed two of my detectives with what's left of the Chinese food?"

"Yes, Chief Inspector." I replied. "Bring them over."

He was referring to the two detectives who had found Chris Collins. They had been working without a break since 4 p.m. The chief inspector said he would be round in ten minutes.

I asked Mrs Wong if she had any takeaway cartons in her car.

She said, "Yes. How many?"

I replied, "If you could do ten cartons of mixed Chinese food for takeaway, please."

Wiwi went to get the cartons from the car. Once filled with the Chinese food, I would give them to the chief inspector to feed his troops.

DCI Heyes arrived, along with Miles Valentine and the two detectives. We talked shop for about fifteen minutes whilst the detectives fed themselves. Charlie made them all coffees, and they thanked her.

Miles and the chief inspector helped themselves to some spare ribs and spring rolls, which they brought to the table where Charlie had set down the coffees.

DCI Heyes then briefly recapped the events regarding Sally and her two fucks, saying, "I've arrested them both for the murder of Chris Collins; their names are Danny and Dave."

I had heard these names somewhere before. I said to the chief inspector, "Did they tell you their names then?"

"No," said the chief inspector. "Two of my detectives were having a drink in the Castle Pub and standing next to them. We soon got their names, which were corroborated later when Sally was talking to Jane in their horsebox. The recording I told you about: Sally told Jane, 'They've just arrested Dave and Danny', and then she added that it was for murder."

"Yes, I remember what you told me, Chief Inspector," I said. I then called Ricky over.

"Yes, Boss?"

"Ricky, where do we know the names Danny and Dave from?" I asked.

He said straight away, "They're those two blokes from Chris's Outside Kiosks& Events, Boss. From Newbury this morning. Don't you remember Allan playing us a bit of audio from the conversation at one of the trailers? 'I'll have an even score with you, go on then, you fat fucker.'"

"Yes, of course that was it! Thanks, Ricky. I remember now. They must have driven from Newbury to Hickstead, and then, when one of the trailers suddenly closed at 2 p.m., it must have been those two, Dave and Danny, who left with a mystery girl."

Ricky agreed.

We told the chief inspector what we had on CCTV and audio from earlier this morning: Danny and Dave working one of the trailers for Chris Stuart's company, COKE, at Newbury – selling drugs to the general public, and it seemed now, touting for business and supplying class A drugs at Hickstead, as well as committing murder.

DCI Heyes was elated with this major breakthrough. "A drop of scotch, please, Steve," he said. "I do not think this would be out of order." He gave his car keys to Miles.

The two detectives had now finished their meal. Miles would drive them back to the Hickstead showground, and also hand out the ten cartons of Chinese food Mrs Wong and Wiwi had previously prepared. He would then come back to collect DCI Heyes.

Mrs Wong was now packing up to go home. All the food was now gone. We said goodbye to Mrs Wong and her daughter, and thanked them for the excellent, courteous service they had provided.

I was deep in conversation with the chief inspector. Laura, Charlie, Gary, and Ricky were on the next table, drinking merrily and enjoying the occasion. Mickey was now on the prowl, wary of this evening's events so far.

DCI Heyes and I were discussing the implications that would link Chris Stuart with Jay Penfold, the drugged-up junkie from Brighton. Chris Stuart, the company director of Chris's Outdoor Kiosks & Events, the company that delivered the drugs to the racecourses, along with his employees, Dave and Danny, were looking at a fifteen-year stretch for murder. We now believed Chris Cobb was the importer of the drugs, and Chris Stuart was probably the distributor. Both were positioned and had the resources to carry out these tasks. But where did they get the money from to set up this operation? It would cost millions if it were as big as we thought it was. Where did my ex, Jane, fit in? Where did Dicky Head fit in? Was Naughty Natalie part of the distribution network in Newmarket?

Miles arrived.

"Okay," said DCI Heyes. He finished his scotch and said, "I will talk to you in the morning, Steve." He went to the other table and said to Laura, "Congratulations, Laura, on today." He kissed her on the cheek as he left.

Very thoughtful of you, Chief Inspector, I thought. *Memories of your daughter no doubt, but a lovely gesture all the same.*

It would soon be midnight. Gary had already gone to bed. Laura had started to yawn, looking at me and smiling at the same time. I knew what she wanted. I was feeling amorous too; the pheromones were running rampant, out of control, in both of us. Ricky and Charlie called it a day and trundled off up the wooden hill to bed. Laura and I went back in-to the house and double-checked all the doors were locked. We then retired to our bedroom.

Laura almost fell over going up the stairs. "Pissed again," she muttered in between giggles, which, for me, was an instant turn-on. She had downed four large vodka and tonics in the last two hours. We undressed and then went into the bathroom to brush our teeth.

Laura only had on her panties and her white high heels as she walked over to the bed, she turned around to face me. I had nothing on, apart from a big hard-on; I was rock hard, and ready to please Laura in any way I could. We kissed, and my erection was now stuck between her legs. Laura let herself fall backwards on to the bed. I pulled her panties down to her ankles and then seductively removed them. Laura spread her legs for me, grabbed my hair, and pulled me down onto her juicy, wet clitoris. I loved my lovely Laura's love juice – my tongue lapped up every drop of this elixir, the slightly salty bodily lubricant, the love juice, that so inflamed our desires and passions.

"Oh!" she groaned as she pulled my hair "Oh wow! Oh!" she groaned as she had her first climax. I moved up her body, licking her inner thighs, her navel, her hard nipples, proudly standing erect to attention on her beautiful firm breasts, and then her throat, and, finally her lips. We shared her love juice as our tongues danced in and out of each other's mouths. The salty liquid sensation inflamed our passions further. Laura put her lovely long legs round my back as I now entered her, pumping her with my rock-hard erection – slowly at first, until I knew her second orgasm wasn't far away, and then I increased the tempo. Laura by now was in a state of ecstasy. "Oh! Oh, Steve, don't stop! I love you so much … oh!" She had her second orgasm as I exploded inside her. We stopped for a short time to catch our breath.

Laura said, "That was beautiful, Steve. Will you give me a 19 now? You did promise. You did say I could have anything I wanted tonight."

I laughed, and Laura started giggling. As always, her giggling turned me on. I was once again rock hard and ready for her.

Laura kept her high heels on as she got onto her hands and knees. I spread her lovely long legs apart, and she then lowered herself onto her elbows as I slipped easily into her, with my rock-hard erection. She was still very wet and ready. "Oh," she said. "Oh, ride me, Steve! Oh yes … yes!" I cupped her breasts and pinched her nipples; I kissed her back and caressed her lovely firm breasts whilst pumping her as she screamed with delirious delight for more. Laura had reached the stage of double ecstasy halfway through her orgasm. I came as well, and emptied myself inside her. She had a consecutive second orgasm immediately.

I told Laura that women orgasm generally for about fourteen seconds, men for only about six seconds, and what she had just experienced was a double orgasm. Lucky Laura! Her double orgasm lasted about thirty seconds.

"Wow!" she said. "Steve, is that so?" she asked, referring to the statistics I'd just cited.

She insisted on kissing her best friend goodnight for all the excitement she had just had. She got down on me and managed to extract some love juice.

We fell asleep, once again, in each other's arms, both of us exhausted.

Chris Cobb had other things on his mind. He was livid because he had been outridden and outthought by Laura Hallett earlier in the day. He had fallen out with Jane too, and it was all Laura's fault. Everything was Laura's fault, as far as he and Jane were concerned. At the moment, though his main concern was, who could he fuck tonight? He had booked a table for 9 p.m. at the Castle tonight, expecting to take Jane. That got blown out the window because of Laura's earlier successes, and then the blazing rows with Jane that ensued. Laura had a lot to answer for and would pay a high price, as far as Chris Cobb was concerned; hopefully, he would have his revenge before the show was over.

Natalie had arrived at Newbury earlier, along with her husband, the trainer Noel Henry. She had purchased two £18 tickets for a place on the favourite in the sprint race. It was time to collect, so she visited two of the trailers to pick up her cans of Coke, but, more importantly, the two lines of cocaine supplied in two straws. At the first trailer, she exchanged one of her tickets for a can of Coke and a straw of cocaine. She asked if they were going anywhere near Brighton after the races were over.

One of the staff said, "No, sorry. As much as I would like to take you, we are staying over tonight for the second day of the meeting tomorrow." He added, "Try one of the other trailers."

"Okay," she said. "Thanks."

At the next trailer, she had more luck. Danny and Dave said they were going that way, but they had a last-minute change of plan and would be leaving in fifteen minutes for Hickstead.

Danny said, "We are actually going to Hickstead for the crack tonight, and driving back here in the morning. Do you want a lift then?" Natalie said yes, and Dave said, "I'm sure a little payment on the way to Brighton won't be a problem, will it?"

"Whatever," Natalie replied. She had already handed over her second £18 Tote ticket and requested two straws.

As far as Danny and Dave were concerned, this was an open invitation, and one of the perks of the job they were into, drug distribution, and sex was one of the payments.

"We are leaving in fifteen minutes," they told Natalie.

Natalie said, "Okay."

It was 1.45 p.m. Natalie went to the toilet, snorted a line of cocaine straight away, and thought to herself, *That's better.* Naughty Natalie had her lift sorted.

She quickly found her husband, told him, "I'm off then," – there was really little he could do about it – and that was that. She had made her mind up she wanted a weekend of fun.

Danny was driving. Natalie was on the back seat with Dave; she had just given him a blow job. They had been on the road an hour. Dave's mobile rang. It was his boss. "Don't say anything, Dave, just listen. When I finish talking, just tell me if you understand what I want you and Danny to do."

Dave replied, "Yeah, okay."

His boss then said, "I want you to kill a horse – Laura Hallett's horse – there will be nobody in the stabling area, and you will easily know what stable it is because there will be an old boy guarding the horse standing outside the box. He will stand out like a sore thumb. Use a syringe of heroin, but make sure you fucking kill that horse – no fuck-ups."

Dave said, "I understand." And the line went dead. Dave would let Danny know later, when they dropped Natalie off.

At the petrol station where Danny filled up with fuel, they switched over drivers. Danny was now in the back with Natalie, where she got down on him and gave him a blow job too.

Natalie's thoughts though were only to fuck Chris tonight – the blonde Adonis – she would ring him about 5 p.m., and surprise him.

They got to Hickstead just after 4.10 p.m. Natalie made her way to the main ring, and Dave and Danny made their way to the stabling area.

Dave told Danny what they were up to, what the boss wanted doing. Their boss was right – yeah, the old man did stand out like a sore thumb. This should be easy enough, they agreed, picking up a pitchfork and walking up to the box. They threatened the old man, pinned him to the ground, and put the pitchfork through his hand. When they couldn't find the key to the stablebox, they panicked. Two grooms appeared, and Dave and Danny ran away.

Natalie rang Chris Cobb's mobile at five on the dot. "Hi, Chris, I thought I would surprise you. It's Natalie … thought I would come down tonight instead of tomorrow."

Chris Cobb thought, *Excellent! I can fuck Natalie tonight, and make it up with Jane tomorrow. Great!* "I'm free tonight as well," he told Natalie. "I will get a table at the Castle. We can have something to eat and a drink. I'll book a table for nine o'clock. See you there, Natalie."

"Okay," said Natalie. "Nine it is then, Chris, at the Castle."

Chris and Natalie met as planned, and they dined in the restaurant at the Castle. During the course of the evening, Chris ordered two bottles of white wine; he wasn't that thirsty, he just wanted to fuck.

Natalie drank most of the two bottles. She went to the loo just after 11 p.m., and snorted the other straw full of cocaine, which she had got at Newbury for her £18 Tote ticket. Right, she said to herself, fuck one of the weekend, the blonde Adonis. She had seen the write-up in the Christmas Edition of the *Horse & Hound,* and had put Chris Cobb on her private bucket fuck-it wish list of people she wanted to fuck. Tonight, she could cross another name off. Ron Kallon had also been on the list, but he was crossed off ages ago.

Back at the table, Natalie said, "Sorry I was so long, Chris. A friend called me on my mobile." She sat down and finished off the wine.

Ten minutes later, they left. Chris settled the bill on the way out, and they left hand in hand, presumably, to go back to Chris's horsebox which had living accommodation. However, unbeknown to Chris and Natalie, one of DCI Heyes's detectives was following them – discreetly, of course.

When Chris and Natalie reached Chris's horsebox, they kissed, went up the two steps, and entered the box. The door led into the small kitchenette, and the kitchen light was already on. It was a warm night, and Chris opened the kitchen window.

Under his breath, the detective said, "Thank you." He switched on his audio recorder to record any conversation the two might have.

Chris led Natalie into the next room, which was a bedroom and lounge. He turned on the light, opened the window, and moved back towards Natalie.

Again, the detective couldn't believe his luck: their voices were crystal clear and audible.

They kissed again as they both got undressed.

Chris said, "How do you like your sex, Natalie?"

Naughty Natalie replied, "Any way you like, Chris. Fuck me whatever way you wish."

Chris said, "Let's start with a 69 – you know the Kama Sutra? – to get the juices flowing and in the mood." He didn't know that this would be Natalie's third blow job in seven hours.

Chris got down on Natalie, blowing up and sucking her pussy, whilst she held his erect penis and sucked him off. After five minutes, Chris came in her mouth. She swallowed straight away.

"Okay," said Natalie. "I'm ready to be fucked now."

Chris got up off the bed and said, "Come with me, Natalie."

He took Natalie into the part of the horsebox where they travelled the horses. There was a line of six metal rings along one side of the horsebox, about 7 feet off the floor. This was where the horses were tethered, and also where the hay net was hung when travelling. Chris tied Natalie's hands together, and then attached the leather strap to one of the rings, so her feet were just off the ground, with her hands now tied and above her head.

He then fucked her against the side of the horsebox. Natalie would have to put her legs round Chris's body and grip tightly to take the weight of her body; this added to Chris's pleasure. And to demean his fuck at the same time, after he'd had enough, Chris undid the leather strap that tied her hands to the ring, and let her down. He then laid her over a bale of straw, pushed her legs apart, and fucked her up the arse.

Natalie was on another planet by now, after the line of coke she had snorted at the Castle earlier.

Not bad, Chris thought.

Natalie just lay there, hardly moving, oblivious to the sex she had just had; she probably never felt a thing.

Chris showered and then dried off. As an afterthought, he threw a horse blanket over Natalie as she slept on the bale of straw. He then went to his bed and fell asleep.

Unfortunately for the detective, there was no incriminating conversation to record for the chief inspector and his ongoing investigation. The detective would return to his designated position at Hickstead until the chief inspector contacted him for an update and a report. He unlocked one of the unmarked police cars that he had keys for, parked in the stabling area, got in, and settled down. He would wait for the chief inspector to call him on the mobile.

The chief inspector, meanwhile, was with Steve Hurst, enjoying a scotch.

The chief inspector called a meeting of all his detectives working this case, for 12.45 a.m. on Saturday. All his detectives were informed, by text or telephone, and they had little time to get back to Brighton Police Station in Edward Street. The detectives never even had time to eat the Chinese takeaway. Four uniformed officers remained on duty at the Hickstead showground, at the stabling area and the entrances and exits, of which there were two. Miles drove the chief inspector to the meeting.

The chief inspector started the meeting off by thanking all the detectives who had taken part in that day's operation. He then explained to them the reason for the operation, and apologised to his officers as to why the operation was so hush, hush. The Home Secretary was aware of this ongoing investigation, and as such, was being orchestrated at the highest level; MI5 was working with the Sussex Constabulary on this particular case. This operation was of national importance, with grave ramifications for the public, if the police did not achieve a result. This is what the chief inspector told his detectives.

He continued, "The outcome would depend on you, my detectives, being vigilant at all times during the rest of this showjumping meeting, which finishes on Sunday evening. The Home Secretary has asked me to keep a lid on this investigation – no press whatsoever – and all my detectives and officers must not talk or speculate with anyone outside this investigation. Any information will only be divulged on a need-to-know basis, do I make myself clear, detectives?"'

One of the detectives said to the chief inspector, "Give us a clue, Chief. Tell us what this is all about! All we have had all day is an old boy with a pitchfork through his hand, and we have caught an old slapper banging a some low-lifers for a few lines of cocaine. For the manpower on this case, that's not a lot of payback, Chief."

Some of the other detectives muttered their agreement.

The chief inspector said, "Look, I know it can be frustrating at times, but this investigation is a very delicate one. I have been given delegated powers to use the MI5 cell which operates out of Gatwick, where they have a holding centre. After tonight's operation, we have three players locked up in what we believe is a nationwide organisation flooding the horse-racing industry and the showjumping fraternity with hard drugs – cocaine and heroin. In the last ten days, we have had three murders in Brighton area alone, and three attempted murders. I am absolutely convinced that more attempted murders will follow sometime over this weekend. I want you, my detectives and officers, to prevent this from happening."

He continued, "We need to take these murderous bastards out of society altogether. It is our duty as policemen to protect society, and what I will tell you is this: I have never in my whole career been as deadly serious as I am now. I even have a sniper near the showjumping arena; he'll be there during the show to take out any would-be assassins if they attack, or try to attack, certain members or operatives of a special agency working alongside MI5 and the Sussex Police Constabulary. So we are, in effect, three government agencies united and sharing information on this ongoing investigation. If it were not for this shared information, we would not have arrested those scumbags tonight, and they would still be at large to peddle their drugs."

Another detective said to the chief inspector, "Okay, Chief, point taken. At least we all feel a bit wiser now, but why did you let that fuck-pig slapper go back out on the loose?" He was referring to Sally Gregory.

The chief inspector slapped the young detective down, saying, "To net bigger fish, my boy."

The detective who had followed Sally back to Jane's horsebox said, "Yes, Chief, and it was the right move. My audio recording suggests it's already paying dividends. At the point of arrest, she flatly denied knowing Danny and Dave, but later, when speaking to her employer, Jane, she referred to them as friends, stating 'they've arrested Danny and Dave for murder'."

The chief inspector thanked the detective for passing on that information to the other detectives. To the entire group he said, "So, you see, we have to be careful and vigilant; we have to be on our toes at all times, and, most importantly, we have to be aware at all times – the lives of innocent people will depend on it."

The chief inspector finished the meeting by informing the detectives that he believed the showjumping fraternity held the key to the main players in a distribution network of imported hard drugs which were then distributed all over the country. He was convinced the main players and the big money investment came from people connected to the showjumping fraternity, and they would be here at this prestigious Hickstead Derby meeting this weekend.

"Now all of you go home and get a good night's sleep," he said. "Uniforms will stay on duty until 10 a.m. this morning. I want you all back at Hickstead for 9.45 a.m. And all of you, make sure you have a good breakfast: it will be a long day tomorrow. Finally, keep your mouths shut – not a word to anyone about this operation which, once again, is of national importance. And my backside is on the line."

The detectives left the meeting now fully aware of the importance of this operation. They were right behind the chief inspector. Most of them had never worked on a case with three murders and three attempted murders within ten days, and a case of such significance – as the chief inspector had said, of national importance. The detectives left to go home to sleep, invigorated and motivated, just as the chief inspector had hoped for.

CHAPTER 20

Laura awoke with a headache. I wasn't surprised. I went to the bathroom and got her an aspirin and a glass of water. It was just after 8 a.m. As I pulled back the curtains, the sun was once again shining brightly. It was going to be another hot summer day. I went downstairs and made two coffees: one for me and one for Laura.

Charlie and Ricky had just got up as well, and they came into the kitchen for some breakfast. Gary was already in the office, and he reported a vast amount of information was coming in from Wharr's.

Charlie said, "Oh no! Not on a Saturday morning."

I said, "A good breakfast for all of us to start the day, and then we'll get to it."

Ricky volunteered to be the chef.

I also indicated we needed to have a team meeting as soon as possible after 9 a.m.

I went back upstairs to the bedroom, carrying the two coffees, and put them on the bedside tables. I got back into bed, and started drinking my coffee.

Laura sipped her coffee as well. "That's better," she said. After another sip, she asked, "Is our sex normal, Steve? Does everybody have sex like we have sex?"

I replied, "No, my beautiful Laura, our sex is very special."

Laura replied, "Is it because we love each other so much?"

"Yes," I replied. "We are so intense and passionate towards each other because our love knows no bounds. We both share the same desire to please each other. Our mind-sets and our deep devotion for each other makes us very special, and that helps us to reach ecstasy very easily when we make love." I looked at her, and then added, "And now you've got me aroused, you naughty girl!"

Laura started giggling, and that made it even worse.

"I'd better have a little talk with my friend then!" she said.

Laura pulled the duvet back, and she got down on my erection. As soon as she had some slightly salty love juice in her mouth, she came up to kiss me. Our tongues danced in and out of each other's mouths; meanwhile, her left hand keeping me hard and erect so that she could return and finish the job. Laura went back down on me as I caressed her breasts. After a few minutes, I could resist no more, as she made me come.

"Steve, you taste so lovely," she said. Laura swallowed, we snuggled up, and then she asked, "So, what's on the agenda for today then, Steve?"

I replied, "Well, firstly, my beautiful Laura, we are going to shower, get dressed, and then have a mega breakfast. Ricky's cooking it right now. I told him you wanted crispy, extra-salty bacon."

Laura started giggling again. "There's only one thing I like salty: you!" she said.

We both started laughing, and we got out of bed and showered together.

We lathered each other up – everywhere – the water cascading down on us. Our arms were wrapped around each other. We *were* special, just as I'd told Laura a few moments before. We gave each other immense confidence and inspiration because of our deep unfettered understanding of each other. Our shared ambition was to be as one, and our beautiful love was just beginning. I thought of what Laura had said to me a few days before: when someone really loves you, that's when your life begins. That was true for both of us; we both knew it. What had started for us ten days ago would last a lifetime.

After we dried off and got dressed, we went down to the kitchen. Ricky had really pushed the boat out: eggs, bacon, mushrooms, tomatoes, sausages, beans, some lovely thick toast, and coffee. Gary came into the kitchen from the office to join us, and all five of us enjoyed a truly sumptuous breakfast.

Breakfast was over, and after the euphoria and sadness of the last twenty-four hours, it was now time to get back to work. Laura went outside to check out Fred; Mickey had mucked him out and fed him, but as usual, was nowhere to be seen. Gary was adding the final touches to his report on Naughty Natalie, trainer Noel Henry's unfaithful wife; though as of yet unbeknown to Gary, an extra few paragraphs would need to be added on later. Charlie was feeding Mother with all the information that had come in from Wharr's overnight. Ricky was tidying up the kitchen after our breakfast. Laura came into the office after visiting Fred, and she dealt with the stack of telephone messages on the answerphone – most of them were messages of congratulations for her achievements at Hickstead. Allan and Billy were due to report in at 10 a.m. We would then make a decision as to whether they would stay down in Berkshire or I would call them back to the office here in Sayers Common. The chief inspector was also due to telephone me this morning, and Charles Paul would be arriving at noon to pay Laura and sign the contracts. We had plenty of work to do this Saturday morning, and I had the sad job of reporting to my employees the death of Chris Collins. However, before I could do so, the chief inspector called.

Charlie answered the telephone. "For you, Steve, she said. "It's the chief inspector."

"Thank you, Charlie," I said. As I picked up the telephone, I said, "Hello, Chief Inspector."

"Morning, Steve," said DCI Heyes. "I am still at Brighton Police Station; however, we will be leaving for Hickstead in a few minutes' time. Some of my detectives have left already. We are using marked cars for the rest of the show, Steve," the chief inspector further informed me.

Hoping he would elaborate, I said, "What do you mean, Chief Inspector?"

"High visibility," he explained. "In your face – police cars everywhere on the showground." The chief inspector went on to say that he was still uneasy and wanted to prevent the possibility of any more unnecessary deaths. "What's your plan for today, Steve?" he asked.

I gave him a brief overview of our plans for the day. I explained about the sale of Laura's horse to Charles Paul's sponsors, and that Laura had secured the ride on Dublin Bay in the big one on Sunday: the Hickstead Derby.

DCI Heyes said, "Damn bloody damn!"

I replied, "Yes, I know exactly how you feel. Believe me, I feel even worse, but we have to show these death-dealing bastards that our resolve is stronger than theirs."

"Quite," he said. "But it's still a bloody problem all the same, Steve."

DCI Heyes then told me about Chris Cobb and Naughty Natalie's antics last night. I knew this would be the final nail in the coffin for Noel Henry's report from my company regarding his unfaithful wife; the trainer from Newmarket would be truly shocked by his wife's extramarital activities.

DCI Heyes said, "I have to go, Steve. I have a meeting with my detectives at 9.45 on the showground."

"Fine," I said. "Why don't you call in for coffee at about eleven o'clock?"

"Yes, okay then, Steve," he said.

We said goodbye, and I put the phone down.

Ricky had finished in the kitchen, and he joined us all in the office. It was now 9.15 a.m.

"Right, everybody," I said. "Office meeting now in progress." I had everybody's attention. "I have a plan of action for today, but firstly, I have some very sad news to tell you."

I was quite emotional. Laura sensed it straight away, quickly came over, and stood by my side, holding one of my hands. I then told them about Chris Collins's death. Charlie burst into tears, and Ricky comforted her. Gary was dumbstruck. Laura sat down next to me lest she fall down – such was the shocking news. I explained about the pitchfork being stuck through his hand as and when he was guarding Fred II, and I explained about his attackers and that those responsible for his attack were caught red-handed gang-banging Sally, Jane's groom, at 10.30 last night, and giving her payment for the sex by means of four lines – or straws – of cocaine. Finally, I informed the team that the two men were no other than Danny and Dave, the two employees from Chris's Outdoor Kiosks & Events who were running one of the trailers yesterday at Newbury.

I relayed what DCI Heyes had told me: Dave and Danny had owned up for the attack on Chris, not realising that the injury they had inflicted on Chris yesterday had induced two heart attacks later in the day, the second of which had proved to be fatal. The unprovoked attack, according to the doctor who treated Chris at the hospital, caused Chris to suffer shock and trauma from which he never recovered. Thus, in effect, Dave and Danny murdered Chris – maybe unintentionally, but I felt a jury wouldn't see it that way. Certainly not with the priors they had, according to the chief inspector, who had already checked them out after their arrests last night. They were, in the chief inspector's words, two vicious thugs with a string of previous convictions for assault and theft. I shared his words verbatim with my team.

Ricky stood up, went into the kitchen, and made five coffees. Laura, comforting Charlie, took her upstairs to give her some space for her grief to dissipate and then to regain her composure. It was an emotional ten minutes for us all; even Gary shed a few tears. We all knew Chris died protecting Laura's horse, Fred II, and as far as we all were concerned, Chris Collins would never be forgotten. He was a lovely man and a good friend.

Ricky came back into the office, with the five coffees on a tray. He took two of the mugs of coffee upstairs, and he stayed with Charlie. Laura returned to the office. I knew what Laura wanted, and I told Gary we were going into the yard for five minutes.

Laura and I walked out of the office and into the yard. We went to the tack room, put our coffees down, and sat down on the couch. Laura then had a good cry. I held her in my arms, feeling the tears rolling down her cheek where her face was next to mine.

"The bastards," she said. "The fucking bastards." If anything, this made Laura even more determined. The tears subsided after a few minutes. Laura's grieving was over, and she quickly regained her composure. "Come on, Steve," she said. "Let's go back to the office. The quicker we put those bastards behind bars, the quicker we can all get on with our lives."

I wiped the remaining tears from Laura's eyes and saw for the first time another side of my beautiful Laura: the steely determination in her, the difference why some of us succeeded in life, but, sadly, the reason why most people failed. Some people were born winners, and I knew then that Laura was one of them. In that moment, I saw what Charles and Becky Paul and Prince Ahmed and his wife could see in Laura. It was better to die in battle than to live in fear; I'd always believed that. If these people were after a fight, they were damn well going to get one.

Laura and I walked back to the office, hand in hand, both of us composed. Charlie, Ricky, and Gary were all seated.

Ricky said, "They've killed one of us, Boss. Let's change the rules: tell the chief inspector there will be no prisoners – when we find the fuckers, let's put them down, there and then."

Little did Ricky know, that was always Mickey's intention. I suspected even the chief inspector would turn a blind eye. I agreed with them to a certain degree; perhaps we were being too defensive and not offensive enough. When the chief inspector called in for coffee at 11 a.m., I would try to get him to change tactics somewhat: high visibility, yes, but we should also go for some high-profile arrests at Hickstead as well. Chris Cobb and Jane Coe were the two I had in mind.

The chief inspector arrived at Hickstead at 9.40 a.m. The police used Doug Dunne's office for the meeting; he was the owner of Hickstead. He was hopping mad, and would have words with the chief inspector once the meeting was over. The team briefing was much the same as the meeting held at the Brighton Police Station much earlier this morning; this time round, though, each team of two detectives had specific areas of the showground to patrol. The police sniper had arrived, and once again, would go to high ground, to observe and to protect certain targets that the chief inspector had identified. As far as the chief inspector was concerned, Laura Hallett and Steve Hurst were on someone's hit list.

During the briefing the chief inspector received some news from police headquarters on his mobile: it was about the vehicle registration numbers of the three cars observed by Gary at the address of Chris's Outdoor Kiosks & Events in Watford. One was registered to Cobblestone Investments, at the Watford address; one was registered to Mrs Amy Cobb, at an address in Northampton Town; one was registered to Miss Lucy Cobb, at an address in Luton Bedfordshire. The last two were probably mother and daughter, in DCI Heyes's opinion; more importantly, though, Mrs Cobb was probably the mother of Chris Cobb. The other bit of news was with regard to Sally Gregory and her mobile phone, which DCI Heyes had confiscated. Some of the stored telephone numbers made him highly suspicious: she had Danny's and Dave's numbers; also stored were Chris Cobb, Pete Gregory (her brother), Jane Coe (her boss), Steve Hurst, Chris Stuart, Dicky Head, and, last but not least, Natalie Henry, the trainer's wife from Newmarket.

It was now 10 a.m., and the detectives were taking up their allotted areas to patrol within the showground. DCI Heyes remained at the offices of the Hickstead arena.

Doug Dunne, the owner, had just arrived. He was furious. He ushered the chief inspector into his office, the one the chief inspector had just used for his briefing. "Now what the fuck's going on, Chief Inspector?" he demanded. "What is this over-the-top police presence at my prestigious derby meeting?"

DCI Heyes gave Doug a brief but descriptive synopsis of the goings-on over the last ten days: the three deaths, the attempted murders, the drug dealing, the murder yesterday of Chris Collins, and so on. (Doug had known Chris for many years and considered him a friend.) "And, furthermore," DCI Heyes added, "Two international riders are coming under increased suspicion of being involved in the criminal activities that have occurred over the last ten days: Jane Coe and Chris Cobb."

Doug Dunne was virtually shell-shocked by the chief inspector's revelations.

Doug immediately made some telephone calls to his sons. He had four sons, all in their twenties, and in his time, he'd had as many wives – four in the last twenty-five years, so one son for each wife. They were all scattered around the vast Hickstead estate that covered some 200 acres. There were eight farmhouses and six cottages on the estate, which either housed his previous wives and their sons, or were let to tenant farmers. Two cottages at present were unoccupied.

"Right, Chief Inspector," said Doug. "Use this office as your headquarters for the duration of the show. My four boys will search the estate for any persons who should not be on it. Please coordinate your operation from here. If you need any backup, I have twenty security guards available. Let's flush the bastards out; they give my sport a bad name."

DCI Heyes shook hands with Doug Dunne, offering his gratitude for Doug's cooperation.

It was now getting near to 10.30 a.m. Chris Cobb had just got up. No need to check on his four horses at the show, though: he had two grooms staying in a caravan near to the stabling area at the show. He was trying to make up his mind whether to give Natalie one before he fucked her off out of it. He was aware she was using and doing drugs in Newmarket, and that she was a distributor for his dad. He had supplied her a few weeks back with some cocaine, and then he'd invited her to Hickstead, promising her that he would fuck her silly. She couldn't believe her luck, and nothing, not even her husband, was going to stop her getting fucked by Adonis.

Chris made up his mind: if she was still on the straw bale, he would give it a quick fuck, and then have a shower. He put on his pants, drank some orange juice he got out of the fridge in the kitchenette, and then went to the area of the horsebox where the horses were tethered when travelling.

Natalie was still in the same position as he had left her last night, with the horse blanket over her.

"Natalie," he said. "Natalie!" He prodded her with his foot, and there was a faint but audible murmur. "Natalie, fancy a fuck for breakfast?" said Chris, but there was no response.

He pulled the horse blanket off her, and knew straight away he wouldn't be fucking her this morning: there was a pool of blood around her crotch; she was in a bad way Chris thought to himself, *I need this like a fucking hole in the head!* He telephoned the office at Hickstead and asked for an ambulance; he told them in the office that his sister had just had a miscarriage. A paramedic would attend within minutes.

Aussie was on the early shift, 8 a.m. to 4 p.m. He attended, and was suspicious straight away of the circumstances surrounding this girl's injuries. Aussie saw the rings and some blood – not a lot, but some – about 4 feet off the floor. Whilst Chris was showering, Aussie took some pictures with a little camera he always carried around with him. He also took some pictures of Natalie lying on the straw bale. Aussie and his partner loaded Natalie into the ambulance and took her straight to Brighton General in Eastern Road. Aussie telephoned me at the office in Sayers Common, as they made their way to the hospital, and he told me of the strange scenario surrounding this girl's injuries. He also told me she had a dislocated shoulder, not usually associated with a miscarriage.

"Thanks, Aussie," I said. I then relayed the information to DCI Heyes straight away.

When Aussie and his partner got to the hospital, Miles Valentine from Police Forensics was waiting for the ambulance to arrive. He collected Natalie's bag from Aussie, her mobile phone was in the bag, and Miles would check out the stored numbers and any text messages from her contacts. The chief inspector had arranged for Miles to meet the ambulance; maybe some more precious information would be obtained.

Chris Collins couldn't stand the sight of blood – it freaked him out. However, he had nobody to clean the mess up, so he would have to do it himself. The straw bale was taken out and placed underneath the horsebox, some Jeyes Fluid and a cloth would clean up the blood on the floor and the side of the box, underneath the ring that he had tied Natalie to before fucking her. He only had twenty minutes to clean the mess up; Jane was due to arrive at 11 a.m. He had to scrub the floor and side of the box in the end to make sure it was as spotless as he could get it; he did not want

265

any hassle from the police, accusing him of assault if they found out about what he had done to Natalie. It was not the start to the morning he had hoped for.

Natalie was in a bad way: apart from overdosing on cocaine, she had indeed miscarried. The doctor attending her thought she had been pregnant for about six to eight weeks. Another hour, and he probably would not have been able to save her. The doctor confirmed she also had a dislocated shoulder, and he believed, from the marks on her wrists, that she had indeed been tied up, raped, and violently assaulted; she had also been buggered. The doctor had collected some DNA evidence, should the girl survive her ordeal and wish to bring charges against her assailant. The doctor relayed all this by phone to DCI Heyes, who in turn relayed it to me.

Miles Valentine had given the doctor the chief inspector's number, and asked him to ring the chief inspector after his initial examination of Natalie, as this was part of an ongoing investigation. The doctor had duly obliged, and the chief inspector thanked him for the information, and then rang me in the office to keep me up to speed. Charlie, hearing everything that was said on the speakerphone, logged it all into Mother.

There was only one person in the frame for this: Chris Cobb, and there was no way out for him. After all, the detective had followed Chris and Natalie last night, on their way back to Chris's horsebox from the Castle. It would have to be up to Natalie, though – that is, if she pulled through – as to whether she wanted to press any charges against Chris. The doctor might be able to save her now, in which case she would live to have a choice and possibly a future. Only Natalie, though, could decide. Besides, it would all depend on whether she did indeed pull through her ordeal.

Allan telephoned the office later than was earlier planned – it was gone eleven – and he gave me a rundown of yesterday's events at Newbury: the Tote had sold three hundred £18 place tickets on the favourite in the sprint race, and the favourite duly obliged, winning the race by 3 lengths – although to finish in the first four, they would have still collected, as they had backed the horse for a place only. The dividend paid £1.80 to a pound stake, which meant an 80 per cent profit. Whoever was running this scam had good information and was really making it pay handsome dividends with the distribution of the cocaine as well.

There was another surprise in store for us in a later race yesterday – a race where Noel Henry had a runner which was a late withdrawal. It was the second-favourite, and three hundred £18 tickets for a place were sold by the Tote on this horse. This was how the organisation ran their plan B: having picked up on the favourite in the sprint handicap, it would appear that this supposed runner was a red herring, so to speak. Well, that was how Allan and Billy saw it: the horse was never going to run anyway, so the punters would get double the amount of cocaine today.

Allan joked, "Well, it is the weekend, Boss! More seriously, though, this distribution method is well organised and smoothly run; and on the gambling side of things, it appears to be valid under the current rules of racing."

I was sure now their regular clients were cashing in as well. As they say, "don't look a gift horse in the mouth"; the punters and drug users would be backing the horses they were told to put their money on.

As the non-runner meant the punters would get their money back, that also meant the COKE employees would have 600 tickets to cash in for the now six employees of the three trailers that were left operating; that would mean at least a hundred tickets each to queue up for and get paid out. Our CCTV operation could not fail to pick out the punters and the employees, through sheer weight of numbers visiting and revisiting the Tote outlets and then buying their cans of Coke and straws full of cocaine.

We would check over the weekend to see if Noel Henry was an active part of the scheme by consistently having late withdrawal non-runners. Was he having an unusually high amount of non-runners on purpose to cover up the illegal distribution of drugs? Was Natalie using her position as trainer's wife and part-time secretary to orchestrate plan B in the event of the gamble on plan A – failing to double their money by being unplaced? I thought it would be best for Allan and Billy to continue the operation and collate further evidence today at Newbury, for the second day of the meeting, and to observe also.

I informed Allan that he should pay special attention to the trailers of Chris's Outside Kiosks & Events. "See if any replacement employees turn up; if so, make sure we have them on CCTV, continue audio coverage," I said. "My gut feeling is, now we have them by the bollocks, and now I want to squeeze them – squeeze them until they beg for mercy, and then squeeze them some more."

"Right, Boss," said Allan.

I further told Allan about the sad death of Chris Collins, and the events surrounding the poor man's death in such tragic circumstances, as well as the arrests of Danny and Dave for Chris's murder.

Allan felt the same as all my employees. "Boss, the police shouldn't put the fuckers behind bars, they should put them down."

We said goodbye, and I put the phone down.

The chief inspector turned up for coffee at 11.15. Laura had dealt with all the messages by now, and had even spoken to her mum, telling her about the invitation to Hickstead tomorrow. Her mum agreed she would love to come, and as the invitation was for Charlie's aunt Doris too, Laura's mum quickly called Doris on her mobile whist still talking to Laura on the landline. Doris told Laura's mum she'd love to come too, and Laura's mum relayed this to Laura. Laura arranged to visit her mother at 4 p.m. today, checked with me that this arrangement was okay, and smiled when I gave her the thumbs up from across the office where I was seated with the chief inspector.

"See you later then, Mum. Bye," Laura said as she put the telephone down.

Laura, the chief inspector, and I then walked into the kitchen. Laura made three coffees, and we sat down at the kitchen table. The chief inspector filled me in further with this morning's events as we exchanged information. He filled me in with more details about Natalie. I just couldn't help but feel sorry for her and the cruel way she had been abused and hung up like a piece of meat. Laura felt some empathy for her as well, and we all hoped she would pull through and then press charges against Chris Cobb for her rape and assault whilst under the influence of drugs. Certainly it could be argued that the sex had not been with her consent. It all depended, of course, on whether Natalie did indeed pull through. Logic prevailed that her only way out would be to press charges.

I wanted Chris Cobb locked up as well for my attempted murder. We would nail the bastard – it was only a matter of time. We talked about maybe some high-profile arrests, about taking no prisoners, and about getting on the offensive, as opposed to being far too defensive for far too long.

The chief inspector then told me of his meeting with Doug Dunne and the extra manpower offered by Doug, with his twenty-strong force of security staff. He explained to me that he had now set up office in the main office for the show, on the third floor of the office block next to the main ring; he had a grandstand view for tomorrow's derby and would be able to observe everything that went on in the main ring. And yet the chief inspector was still uneasy.

"Steve," said DCI Heyes. "As of this time, Doug Dunne's four sons are scouring the estate for people who should not be there. Trespassers are a fact of life, unfortunately, and if there are some people on the estate who should not be there, Doug's sons will find them."

I was glad to hear this.

It was now fast approaching 12 p.m. The chief inspector left to go back to the showground, but he said he would keep me posted as to any further events that he felt I would need to know about. I said I would do the same with regard to the Newbury operation. It was becoming increasingly apparent that our separate investigations were overriding each other and linked together.

Charles and Becky Paul arrived. Laura greeted them and showed them into the lounge. Charles and I shook hands, and I kissed Becky on both cheeks. Charles did the same with Laura. We sat down, and Laura asked Charles and Becky if they would like coffee. Both of them said yes, so Laura went to the kitchen to make the coffee.

Charles told me that they always stayed at the Gatwick Hilton with Prince Ahmed whenever they came to Hickstead; it was so easy to just fly in and fly out again whenever there was a show on of which they had an interest. Of course, it was only a twenty-minute drive from the airport to the showground. The Ahmeds' chauffeur was based in Crawley and employed full-time, even though he hardly saw Prince Ahmed from one week to the next. It was the same situation in Ireland, where he had a full-time chauffeur as well.

Laura returned from the kitchen with the coffees.

Charles took out from the inside pocket of his jacket the two contracts, along with Laura's cheque for the purchase of Fred II, which was made out to Miss Laura Hallett for the sum of £150,000. He also had an invoice for the purchase of the horse, which Laura needed to sign. Laura signed the invoice and then handed over Fred II's passport. All competition horses, whether racehorses or showjumpers, must have passports for identification purposes; the passports also kept a record of vaccinations and inoculations, and the horses had to have these up to date, or they would not be allowed to compete.

Charles handed Laura and I the two contracts, which were identical. We would need to read and then sign them. The contracts stated the terms and conditions of that which was previously agreed last night; we both spent about five minutes digesting the details as outlined within the contracts. Word for word, the contracts were just as Becky had first described last night: the contract would be for a minimum of four years, at which time, subject to a new contract being issued, the new horsebox (for two horses) would be replaced with another new horsebox in another four years. The contract would start on 1 September 2004, a few weeks from now. Laura's first two horses would arrive on 2 September, and every month thereafter, for the period of the contract. We looked at each other after reading the contracts, and we both approved of them.

Laura signed and dated both contracts in acceptance of their terms and conditions. Becky did the same. As I was an independent party unrelated, I signed both contracts as a witness and duly dated them.

Charles said, "Congratulations, Laura!"

Laura and Becky exchanged another round of kisses on the cheek.

We finished our coffees and walked out into the yard to go and see Fred II. Laura held my hand as we walked across the yard to Fred's box, and then, as if on cue, Fred poked his head out to say hello. Laura fed him a few carrots. Charles indicated that Fred would be collected tomorrow afternoon between five and six, after the derby had finished. Mickey was observing us from a distance.

It was now 12.30 p.m. Allan was on the telephone from Newbury: two new faces had appeared to work one of the trailers. Allan said it was two women. I told him to make sure he had some CCTV and audio once again. I was thinking it could very well be Mrs Amy Cobb and her daughter, Lucy, from the Watford office of COKE.

I quickly looked at the runners today at Newbury. There was nothing which sort of stood out to suggest another scam, but if that was the case, then why had Mrs Cobb and her daughter turned up? I looked through the runners again: the third race was a nine-runner affair, and Noel Henry had the second-favourite – perhaps that was the horse they would back for a place. I made Allan aware that it was his only runner of the day; Noel Henry had sent three horses down the day before, and this was to be the last of them.

I gathered he must have stayed over the night, but not with his wife, obviously. I wondered if he had received any news from the hospital. The chief inspector had just texted me to say that Natalie was now in ICU. I relayed this information to Allan, although Noel Henry would find out about last night's events in his own time, or as I suspected, when the chief inspector informed him. If it were at all possible to speak to Natalie, if indeed she pulled through, DCI Heyes would no doubt do so.

Allan said he would call again to update at 2 p.m.

Meanwhile, Doug's four sons were now conducting their search of the vast estate, looking for any trespassers or vehicles that should not be there. They telephoned their father every half hour, each time saying "Nothing to report so far." DCI Heyes was in the office with Doug, who passed on his sons' messages to the chief inspector.

During the small talk in between updates, the chief inspector told Doug about his daughter's showjumping career from more than twenty years ago. Doug remembered Penny Heyes very well, and asked where she was now. DCI Heyes said that Penny was a jockey's agent in America; she was based in Chicago, and had a daughter called Belle who was 8. He also told Doug that when Penny had enough of showjumping, she took out a National Hunt licence and became a jockey; she rode many winners around Plumpton and Fontwell, and even rode in two Grand Nationals.

Chris Cobb and Jane met in Chris's horsebox at 11.30 a.m. Jane had called him to say she would be late, and he made good use of the added time by changing the bed linen and tidying up the living area of the horsebox. His dad was due to arrive at 2 p.m.

"Hi, Jane," Chris said when she arrived. "Come in."

She climbed the two steps, and entered. "Have you heard, Chris?" said Jane.

"Heard what?" replied Chris.

"Danny and Dave were arrested late last night, for murdering Chris Collins. They were both caught fucking my groom, Sally, last night in the back of my trailer."

"No," said Chris. "I hadn't heard."

What Chris wasn't telling Jane was that his dad had sent Danny and Dave to kill Laura's horse, Fred II. Chris's dad had telephoned him on his mobile at 2 p.m. yesterday, to tell him what he intended to do. It was Chris Collins who had prevented them from doing so, with his lock on the stable door. They panicked, and the pitchfork was used to pin Chris Collins to the ground by sticking it through his hand while they tried to search him for the key to the lock. They couldn't find the key, and as two grooms were passing, they ran away. The two grooms had been about to ring the police when the two detectives arrived.

Chris laughed. "So they got caught fucking that old blind dog," he said, referring to Sally.

Jane said, "It's not funny, Chris. What if the police put two and two together? We're both in the frame."

Chris said, "It's all your fault, Jane, with your obsession with Laura fucking Hallett!"

Jane replied, "I am not obsessed with her – I just fucking hate her!"

"Why?" said Chris. "What has she done to you?"

"She's fucking better than I am in everything I do! She makes me look like an idiot on a horse, and yesterday, she did it to you too. That's why I fucking hate her. I wish she was dead!" said Jane, adding, "They know about Jay Penfold, you know, Chris."

"Well," said Chris, "he's dead, so he won't be telling anyone anything."

"Why the fuck could you not have used someone who was sober to run Steve over in the car park? That fucking idiot nearly killed me!" said Jane.

"Yeah," said Chris. "That's why I killed him and set fire to all the evidence."

Jane said, "You're the one obsessed, Chris. You're so obsessed with Steve Hurst."

"Yeah," said Chris. "I want him fucking dead. Chris Stuart wants him fucking dead for insulting him with that horsebox routine outside his night club in Brighton, the Konkordski Bar. And my dad wants him dead as well. The six Tote employees who have been fiddling some tickets have been uneasy the last few weeks. They feel they are being watched, and they think it is your ex's company, DIRTS, that is watching them."

"I tried to kill him last week, and I would have succeeded too, if it were not for that fucking Laura saving him," Jane said. "When's the next shipment of cocaine and heroin due in?"

Chris replied, "It came in yesterday, concealed as usual in the pre-packed horse feed – the HorseHage – 100 kilos of cocaine and 50 kilos of heroin. It's at the offices in Watford, awaiting packing for distribution. My mum will be on the job tomorrow; my mum and sister are covering for Dave and Danny at Newbury today. Until we can get more staff, they couldn't get anybody today at short notice."

Jane said, "Don't treat Steve like a fool, Chris. His logic is far superior to ours."

Chris replied, "My dad will take care of Steve and Laura. And by the way, why didn't they arrest Sally then?"

Jane replied, "Sally used the 'they got me drunk and sexually abused me' routine, then started crying, and the police fell for it. They were making so much noise in the trailer, and some people passing called the police; that's how Sally got caught fucking those two idiots. Chris Collins must have given the police good descriptions, because the police were all over the arena looking for them. I bet they wished they had stayed at Newbury now."

Chris moved over to Jane and kissed her. She responded by undoing his zip and freeing his hard-on. Jane slowly went onto her knees and took him in her mouth, massaging him until she felt the slightly salty semen hit the back of her throat. She swallowed. She also swallowed her groom's story of events of how Danny and Dave were nicked. But Sally had forgot to tell Jane that her mobile had been confiscated by the police.

In the meantime, Sally was busy grooming Jane's two showjumpers that were at the show. She had been trying to contact her brother, Pete, for ages now. *Why the fuck can he not answer the phone?* she wondered. She left a few messages, but thought, *Well, if he can't be bothered to ring me back, then fuck him!* She had a replacement mobile, and nobody would be the wiser. She was looking forward to getting pissed down the Castle again tonight. She also needed a fix. She couldn't ask Jane at the moment because she was still mad at her; maybe, though, she might score, if she could locate Natalie.

CHAPTER 21

It was now 1 p.m., and all five of us were still working in the office. Ricky went to the kitchen, and made five rounds of cheese sandwiches and five coffees. Gary had finally finished his report on Naughty Natalie Henry. However, now it would have to wait for at least until Monday, subject to whether DCI Heyes was able to talk to Natalie, if she were to pull through from her injuries and miscarriage, not to mention her overdosing on cocaine; he wanted badly for Natalie to accuse Chris Cobb of rape and assault. In short, we couldn't present our report to Noel Henry, her husband and our client, until DCI Heyes spoke to Natalie Henry.

Charlie was of the opinion that Mother had enough data and factual evidence to suggest that the ten employees of the COKE trailers at Newbury – including Danny and Dave, – had already been arrested for other offences, enough to put them all behind bars for a long time. Amy and Lucy Cobb had already been caught on CCTV and audio exchanging £18 Tote place tickets for cans of Coke with two straws each on ten occasions so far. The punters on five occasions had been caught on CCTV throwing the cans of Coke away in the toilets, and then snorting the cocaine out of the straws in the toilet cubicles. I would have to speak to Lord Oakley very soon. I tended to agree with Charlie, though: if we wanted to, we could take this down this very afternoon. I would get Lord Oakley's views, but my men in the field would have the final say.

Laura had started clearing out all the boxes in the yard. It was her intention to redecorate them so they would be ready for the new crop of horses that would start arriving in a fortnight's time. The boxes would be painted in traditional white over black: white walls and ceilings, with a 3-foot black skirt around the bases of the boxes; the stable doors would be painted in black gloss, and new furniture for the doors would be included in the refit. The tack room would need a refit as well, with some new shelving, a new fridge, and a new sink, and also a lockable cabinet for any drugs for the horses and other veterinary products; the old couch would have to go soon as well, but not until this was all over and Mickey was no longer required. Mickey helped Laura with the clearing out. We set a deadline for us all to stop work at 3 p.m. Laura and I would have to leave at 3.30 to visit her mum in Ringmer, just outside Lewes.

Meanwhile, Chris Cobb had other problems on his mind. Jane was right: Steve Hurst was methodical and logical, two things Chris never was. Chris was brash, illogical, and had all the airs and graces of a spoilt brat. He had inherited this attitude from his father, Fred, and so had his sister, Lucy. Both were in their mid-twenties, and they were of the opinion that the world revolved around them. They were the centre of the universe, and so they could see no wrong in their logic or actions, no matter how twisted and warped their minds had become. Their father never gave them a proper education, and, therefore, never gave them a chance to have a normal upbringing.

Chris and Lucy Cobb both did poorly throughout their schooling, and had no ability whatsoever in any subject. Their levels of concentration were virtually nil, so they spent most of their time at home playing games or running around the farm on quad bikes, rather than learning any gainful knowledge to prepare them in later life. Chris became interested in horses when his dad took him to the races one day, and so he focused on that instead of going to school. Both Chris and Lucy left school hardly able to read and write – they were virtually illiterate. Their dad promised them everything, even thinking he could buy them an education like everything else in life. He thought he was giving them everything but ended up giving them nothing, and that's how they ended up illiterate and psychotic. Again, they believed they were the centre of the universe and only they mattered, such were their massively inflated egos.

Frederick William Cobb left for Hickstead at 11 a.m. His wife and daughter would not be going; Amy had to fill in at Newbury, and so did Lucy. Fred had not heard from Dave or Danny since he had ordered them to kill Laura Hallett's horse. Chris was the messenger boy: he did what his dad told him. Obviously, they had fucked up, so his wife and his daughter had to fill in at Newbury today. Fred gave himself thee hours to get there from Northampton, but he would do it easily. Traffic on the M1 was always light on a Saturday morning.

Before he left, he had hired a hitman to take out Steve Hurst and Laura Hallett sometime this weekend. Fred Cobb was a vile, sadistic thug; his children had inherited his genes and were no better than he. *Lucy had been thrown out of school and college for selling drugs. Now, with her mother, father, and brother, she was at it again. They were all selling drugs, wholesale and retail. Fred Cobb had raised the capital through selling his share of the family business, Cobb's for Classic Footwear. The company had been started more than forty years ago by Fred's father when Fred and his older brother, George, were aged 7 and 4. Forty years later, both the sons were directors, but it was the oldest son, George, who did all the work, whilst the younger, Fred, was always lolling about and pleading poverty.*

Both their parents had died in short succession; they'd both been in their seventies. Before the father died, though, he had beckoned George to his deathbed, telling his eldest son, "George, your brother has the devil in him and has passed it on to his children. In my will, I have left you 67 per cent of the business, and Fred the other 33 per cent. Run the business down by setting aside profit for a few years, and then let Fred have his way and float the company. Put the excess profit that you set aside in a holding company, and use that to purchase shares when they are floated. Don't let your brother find out; he is not educated like you. Just pay him off, and get him out of your life! George, you're a good son. I just wish your mother had loved you like I did. At least I gave you a good education. Now make use of it."

The mother had died three weeks before the father, and so, within a month, both parents had died. That bedside conversation was the last time George saw and spoke to his father before the man died, and he followed his father's instructions to the letter. That had been more than two years ago.

The company was floated, and 73 per cent of the shares were available to be purchased. George had retained some 27 per cent; however, the shares were undersubscribed by potential investors – as George had figured out they would be – by almost a third of the 73 per cent. The opening price for the shares the next day would be low – very low – and as soon as they started trading, they dropped another 10 per cent on the issue price. That was when George pounced: he purchased another 24 per cent, giving him a controlling interest of 51 per cent. His brother, Fred, hand been ousted from the company and would be paid off with the smallest amount possible for his 33 per cent of the company.

George and Fred's father was indeed a canny man, and George was a highly skilled and intelligent accountant, so he was just the man to pull it off. Fred never was any the wiser.

Fred was now able to go into business on his own and away from his "fucking prick of an older brother, George", as Fred called him. When George was at university, Fred was doing the racetracks. George studied mathematics and accountancy; Fred studied the horses. That was just the way they grew up.

Chris Stuart was a different kettle of fish altogether: he had been a con man all his life. His club, the Konkordski Bar, was a front for selling drugs, both the importation and the distribution, especially cocaine and heroin. They would be shipped in from the Far East, where they were harvested and cut, refined and tested for purity and consistency, and ready for use when they were shipped to Rotterdam in Holland. They were shipped in 5-kilo flat, oblong lead boxes that were sealed by lead welding. They were then packed into a horse-feed product called HorseHage. Each packet of feed weighed approximately 25 kilos, and 5 kilos of HorseHage would be taken out, the metal container would be placed in the middle of the feed supplement, and then it would be resealed in new plastic packaging. It was a very smart operation because the feed, once opened, let off a very pungent smell.

They had thirty packets of the feed delivered to the port of Newhaven, twice a month now to keep up with demand. Once unloaded at the port, the feed would be transported to the Watford address to be readied for delivery in the straws for the cocaine or in syringes for the heroin. Once the drugs were separated from the feed, Chris Cobb would pick up the feed and take it to his dad's house and yard in Northampton, where he kept his showjumpers.

Chris Stuart had operated the trailer hire and COKE business now for four years. He had met Fred Cobb a little more than a year ago at Plumpton, where Fred had set a horse up to sting the bookies in a coup. The race was a 2-mile chase for novices. Fred's horse, Hessinger, was trained locally to the track at the time, and his opening price was 33 to 1. The trainer was not known for having first-time-out winners, especially in a 2-mile chase with sixteen runners. Chris Stuart latched on by seeing the odds tumble, 33s to 25s, then to 20s; he eventually got his £500 each way on at 16s. He was pissed off at the time for not getting 20s, but smug by the end of the race, as the horse bolted up at a return price of only 8 to 1. Chris cleared a profit of £9,600.

He was enjoying a drink after the race, found himself in Fred Cobb's company, and invited him back to his club for a drink, with his wife too, of course. They hit it off, and by the end of the night, Fred had booked in across the road at the Hilton and met Chris and his girlfriend the following day for lunch. They became firm friends. As soon as Fred had been paid for his share of the shoe business, so ensued this devious business of drug dealing on a vast scale. The business had grown into a multimillion-pound franchise, with the Brighton Triads community trying to muscle in for some of the action. They were also the local law enforcers for the Far East suppliers of where Chris Stuart imported his drugs from. Fred and Chris both played their cards very close to their chests.

Fred Cobb, whilst driving down to Hickstead, received an incoming call from his son, Chris, on the mobile.

"Dad, Jane's just told me that Danny and Dave got arrested last night for murdering that old boy that was guarding Laura Hallett's horse."

Fred just replied, "You really are fucking useless at times! I will take care of it when I arrive."

It was 1 p.m., and Fred told his son he would be down within the hour; he was just passing the turn off for Heathrow on the M4. He was aware his son's addiction was getting out of hand.

Chris Cobb never said a word about Natalie; he was in enough trouble with his dad already.

Chris Stuart was already being hassled for the last shipment of drugs that arrived at the Watford office yesterday. It was cash on delivery, with forty-eight hours' grace to pay or forfeit your life: this was the wholesale arrangement. The drugs were supplied at £1,000 sterling per kilo, 150 kilos was £150,000 pounds, cash. The delivery was Friday, so they had until Sunday, and close of business was 5 p.m. – then it was your life, regardless of the money. The Chinese wanted the franchise and to be Fred's partner; they knew he was good for a few million. But Chris he never liked parting with money unless he had to, and the Chinese knew it, and would one day they would use it to their advantage. Their masters were in their native country, and they pulled all the strings. The Brighton Triads were obedient to their every word – no favours, no friendships, strictly business.

Chris Stuart wasn't too bothered; he already had his half in readies. Fred had already contacted him on his mobile to say he would bring the other £75,000 in readies with him down to Hickstead this afternoon. He also let Chris, his partner, know that business was fantastic at Newbury yesterday and that their turnover was hitting new heights. The September shipment should be increased to 200 kilos. They were setting up a Midland circuit of tracks to flood with cocaine and heroin; business was expanding, and so were the profits.

DCI Heyes was becoming more uneasy by the minute. He looked over the arena from Doug Dunne's office on the third floor. Opposite the offices were the six private boxes, one of which was Fred Cobb's. DCI Heyes went down the stairs and out of the show offices. He wandered over to the private boxes, past the members' bar where he'd lunched with Steve Hurst and his friends yesterday, and then further on to where he saw the entrance to the members' private boxes. The showjumping in the main arena would not start until 3 p.m., and he hoped that none of Fred Cobb's guests had turned up yet. He went in, and on the wall of the private box facility was a list of names and numbers. Fred's box was number 3 on the second block, the top one. The chief inspector made his way up to the top floor. Nobody was around, it was too early, and he thought that was lucky. He let himself in and stood in the middle of the box. He did his sums, surveyed the possibilities, and went out onto the viewing balcony, taking in the panoramic view – all 180 degrees of it. He went back to the door, into the box, and locked it; the key was in the door in the inside lock. He did not want to be disturbed for a few minutes.

DCI Heyes had three audio bugs in his jacket pocket. He wanted to have the bugs in places where the guests would congregate and talk to one another. He placed one underneath the dining table, another behind the curtain pelmet of the door that led onto the balcony, and the third in the kitchenette, where the food and drink would be prepared. He placed the bug under the cover of a fire alarm, replaced the cover, and then went back out onto the balcony. He could easily spot Doug Dunne's third-floor office to his left; it was virtually eye level with Fred Cobb's private box The distance was no more than 140 yards. DCI Heyes glanced over to his right, he could see the derby bank easily, about 130 yards away and to his right. He calculated that if you were riding a horse and you were on top of the bank, you were virtually at eye level with the rider; the water jump was in front, though slightly to his left, and about 60 yards away. He looked back at the derby bank, deep in thought, and then he left the private box as he had found it, with the key still in the lock in the inside of the door. Shuddering at the thought of his perceived scenario, he hurried to get back to Doug Dunne's office.

It was now 1.30 p.m., and DCI Heyes still had no news about Natalie Henry from the hospital. He sat down, thinking, *The bastards! They wouldn't dare – would they?* He couldn't answer his own question because he didn't know he was dealing with a family of psychopaths and murderers.

Despairingly, he telephoned Doug on his mobile. "Any luck with the search yet, Doug?" DCI Heyes enquired.

Doug replied, "Yes, Chief Inspector, we have found an old grey Maestro van like the ones BT uses. It had a cover over it, and one of the boys found it at one of the cottages that is not being used at the moment. We have not touched it in case you wanted your forensics team to go over it."

DCI Heyes replied, "Give me ten minutes on that one. Anything else, Doug?"

"Yes," Doug replied. "A Ford Focus estate car left the cottage in a hurry as two of my boys pulled up. We got both registration numbers for you, Chief Inspector." Doug then gave DCI Heyes the registration details of both vehicles.

DCI Heyes knew both numbers by heart. The old grey van was the one that had been snooping around Steve Hurst's property; it was probably a false number plate from one similar they had seen in the area. MI5 had a grey Maestro van with the same registration number, which they used at the Gatwick holding centre, and Mickey had an identical one he used for running around in. DCI Heyes thought that this line of enquiry would not be necessary at the moment. However, the connection between the old grey van and the Ford Focus estate car was vital information, as it linked Dicky Head – somehow – to the showjumping and the drug ring that was operating. The registration number of the Ford Focus was that which the police had been searching for, for nearly a week now.

DCI Heyes thought, *Dicky Head has probably been here since Monday night. So this is where he's been holed up all week! Where's he gone now?* Into the phone he said, "Thank you, Doug. Your boys have been most helpful. Don't touch the van, and put the cover back over it. I will get Miles Valentine from forensics to arrange to have it picked up tomorrow." He then added, "By the way, Doug, there is something I want to tell you which I never told you this morning. I have a police sniper in the showground, and he's been here two days. I want to have two snipers here for tomorrow. I think we have a hitman on the loose, and we need to take him out before he kills more innocent people. I want to put a sniper in your office on the third floor, and I intend to put the other one in a cherry picker, next to the television platform behind the derby bank." He paused, and then finished by saying, "Doug, I wouldn't ask you unless I thought it was absolutely necessary."

Doug Dunne was stuck for words; this was beyond his comprehension. He replied, "Just do what you think is necessary, Chief Inspector. I will back you up all the way."

"Thank you," said DCI Heyes.

He put the phone down on the desk, and prepared for his next call, which was to the Home Secretary. He dialled the direct line, and then explained his plans to the Home Secretary. "Yes, sir, I think it's absolutely necessary," said DCI Heyes. "I want a full squad of twelve armed officers in full military combat uniform and bulletproof vests, and I want another six bulletproof vests for civilians. And I need another sniper for tomorrow." When the Home Secretary questioned this, DCI Heyes confirmed, "It is *that* serious, sir, yes – we had another murder yesterday, and a rape and assault. We have also had drug dealing taking place, and the drug dealing is getting out of hand, sir – and not just at Hickstead, but at the racecourses that DIRTS has been monitoring for the Jockey Club." The Home Secretary seemed concerned, asking if the crimes were linked. "Yes, sir," said DCI Heyes. "We now believe it is the same drug ring, yes, sir. I will keep you informed, sir. Thank you for your cooperation, sir, I am much obliged."

DCI Heyes put the phone down. He had got his way with the Home Secretary. He made himself a coffee, and checked the time. It was near to 2 p.m. Unbeknownst to the chief inspector, Fred Cobb had been held up in traffic and would be late arriving at Hickstead.

DCI Heyes need to speak to Steve, immediately.

Steve had earlier telephoned Lord Oakley, who was attending the race meeting at Newbury today, and outlined his proposals, which included the round-up of the punters purchasing the £18 Tote place tickets and segregating them throughout of the meeting during the rest of the afternoon, after the proposed, major delay that Steve had already explained to Lord Oakley: a bomb scare. This was so that the police could organise and run a convoy of arrested punters away from the racecourse, to a large, unused, and totally secure military defence building at Greenham Common, just outside Newbury.

The first race today at Newbury was at 2.30 p.m. Noel Henry's runner was in the third, at 3.30, and so a bomb scare at 3.15 p.m. was necessary.

Steve explained all this to Lord Oakley, and then added that when they had weighed out for the 3.30, Noel's runner would eventually be a non-runner. Lord Oakley agreed to the request, and a bomb scare would be broadcast at exactly 3.15 p.m., before the jockeys got mounted and went down to the start for the third race. The bomb scare would be for the members' enclosure, and racing would be put back an hour. This meant the 3.15 would not be run until 4.15, and the last race nearer to 6, which meant the Tote this evening would not officially close until 7 p.m., one hour after the last race.

Allan and Billy had devised this course of action, having consulted with Steve sometime earlier. They needed some extra time to organise and plan, and they needed to at all times be in full cooperation with the DCI Heyes, based at Hickstead. The direct contact he had with the Home Secretary at the Home Office cut through all the red tape; all services would therefore be on red alert in an instant, including the police and the military.

All of the assembled team were now aware that the showdown was to be later on in the afternoon. Allan and Billy's plan was that the punters would firstly invest and purchase their £18 Tote tickets, and it was immaterial whether the race was run or not: their currency was the £18 Tote tickets. The bomb scare delay would enable the punters to exchange their tickets for the cans of Coke and the straws of cocaine; once they had obtained the drugs, they could be and would be arrested at any time thereafter – either on their way to the toilets or on their way out of the racecourse. Once arrested, they would be taken to the local police station, where they would be cautioned; their drugs and mobile phones would be confiscated, their details would be logged, and then they would be taken to the airbase at Greenham Common to be detained under the Prevention of Terrorism Act. This would be approved by the Home Secretary to protect national security, and it would thereby allow the police to cut through the protocols of usual arrest directives.

They, the punters, would be charged later. The police could now hold them for forty-eight hours; this meant Monday afternoon, at the earliest, they would be released. DCI Heyes was pleased. Time was now on their side with the Newbury operation. The Greenham complex meant that the punters could be detained, fed, and watered, and then they could spend at least two nights in detention. If anybody telephoned the local police at Newbury as to where a relative was, they would be told that the individual was helping police with enquiries regarding the bomb scare this afternoon. It was vitally important to keep all these people away from any form of outside communication, and all the punters' mobiles would be checked for the stored numbers, and cross-referenced. DCI Heyes was now on the offensive; he was going to nail the bastards this weekend.

The six Tote employees would be arrested at 7 p.m., after the Tote closed for the day. They would be taken straight to Gatwick, to the MI5 holding unit, and interrogated. They would then be charged with conspiracy to commit fraud and deception – and with anything else they owned up to, subject to, perhaps, some of Mickey's persuasion. They would not be released. The police would, on Monday morning, ask the magistrates for a remand order.

The Chris's Outdoor Kiosks & Events employees would be arrested as they shut up the trailers and prepared to leave sometime around 7 p.m. They would be allowed to collect their money before the police arrested them and seized their trailers, together with the drugs and the money they had accumulated throughout the day's illegal activities.

The eight trailer operatives would be charged with dealing and supplying class A drugs. They too would be taken to the Gatwick MI5 holding centre and detained indefinitely, or at least until the investigation was closed. All communications would be closed for these eight operatives. Amy and Lucy would be arrested last, only after Amy had contacted her husband on her mobile at 7 p.m., as she had earlier arranged and of which the chief inspector was aware because of the bugging devices in her husband's private box at Hickstead. Their mobiles would then be seized immediately; nobody would be given the chance to telephone any solicitors.

Allan and Billy had previously agreed with Charlie's assessment that the evidence was now overwhelming, and although most of the punters would get off with a slapped wrist and a fine, a great deal of them would do time if they had criminal records with past drug offences or past criminal acts likely to result in a custodial sentence this time round.

This Saturday from lunchtime onwards was becoming quite frantic, to say the least, with the developments and information that was coming into the office. Charlie and Ricky were almost unable to keep up with what was going on, and where. The same could be applied to the chief inspector's situation. It was indeed a godsend that Doug had given DCI Heyes his office on the third floor to use. DCI Heyes was on the mobile to Steve at regular intervals now, as they cross-referenced information and updated each other with their separate operations overlapping each other and running in tandem at both Newbury and Hickstead.

At 2.15 p.m., DCI Heyes telephoned Steve on his mobile. They needed to speak to each other urgently. Steve told the chief inspector to pop in for a coffee right away, and the chief inspector said, "See you in ten minutes."

I saw DCI Heyes turn up at the farmhouse, and met him at the kitchen door, near to the yard. We walked into the yard.

Laura and Mickey had cleared out six of the boxes in the yard, readying them for redecoration. Laura said, "That will do for now, Mickey. Thank you for your help." She turned to me and said, "Steve, I want to have a soak in the bath for half an hour."

"Okay, Laura," I replied. "I will be with the chief inspector for at least that time."

We walked over to the tack room and sat on the couch. Mickey joined us as the chief inspector asked me first what my news was. I told him about Allan and Billy's plan, and the bomb scare to delay the race and also give us more time to organise.

The chief inspector said, "I will speak to the Home Secretary again before I leave you. He will speed things up and cut out the red tape."

I said, "Thank you, Chief Inspector, we double-checked on everything."

DCI Heyes and I both came to the same conclusion that today would be the day for the Newbury illegal operation to be shut down completely.

We would wipe out the drug dealing and fraud, he agreed to the Tote employees, all six of them, being taken to the MI5 holding centre at Gatwick and detained, and also the trailer operatives being detained at Gatwick.

DCI Heyes said, "We will get them all together, and listen to them squeal as they blame each other."

The chief inspector agreed that a blackout from Newbury was vitally important, and he wanted to keep Amy Cobb and her daughter away from Hickstead if at all possible. His bugs were set, and with the bomb scare created, the time was there for the chief inspector to get his wish. Our plan was slowly coming together. He needed Amy and Lucy Cobb locked up for the weekend so that he could search the premises at Watford, where my operative, Gary, had previously visited. This would be a raid of which the Home Secretary would have to sanction with a search warrant. The chief inspector whilst now on the telephone to the Home Secretary accepted it would have to be for 11 a.m. on Monday morning; it could not be done any earlier than that. What worried the chief inspector, though, was if Fred Cobb got wind of his wife and daughter's arrest before Monday morning, then what?

The chief inspector thanked me for all the help we had given him on these investigations, and then he dropped the bombshell of what he wanted to see me about which was so important. He outlined his suspicions, and then he said, "Steve, I want you to stop Laura from riding in the derby tomorrow."

"I have my reservations as well, Chief Inspector," I said, and I had to admit it was true. "However, I must also point out that all my employees this morning unanimously agreed that we will not live our lives in fear; we will carry on as normal – with caution, yes, but with no fear."

"I thought you would say that, Steve," said DCI Heyes. "So I made other arrangements earlier today, with Home Office approval."

The chief inspector then outlined his plan for tomorrow at the Hickstead Showjumping Derby. He told me about the specially trained and armed unit of twelve officers that would be arriving first thing in the morning. He told me about Doug's boys finding the grey BT van, and also about Dicky Head driving at speed away from one of the unused cottages on Doug Dunne's estate, where he had been holed up possibly since Monday. We still did not know where he was or what he was up to, though. The chief inspector further told me about the two snipers he would have on duty tomorrow, and where they would be positioned. Next, he told me he had earlier today bugged Fred Cobb's private box, and he wanted to be back in Doug's office later this afternoon to listen in on any conversations that took place whilst the showjumping was on. Last but not least, he told me about the stab-proof vests. He wanted Laura, Charlie, Ricky, and me to wear them at all times tomorrow while on the showground.

"I don't want anybody else getting hurt with pitchforks, Steve," he said.

Dropping all formalities, I said, "Cut the bullshit, John. You're deadly serious about tomorrow, aren't you? You think Fred Cobb has hired someone to shoot us!"

The chief inspector replied, "Well, if you put it like that, Steve, yes, I do. I think Fred Cobb and his son are a pair of maniacs, and if we get the chance to take them out tomorrow, we will shoot to kill – no court cases, no short-term jail sentences. I want to put these two evil fuckers down."

Mickey looked at me with a grin.

"Okay," I said to the chief inspector. "We will wear the stab-proof jackets, which are really bulletproof. But we are meant to be having lunch tomorrow at one o'clock with Prince Ahmed in his private box, which is close to Fred Cobb's."

"Leave that to me," said DCI Heyes. "I will sort something out with Doug for you with regard to your private lunch tomorrow."

CHAPTER 22

The chief inspector was at last beginning to see some light at the end of the tunnel. "I want you at Hickstead tomorrow, Mickey, he said. "And I want you in the stabling area tonight. Check out what's going on at the Castle Pub, and sleep in your van tonight, near to Chris Cobb's horsebox. Try to earwig and record any conversations. I really do need to know exactly what Fred and his son are up to, and what they have got planned. And I want to know where Dicky fucking Head is, and where he fits into this operation."

Mickey said to the chief inspector, "What time shall I leave here tonight?"

The chief inspector replied, "About ten o'clock. DS Harman and PC Hoad will again be on duty here from ten this evening." He turned towards me, saying, "Steve, if you could let them use your tack room for tea, coffee, and biscuits, I would be much obliged."

I replied, "Yes, of course, Chief Inspector."

It was now just past three o'clock, and the chief inspector left to go back to Hickstead.

Ricky was in the office with Charlie and Gary. The second race at Newbury had just finished.

"Boss, the first two favourites have won," said Ricky.

I replied, "Thanks, Ricky. Keep me informed. I'm going to have a bath and a shave, and then, after dressing, we will be leaving at 3.30. I'm taking Laura to see her mum. We have to be in Ringmer for 4 p.m."

"Okay, Boss," Ricky replied.

I went upstairs and got undressed. Laura was still in the bath. It was a triangular bath, with plenty of room for two people. Laura turned the

287

hot tap on as I got in, and then she sat between my legs, with her back against my chest. A soak for twenty minutes or so seemed like a good idea. I kissed Laura behind her ears and rolled her nipples playfully between my fingers and thumbs.

Laura said, We haven't got time, Steve." A pause followed, and then she added, "Have we?"

Before I could answer, Ricky shouted up the stairs: "Bomb scare at Newbury, Boss. Racing has been put back an hour."

I shouted back my acknowledgement.

Laura and I settled for another ten minutes of soaking, and then she got out of the bath, dried herself off, and got changed. I got out too, dried off, had a quick shave, and then put on some jeans and a crew-necked jumper over a shirt – casual but smart.

We were both in the office for 3.30, looking at the television on the wall. The images were of police officers carrying out a search of the members' area.

Good, I thought.

Laura and I then left to visit her mum in Ringmer.

Meanwhile, Fred Cobb had arrived at his son's horsebox at around 2.30 p.m. He had trouble getting in to the arena, and then further trouble parking. "Fucking people," he muttered to himself as he drove off the A23 into a queue of traffic. He thought because he drove a brand-new silver Mercedes 230SLK automatic sports car, he had a divine right to bypass traffic queues, just like royalty. He also thought he shouldn't have to queue, and it had put him in a bad temper from the outset. He was eventually forced to park near to his private box, and then had to walk 300 yards to where his son's horsebox was parked in the stabling area.

He never bothered knocking; he just walked straight in. "Chris!" he shouted. "Where the fuck are you?!"

Chris shouted back, "In the back of the horsebox!." He was getting his tack ready for this afternoon.

Fred kicked the door open into the horse's section of the box. "What the fuck went wrong?" he said to Chris, as if it were his fault.

Chris just shrugged his shoulders. "Too much security and too many police here, Dad," he said.

Fred slammed the door. "At times, Chris, you are so fucking useless. Just like your fucking sister! You've just cost me another twenty fucking grand."

"Why, Dad?" Chris asked.

"To get rid of those two! Because you're so fucking stupid, I've had to hire a hitman to shoot them," he said, adding, "I will be in my private box. I have some business to attend to. I'll see you fucking later, when you've finished riding. I trust you won't fuck that up this afternoon as well."

Chris didn't respond.

Fred stormed out, headed towards his box.

It was getting near to the time for the first class in the main arena.

They were running late at Hickstead too. Following the chief inspector's request, Doug Dunne had delayed the start of the showjumping in the main arena. Doug got the course builders to rebuild three of the fences because of a discrepancy with regard to related distances between the fences, and, consequently, the stride pattern of the horses. The showjumping would be delayed by forty-five minutes, and would not start until 3.45 p.m. The public was informed over the loudspeakers surrounding the arena.

Steve was passing through Lewes when the chief inspector called him on his mobile. "Just thought I would update you, Steve, with some news," said the chief inspector. "The Daihatsu Hijet registration number you sent me, with regard to Natalie and her mystery lover, the vehicle is registered to Cobb's for Classic Footwear, with their Northampton address. My guess is that Fred Cobb's been having a bit of Natalie, as well as supplying her with drugs to distribute."

Steve replied, "That's interesting; it sort of all fits in. By the way, Chief Inspector, the bomb scare at Newbury is now official. Laura and I will not be available from now until about six o'clock. I will call you when we leave Laura's mum's."

The chief inspector told Steve he had arranged a similar scenario at Hickstead to delay time, organised by Doug Dunne: the showjumping had been delayed by forty-five minutes.

Chris Cobb was severely pissed off with the delay. He made himself a coffee in the kitchenette of his horsebox, thinking about how put out he was. He soon cheered himself up, though: he was hoping to soon see Laura Hallett and Steve Hurst both take a bullet. *Yeah,* he thought, *and that will cheer Jane up as well. Maybe Dad's arranged for it to happen in the main ring.* He finished his coffee, and tuned in to the racing from Newbury. Noel Henry had a non-runner in the third race – the 3.30. *Ha-ha!* Chris laughed to himself. *Fucking bomb scare! We will probably sell loads more cocaine now … things just keep getting better and better.* He was looking forward to fucking Jane tonight as well.

Meanwhile, Fred Cobb was in his private box overlooking the arena. His mobile rang; it was his wife, Amy.

"What do you mean, there's been a bomb scare? The police are searching the members' enclosure! Fuck!" said Fred. "What time do you think you will get away then?" he asked his wife.

Amy replied, "Well, not before seven o'clock, Fred."

"Well," said Fred, "there's no point you coming all the way to Hickstead then is there? You have a full day's work tomorrow at the Watford office. I have a meeting later on with the Chinese, and I have to see Chris Stuart tomorrow morning to butter him up. Payment for yesterday's delivery has got to be sorted as well, if you see what I mean."

"Yes," said Amy. "But I still think you are playing with fire, all the same."

DCI Heyes couldn't believe his luck: he was recording all of the conversation. Fred Cobb had even turned the loudspeaker on his mobile, so all that Amy was saying was loud and clear as well. Everything was falling into place that had been pre-planned earlier in the afternoon. The operation at Newbury was being coordinated by Steve's team in exemplary fashion. DCI Heyes was willing Fred to be more specific, though.

Amy said, "Trades been really good today, so maybe we will give Hickstead a miss. We will go back to Watford tonight, and make a start on the shipment in the morning. Lucy won't mind; she hates fucking showjumping anyway. I will ring you when we leave Newbury, Fred, and calm down."

Fred said, "As you and Lucy are not going to be here tonight, I will try to sort Chris out. Speak to you later then, Amy."

"Yeah, okay," she replied.

DCI Heyes was pleased with the outcome; the delaying tactics at Newbury racecourse and the Hickstead showground were working out a treat.

Laura directed me to her mother's house as they entered the village of Ringmer. "Directly opposite the cricket green, Steve," she said. "Turn right into Springett Avenue, and my mum's house is 300 yards down the road, on the left."

It was now a few minutes after 4 p.m. I pulled up outside the house, and turned the engine off.

Laura seemed a little apprehensive. "Steve," she said, "I feel like I have butterflies in my stomach."

I replied, "It's because you don't know what to expect."

Laura's mum came out to greet us.

Laura gave her mum a cuddle by the front door of the house, and then she introduced me to her mum. She said, "Mum, this is the man I am going to marry in the next few years. Steve, meet my mum, Jacky."

Jacky and I shook hands, and I said, "It's a pleasure to meet you, Jacky." Jacky smiled, returning my greeting, and I added, "I love your daughter very much."

Jacky said, "Do come in, both of you. I've made some sandwiches and baked a chocolate cake. That was always Laura's favourite."

Laura and I followed Jacky into the lounge. The showjumping had just started on the television. Jacky turned the sound down.

"Now then, Steve," Jacky said. "What do you prefer, tea or coffee?"

Before I could answer, Laura said, "Coffee. He loves the stuff, Mum. White, with a sweetener, if you still use them, Mum."

"What about you, Laura?" said Jacky.

Laura replied, "I will have the same as Steve, please, Mum: white coffee, with a sweetener."

Jacky went into the kitchen to prepare the coffees, and within minutes, returned with them on a tray. She had made herself a tea.

"Steve, Laura, please help yourselves to sandwiches and cake," Jacky said as she put some side plates out.

I put some salmon and cucumber sandwich quarters on my plate, along with a piece of the chocolate cake. Laura did the same.

Jacky didn't seem hungry. I sort of perceived that she dearly wanted to talk to her daughter in private, just the two of them. With luck my mobile rang, and I excused myself, walked out of the lounge, and answered the call in the kitchen. I poked my head back into the lounge to signal Laura that it was Allan, and I needed to take the call. I then walked out the kitchen door and into the garden.

I left the door open, so I peripherally heard Laura tell her mum that we had three investigations going on at the moment. Laura further elaborated, "Mum, Steve is the boss of a security company that works with the police, in conjunction with the company's main client, the Jockey Club, which basically runs the horse-racing industry in this country. A lot of the work is sort of, hush, hush, Mum."

I didn't hear Jacky's reply, but as I was talking to Allan, I heard her start to cry. She sounded so remorseful, and I was hoping Laura would be forgiving and give her mum a bit of slack.

I then turned my full attention to my conversation with Allan. He told me that Noel Henry's runner in the delayed 3.30 race now being run at 4.30 had bolted going down to the start, and pulling up by the starting stalls had unshipped the jockey, Ron Kallon. The starter, seeing that Kallon appeared to be injured, had no alternative other than to declare the horse a non-runner. It was now close to the start time of 4.30, and Allan said the horses were being loaded into the starting stalls. "I have to go, Boss," he said, and the line went dead.

I pretended I was still talking, though. I wanted to give Laura and her mum some more private time together.

I walked down to the bottom of the garden, admiring the flowers and the rose bushes. It was a lovely, neat garden, with a little shed in the corner. *It must be Jacky's pride and joy,* I thought, imagining Laura's mum and Charlie's aunt Doris sitting out here on a day like today, sharing a cup of tea and a piece of cake. I walked back to the kitchen; it sounded like the tears had now passed.

Jacky was now back in control, and by the sound of it, once again composed. Laura, to her credit, had cuddled her mother until the tears had subsided, as she later told me in the car whilst driving back to Sayers Common.

I walked back into the lounge, and we all once again sat down. I told Laura what had happened at Newbury, and that Noel Henry's runner had been withdrawn.

Laura just replied, "Well, much as we expected." She then asked her mum how long she had been friends with Charlie's aunt.

"Oh," said Jacky. "It was when Charlie was staying here with you, just before you were banned from cricket. I saw Charlie outside the shops with her aunt, and then bumped into her aunt again in the post office. I told her I was your mum, and ever since then we have met a few times a week in the cake shop next to the post office, where we would have a coffee. And every Friday, we have lunch at one of the two local pubs in the village, the Green Man or sometimes the Anchor. We have become really good friends."

Laura replied, "That's really nice, Mum." She then added, "What's my dad up to these days?"

Jacky cut her daughter short. "I don't wish to talk about your father, Laura. I can give you a telephone number if you want to get in touch, but I'm more interested in getting to know my daughter again. And, of course, I will be following your career now as your number 1 fan!" she added.

Laura said, "Yes, Mum, please follow my career. I have just signed a contract with one of Steve's associates to school his showjumpers for him at our base in Sayers Common. You will meet him tomorrow over lunch. You will be ready, won't you, Mum?"

"Yes, of course, dear," her mum replied.

Laura said, "Charlie will most probably pick you and her aunt up at 12.15, Mum. We have a hectic day tomorrow. Oh, and by the way, Mum, Steve's friend Charles Paul is letting me keep the ride on Dublin Bay in the Hickstead Derby tomorrow."

Jacky was stuck for words. "Oh, Laura, I am so proud of you."

Jacky then turned her attention to me. "And you, Steve, are the man who has made this all happen for my daughter – and from what Doris tells me, for Charlie as well. How can I ever thank you enough?"

I waited for a few seconds before I answered. "Jacky, I do intend to marry your daughter sometime in the very near future, and your blessing would be all that the both of us would require."

Laura moved to my side, and held my hand.

"Well," said Jacky. "I can see my daughter's found the man she truly loves, and I can see you truly love my daughter, Steve. Of course you have my blessing, although I feel it's a small price to pay. Perhaps I will do something special for your wedding day."

Laura and I agreed, and said to her mum, "That would be really lovely."

Laura said, "Mum, we have to go now. We are really busy at work. But can I ask a favour?"

"Yes, of course, dear."

"Can I take the rest of the chocolate cake back with me," Laura asked. "I still love and miss your chocolate cake, Mum."

Jacky replied, "Yes, of course, my darling." She sliced the cake, wrapped it in bacon-foil, and gave it to her daughter.

We said our goodbyes. I kissed Jacky on the cheek, and mother and daughter exchanged another cuddle.

Laura and I headed back to Sayers Common, and she told me how her mum had a good cry during my absence because of my phone call. Laura couldn't resist another piece of the chocolate cake.

Time was getting on; it was just after 5.30 p.m. when we got back to the farmhouse at Sayers Common. We parked the car in the yard, next to Laura's MGB, and then walked across the stable yard towards the office.

Mickey was in the yard, and he told Laura he had just fed Fred II and tidied up his stable box. Laura thanked Mickey, and she and I went inside. I went into the office, and Laura went into the kitchen. She left her chocolate cake on the kitchen table, and then she made two coffees, brought them into the office, and sat next to me.

Charlie brought us up to date. "Plenty of action at Newbury, Steve," she said.

"Yeah," added Ricky. "And plenty of arrests too, Boss."

Gary said, "Boss, it was a good call to take this operation down today, what with tomorrow being Sunday."

We all agreed the planned procedure was working like a well-oiled machine. According to the chief inspector, the police had already arrested, charged, and detained 150 punters in possession of an illegal substance – namely cocaine – they were all so far being detained by plain-clothes detectives, as they would be all afternoon. They were all detained in the following manner: After they had obtained their cocaine from the trailer outlets, and as soon as they were out of sight from the trailers or coming out of the men's and women's toilets, they were arrested – some were even arrested as they idly walked around the enclosures and paddocks. All the detectives making the arrests acted as discreetly as possible, and in such a manner that the punters knew they had been caught, and bang to rights. They were informed of their rights, and that they were on CCTV and had been filmed and observed over many hours, and in many of the cases, at two different courses on two different days – not just Newbury today, but at Ascot on the previous Wednesday.

There really was no defence for them to plead; thus, for the most part, the punters accepted the situation as an occupational hazard. Little did they know at the time, though, that they would be detained for at least forty-eight hours; perhaps if they had known, they would have kicked up more of a fuss.

They were ushered into a holding area well away from the racing, the Tote buildings, and the paddocks; they were then loaded into a coach and escorted to Newbury Police Station, where they would be formally charged. All mobiles were confiscated immediately at the point of arrest on the racecourse. Their personal possessions were itemised on the charge-sheet, and only medicinal items like inhalers were handed back. The punters were then loaded back onto the coach and taken to Greenham Common's old airbase, where they would be detained for at least forty-eight hours.

The confiscated phones had all their individual contacts and telephone numbers, and police secretaries logged all the data onto computers. These secretaries were specially assigned at the airbase to the correlation of this information. The cross-referencing threw up at least three matching numbers on each and every mobile phone. The whole operation regarding just the punters was completed by 8.30 p.m., by which time the police had arrested, charged, and detained 284 of them.

The commander of the police operation informed them at this time of the gravity of the situation and the reason for their detention. Furthermore, he stated, "All of you arrested are going to be detained under the Prevention of Terrorism Act; you will be held for at least forty-eight hours before release, so the earliest any of you can expect to leave will be Monday evening. There was utter disbelief amongst the punters. The commander then added, "A hot meal will be served at 9 p.m. These two holding areas, one for women and one for men, have all the facilities you will require for your detention period. Breakfast tomorrow will be between 8 and 9 a.m.

Whilst I was out of the office, Charlie kept the chief inspector up to speed, apprising him of all the information Allan and Billy relayed to her. She told the chief inspector I would be back in the office near to 5.30 p.m.

Amy Cobb telephoned her husband from her mobile at 7 p.m., as previously arranged. She told him they were now packing up for the day; they had taken 612 Tote tickets during the course of the afternoon. She further told Fred it was becoming embarrassing to pick up the winnings and the refunds for non-runners, with only eight people trusted to collect the money. Fred said that he would sort it out next week; he would get twice the amount of staff in.

Amy then said, "Lucy and I will stay at Watford tonight, Fred, so we can make an early start on the shipment tomorrow.

Fred replied, "Yeah, okay." After a pause, he added, "Did you have much charlie (cocaine) left over today then?"

Amy replied, "Only twenty straws, Fred, from all the trailers."

295

"Well," said Fred. "We will need to step up production for next week then."

Amy said, "Yes, we will, Fred.

Lucy said, "Come on, Mum, let's fuck off. I'm getting so tired."

Amy said to Fred, "Look, I've got to go. I'll call you tomorrow lunchtime, Fred."

"Yeah, okay," Fred said.

Amy pressed the Disconnect button, and the line on her mobile phone went dead. Moments later, she was arrested, along with her daughter, Lucy. The other three trailer occupants suffered the same fate at exactly the same time: 7.10 p.m.

All mobiles were confiscated immediately, labelled with the owners name, and set aside for the information collection. The four trailers were seized and taken to Greenham Common for safe and secure storage; forensics would be all over them in the morning. The eight operatives of the trailers were all handcuffed, including Amy and Lucy Cobb, and loaded into a waiting minibus which delivered them with a police escort of outriders on motorcycles to the secure MI5 holding centre at Gatwick, where they would be interrogated and detained indefinitely.

The six Tote operatives were all arrested at precisely 7.10 p.m. also, and suffered a fate similar to that of the eight trailer operators: they were also handcuffed, all their mobiles were confiscated immediately, and they were put into a minibus and transported to Gatwick, where they too would be interrogated and detained indefinitely.

All in all, DCI Heyes was well satisfied with how smoothly the operation had been accomplished by the DIRTS team working in unison with Wharr's and the Berkshire Constabulary. He was hoping he would pull off a similar result at Hickstead tomorrow. The whole operation at Newbury had a final twist: on DIRTS' recommendation, at 6 p.m., DCI Heyes gave instructions to the Berkshire Police Operations Commander to arrest the racehorse trainer Noel Henry and the jockey Ron Kallon for aiding and abetting the supply of a banned drug – namely cocaine – they were also taken to the holding centre at Gatwick, and their detention would be indefinite as well.

DCI Heyes was in Doug Dunne's office waiting for the Chinese to arrive at Fred Cobb's private box, which he could see quite clearly opposite; he also had a zoom-lens camera mounted on a tripod to take images – if he was lucky – of the three Chinese gentlemen who would eventually turn up.

The showjumping had now started in the main ring. Chris Cobb had been drawn high, so he would not be jumping in the main ring until much later. After watching the showjumping now for an hour or so, Fred Cobb seemed to get bored. He took his mobile out of his pocket and dialled a number. Miles Valentine telephoned DCI Heyes at the same time.

"Yes, Miles," said DCI Heyes.

Miles replied, "Fred is trying to contact Natalie; he has just tried her number two times in succession."

The chief inspector replied, "Yes, I can see him opposite. His son had her last night, and Fred wants her tonight now that his wife is not coming to Hickstead. Obviously, his son did not let on what he did to her last night when he met his father earlier this afternoon."

"Yes," said Miles, "it would appear that way, Chief Inspector."

"Any news from the hospital yet, Miles?" asked DCI Heyes.

"Yes," said Miles. "Natalie has regained consciousness, though she is still very weak. The doctor said he didn't want her disturbed until the morning."

"In that case," said the chief inspector, "I will call in and see her at about nine o'clock tonight. We cannot wait until the morning. Will you come with me, Miles?"

"Yes," Miles replied.

"See you at the station at 9 p.m. then. DCI Heyes said. "Was there anything interesting on her mobile then?" he enquired.

Miles said, "Yes. There appears to be a bucket fuck-it agenda on her mobile, with a list of about twenty male names, eight of which have asterisks next to them."

"Miles, please read me out the names," DCI Heyes said.

Miles obliged. "The ones with the asterisks are Fred Cobb; Ron Kallon; Taffy the head lad; Chris Stuart; and the next four names are of other well-known jockeys. Chris Cobb's name comes next, along with eleven others which have no asterisk beside them."

"Maybe Natalie hadn't got round to putting an asterisk next to Chris's name yet," DCI Heyes said.

Miles agreed.

Included in the eleven other names were not only well-known jockeys but also trainers from the Newmarket area. DCI Heyes said, "I'll have to let Steve know about this when I speak to him later."

Again Miles agreed. They said goodbye.

DCI Heyes checked his zoom camera. The Chinese had arrived. He activated his audio bugs and listened in on their conversation for the next half hour or so. Fred Cobb had hatched up a plan to get rid of his partner, Chris Stuart.

No honour among thieves, the chief inspector thought to himself.

The three Chinese gentlemen that turned up to Fred Cobb's private box were all smartly dressed. DCI Heyes knew one of them. His name was Wong Fat, and he was one of the kingpins of the Brighton Triads. The other two he would get images of and then try to find out who they were. He didn't associate them with the Brighton area. The gist of Fred's conversation with Wong Fat was that Fred intended to double-cross his partner, Chris Stuart; Fred wanted the Brighton Triads as his new partners. He wanted to take control and expand; he just didn't think for one minute what he was getting into – he wanted to expand, and to eventually cover every racecourse in England, supplying cocaine and heroin at every race meeting. He also wanted to take control of Chris Stuart's Konkordski Bar, and supply all the south coast, from Margate to Bournemouth. Fred Cobb indeed had big plans – far too big for the likes of Chris Stuart – the Brighton Triads would be his perfect partners.

Wong Fat said, "Mr Fred, we can get the Midland racecourses serviced and up and running by next weekend – Stratford, Warwick, Towcester, Worcester and Leicester. We can get a crew to do the circuit with four trailer retail outlets. We have Chinese boys to run the trailers; they will be based in Luton. My bosses in the Far East say you get 10 per cent for doing nothing, with no investment necessary. Also, we will take care of Chris Stuart. We are willing to share his club with you and divide the profits fifty-fifty. We will also set up the south coast drug delivery service from Margate to Bournemouth. We have people ready and waiting to start implementing the operation. Mr Fred, my bosses say you don't need to purchase and pay within forty-eight hours anymore; you can pay in future out of profits when drugs are sold, with no time limit."

Wong Fat paused, and then he added, "My bosses also tell me to tell you the shipment that arrived yesterday, that was delivered to your Watford office, is free of charge. You do not have to pay us £75,000. If Mr Chris wants, he has to pay us £150,000 instead by five o'clock tomorrow; or else we take care of him."

Fred couldn't believe his luck. He was getting rid of his partner, and got himself a much better deal with the Brighton Triads. He ordered one of the waitresses to go and get him a bottle of champagne. To the main man, Wong Fat, he said, "Let's have a toast."

"No," said Wong Fat. "Business over. We go no drink."

Wong Fat shook Fred's hand, and said, "We tidy up loose ends tomorrow. We now partners."

Fred said, "Yes, agreed."

Fred saw his guests out, thanking them as they left. The waitress delivered his champagne. He sat on the balcony, watching the showjumping and sipping his champagne. His son then entered the ring; there had been three clear rounds so far, would his son be the fourth? Fred urged his son on, and although clear to the last, he met the final fence all wrong and knocked the top bar off for four faults. Fred said under his breath, "Dopey fucker."

All the private boxes were now full of people, and so were their balconies. Fred picked up his mobile and tried again to contact Natalie. "Where is the dopey bitch?" he muttered once again under his breath.

Miles knew, though, that Fred had tried to contact Natalie again; he had her mobile phone, and was making a note of all the people who had tried to contact her. Sally Gregory had also called a few times and left messages.

DCI Heyes called me on my mobile. It was now just after 6 p.m. "Hi, Steve, he said. "I have some news for you regarding Natalie." He then read out the list Miles had given him off her mobile. "It's a bucket fuck-it list. Evidently, you give yourself a list of people you want to fuck, and then as you fuck each of them, you cross the name off your list. So far, Natalie has done eight of a list of twenty. She never got round to crossing Chris Cobb off the list, though."

I thanked him for the information. Gary would have to rewrite some of his report possibly.

"Miles and I will be visiting Natalie tonight, Steve," DCI Heyes said. "I have something to trade with Natalie. I'll tell her that the bucket list will remain secret if she is willing to bring charges of rape against Chris Cobb."

"Good idea, Chief Inspector," I said. "I think it will work a treat." I asked him, "Would you relocate Natalie then, and give her a new identity?"

The chief inspector said, "She doesn't deserve it, but that is a possibility. It depends on whether she's agreeable to attending a rehabilitation clinic and getting herself clean of drugs."

Finally, the chief inspector told me about Fred Cobb's meeting with the Chinese; how Fred intended to have his partner, Chris Stuart, taken out of circulation, and that he planned to become partners with the Brighton Triads.

"Well," I replied. "It seems there is no honour among thieves."

DCI Heyes said, "My thoughts exactly."

Time was getting on. It was now well after 6 p.m. Laura suggested we have steak and chips for supper, followed by some of her mum's chocolate cake, with some cream. Her suggestion was met with unanimous approval. Ricky offered to be the chef and went into the kitchen to start preparing our meal.

Allan phoned me from Newbury: the team of operatives at the course, in collaboration with the police, had matters well under control. The chief inspector was monitoring the situation at Hickstead, from his command post that was Doug Dunne's office in the office block on the third floor. The whereabouts of Dicky Head, though, still remained a mystery.

Charlie and Gary left the office to shower and get changed for supper.

I looked at Laura at the same time as she looked at me. Laura said 19 at the same time I said 20. We both burst out laughing, ran upstairs to our bedroom, and within seconds, were completely naked. We fell onto the bed. We just couldn't keep our hands off each other, and we settled for a 69, a nice juicy starter. We would have the main course later.

CHAPTER 23

DCI Heyes left his office at Hickstead at 8.30 p.m. He had let all his detectives on the investigation go home at 7 p.m., apart from the two who would man his temporary office until 10 p.m. tonight, at which time Mickey would be on the prowl. The detectives all were told to be back on duty tomorrow at 10 a.m.

DCI Heyes then drove to Brighton Police Station, where he met Miles Valentine, his forensics expert. Miles updated DCI Heyes with regard to the condition of Natalie Henry, and DCI Heyes then brought Miles up to speed with events at Hickstead. He informed Miles of the grey Maestro van that had been found on the Hickstead estate, and Miles said that he would detail a team in the morning to recover the vehicle back to the station for an in-depth examination. At 9.10 p.m., they left the station together to go to the hospital and pay Naughty Natalie a visit.

The doctor on duty was not at all pleased with the chief inspector's choice of time to visit; however, he allowed the chief inspector twenty minutes with Natalie. She had been moved out of the ICU, and was now in a small ward of four beds. Thankfully, the other three beds were empty. Natalie was sitting up in bed, reading a magazine.

DCI Heyes introduced himself and Miles Valentine.

Natalie looked up, attempted to shrug her shoulders, and immediately found out one of them wasn't working properly. The one that had been dislocated was now being propped up by a sling, and the sudden jolt of pain from the attempted shrug seemed to bring Natalie back to reality. She suddenly appeared to realise she was in hospital and would be there for a good few days more.

The first question the chief inspector asked Natalie was, "Have you spoken to the doctor yet who saved your life?" Natalie didn't answer; it seemed as if she couldn't think of anything to say. The chief inspector forced home the point because of Natalie's indecision. He added, "If it had not been for the paramedic who got to you firstly with on the spot emergency treatment, I would not be here talking to you, Natalie. You would be in the morgue now, with a tag tied to one of your toes, with a number on it, not even a name." After a pause, the chief inspector finally rammed the point home, although in hindsight, he realised he never needed to. "The paramedic saved your life, Natalie. He didn't want you to die, although, personally, I don't think you deserved being saved."

Natalie burst into tears, and Miles quickly gave her a tissue.

DCI Heyes got up, turned towards Miles, and said, "Come on, let's go. We should have let the fucking whore die in Chris Cobb's horsebox."

They both started to walk away.

Natalie shouted, "Stop! Stop! I don't want to die!."

Miles and DCI Heyes returned to their chairs next to Natalie's bed.

DCI Heyes never relented. "Natalie, your life at the moment is absolutely worthless," he said. "You're a drug addict and virtually a prostitute. What is the point of you wanting to live? Why should we waste our time on you when there are many more deserving people in the world that need help?"

Miles switched his recorder on, with neither the chief inspector nor Natalie noticing.

Natalie said to the chief inspector, "In the last ten hours, I have visited both heaven and hell. Heaven was so lovely, so peaceful; it was quite tranquil and beautiful, and that was where I wanted to be and perhaps die. Suddenly, I was somewhere else. It was hell; it was mayhem. Lost souls screaming all the time – fire; horror; souls ablaze, burned alive but never dying. I travelled down the road. They wouldn't let me into heaven, and I don't want to go to hell. Then I woke up, and I knew I wanted to live," Natalie asked the chief inspector, "What's your name?"

He replied, "My name is John."

"And what's your name?" asked Natalie, looking at Miles.

"My name is Miles Valentine," he said.

Natalie replied, "That is such a lovely name."

The chief inspector said to Natalie, "My full title is Detective Chief Inspector John Fitzwilliam Heyes of the Sussex Constabulary. Miles is my forensics expert. We obviously know who you are, Natalie. Is there anything you want to tell us before we charge you with drug offences and prostitution?"

Natalie paused, seeming to gather her thoughts, and asked Miles if he would pour some water from the jug on the side into a glass for her. Miles poured the water into the glass and handed the glass to Natalie. She took the glass, sipped some water, and then said to the chief inspector, "My husband, Noel, got me hooked on cocaine. He used to take it with a Viagra tablet after a year or two of marriage. He was great in bed to start off with, but then he put on a lot of weight and became useless. In frustration, I started an affair with our stable jockey, Ron Kallon. Noel became suspicious, so I started going out around the town, and soon I was able to find my own supply of cocaine. It was quite easy to get hold of. But then, Noel stopped giving me money, so I would fuck or give blow jobs to score. I met Fred Cobb a few months ago, and he offered me free cocaine if I distributed it and sold it around the town for him. Before long, I had a network of customers in Newmarket, and I really fancied his son, Chris Cobb the showjumper. I saw him on television last Christmas. I kept a file of my top twenty fucks – my bucket fuck-it list—"

"Yes," the chief inspector interrupted. "We are well aware of that list."

"How?" asked Natalie.

The chief inspector replied, "We have your mobile phone, Natalie, and I can tell you now, this game is over. Fred and his son will both be arrested tomorrow for their part in three murders in the last ten days, together with Chris Stuart. They will all probably spend the rest of their lives in prison."

Natalie was visibly shocked by what the chief inspector had just said. She said, "Well, I won't stand in the way of your investigation, Chief Inspector. For the first time in months, I have gone ten hours without having to resort to cocaine. I've been to death's door and seen what death is like, and I don't want to go to hell. I will own up to the drug dealing with Fred Cobb. I will cooperate with you in every way I can. I know I will probably go to prison for a while, but that's a small price to pay for the misery I've no doubt caused to other people and for the deplorable way I've lived my life in the last six months."

The chief inspector got up from his chair and beckoned Miles to do the same. They walked outside the ward to confer for a few moments.

The chief inspector said to Miles, "Shall we give her a chance?"

Miles replied, "I think there is a lovely girl in there. She has been totally honest with us, without any prompting. I would say on this occasion, yes, we should give her a chance."

"Very well," said DCI Heyes.

They returned to the ward, and sat down once again at Natalie's bedside.

The doctor looked in and said, "Five more minutes, Chief Inspector."

"Now then, Natalie," said DCI Heyes. "We know all about the scam at the racecourses."

"Oh," said Natalie. "That's how Noel gets his free supply of cocaine from Fred. Every now and again, if there is no sure bet to collect on at the races, we supply a non-runner so that the trailers can supply the cocaine with no money being exchanged. Noel also tells Fred what horses are virtual certainties to be placed in big field handicaps. If Noel was ever good at anything, it would be horses. In all the time I've been married to him, he's never backed a loser or failed to collect. He always backs horses for places only, never to win. Our stable jockey has lots of ways to stop a horse from coming under starter's orders and to be able to get refunds on the Tote tickets – they are exchanged for cocaine at the trailers."

The chief inspector was overjoyed at Natalie's confession: he already had enough to put Fred Cobb, Chris Cobb, and Chris Stuart away, probably for life. DCI Heyes then said to Natalie, "And what about last night?"

Natalie told the chief inspector about her lift from Newbury to Hickstead with Danny and Dave, as well as her opportunistic date with Chris Cobb for supper in the Castle Pub. She said, "The last thing I can remember is sitting at the table with Chris when I returned to the table after going to the loo, and thinking that the wine tasted funny. I remember going to the loo just to snort a bit of cocaine; I just wanted to enjoy fucking Chris. He just said, 'Finish the wine, and then I will fuck you. You can stay the night with me in the horsebox.' Chris hardly drank any wine at all. We walked back to his horsebox, and I could hardly speak. When we got into the horsebox, everything was a bit blurred; my mind went to sleep, and I just couldn't function properly. I have no idea what was going on or what happened to me. The next thing I knew, I woke up here in hospital, just a few hours ago, recalling my strange dream of heaven and hell. The doctor told me I had suffered a miscarriage and had lost a lot of blood; he also told me I had been tied up and sexually abused. Well, to be precise, he told me I had been raped and buggered. I do not remember anything that happened in the horsebox, Chief Inspector. I don't remember being tied up or hung up or having had sex with Chris."

The chief inspector said, "Are you saying, Natalie, that the sex you had with Chris was against your will? That it was without your consent?"

"Yes, Chief Inspector," said Natalie. "I was drugged, and then he tied me up and raped me. I knew nothing about it."

DCI Heyes said to Natalie, "Would you excuse us for a minute?"

He conferred with Miles, and then they once again returned to Natalie's bedside.

"Natalie, what you have told us is of your own volition and was offered to us voluntary, is that correct?" asked DCI Heyes.

"Yes," replied Natalie. "And I would be prepared to sign a statement to that effect."

"In that case," said the chief inspector, "we would be prepared to offer you a deal where you will not go to prison. This is a one off chance in a lifetime for you. We are going to give you the chance of a rehabilitation programme, with a new identity; we will also relocate you in some other part of the country away from Newmarket. We will destroy your bucket fuck-it wish list; it will never be made public. Your husband is now in custody, and so is jockey Ron Kallon. You really do have nothing to go back to in Newmarket after you're fit enough to leave hospital. What we are offering you is the Witness Assistance Programme. When you leave hospital, you will be booked into a rehab clinic for a few weeks, and then we will set you up with a new identity, a house and a job. What do you say?"

Natalie really did not have a choice, obviously, and so she agreed to the chief inspector's proposition.

DCI Heyes and Miles Valentine got up to leave as the doctor walked in. "I'm afraid you will have to go now, gentlemen," the doctor said. "You've been here over half an hour already."

Miles turned back towards Natalie. He picked up her hand, which was lying by her side, and smiled at her. "I will call back to see you in the morning," he said. "I'll bring a written statement for you to sign." He turned his recorder off and followed the chief inspector out of the ward.

They walked along the corridor, got into the lift, and pressed the button.

As the lift descended to ground level, the chief inspector said, "You like her, don't you, Miles?"

Miles replied, "is it that obvious, Chief Inspector?"

Meanwhile, Ricky had all the cooking sorted by 7 p.m. The five of us congregated in the kitchen to eat. The Foster's lagers came out, as did the strawberry cider and the Bacardi Breezers. Gary had a glass of red wine. The talk around the table was all about the Newbury operation, which was going to be a complete success. Lord Oakley was going to be ecstatic with the outcome. However, where was the elusive Dicky Head? What was he now up to, what was he planning, and what was he now scheming? Nobody around the table could hazard a guess at his next move: Dicky Head was unpredictable.

I changed the subject. "Right, I said. "I am going to get a new car. What shall I buy?"

Everybody around the table agreed that the line of work we were in meant that an estate car would be the most suitable. The vets had started to use the new Volvo Estates that had been winning all the touring car races on the television, so a new Volvo would be ordered next week. Laura had the final say on colour: it had to be teal blue like her MGB, and it had to have leather trim.

We started on Laura's mother's chocolate cake, with some cream, and then had a few more drinks.

Laura said, "Look at the clock! The time has certainly flown tonight. It's *nineteen* minutes past nine!" She put a strong emphasis on the *nineteen.*

I knew what she wanted, so I replied, "We will go to bed at *twenty* to ten." I emphasised the *twenty,* of course.

We both laughed at our little secret. Charlie, Ricky, and Gary were none the wiser. We spent the next half an hour talking about Hickstead tomorrow. Charlie offered to go and pick up her aunt and Laura's mum up in the Vitara; Ricky would go with her.

"What time?" Charlie asked.

Laura replied, "I told Mum about 12.15. Steve and I will meet you at the arena."

Gary volunteered to babysit the farm and watch the showjumping on the television.

So, all in all, we had a good end to the day. One last job to do today before we went to sleep: I had to give Laura her main course. It was now ten o'clock.

We left Gary, Charlie, and Ricky still sitting at the kitchen table, drinking. We said goodnight and went up the stairs to bed.

After the usual ablutions, we quickly took our clothes off; we couldn't wait to get hold of each other. Laura turned on the CD player. Sade once again provided the background music for our intended lovemaking. We gently caressed and stroked each other; we lay on the bed and kissed, slowly passionately. Laura filled up my mouth with her tongue, and I sucked on it; I then did the same to Laura with my tongue, and she sucked on it. We then did it in unison, kissing and sucking each other tongues. We were arousing each other rhythmically to the music, our tongues pleasuring each other as they danced to Sade's dulcet tones. Laura's nipples were once again standing up to attention, and I began to suck on them whilst fondling her beautiful breasts; they seemed to get fuller and harder with the sudden rush of blood.

"Oh," Laura sighed. "Oh … oh!" She moved her lovely long legs apart, and I felt her beautiful wet clitoris. I lowered my head to her navel, kissing her all the time, lower and lower still, until I could taste her slightly salty wetness. I buried my tongue inside her clitoris, lapping up her beautiful love juice. I felt her first orgasm. As she came, I returned to her lips. We kissed again, passionately, with the slightly salty taste of her love juices lingering.

We paused for a few minutes, and then I lay on my back. Laura straddled me, sitting on top of me, and my erection slid easily inside her. She sighed again, leaning back for extra penetration, and swayed to the rhythm of "Your Love Is King". It wasn't long before Laura had her second orgasm. I felt huge inside her. Laura leant down to kiss me, her beautiful breasts dancing tantalisingly in front of my mouth. I playfully sucked on her nipples, and she then sat upright again and put her arms out beside her, resting her hands on the bed slightly behind her and pressing into me for even deeper extra penetration. It was then I came inside her.

"Oh my beautiful Laura!" I exclaimed., "I love you so much."

We snuggled up together, kissing each other all over. It wasn't long before Laura was on her hands and knees, with her tongue out, panting.

I laughed, knowing exactly what she wanted now. Laura started giggling too. That was it – I was now rock hard again. Another serving of 19 was coming up.

I slipped into her easily, and she let out a slight scream of delight as I started pumping her to the rhythm of "Smooth Operator". Laura was reaching ecstasy once again, with my incessant pumping. I cupped her breasts with my hands and tweaked her nipples, still pumping, pumping.

Laura was having another double orgasm which lasted a good thirty seconds. Laura was groaning with sheer unadulterated pleasure, "Oh … oh … oh!" After twenty seconds of her double orgasm, I came too. I exploded inside her; I could feel myself empty inside her. I sighed and cupped her breasts again, playing with her hard erect nipples. I pushed even harder inside her, and Laura screamed with delight.

"Oh Steve! That was lovely," she said, adding, "I love you so much."

We lay down together, side by side, to get our breath back.

After a few minutes, Laura said, "I'd better kiss my friend goodnight."

Laura got down on me to suck her friend goodnight. She sucked out the very last of the slightly salty love juice. We then had a last passionate salty kiss before falling asleep in each other's arms.

Chris Cobb spent the evening in his horsebox, with Jane. He ordered and collected some Chinese takeaway from the Castle Pub. He told Jane that his father had paid for a hitman to take care of Steve Hurst and Laura Hallett: sometime tomorrow, they would both be shot dead.

Jane was unmoved by Chris's comment; she absolutely despised both of them, and couldn't give a damn.

They finished their Chinese takeaway meal. It was now Jane's turn to be tied up and fucked. But Jane would be fucked consciously and willingly, unlike perhaps Natalie the night before. Not that Jane knew. She thought her shoulder would be okay now; after all, it had been ten days since the dislocation. They undressed each other in Chris's bedroom, and then Jane got down on her knees to give Chris a blow job. She sucked him off until he came in her mouth and she could taste the salty semen, which she swallowed.

Good, she thought. *Now he's ready.* She didn't want him coming inside her too quickly; she wanted a good fucking tonight.

Chris never bothered with wearing a condom; he probably didn't have the brains anyway to know how they worked. He tied Jane's hands together firstly, and then led her into the horsebox area and attached her to one of the six rings on the side of the box used for attaching hay nets. He then virtually suspended her until she could barely touch the floor with an outstretched foot. Chris then sucked her pussy, and she wrapped her legs round Chris's neck. When he considered she was wet enough, he rammed himself inside her and banged her against the side of the horsebox as he had done to Natalie. He really didn't give a damn about Jane's shoulder, even when she screamed at him to let her down because of the pain she was now in. Jane pleaded with him to stop, but he just ignored her. Jane started to cry, and Chris thought it was just a game, her tears adding to his demented sadistic pleasure. Only after he had come inside her did he let her down, and then he realised her tears were genuine. She fell down into a heap on the floor.

Chris said, "What's the matter with you?"

Jane replied, "Sometimes you are just too fucking rough. This is the first time in ten days my arm hasn't been in a sling, and you string me up like a chicken and fuck me like a piece of meat on a hook. When I asked you to stop, you just carried on. That was fucking sheer selfishness, Chris! Why did you do that?"

Chris replied, "I thought you loved me, and if you do, why complain when I fuck you?"

Jane said, "That's the point, Chris. We fuck, we don't make love. You don't care about me, do you, Chris?"

Chris said, "Of course I do. My dad's looking after both of us as well. He is, after all, spending £20,000 on getting rid of Steve Hurst and Laura Hallett. What fucking more do you want, Jane? Surely that proves how much I love you."

Jane had stopped crying, and the pain in her shoulder had subsided.

Chris helped Jane off the cold floor, and said, "Come on, Jane, let's go to bed."

They showered firstly, and then went to bed.

Chris went out like a light, without a care in the world. Jane, however, just couldn't sleep; she was deep in thought of the reality of the situation she had let herself become embroiled into. The realisation of the seriousness was beginning to hit home, and she asked herself, *What do I really want? Well, I wanted Chris; yes, that's true, but am I any happier? No.* She was being truthful with herself at least. She got up out of the bed. The light in the bedroom was still on; Chris didn't like to sleep in the dark. She looked into the mirror on the wall, and then she turned around and looked at Chris in bed. He looked like a child, without a care in the world. She knew then she had made the worst decision of her whole life when she left Steve. She then asked herself what she could do now. Her options were limited, and she was hooked on cocaine and heroin. She had a choice to make: she could quite easily walk out now, perhaps go to the police and tell them about Chris and the fact he was a murderer and psychotic; she could also warn them of the double murder Fred Cobb had paid for that was going to be attempted tomorrow sometime. On the other hand, she could just get back into bed with Chris and pretend it was not her problem. She decided on the latter, and virtually cried herself to sleep. Chris was oblivious to Jane's thoughts, and Jane knew she would be in the same frame of mind when she woke up tomorrow morning, so she would have to deal with it then.

Fred Cobb stayed in Brighton Saturday night; the chief inspector was aware, thanks to his audio bugs. It was the last piece of information he had got from Fred before he left his private box and headed for Brighton. Fred had already booked a room at the Metropole, on the seafront. He left for Brighton soon after his meeting with Wong Fat; he had nothing to stay for in Hickstead. Chris having the last fence down meant he would not be in the jump-off. Fred thought, *Fuck.* He then rang his hotel, the Metropole, and told them he would be down within the hour; he could then go to the greyhound meeting at nearby Hove. He did exactly that, not knowing, of course. that two of the chief inspector's detectives followed him everywhere. The chief inspector had detailed two detectives directly from the police station in Edward Street, just round the corner from the Metropole. They waited in reception for Fred to arrive, and would stick with him until he went to bed, detailing his every move.

Mickey was in the Castle Pub bang on ten o'clock. Sally was the first person he recognised. She was drunk, leaning on the bar.

Sally had been looking for a fuck but tonight couldn't find one. Jane had also had a go at her earlier this evening. Sally had told Jane to get a grip; she had been hitting the cocaine far too much recently, and it was getting out of hand.

Mickey then spotted Chris Cobb; he had arrived to pick up his Chinese takeaway. Mickey watched him collect and pay for his food, and then followed him back to his horsebox. As soon as Chris entered the box, Mickey switched on his recorder. He guessed Jane would be there, and he was right. It was another warm night, and most of the horsebox windows were open. The recording was crystal clear, and Mickey would report the conversation to the chief inspector as soon as Chris and Jane went to bed.

The chief inspector had another job for Mickey that would be undertaken in the early hours of the morning: he was to pay Pete Gregory a visit at the MI5 holding centre at Gatwick. The chief inspector instructed Mickey to lean on Gregory hard, get him to tell all he knew about Dicky Head.

"We need to know where he fits in and what he is up to and what he is capable of," the chief inspector had said. "Tell him his sister, Sally, has been nicked as an accessory to murder and drug dealing; tell him she's looking at a minimum ten-year stretch. Just get the fucker to talk."

It was now after 11.30 p.m., and Chris and Jane it seemed, had already gone to bed. Mickey gave it another ten minutes; he hung around a bit longer; he saw Jane get up and look in the mirror and then at Chris. Mickey was standing on the straw bale that Chris had left underneath the horsebox earlier that morning. He then saw Jane go in to the little kitchenette and make herself a cup of coffee. She sipped her coffee, seemingly lost in thought. He wondered what she was thinking about. Perhaps what Steve had told her on Tuesday when she collected her horse and belongings: that the police knew about Jay Penfold, and who killed him, and would be making arrests before the weekend.

Jane also pondered the fact that they had Danny and Dave, and they had been charged with murder; she thought of Sally's brother, Pete, and wondered if they had got him as well. Did the police know about her uncle Dick? Jane knew all about Pete Gregory beating up Giles Holland on her uncle's orders; that was why she went down to Gloucester last Easter with Steve – to find out what they knew for her uncle Dick. It was Jane who got her uncle to hire Pete to kill Laura's horse with a lethal injection of heroin. Jane was beginning to believe it was all circumstantial, and she might just get away with it if she went to the police in the morning and handed herself in.

If Fred Cobb succeeded in killing both Steve and Laura tomorrow, Jane now knew it would be inevitable that within weeks, if not days, she would be arrested and go to prison for a very long time – perhaps the rest of her life. Jane decided to leave a note for Chris, saying Sally had rung her and told her she was pissed and couldn't get in the horsebox, that Jane had to go and sort Sally out, and that she (Jane) would see him later on in the morning. She left his horsebox, knowing she would never set foot in it again, and she returned to her own horsebox.

Sally had just got back from the Castle Pub, and, yes, she was well and truly pissed. Jane went to bed; she would sleep better tonight in her own bed, and tomorrow she would give herself up to the police, and confess all she knew about Chris Cobb and his lunatic father. Jane knew the game was up, and the exercise now was damage limitation and to try to salvage her reputation. If she managed to hang on to her freedom, the first chance she got, she would book into a rehab centre, and then try to save her career.

Mickey by now was on his way down the M23 to see Pete Gregory and give him some hell. He got to the holding centre, which was quite full now, at about midnight, Mickey then went straight to Gregory's cell. He was still asleep, so Mickey threw some water over him. Gregory woke up, and then Mickey slapped him across the face.

Mickey said to him, "Do I have your attention?"

Gregory said, "Yes, yes. Leave me alone! Go away, and leave me alone."

Mickey said, "I'm not going until I beat you to death or you give me some answers, and I don't really give a fuck which way it is."

Gregory said, "I don't know anything more. I've told you everything."

"Not quite," said Mickey. "Why didn't you tell us Sally, Jane's groom, was your sister? We have just arrested her as an accessory to murder, and also for drug dealing and prostitution. Looks like she will get at least ten years. Now tell me more about Dicky Head, or I'll kill you here and now."

Mickey got a syringe out of his pocket and tested it in Gregory's face. "Please, no!" Gregory whimpered. "What do you want to know?"

"What's his connection?" said Mickey.

"He's Jane's uncle, and he has an interest in Chris's Outdoor Kiosks & Events. Now please leave me alone!"

Mickey gave him another slap, and told him he would be back in the morning. Mickey drove back to Hickstead and parked near to Chris's horsebox. He telephoned the chief inspector, conveyed all the interesting developments, and then he got in the back of the van, into his sleeping bag, and went to sleep.

CHAPTER 24

We woke up to bright beautiful blue skies and lovely sunshine this fine Sunday morning. Laura woke up first and gave me a nudge. The bedside clock said 8 a.m. We showered together, dried off, and brushed our teeth, and then we got dressed – the usual: jeans and T-shirts. We were both in need of a good hearty breakfast, so we went downstairs to the kitchen.

DS Harman, PC Hoad, and Mickey were seated at the kitchen table, as was Gary, who then had to go and make a quick telephone call from the office. Ricky had cooked them all a fried breakfast.

DS Harman said, "Come on then, Marcus. Back to work." They had finished their meal. DS Harman looked at me and said, "Thank you for the coffee, tea, and biscuits throughout the night in the tack room, Steve. That was very thoughtful of you." He looked then at Ricky, thanked him for the breakfast, and turned to walk outside. As they left the kitchen, DS Harman informed me they would be on duty until 10 a.m., a twelve-hour shift.

Mickey thanked Ricky for his breakfast too, and then he told me that the chief inspector would be calling me on my mobile at 9 a.m. I said okay. Mickey then went into the yard, and Laura and I sat down at the table. Ricky brought us over some coffees.

Laura said, "I'm famished! I could eat a great big breakfast now."

"Right," said Ricky. "Leave it to me."

He fired up the frying pan, and got to work.

"Where's Charlie?" asked Laura.

Ricky replied, "She's still in bed. I thought I would let her sleep in for an extra hour this morning. I told her I would wake her at about nine o'clock."

Gary came in from the office after his call, finished his breakfast, and asked me what he should do about the Natalie Henry case. I told him to hold fire until I had spoken to the chief inspector; I also informed Gary that the trainer Noel Henry had been arrested at Newbury, along with his stable jockey, Ron Kallon, late yesterday afternoon, and that both had detained overnight by the police.

Ricky brought over Laura's and my fried breakfasts of eggs, bacon, mushrooms, tomatoes, beans, and sausages, along with some toast. Within fifteen minutes, both plates were wiped clean. We had both obviously used up a lot of energy the night before.

Gary turned to go back into the office, as Allan would be calling him on his mobile at8.30 to update him on the Newbury operation. Before Gary left, I asked him if he would contact Ginger Martin at Edenbridge to ask him if he would come over to pick the horsebox up that Chris Collins had hired for the month. Sadly, Chris obviously would not be needing it anymore.

Gary said, "Yes, Boss, will do."

Laura was now in the fridge, foraging for that last slice of chocolate cake. "Ah," she said. "There it is." She returned with it to the kitchen table, undid the bacon-foil wrapping, and devoured the cake within minutes, along with her second cup of coffee. Ricky looked at her in amazement. Laura looked up, and in all innocence, said, "What!"

Ricky said, "I just don't know where you put it all."

Laura replied, "Well, I'm a young girl with a healthy appetite, and I'm going to need lots of energy for this afternoon." After a few seconds' pause, she added, "And for tonight as well!"

Ricky started to laugh, and I joined in as well, as did Laura, who really can be quite funny at times.

Ricky made me another coffee. I told Laura I would now be in the office for a good hour; it was 8.45. Laura said she'd be out into the yard after she finished her cake and coffee; she wanted to make a start on the rest of the horseboxes, clearing them out to ready them for the redecoration and refit later on in the week. First of all, though, she would feed her horse, Fred II. She would turn him out in one of the paddocks a little bit later, for an hour, and let him have a stretch and a run round.

At 9 a.m. on the dot, DCI Heyes telephoned me on my mobile. He was still at the Brighton Police Station in Edward Street, and he relayed every bit of the conversation he'd had with Natalie Henry the previous night at the hospital, where she was interviewed in her hospital bed. He also informed me Miles would be seeing her later this morning so that she could sign a sworn statement, and then Chris Cobb could be arrested later today. The chief inspector also told me of Fred Cobb's wicked intentions with regard to me and Laura, and that he had planned to have his partner, Chris Stuart, murdered by the Brighton Triads gang. They were to be his new business partners. He then told me in greater detail about Mickey's eavesdrop on Chris Cobb and Jane last night, and their conversation whilst they were eating their late-night Chinese meal.

"Fred Cobb paid a hitman £20,000 to have you and Laura shot and killed sometime today in the arena at Hickstead, Steve," said DCI Heyes. I suddenly felt like throwing up all that breakfast I had just eaten. "Don't be alarmed, though, Steve," he added. *Yeah, right!* I thought. Alarmed to fucking right I was! DCI Heyes continued, "I promise you it won't come to that. I'm in the middle of planning how to put an end to all this and wipe out these vicious bastards. The Home Secretary doesn't want any trials with clever lawyers, Steve. His exact words to me were: 'Take these evil bastards out of circulation for good.'"

I thought of Pete Gregory; his days were now surely numbered, thanks to Mickey.

DCI Heyes elaborated further. "Your lunch today with Prince Ahmed will now be held in Doug Dunne's private function room, which is adjacent to his office on the third floor of the offices, next to the entrance to the main ring; there is a much larger balcony as well, where you can view the main event this afternoon. Prince Ahmed's private box is next to Fred Cobb's, and we have taken over the prince's box; he has already been told of a major plumbing problem that cannot be fixed in time. Doug Dunne has kindly offered the use of his private box, which the prince has already accepted. I will have a crack team of armed officers in there, Steve, before and during the day's main ring events. We have placed some spy cameras in Fred's box overnight as well, so we will know at all times what is going on."

I asked the chief inspector for his assessment on the Newbury operation next; I had to produce a report on my company's behalf for Lord Oakley at the Jockey Club. The chief inspector implied that most of the punters could be released later on this evening; it all depended on how the situation unfolded today at Hickstead.

"If, and it is a big if," said the chief inspector, "there are no loose ends, then and only then, would we consider releasing the bulk of the punters."

He then added. "However, Steve, should the operation here at Hickstead go pear shaped, then the punters would once again be detained overnight."

I asked the chief inspector what he considered to be the best outcome for us, in consideration of our joint operations and investigations.

He said quite candidly, "I want Chris Cobb, Fred Cobb, Chris Stuart, Wong Fat, and Dicky Head dead by the end of the day. My officers will be shooting to kill today, Steve, make no bones about that!"

Just out of curiosity, I asked about the fate of my ex, Jane.

The chief inspector said, "She has a lot of questions to answer, and there is no doubt she was involved; it will all depend on the level of her involvement." He paused for a second, and then added, "By the way, Steve, we heard from two different sources last night that Dicky Head is in fact Jane's uncle; Jane's father is Dicky Head's brother. We heard this firstly from Jane herself and then from Pete Gregory when Mickey further questioned him last night at around midnight at the MI5 holding centre at Gatwick. Gregory confirmed that fact to be true. We believe now that Dicky Head is staying with his brother at the riding school that Jane's parents run at Irons Bottom just outside Reigate."

I said, "Yes, Chief Inspector, I know the place well."

As the chief inspector continued talking, I started to wonder whether there would be any need at all to make any written reports with regard to my cases and clients.

Natalie Henry would be set up with a new identity. Noel Henry was facing criminal charges and would probably be banned for life from ever again holding a trainer's licence; his stable jockey, Ron Kallon, also looked like he was facing a lengthy ban. The last thing Noel Henry would want right now was a report on his wife; he would probably never see her again anyway. As far as my employee's report on Natalie was concerned, Gary could probably now throw it in the bin.

Tim Holland had already been sent a report on his son's assault at Christmas, so that case was now closed. Giles Holland's assailant, Pete Gregory, was at the MI5 holding centre at Gatwick. Given Mickey's intentions, suffice it to say that Pete Gregory's days were now numbered; to put it bluntly, they were now in single figures, and nearer one than nine. Dicky Head, who had paid Pete to carry out the assault, would face several charges as soon as he was apprehended, and he would then spend a long time behind bars.

The Tote scam would need a report, and no doubt the Home Office would receive one from the police, in due course and for the eyes of the Home Secretary; after all, this case carried significant national importance as to its final outcome, which was still in the balance. That said, I would still have to send in a report to Lord Oakley, and Gary could start preparing it now. Billy and Allan could and would supply Gary with any information that Charlie did not have on file.

The chief inspector further informed me that he had two detectives already on watch at the riding school, keeping an eye out for Dicky Head. "I must leave now to meet my detectives at Hickstead, Steve," said DCI Heyes. "We have a meeting at 10 a.m. One last bit of news, though: I also have two detectives in plain clothes following Fred Cobb. He stayed at a hotel in Brighton, last night; he went to the dogs at Hove greyhound stadium, and by the looks of it, he has not got up this morning yet – he certainly has not been down for breakfast anyway."

I thanked the chief inspector for all the information, we said goodbye, and I put the phone down. I would now update my team in the office; it was now 9.30 a.m.

Charlie had got up at nine, and Ricky made sure she had a proper fried breakfast as well. He tidied then up in the kitchen, and he and Charlie, now fed and nourished, joined us in the office. Laura joined us also, and we had an impromptu team briefing right away. The whole team was filled in with all the details of what the chief inspector had relayed to me over the phone in the previous half hour; the one main item I omitted from telling my team was what the chief inspector had said about Laura and me being the targets for a would-be assassin who would be or already had been paid the sum of £20,000 to kill us both. Evidently, according to the chief inspector, we would both be shot in the arena sometime today. Our lives then, it would appear, were now in the chief inspector's hands.

There were several gasps of amazement when I revealed that Dicky Head was in fact Jane's uncle.

Laura said, "The lousy cow. She must have only gone with you to the Hollands in Gloucester at Easter to find out what and how much they knew, if anything, about Giles's beating last Christmas, Steve. All she wanted was to know whether they had anything on her uncle. What a bitch."

Everyone around the table agreed.

I also told the team that the luncheon with Prince Ahmed would now be in Doug Dunne's private function room, next to his office on the third floor of the office block next to the entrance of the main arena, and those that were attending needed to be there by 12.45 p.m. It was now nearing 10 a.m., and DS Harman popped his head inside the office door to say goodbye and wish Laura luck this afternoon. PC Hoad wished Laura luck as well. DS Harman told us he would watch the showjumping on the television at home with his wife; she liked to watch the showjumping. DS Harman and PC Hoad then left in their panda car parked round the back in the ten-vehicle car park next to the yard. The white police Mercedes estate car was still parked outside the front drive, the officer patrolling in uniform, with his submachine gun strapped to his body and his finger on the trigger.

Meanwhile, DCI Heyes had just started to brief his team of detectives in Doug Dunne's office when his mobile rang. It was one of his detectives in the hotel lobby in Brighton: Chris Stuart had turned up and was having breakfast with Fred Cobb.

"Okay," said DCI Heyes. "One of you tail Chris Stuart. When he leaves, the other one stays with Fred Cobb."

The detective with the mobile said, "Okay, Boss."

DCI Heyes then continued to brief his detectives, telling them of the brilliant success at Newbury yesterday, which had resulted in 300 arrests, for drug offences, fraud, and murder. He also told them that a hitman was on the loose at Hickstead today, and his two targets were Laura Hallett and Steve Hurst. He told them he had drafted in an elite armed unit of twelve specially trained officers in full-battle uniform, four of which would be positioned inside Prince Ahmed's private box, which was next to Fred Cobb's. He further told them that CCTV cameras had been installed in Fred's box overnight, and discreetly positioned. The eight remaining armed police would be positioned north, south, east, and west of the arena, in groups of two officers in unmarked police cars. A sniper would be in a cherry picker, 30 feet up and behind the derby bank; another sniper would be positioned here in this office on the balcony.

He finished by instructing his detectives: "Be extra vigilant on today of all days, as two very special people's lives depended on you detectives gathered here now; they are depending on your expertise and professionalism. Don't let them down."

The detectives acknowledged the chief inspector's words as they left to go to their allotted areas to patrol.

DCI Heyes made himself a coffee, and went and sat down next to Doug's desk. There was a knock on the door, and DCI Heyes got up to answer it. He opened the door, and Jane Coe was standing there.

"Remember me, Chief Inspector? I'm Jane Coe, and I would like to give myself up to you. As you know, I was an International showjumper, and in the last few weeks I have completely ruined my life. In the last few months, I have also become a drug addict."

DCI Heyes invited Jane into the office, offered her a seat, and made her a coffee. Jane then burst into tears. DCI Heyes was completely unmoved by Jane's sudden bout of crocodile tears and remorse, but he gave her a box of tissues, sat down opposite her, and waited for her to stop crying. After a few minutes, Jane was a little more composed.

DCI Heyes then said, "So what have you come to tell me then, Jane, that I don't already know?" He switched his recorder on to record the conversation that would ensue.

Jane gave the chief inspector her version of events, which would hopefully stop her going to prison for a very long time; it was her carefully thought-out and contrived damage-limitation speech.

"Well, Chief Inspector, I first met Chris Cobb at the Horse of the Year show, last Christmas. At that time, I had been seeing Steve Hurst for about a year, and we had become engaged. I have been seeing Chris Cobb off and on for about the last four months; certainly since the spring show in Hampshire at Stocklands in April this year. I broke off the engagement with Steve nearly two weeks ago now. I first had sex with Chris in April at that show, and, yes, I know I have fucked my life up and that it was the biggest mistake I have ever made leaving Steve for that psychopath Chris Cobb – and his father is just as bad."

DCI Heyes said, "Yes, well, we all know all that, so what have you got to tell me that I don't know, Jane? I thought you had some news for me. I might as well arrest you now as an accessory to three murders; you will do at least fifteen years, Jane."

The tears started again. DCI Heyes got up, made himself another coffee, and sat down again. "What you're now telling me, Jane, I already know." He passed the coffee to Jane.

Jane decided to play one of her trump cards. "Did you know, Chief Inspector, that Fred Cobb had hired a hitman to kill both Steve Hurst and Laura Hallett later today?" Jane thought that info should knock at least ten years off her sentence.

"Oh yes," said DCI Heyes. "We know all about that. It's costing Fred twenty grand, isn't it?"

Jane's trump card was a spectacular own goal. She tried again. "Did you know that Chris Cobb had murdered the car park attendant?"

"Yes," said DCI Heyes. "Along with Jay Penfold, who Chris murdered with a syringe full of heroin and then set his car on fire in Lewes. He murdered Jay because Jay nearly killed you in the car park. Am I right so far, Jane?"

DCI Heyes was spot on, and Jane was now utterly deflated; she had no more trump cards to play. The chief inspector was always one jump ahead of her.

Jane continued, "It appears I have nothing new to offer you then, Chief Inspector."

"Oh," said DCI Heyes, "if you keep thinking, I'm sure you will find something to interest me and help us with our enquiries. I'm sure Chris must have told you some little secrets." He then gave Jane a little snippet of information. "Did you know that Chris fucked a racehorse trainer's wife in his horsebox two nights ago, Jane? He drugged her, fucked her, buggered her, and caused her to have a miscarriage. Did you know Natalie Henry, Jane?" enquired the chief inspector.

Jane was knocked out by this revelation. Jane sipped her coffee, and said, "I know of her. She sells drugs for Fred in Newmarket," Jane said. "You asked me 'did I know her'; is she dead then?"

DCI Heyes replied, "Not quite yet, but she is on a life-support machine in the hospital as we speak. She was found covered in blood in the back of Chris's horsebox Saturday morning. Chris had tied her up, strung her up on one of the rings, raped her while she was unconscious, and then viciously buggered her." Jane by now was a completely broken woman, and the chief inspector drove the final nail into the coffin. "Chris and his father had been taking it in turns to fuck her, without either of them letting on. Fred rang her three times last night, wondering where she was; he had arranged to fuck her in his private box last night, but his son fucked her the night before, because you were not available as a result of your argument over Laura's success. Natalie then, of course, couldn't answer Fred's calls because she was in hospital. But Fred doesn't know any of that." The chief inspector paused, and then added, "Am I right, Jane? Fred doesn't know that his son raped her and nearly killed Natalie; they are, as you say, Jane, both 'demented psychopaths'." Jane was crying again. "The poor girl," Jane said. "Please help me, Chief Inspector," she pleaded.

"I need something from you, Jane, if I am to help you," said DCI Heyes.

Jane said, "What else can I possibly give you? You know everything already."

The chief inspector said two words: Dicky Head. He then repeated, "Jane, give me your uncle Dicky Head before he kills someone."

Jane said, "Oh him. He's another psychopath. He collects and carries grudges more than any other person I know."

"Well, then," said the chief inspector. "Why don't you tell me all about him, and where he is at the moment. He's been staying at one of the cottages on the Hickstead estate most of the week, hasn't he, Jane?"

Jane replied, "You know everything, don't you, Chief Inspector?"

DCI Heyes replied, "Well, try to tell me something I don't know, Jane."

Jane told the chief inspector about uncle Dick getting Sally's brother, Pete Gregory, to beat up Giles Holland the previous Christmas.

DCI Heyes said, "Oh, that's old news, Jane. Pete Gregory is already in custody for that. Did you know, Jane, that he tried to kill Laura Hallett and her horse by filling them both up with a syringe of heroin? Come on, Jane, tell me something I don't know!"

Oh fuck! Jane thought. *So that's why Pete hasn't been around.* "No, Chief Inspector, I know nothing about that."

"Pete told us it was your idea, Jane, and you gave your uncle £500 to give to Pete for doing this job for you." The chief inspector was now spoofing Jane.

"No, Chief Inspector! I wouldn't stoop so low as to do a thing like that."

The chief inspector now had Jane on the ropes, and he asked her, "What about Friday then in the Grade C Final, did you not make a public comment on Laura: 'Go on, fall off and break your fucking neck!' Is that what you think of your fellow competitors, Jane? Don't you remember watching the class with that fuck-pig groom of yours called Sally, whose brother you sent to kill Laura and her horse because you are insanely jealous of her ability?"

"Chief Inspector, you have it all wrong," Jane insisted. "I only said that because Chris and I were arguing."

"What about?" said the chief inspector. Jane didn't speak. "I will tell you what you were arguing about, Jane. Laura is an exceptional talent, with more skill in the saddle than you and Chris put together, and the pair of you are insanely jealous."

Jane replied, "Yes, I am jealous of her ability, Chief Inspector. Laura now knows more about horses than I will ever know. I envy her so much."

DCI Heyes said, "Jane, Laura offered you her friendship. She even said nothing when you got engaged to Steve. She had been in love with Steve for two and a half years before you arrived, but she said nothing because Steve's happiness meant more to her than her own. She gave you Steve on a plate, without a bad word about you. She sorted out your horse problems as well. And you repay her by hoping she breaks her 'fucking neck'! You even tried to have Laura and her horse killed by a lethal injection of heroin, hiring Pete Gregory as a hitman."

Two of his detectives walked into the office, and DCI Heyes said, "Take Miss Coe down to Brighton Police Station, and charge her with being an accessory to murder on three counts, and conspiracy to murder on one count. That should put you away for twenty years, Jane."

Jane then called the chief inspector a fucking wanker.

DCI Heyes didn't care. Jane Coe had nothing to give him; her arrest meant one more drug addict out of the way. It was now after 11 a.m. He went and made himself a nice hot cup of coffee. The morning was going better than he could possibly have hoped for, and he would inform Steve, after he'd had his coffee, that the detectives had handcuffed Jane and taken her off to the Brighton Police Station. She would be charged and then brought to the holding centre at Hollingbury, where she would stay indefinitely as a remand prisoner until a trial date was set by the magistrates.

Miles telephoned the chief inspector to let him know that Natalie had signed the statement. What with the recording DCI Heyes had just made of Jane Coe's interview, he might arrest Chris Cobb sooner rather than later; it all depended on what Fred Cobb was up to. DCI Heyes would let Jane stew for a bit in holding as well, just in case he needed her later. A few hours in the cells for Jane, and let's see how this afternoon would turn out.

One of the detectives telephoned the chief inspector from the hotel where Fred Cobb was staying. The detective reported that Chris Stuart had just had a blazing row with Fred Cobb. Fred had told Chris that his Mercedes was broken into last night, and his seventy-five grand in readies was stolen. Fred blamed Chris, as he was the only person who knew about the money. Chris protested his innocence, and he further told Fred that if the £150,000 was not paid by 5 p.m., he would be dead at 6 p.m. Fred replied, "Well, where the fuck am I going to get seventy-five grand in readies from in six hours on a Sunday afternoon?" Chris then told Fred he was a liar and had done a deal with the Chinese, – the Brighton Triads behind Chris's back adding that the Chinese had been after his business for years. Chris stormed out, shouting "You've sold me out, Fred! I'll be dead before five o'clock!" He was then followed by a certain Chinese man, called Gary Sui. Fred's final words to Chris were "go fuck yourself".

Barry, one of the detectives, told DCI Heyes he would tail Chris Stuart. Colin, the other detective, said he would stay with Fred.

"Okay," said DCI Heyes. "Both of you now keep me informed with all further details."

The chief inspector put the phone down, and then he had one of those moments of inspiration: he would use Jane to flush out Dicky Head. Before Jane had left the office after being arrested, he had confiscated her mobile phone and her Range Rover keys from her bag. He now had the mobile number for Dicky Head which was stored on Jane's mobile. He would send him a text at about 2 p.m., purportedly from Jane, saying Fred Cobb wanted to see him. It was a bit of a gamble, because DCI Heyes didn't know how bright Dicky Head actually was; however, it was, in the chief inspector's mind, worth a try. Head was probably close to Jane, so he would not suspect anything.

The chief inspector telephoned Steve on his mobile, and gave him the news of Jane's arrest. It was about 11.15 a.m. Jane would be charged on three counts of accessory to murder, and one count of conspiracy to murder. "In my opinion, Steve, Jane paid Pete Gregory for the attempted killing Laura's horse, and probably Laura as well, with the syringe of heroin that Gregory had on him when apprehended by Mickey. Jane is also linked to Chris Collins's death, through her association with Fred and Chris Cobb." The chief inspector further implied that Jane was her own worst enemy. He also explained his plan to draw out Dicky Head.

Steve was in full agreement; however, time was of the essence. It was now 11.30 a.m.

Steve, Laura, Ricky, and Charlie were now getting ready for Hickstead. Mickey had brought Fred II in from the paddock; he was now being collected at 12.15 p.m. by Charles Paul's horsebox driver. Gary manned the phone in the office and got on with preparing the report for Lord Oakley at the Jockey Club on the company's behalf regarding the Tote scam; he had most of the details and would set the report out in an orderly fashion.

Meanwhile, Chris Stuart sat in his bar, visibly shaking, with a lager in front of him. He had just had a call on his mobile phone from Wong Fat. "One hundred fifty grand in readies, Mr Chris, by five o'clock, or you dog meat." Chris had heard rumours that the Brighton Triads ran a processing plant for animal feed; they bought all the old carcasses from Masnun's, the horse slaughterers in Crawley, and crushed them to provide bonemeal for the pet-food products and supplements they sold. He did not want to find out if it were true. He had found another 25,000 in readies, but was still 50,000 short, with no way of finding it. He had another lager.

DCI Heyes had a call on his mobile; it was Miles.

"The two images of the Chinese men with Wong Fat who met Fred Cobb at Hickstead in his private box," said Miles.

"Oh yes," said the chief inspector. "Go on."

Miles said, "We now have positive identifications: their names are Zang Zai and Gary Sui, and they are both hired killers who work only for the Triads and on a contract basis. Once they accept a contract, it's kill or be killed – there is no in between, Chief Inspector, you either take them out, or they will honour their contract."

"Thank you for the information, Miles," said the chief inspector.

"Finally, Chief Inspector, I have sent a team of forensics to recover the grey van from Hickstead. I thought I'd better let you know."

Once again, DCI Heyes said, "Thank you, Miles, please keep in touch."

The mood of the chief inspector changed in a flash. He made himself another cup of hot coffee, and he sat down and pondered his next move. As the pictures came through on Doug's printer of the two hitmen, he photocopied a dozen of each. Had Fred Cobb paid for two contracts or one? Did Zang Zai and Gary Sui each have a separate contract for different hits? Was one contract for Steve and Laura, and another one for Chris

Stuart? It was fast approaching noon, which meant Chris Stuart only had five hours to live.

Charlie and Ricky left the farmhouse in Sayers Common at 11.45 a.m.; they would be in Ringmer easily by 12.15 p.m. to pick up Charlie's aunt Doris and Laura's mum, Jacky. The traffic was light, and they arrived in plenty of time. Charlie's aunt Doris had never met Ricky.

When Ricky asked if he could use the loo, Doris said to Charlie, "Is that your man?"

Charlie said, "Don't say anything, Aunt Doris, but I intend to marry him within a year from now."

Ricky came out of the loo.

"Oh good," said Doris "I've not been to a wedding in years, and then two come along!"

Charlie looked puzzled. Who else in the village that Aunt Doris knew was getting married?

They all got in the Vitara and set off round the corner to pick up Jacky. Within minutes, they were all in the car, and they set off for Hickstead to enjoy a nice lunch and to watch an afternoon of top-class showjumping.

CHAPTER 25

There were a number of people at Hickstead at the moment with serious decisions to make. DCI Heyes was one of them. Chris Stuart was one of his problems, and Fred Cobb was another; they each had problems of their own also. Fred's wife, Amy, was not answering her phone, which was not like her. He tried his daughter, Lucy; no answer as well – he would have to try them both again later.

DCI Heyes was aware he had the mobiles of Amy and Lucy Cobb on his desk: all the confiscated mobiles were labelled with the names of the people they belonged to. Mickey had brought them back with him from the MI5 holding centre at Gatwick last night. DCI Heyes could see the mobiles ringing; no doubt Fred was calling.

Meanwhile, Chris Stuart consoled himself with another lager in his bar in Brighton.

The lunch idea was a smart move by the chief inspector. Charles Paul seemed very impressed with Doug Dunne's generosity at such short notice. Plus, Doug's function room was much bigger and with a larger balcony to watch the showjumping. Seated around the table for lunch were Prince Ahmed and his wife, Charles and Becky Paul, Doris, Jacky, Ricky, Charlie, Laura, and I. We were ten in all.

Lunch would consist of a hot or cold buffet, with apple pie and cream or a lemon sorbet; cheese and biscuits, tea, and coffee would follow. Laura and Charles declined to eat, as they would be competing later in the afternoon. They left us at 1.30 p.m. to walk the course and to warm up their horses in case they were drawn early on in the competition.

The Hickstead Derby would commence at 2 p.m., and the whole competition would take about three hours, including a jump-off, if necessary, to decide the winner.

The chief inspector was having second thoughts: he had two possible hitmen out there, with two possible targets. He issued the pictures of the hitmen to all his detectives on the ground at the arena, and to all the officers in the special unit; both the snipers received images as well. However, what the chief inspector did not know was that Zang Zai was already on-site: he was a waiter setting up Fred Cobb's very own private box. The CCTV pictures were live next door in the commandeered private box of Prince Ahmed, which had the supposed plumbing problem; none of the four armed officers were aware, though. They were not paying that much attention to the television screen showing live pictures of a waiter laying a table for six people.

The way in which the afternoon unfolded would all depend on the draw. Charles Paul was drawn last to go, at number 20, which was a good draw to have. Laura was lucky with her draw as well, at number 18. Chris Cobb was drawn 16. After walking the course, Charles and Laura returned to the private luncheon box in the office complex. Mickey, at all times, was never far behind Laura or indeed Charles.

The chief inspector was about to send a text to Dicky Head's mobile number. He decided to keep the message short and sweet: "Uncle Dick, Fred Cobb wants to see you at Hickstead this afternoon. Most of the police now have gone. He says he wants to buy your bit of the COKE business, and he's got seventy-five grand in readies for you." DCI Heyes typed out the message on Jane's phone, pressed Send, and the text was on its way.

Within ten minutes, he had a reply on Jane's phone: "Jane, why does he want my share of the COKE business?"

DCI Heyes replied from Jane's phone, "He's getting rid of Chris Stuart. He doesn't think big enough. He's got a new partner; he's going in with the Brighton Triads. They are starting the Midland operation next week, and they are going to double production and profits. Are you in or out, Uncle Dick? It's all being reorganised, and the drugs are now paid for out of the profits, so no investment. Wong Fat has given Fred seventy five grand to give you."

Within five minutes, Head replied, "I'm in, Jane. I will be at Fred's box at 4.30 to pick up my money. I'll be dressed as a rider to blend in."

Jane's phone replied, "Yeah, okay. See you there."

Bingo! Dicky Head had taken the bait. DCI Heyes had been right about Dicky Head all along: he was a psychotic idiot with a big chip on his shoulder. DCI Heyes let out a little laugh as he made himself yet another coffee. So he was going to dress up as a rider to collect seventy-five grand in readies, and he thought he would blend in. As there were ten male riders and ten female riders, of which of the police knew two, Dicky Head was going to stick out like a sore thumb! What a dumb bloody idiot! DCI Heyes smiled and then sipped his coffee.

The sniper in the office on the balcony floor told the chief inspector that Fred Cobb had just arrived with the fat man – Wong Fat – and the chief inspector looked through his zoom lens to confirm. Sure enough, the only other person in the room was the waiter; no other guests had yet arrived.

The chief inspector saw Fred use his mobile phone again. Amy Cobb's mobile rang on his desk; a few minutes later, Lucy's mobile rang. Neither was answered.

Chris Stuart was now on his third lager. His bar was beginning to empty from the lunchtime trade. Gary Sui went into the bar and ordered an orange juice and soda. "A pint please," he said to the barman.

At Hickstead, the Derby was now under way. Doris and Jacky were enjoying every minute of it. Laura sat on the second row of seats positioned on the balcony, behind Prince Ahmed. Charles was sat next to Laura on one side, and I sat next to Laura on the other side. If we were to be shot, it was going to be very difficult for the hitman. I was aware that DCI Heyes had a sniper next door, and another sniper in the cherry picker. Also, at the insistence of DCI Heyes, both Laura and I were wearing bulletproof, stab-proof vests. Ricky and Charlie wore vests as well. Laura and Charles got up to go and warm up their mounts. Ricky, Mickey, and the two detectives followed the two of them everywhere; it would not be long now before they were competing.

The afternoon was not as warm as it had been earlier in the day. Clouds were now blocking out the sun more often than not. Chris Cobb had not seen Jane all morning. Sally told him Jane went out and about just after 10 a.m., and Sally hadn't seen her since; maybe she went back to her parents' place to see her uncle Dick. Jane's Range Rover and trailer were not there. Chris agreed that must be what Jane had done.

DCI Heyes had confiscated the Range Rover and trailer after Jane was taken away and charged earlier in the day. He did this hoping that Chris and Sally would think that Jane had driven the Range Rover to her parents' home just outside Reigate; their reaction was exactly what he desired – they had no idea that Jane had been arrested.

Meanwhile, Aussie rang DCI Heyes on his mobile. He answered, and Aussie said, "Chief Inspector, I've done as you asked: I've got four emergency ambulances with paramedics on board."

"Thank you, Aussie," said DCI Heyes. "Will you now park them at three, six, nine, and twelve o'clock? The office block is six o'clock. You will be parked by armed police units; they will acknowledge you."

"Well," said Aussie. "What are you expecting – World War III?"

"If you please, Aussie. Just do as I ask."

"Yes, Chief Inspector, right away," said Aussie.

The three ambulances went to their positions. Aussie's ambulance went to six o'clock, the office block and the riders' entrance to the main arena.

Back in Brighton, Gary Sui had finished half of his pint of orange juice and soda. Chris Stuart was on his fourth pint of lager. Barry, the detective who was following Chris Stuart, reported in to the chief inspector.

"Ah good. Glad you rang in Barry," said the chief inspector. "What's the situation with you?"

"Chris Stuart is sitting in the bar at his club, getting drunk. My colleague Colin just texted to inform me has followed Fred Cobb back to Hickstead."

"Yes," said the chief inspector. "We have Fred Cobb in sight."

Colin, the detective following Fred Cobb, entered the chief inspector's office. He made himself a coffee whilst the chief inspector was on the phone; he was awaiting his new orders from the chief inspector. Colin noticed the photo on the desk of the two Triad hitmen. "Chief Inspector," said Colin, pointing to one of the men in photo. "I saw that one in Brighton this morning. He was in the same hotel as Chris Stuart and Fred Cobb. I think he followed Chris Stuart out of the hotel."

"Are you sure, Colin?" said the chief inspector.

"Absolutely," replied Colin.

The chief inspector was overjoyed: he only had one hitman in the arena after all. He talked further to Barry, the detective on the phone, updating him with what Colin had just said. "Barry, are there any other Chinese people in the bar?"

Barry said, "Yeah, one. He's been sucking on a pint of orange juice and soda for about an hour."

"Describe him to me," said the chief inspector. From Barry's description, the chief inspector was fairly sure it was his hitman.

Now DCI Heyes had to decide what to do.

He told Barry to keep him posted, said goodbye, and almost immediately received a call on his mobile from Mickey. "Come to the office, would you, Mickey? I have a job for you," said DCI Heyes.

Mickey was in the office within a minute; he let Ricky know where he was going. On seeing Mickey disappear, the two detectives on the detail paid Laura closer attention.

The chief inspector asked Mickey if he had a silencer for his gun.

"It's in my van," Mickey said.

"All right," said DCI Heyes. "Here's a picture of a hitman I want you to kill immediately. His name is Gary Sui, and he's been hired to kill Chris Stuart at the Konkordski Bar in Brighton, on the seafront. Can you go immediately?"

"Yes," said Mickey, and then he enquired, "This Chris Stuart, is he a good guy or a bad guy?"

DCI Heyes said, "He's bad, Mickey."

"Okay, message understood," Mickey said. "Please get the boys at Gatwick to send a laundry van."

"Right away," DCI Heyes said.

Mickey left to do what he was good at.

Mickey was at the Konkordski Bar within twenty minutes. He parked outside, got the silencer out of the glove box, and attached it to his handgun. After checking that there were at least four rounds in the gun, Mickey placed it in a newspaper underneath his arm, and then he got out of the van and walked into the bar. Barry silently acknowledged Mickey and then walked out of the bar. Mickey ordered an espresso coffee, and the barman went to make it. Mickey then shouted, "Hey, Gary!" Gary Sui turned round to face Mickey; he was dead before he could see who shot him. Mickey put one bullet right between Gary's eyes and another one in his heart.

Chris Stuart said, "Oh thank you! Thank you!"

Mickey searched the dead man: he was packing a handgun too. Mickey checked to see if it was loaded. He then he used Gary Sui's gun to give Chris Stuart the same treatment that Gary had just received. Mickey wiped the gun clean and placed it in Gary Sui's right hand; the report would say Mickey got there too late and couldn't prevent Chris Stuart's death, but he did get the hitman. There were no witnesses; the bar was empty as the barman who brought Mickey's expresso coffee found out upon his return. He told the laundryman later that he knew nothing and saw nothing.

Mickey then gave Barry a lift back to Hickstead. As they left, the laundryman arrived from Gatwick to clean up the mess. No one was any the wiser except for the chief inspector.

Fred Cobb's son, Chris, would soon be entering the arena. Fred seemed anxious as he sat on the balcony, watching the showjumping with Wong Fat. It was just past four o'clock: another five riders to go. Once again, Fred tried Amy on her mobile, but there was still no reply; this was so unlike his wife that Fred didn't know what to think.

DCI Heyes continued to watch Fred Cobb, and then Amy Cobb's mobile ringing on the desk. The chief inspector now was calling the shots. But where was Zang Zai, the other hitman?

The announcer's voice via the loudspeaker said, "Twelve faults for number 15, and into the ring now is Chris Cobb on his father's Final Chapter. Can he go clear? He must be one of the favourites; he has been in the money all year, and goes well here."

Fred was cheering Chris on, as he was going so well; he was clear to the last, but then, just like Friday, he took the pole off the top of the last fence, for four faults.

"Well," said the announcer. "Is anybody going to go clear? Hard luck there for Chris Cobb; that's three horses now on four faults."

Crestfallen, Chris left the ring. Sally ran up to him and told him Jane had left a note saying she'd given herself up to the police.

"Now let's see," said the announcer. "Can the new kid on the block do the double with Dublin Bay? Laura Hallett won the Hickstead Derby Trial on him on Friday. Can she give us a repeat performance?"

Laura's mum, Jacky, said she had everything crossed. Charlie's aunt Doris said she hadn't had this much fun in years. Prince Ahmed and his wife were looking on with intensive interest, as was Becky Paul. Charles Paul had come up from downstairs for a better view. Ricky and Charlie had their eyes all over the tunnel area, waiting for something to happen. I stood next to Charles.

Rosie, the same waitress from Friday, approached me. "Would you like a coffee, Mr Hurst?"

I said, "Thanks, Rosie. In about five minutes, please."

The bell went, and Laura was off. At the same time, Dicky Head was walking towards the members' private boxes, wearing his scarlet-red riding jacket. He went and spent a penny before proceeding up the stairs to Fred Cobb's box. Laura was clear as she now approached the derby bank. She stepped up the bank; Dublin Bay had done it all before on Friday, and now he didn't care. Fred Cobb and Wong Fat left the balcony; the balcony doors were now wide open. The chief inspector's snipers were primed. The chief inspector saw Zang Zai for the first time, just as the hitman whipped the cover off his tripod-mounted telescopic rifle: he had Laura in his sights as his finger tightened on the trigger. Suddenly, there was a thud, and then somebody knocked on the door. Laura sat there motionless as Dublin Bay slithered down the bank. Zang Zai reeled backwards from the bullet hitting him between the eyes. Dicky Head opened the door, and Fred Cobb said, "What the fuck do you want?" Fred went and looked out of the balcony doors; that was when the sniper in the chief inspector's office took out Fred Cobb. The cherry-picker sniper's second shot was an easy one: just for good measure, he took out Wong Fat as well. Dicky Head was taken care of with two bullets through the heart by the elite officers who burst in from the private box next door, the four of them crashing into Fred's box together.

Laura was still clear and on her way to the triple with ditches at Devil's Dyke. She was perfect. "Go on, Laura!" everybody screamed as she passed our box on the third floor of the office complex. Even Prince Ahmed was now on his feet, willing Laura on. She met the water perfectly, and cleared it by a foot; just a double now, then the gate, and the final fence. The double was no problem, and she met the gate perfectly as well. Now, just the last. Laura had said she was going to tell herself to remember what Charles had advised: aim for the fixed upright in the middle of the fence. And now Laura did just that, on a good stride, and never touched the fence. She was clear, the first clear round of the day.

The announcer said, "Wonderful! Absolutely wonderful! What an exhibition, Laura Hallett!"

The chief inspector later told me that he had tears in his eyes watching Laura ride. Not to mention the tears of pride and joy shed by Jacky and Doris. Prince Ahmed patted me on the back, and Charles said he had to go. I watched as Laura soaked up the applause.

Not everyone was jubilant, though. For Chris Cobb, watching Laura going clear was like putting a red rag in front of a bull: he was red with wild rage. As Laura entered the exit tunnel to leave the ring so that the next rider could go in, Chris Cobb attacked her. He drew a knife from inside his jacket pocket, pulled Laura from off the back of Dublin Bay, and stabbed her repeatedly – three times in the lower abdomen area – before Ricky had a chance to hit him with his truncheon.

Remembering that the chief inspector had said "don't take prisoners", Ricky hit Chris Cobb three times in all, cracking his skull. The ferocity of Ricky's blows to Chris's skull killed him.

Laura was covered in blood. Aussie was on hand to quickly get her into the ambulance and assess the damage. He undid her coat, took it off, and then removed her white shirt. Aussie didn't realise she had on a bullet- and stab-proof vest. "Oh fuck! Thank heavens!" he cried out.

Laura had a few puncture wounds, but they were superficial.

Aussie said to Ricky, "I can patch her up, mate. Go and get her a new shirt."

Aussie stopped the bleeding with some stick-on sutures and then covered them with larger plasters. Ricky was back in no time with a new shirt purchased from one of the many retail outlets at the show. Aussie put the blood-soaked one in a bag. "No point worrying your mother now, is there, Laura?" Laura agreed.

Meanwhile, Charles had come back to the box and pulled me to one side to tell me what had happened. He had also immediately withdrawn his own mount. It was only then that the judges were made aware of the situation. The previous rider was already in the ring and had started his round; he refused at the derby bank, so the contest was over. Laura had won the Hickstead Derby, but I still didn't know whether she was alive or dead.

I ran to the ambulance, crying my eyes out. *No, God, no – not my beautiful Laura!* I had never cried so much in my life, tears of grief, followed by tears of relief, and then tears of happiness and joy as I held Laura tightly. Aussie and Ricky vacated the ambulance and left us alone.

"My beautiful Laura, I love you so much."

Laura replied, "As I do you, Steve."

When someone really loves you, I guess that really *is* when your life begins. And ours was just beginning.

EPILOGUE

Aussie attended to Chris Cobb and pronounced him dead at the scene. Within minutes, another ambulance arrived to take the body away. Some two hundred people had gathered at the mouth of the tunnel, and the detectives did their best to control the crowd. Ricky stood patiently with Charlie, and the groom waited, holding the reins of Dublin Bay. Jacky and Doris were aware something was wrong, but they didn't know quite what.

Charles Paul broke the tension. He opened the ambulance door and said, "Come on, Laura! You won! The crowd wants a lap of honour."

I was back in control of my emotions. "Yes, do it, Laura, if you can," I said.

"Okay, Steve," Laura said. "Let's do it."

We got out the ambulance to a massive ovation. People were clapping and cheering. All the other riders formed a guard of honour. It was Laura's moment alone. As word of what had actually happened spread round like wildfire, Laura mounted Dublin Bay and did her lap of honour on her own. When she returned to the tunnel this time, all the riders were still there clapping; so were the detectives, the special armed officers, and Doug Dunne and his sons. I helped my beautiful Laura dismount, and all we wanted to do was go home. Charlie took Doris and Jacky both home. Laura hugged her mum before they left. "Don't worry, Mum. I'll be fine. I just need to sleep."

As for the three dead bodies in Fred Cobb's private box, of which he was one, the laundryman from MI5 at Gatwick would pick them up later, after all the crowds had gone home. Fred's Watford office with the stash of cocaine and heroin would be raided at 11 a.m. the following day, as planned by the Home Secretary. All vehicles recovered would be auctioned off and go into the national purse as proceeds of crime, including Fred's new Mercedes with £75,000 in the boot.

The punters detained at Greenham Common were mostly let out Sunday evening, with fines. However, about thirty of them were detained and then released on Monday on bail; they all would receive custodial sentences of two to four years.

The six Tote operators were all charged with fraud and conspiracy to defraud; they were all given three years.

Amy Cobb and her daughter, Lucy, were convicted of drug dealing and supplying class A drugs; they were each given eight years.

Noel Henry was banned for life from holding another trainer's licence. He also received a custodial sentence of three years for dealing and supplying class A drugs.

Ron Kallon was banned for six years by the Jockey Club for race fixing and riding under the influence of class A drugs; no criminal charges were brought against him.

All six of the trailer employees were convicted of supplying class A drugs; all of them received six-year sentences.

Sally Gregory was arrested that evening, and convicted of drug dealing and prostitution; she was sentenced to four years.

Danny and Dave were found guilty of the murder of Chris Collins; they would serve a minimum term of fifteen years with no remission.

Jane Coe was acquitted of the murders of Chris Collins and Henry Hall; however, she was found guilty of being an accessory to the murder of Jay Penfold, for which she received six years. She was also found guilty of conspiracy to commit murder, that of Laura Hallett, for which she received an eight-year sentence. The terms would run concurrently.

Pete Gregory never did get to see the back of a courtroom again. He was taken out for a walk in the country by Mickey, on Epsom Downs, and has never been seen since.

ABOUT THE AUTHOR

Ronald Moore had the incredible experience of working as an assistant trainer in a racing yard during the late 1980s and early 1990s. He has also held a jockey's licence during that time and rode in races. His niece was an international showjumper who represented her country many times before turning to race riding; she rode in two Grand Nationals. Ronald has always been interested in horse racing and showjumping, and has owned many racehorses and showjumpers over the years.

One of his favourite authors is Dick Francis, who wrote many novels based on the horse-racing theme. Jilly Cooper, famed for her book *Riders,* set in the promiscuous showjumping world, is another author he admires.

Vengeance is Ronald's first novel, and he sought to blend racing and showjumping as the story's backdrop, peppering the action with romance, as well as various criminal activities regarding the illegal sale and distribution of drugs. This provides a unique spin on this tried-and-trusted equestrian theme that has served countless authors so well in the past. Ronald intends to utilise the main characters in this novel in the sequel which he is writing at the moment. He hopes the poignant scenes and moral issues threaded through the story, together with the romance and fast-paced action, will make *Vengeance* a memorable and enjoyable read.

If you enjoyed *Vengeance,* the sequel, *The Secret Syndicate,* is under way! It's set in Sussex and filled with more intrigue regarding the horse-racing industry. (Release date: September 2015.) Find out how Steve and Laura, Ricky and Charlie, and DCI John Heyes crack their second case. Will Miles and Natalie get together? And how will Laura deal with a yard full of horses?

Lightning Source UK Ltd.
Milton Keynes UK
UKOW04n1447180115

244670UK00001B/1/P